Praise for Nick Triplow

'Mesmerising'
Financial Times on *Never Walk Away*

'Like a darker, grimier version of Mick Herron's Slough
House novels, this is a highly promising debut'
Mail on Sunday on *Never Walk Away*

'An astute and relevant thriller with real psychological
depth and plenty of atmosphere. Highly recommended'
Crime Time on *Never Walk Away*

'A lesson in top-notch thriller-writing'
Carolyn Kirby on *Never Walk Away*

'Triplow's excellent biography rightly puts the
spotlight back on one of the crucial figures of
British crime writing'
The Spectator on *Getting Carter*

'Triplow does a fine job of demonstrating why
Lewis's work should be rediscovered'
Jake Kerridge, *Daily Telegraph*

ALSO BY NICK TRIPLOW

Getting Carter
Never Walk Away

THE
LAST DAYS
OF JOHNNY
NUNN

NICK
TRIPLOW

NO EXIT PRESS

First published in the UK in 2024 by No Exit Press,
an imprint of Bedford Square Publishers Ltd,
London, UK

noexit.co.uk
@noexitpress

ISBN
978-1-915798-44-2 (Paperback)
978-1-915798-45-9 (eBook)

2 4 6 8 10 9 7 5 3 1

Typeset in Times New Roman by Palimpsest Book Production Limited,
Falkirk, Stirlingshire

Printed in Great Britain by CPI Group (UK) Ltd, Croydon CR0 4YY

In fact you are secretly somebody else.
You live here on the city's edge
Among back lanes and stable-blocks
From which you glimpse the allegations
Of the gardening bourgeoisie that all is well.

Sean O'Brien – *'Somebody Else'*

DRAMATIS PERSONAE

Specialist Crime and Operations, Metropolitan Police, Scotland Yard

Assistant Commissioner Douglas Kilby, Specialist Crime and Operations

Commander Tessa Harding, Intelligence and Covert Policing

DS Max Lomax, intelligence analyst and former covert operative

DC Maggie Denny, seconded from Operation Trident Team

South Area Major Investigation Team, based at Lewisham Police Station

DI Andrew Conway, Investigating Officer

DS Ben Tait, Case Officer

DC Shannon Reed, Family Liaison Officer

DS Lloyd Ferris

DC Roy Tolly

DC David Cobb

Marlowe Estate / New Cross

Fraser Neal, community leader and campaigner

Alison Barnes, Marlowe Estate development worker

Johnny Nunn, former professional boxer

Alec Barnes, Alison's father, Johnny's old trainer

Lorraine Barnes, Alec's wife

Jerome Standing, victim of wrongful arrest
Marcia Standing, his mother
Father Sam Downey, Parish Priest, St Mark's Church
Shelly Dowd, St Mark's Church volunteer
Nathan Dowd, her son
Sheila Okenia, St Mark's Church administrator
Dwight Payne, drug dealer and philanthropist
Chris Clark, community centre manager
Lukshana Dahir, Marlowe Estate resident
Mrs Stearns, Marlowe Estate resident
Mr Tousi, Marlowe Estate resident
Rosco & Muhammed, youth project music producers / youth
  workers
Mrs Kathleen Archer, displaced Marlowe Estate resident
Carol Archer, her daughter

City Hall
Martin Dyce, Jamaica Dock project lead
Greg Walsham, elected member of the London Assembly
Rod Hutchings, Strategic Director of Planning and Regeneration

Kingdale Developments Ltd
Gavin Slade, business leader and driving force behind Jamaica
  Dock Development
Stuart Slade, his cousin
George Laska, private security contractor
Tony Fitzpatrick, private security contractor
Pallo Gashi, private security contractor
Stan Moffatt, their associate

Edinburgh
Kenneth Neal, Fraser Neal's father
Susan Neal, Fraser Neal's sister

Calum Neal, Fraser Neal's uncle
Craig Neal, Fraser Neal's uncle

Delaney & Coles, Solicitors
Jonathon Coles, human rights lawyer
Liz Delaney, human rights lawyer and associate of DS Lomax
Hannah Rees, Security and Intelligence Executive, ID
  International
Dominik Saski, electronic and surveillance specialist

Saturday 16 October, 1993
Woolwich, south east London

It was dark as they waited for the off. A dozen blokes in riot fatigues in the back of a Transit, sweating out last night's beer and curry. Max had two sticks of Airwaves menthol gum on the go. It wasn't working, not even close.

He checked his watch and got a dig in the ribs from McFarland, the senior man. 'Will you sit still. Every time you fidget, I get your fucking elbow in my ribs.'

'Just making sure you're awake.'

McFarland appealed to the others, 'You hear this? College wanker's telling me to stay awake. You want to mind your mouth, son.' He sniffed. 'You smell like a dentist.'

Max chewed in silence as the convoy rolled into pre-dawn streets.

The brass had briefed the press. Today's operation would send a message the Met was tackling extremism at its roots. Commissioner Condon and the Home Secretary had been all over Friday night news, priming Londoners for public-order unpleasantness. McFarland's squad arrived in Welling ready to make sure of it.

Ron Forest nosed the Transit into its designated parking space. A slap on the side, handbrake on, and they waited to disembark. Gibson and Callard were nervy. Max wanted away. Get deployed and put into practice what they'd learned on tactical training, taking bruises from rent-a-mob squaddies on an earner at Gravesend.

A hurry-up shove from McFarland and Max was out in the morning chill. He helped unload the stowed gear and went to stretch his legs. He grabbed a brew from the tea van, sparked up a fag and wandered, coming across a line of old green buses last seen South Yorkshire, 1985. Kent boys up for the day were telling war stories: Betteshanger; Orgreave; Poll Tax. McFarland called Max for the boss's final briefing.

Chief Inspector Whitley stepped up on a camera crate and brought the lads round. London was their city. These streets were theirs and God help anyone who thought otherwise. 'Gentlemen, the British National Party headquarters and book-shop is on Upper Wickham Lane. The protestors intend to proceed along Upper Wickham Lane. We believe there are significant numbers of extremist agitators who are intent on staging a violent confrontation with the BNP. That is not going to happen. You'll have memorised the alternative route the commander has ordered the march to take, diverting away from the bookshop. It will leave the rallying point on Winns Common at 10 o'clock. Protestors will be funnelled between our lines, which will be unbroken along the entire route, blocking potential exits. There will not be a metre we do not control. Once the march begins, these people are committed. Mounted officers and dog section will close in behind. No one leaves.'

Another departure from their earlier briefing.

Whitley asked, were there any questions?

A sergeant Max had got to know at Gravesend raised his hand. 'Sir, what's the contingency if we need to get people out, say, for medical reasons?'

Whitley again: 'Let me be clear, no one is to leave the

march. Those are the commander's orders. I expect them to be carried out.'

The squad spread at regular intervals on Wickham Lane. Max was posted with Gibson a few metres to his right, Wayne Ackley and Callard farther on. Directly behind him, Plumstead Cemetery. 'Must be the dead centre of town,' cracked McFarland. A joke so funny he repeated it two minutes later.

The head of the march passed by on schedule. Up front, a Justice for Stephen Lawrence banner. Then the mass of protestors, Socialist Workers, TUC and Anti-Nazi League, Socialist Students and more Justice for Stephen Lawrence banners.

Veterans of previous demonstrations eyed the police with suspicion, unsettled by the changed tactics, unused to ranks of men in full riot kit, helmets, shields and two-foot batons on their belts. The message was explicit: you're going nowhere we don't want you to go. The boss told them, no chat. Expect violence. Be vigilant. Within half an hour, the miscalculation was obvious. For starters, numbers were higher than expected. These were no more anarchist agitators than he was. Parents with kids in buggies walked alongside mums and daughters. An older couple, tweedy, well-to-do, strolled by arm in arm as if they were on the prom at Eastbourne. The woman smiled. Max was stony-faced. She looked away.

On the opposite side of Wickham Lane, at the ridge of the hill, mounted officers appeared, silhouetted against weak sunlight. More units moved into place at the brow of the hill. Dogs barked constantly, their handlers winding them up.

Max received word police units had sealed off the agreed alternative route along Lodge Hill. Reserve squads were assigned to the barricades at the junction, creating a dead end that gave the body of the march no means of exit. At the cemetery, Max was ordered to maintain his position. The demonstration came to a standstill within minutes, thousands still making their way up the hill without realising the route ahead was sealed off.

As the crowd packed closer, a lad in a light blue anorak, Saltire flag patch on the sleeve, asked McFarland to let his sister out. She was sick, she couldn't breathe, she had asthma. From where he stood, Max could see her expression, pure white-out panic. The Scots lad's reasoned argument fell on deaf ears. McFarland used his shield to drive them back into the crowd. The brother protested. His sister pulled him away, 'Leave it, they don't care.'

Scuffles broke out in Max's section. Plywood placards arced through the air. Demonstrators packed tighter as others joined from the rear.

An elderly gent wearing a black beret, Tank Corps badge polished to a shine, asked Max how they were dealing with the build-up? Behind him, a young woman with a kid in a buggy pleaded with Max to let her out. Police reinforcements, until now in reserve behind the cemetery, deployed forward. From the rising noise, the shouts and cracks of batons on shields, it was kicking off at Lodge Hill junction. Police loud-speakers, mounted on an overhead scaffold and intended for crowd control, were silent.

The Tank Corps veteran was back, the mum with the buggy clinging to his arm.

'I'm sorry sir,' said Max, 'you can't leave the demonstration. Stay patient, you'll be fine.'

'I know I will, son. It's for this lady and her little girl.'

'Just the same, sir, step back and you'll be all right.'

It was bullshit and the old soldier knew it.

A grey-haired woman in a yellow ANL T-shirt and steward's armband pleaded for the demonstrators to stay calm. Some sat down in the road. She raised her hands passively as she walked towards McFarland. He ordered her back.

'I have to speak to someone about this. Who is in charge?'

'*Step back now.*'

She put a hand on his arm. 'Please.'

'*I'm telling you, step off.*'

Her voice rose above the agitated crowd. 'Let these people out. Can't you see this is dangerous? It's a disgrace. People are going to get hurt.'

'*They shouldn't fucking be here, then.*'

A bottle flew over the crowd and smashed against the cemetery wall. As the steward turned to see where it had been thrown from, McFarland hit her with his baton. She went down heavily, blood across her face.

Max heard hooves, hard and hollow on the road. Mounted officers riding through the penned-in crowd. Standing protestors dragged those still sitting to their feet. Max flexed his grip on the baton. The crowd surged, lifting him off his feet, carrying him back against the cemetery wall. He heard himself groan, winded by the press of bodies on his chest. Old London brick ground on crumbling mortar at his back. The wall shifted and buckled. Its top two thirds gave way. Max fell backwards, pinned under bodies over the broken wall. He was certain his spine would crack. Counting the seconds, until a hand reached through and hauled him free.

He doubled over, flung his helmet aside and caught his breath. McFarland and the others were nowhere to be seen, and neither were his shield and baton. He gained his senses, helping a man to his feet, blood smeared across his face, a deep gash across the bridge of his nose. He threw off Max's hand. 'You people make me sick.'

Class War activists in full-face crash helmets stepped through the chaos from the rear. Whitley's anarchists had chosen their moment. Collecting armfuls of bricks from the half-demolished wall, they made their way towards the front line at the Lodge Hill crossroads. A big lad patted Max on the shoulder in passing, 'Cheers, mate, ammo, nice one.'

Max recognised the Scottish girl he'd seen earlier, wheezing through tears. He held her steady as her legs buckled under. 'Where do we go, please tell us where we go?'

Her brother pushed his way through the crowd, his anorak hood ripped and an ugly red welt around his throat. 'For Christ's sake, man, get us out.'

Max helped them across the wrecked wall at its lowest part. 'Go around the cemetery and double back. Take a wide route, get on a bus, get a cab, go anywhere, get away.'

The sister wasn't sure. 'Our coach is at the car park. We've left our things.'

'Do not go back to the car park,' said Max.

They got the message.

Others followed. Max moved through the crowd looking for the woman with the buggy, but couldn't find her. He came across a young boy, separated from his parents, maybe eight years old. He'd lost a shoe. Max carried him to the side and crouched down. What was his name? Who was he with? Max shouted above the noise. 'Daniel Shaw's dad, your son's here, Daniel's here.' He was clear-voiced, composed. Daniel's dad fell through the crowd and took the boy in his arms. 'Where do I go, where do I go?'

Max helped them through the gap, 'Keep going, mate. Keep walking, take a wide berth and stay away from the car park.'

He made sure they were safely away and was ready to go again when he felt himself grabbed from behind and dragged backwards, hit hard around the side of the head and knocked to the ground.

McFarland stood over him. 'What the fuck are you doing?'

Part One

Friday, 21 October 2011
London SE14

1

Max

MAX LEFT THE DEAD man in the alley and walked into daylight.
He took a hard moment to process what he'd seen. Hidden
from view behind a phalanx of wheelie bins, Fraser Neal's
body lay slumped at the side entrance to the flats above the
Tennessee Fried Chicken takeaway, his shirt sodden with blood
and rain, a fatal stab wound to his chest.

Detective Inspector Conway followed Max out. 'Bit grim.'

'Fucking idiot,' said Max.

Conway stopped writing. 'Excuse me?'

'Neal.'

'You want to try showing some respect?' Conway made a
circular motion with his hand. 'And elaborate while you're
doing it.'

'He never knew when to keep his mouth shut.'

'Enlighten me.' Conway playing the innocent. It didn't suit
him.

'He made a habit of airing grievances in public, but you
already know that. It's all over his socials and his press file.
Better still, talk to anyone on the Marlowe Estate.'

'Is that where he lives?'

'And works.' Max stepped to the kerb. Friday-morning rush
hour in south east London, City-bound traffic was at a standstill

'So you're saying he's off his ground.'

'I'm not saying anything.'

'Any thoughts as to what would bring him here?'

'Maybe he had a train to catch.' They were a stone's throw from New Cross Station.

Conway wasn't sure if Max was taking the rise. 'I assumed he was one of yours.'

'In what sense?'

'A source, an informant. That's what you deal in, isn't it? Your *thing*. We found a mobile phone in his jacket pocket. Last number in the call log was yours. The only number, in fact.'

Max turned up his raincoat collar. His *thing*, as Conway put it, was whatever Assistant Commissioner Kilby decided at any given time. Conway didn't know what he didn't know.

Max stood back. Left of the alleyway, mid-refurbishment, stood 489 New Cross Road, a three-storey townhouse encased in scaffolding and plastic sheeting. Right side, 491. Three flats over the chicken shop, one occupied. A cashpoint so exposed it might as well have had a sign saying, 'take my money, please don't fuck me up', then Red Cherry Cabs. The next three shop fronts were vacant, shuttered and graffitied, the third badly scorched – someone had set fire to junk mail shoved through the grille. If they were lucky, the last to sling the Tennessee's rubbish or one of the Red Cherry drivers would have seen Neal arrive, or chosen not to. He moved in closer. The cashpoint's street-facing camera was glued over. Best chance of CCTV would be the camera above Red Cherry's doorway. He'd have started there, but the case belonged to Conway.

He surveyed the scene one more time, taking in access routes and exits. The alley gate was pinned open by the bins. He turned back to Conway. 'Who called it in?'

'One of ours. PC Des Aitken, driving off shift shortly after three this morning, saw something as he was passing. He doubled back and found Neal as you see him now. He phoned it in and did what he could, which wasn't much. We got down here, set the cordon and made an initial search. Found the phone and called your number.'

A news crew was setting up on the corner of Wilshaw Street. Behind them, a solitary light came on upstairs in the Star and Garter. Max remembered it as a sticky-carpet boozer, an occasional stop-off when he couldn't handle the thought of going home. The memory made him shiver. 'Neal wanted everyone to tell him he was right, that he was entitled to speak truth to power as he saw it, irrespective of whether he could back it up. A lot of the time he missed the mark. If he didn't get what he wanted, he went his own way.'

'But he was your informant?'

'He liked to think he was, but I never recruited him.'

'Really?'

'He came to us on spec. He'd been told we would be interested in what he had to offer. Turns out we weren't.'

'Interested in what?'

'Something to do with dirty money and property developments south of the river. We didn't get much further than that.'

'Who put him on to you?'

'He never said.'

'Jesus, Lomax, it's like pulling teeth. Educated guess?'

'I don't know, a wind-up merchant.'

The lights at Lewisham Way turned green. Whatever was snarling the traffic must have cleared. The cars moved forward slowly at first, steadily picking up speed, headlights reflecting in slick tarmac.

The CSI photographer emerged from the alley and dropped his mask. DS Lloyd Ferris did the same, shaking his head. 'We're ready to move the body.'

'I'll be there in a minute.'

Ferris guided the coroner's ambulance onto the pavement, reversing close to the alley entrance.

A woman wearing bedroom slippers stepped out from a flat further along the street, feet scuffing as she walked, her hands resting in the front pocket of a grimy red tabard. She caught Conway's eye and quickened her pace. Conway indicated to a uniformed officer, tipping his notebook towards the woman. The uniform walked alongside, asking had she been around late last night? Maybe seen a skinny white guy hanging around? She was just home from a night shift, she said. He took her name and contact details and came back to his post with the air of someone used to keeping his expectations in check.

Max turned to Conway. 'Anything more you need from me?'

'Absolutely there is. I want details on Fraser Neal's connection with Special Operations, your peculiar set-up in particular. What was your arrangement? As it stands, we're dealing with murder by persons known or unknown to the victim and that's as wide open as it sounds. I want what you have. Was Neal connected to a specific case of yours? If so, I want chapter and verse. What's the subject and who is involved?'

Max needed Kilby's say-so before relaying information related to their work. Conway was well aware of it. 'I'll clear it with the boss and get back to you. Is that it?'

'One other thing, Neal's family are in Edinburgh. Does he have people locally we should contact?'

'I've no idea.'

'He's one of yours. Maybe try giving a shit.' Conway disappeared into the alley, cursing under his breath.

Max kept his head down against the rain as he walked the short distance from Westminster to his office in Carteret Street. Kilby's text arrived as he climbed the stairs to the first floor: *Your office, 11 am, K.* He switched on the desk light and pulled Fraser Neal's file from the live cases. Until that morning they'd agreed, for all Neal's claims of inside knowledge, corrupt practice and dark money investments, he was too high-risk, too good to be true. Now he was too dead to be otherwise.

Kilby arrived, accompanied by Commander Tessa Harding. Six months since she'd taken over from Rothwell, this was the first time she'd made the trip across from the Yard. She took in his poky home from home, his books and radio, the collage of notes and reminders that took up the length of one wall. She pushed open the door to the anteroom, revealing the eight Chubb combination cabinets that held the SDS case archive. In there were names and cases that didn't exist on any official database, nor would they ever if Kilby had his way. She gave Fraser Neal's case file a dismissive glance. Television news ran quietly on Max's PC. He went to switch it off.

'No, leave it.' Harding repositioned her chair to keep the screen in view.

There were other influences at play in Harding's unexpected presence. Kilby was making a peace offering, though his motives were unclear. 'Commander Harding has prior interest in Fraser Neal's corner of south east London. We thought it would be useful for you to brief us both at the same time.'

Max began, 'Detective Inspector Conway is treating Fraser Neal's death as murder and is aware of his link with Special Operations. Neal had my number in his phone log – I gave it to him to contact me. Conway's team are hitting the investigation hard, as you'd expect. Forensics are making the most of what they can at the scene, but it'll be limited. It rained heavily overnight.'

'There's no doubt?' said Kilby.

'None at all. Cause of death a single stab wound to the chest, time of death provisionally between midnight and 3 am. No weapon at the scene – they were finishing the search as I left. Nothing helpful on CCTV so far. Officers are going door to door for potential witnesses. We'll know more in a few hours.'

Nick Triplow

Harding was distracted by the TV news. Kilby asked Max to recap their recent history with Neal.

'Neal was a career campaigner, based on the Marlowe Estate. He's been critical of Lewisham, Greenwich and Southwark Councils' joint development policies, calling it "urban cleansing". If he's known beyond that, it's for campaigning against stop-and-search tactics, triggered by the in-custody beating and hospitalisation of Jerome Standing in December 2010. He ran a fundraiser, organised street protests and wrote several articles, most notably the one published in the *Guardian*, bringing the case and himself significant media attention.'

Harding's shoulders stiffened visibly at the mention of Standing. The officers who'd put Jerome Standing in Lewisham Hospital had been under her command. Andrew Conway had been senior officer on duty. 'We can't avoid the media revisiting the link between Neal and Jerome Standing. But our connection with him has been around corrupt practice. Development contracts, corruption of public officials, money laundering and cover-up. If you're jumping to conclusions about motive for his murder, those are most likely. They won't be flying flags at half-mast over City Hall, but pissed-off bureaucrats tend not to resort to murder.'

Now Harding spoke. 'You say corrupt practice. What's his specific relationship with your work?'

Kilby said, 'Lomax has been looking into dark money sources.'

Harding's set expression told him this was news. Kilby gave Max the go-ahead to fill in the gaps.

'We're seeing a rise in numbers of tier one investors coming into the UK, entering on visas no other entrant would have access to. About half are Chinese, a large proportion are Russian and there are a mix of others. BRIC countries, Eastern Europe. It's reasonable, given what we already know, to assume a fair chunk of what they bring is dirty. Billions in criminally gained capital. The kind of wealth that buys anonymity.'

'Surely, none of this is new information, DS Lomax. Quite the contrary, it's been this way for some time.'

'Not on this scale. Gaining inside intelligence is nigh-on impossible. These people's lawyers, accountants, bankers, estate agents, advisors and fixers are too deeply invested to call it out. Many rely on family connections.'

'But it's not *dark money*, is it? That's peculiar to the US. Laws here—'

'Are slow and ineffective – even when the intention's there, and that's not guaranteed, not by any means.' Max weathered Harding's stare and carried on. 'We're talking unaffiliated groups and individuals that exist to influence political process, using money we can't trace to source. Offshore investors in jurisdictions we can't touch. It amounts to the same thing, criminal capital buying influence with an eye to the political future.'

'And this is your connection with Neal?'

Kilby took up a position by the window, his back to the street. 'It's more than that. Neal believed the Jamaica Dock Development in south east London was criminally funded. Dark-money payments used to silence opposition. We don't think it stops there.'

'He came to us with that proposition,' said Max. 'We gave him the opportunity to back it up.'

'But he wasn't officially an informant?'

Max shook his head. 'I couldn't take a chance on someone as unpredictable as Neal without being sure he could deliver. I told him back in June, unless he produced substantive evidence, we'd taken things as far as we could. After that, we had no contact until a month ago. He called and told me he had what we'd asked for, but he wanted money. We spoke again last week and he repeated the request.'

'Had you paid him previously?'

'Three thousand pounds' seed funding. He had someone prepared to give us contract documents.'

'And did the documents materialise?'

'No.'

'He wasn't your registered informant, yet you gave him seed funding to bribe someone – let's assume a public official liable to dismissal and investigation had they been exposed, which would, in turn, have led back to this office, to you.'

'In my view, Neal was smart enough to know what the stakes were.'

'I was told you called him a fool.'

Evidently, the hotline to Conway was in working order. 'I said he was a fucking idiot. You can be both.'

'So, you played him for as long as you could and cut him loose.'

'We were in the process of doing that.'

'While paying for non-existent information. That's terribly generous of you.'

She gestured to Kilby. 'I take it this was done without your knowledge?'

Kilby smiled. 'Be assured, nothing is done without my knowledge. Fraser Neal included.'

2

Max

NEAL'S MURDER ROLLED IN and out of Friday's afternoon and early evening broadcasts. With no new information from the police investigation, reports were a tearful parade of grieving friends and Marlowe Estate residents. A London News team doorstepped Jerome Standing's mother. 'It's truly a sad thing,' she told the reporter, who left her microphone hanging under Mrs Standing's chin – *if you could manage to blub for the cameras*. Marcia Standing folded her arms and made it plain she'd say no more.

Max pulled up video clips of Neal in action: a *Newsnight* interview amounted to an adversarial set-up opposite the Jamaica Dock Development lead, businessman Gavin Slade; the *ITV London News* programme coverage at the march for Jerome Standing; and a YouTube clip from the summer's opening of Clara James Community Garden on the Marlowe Estate.

For *Newsnight*, Emily Maitlis framed the dispute with a piece to camera. Behind her, a blue and black backdrop of Marlowe Estate and an image of the proposed refurbished high-rise, divided by a ragged diagonal slash. Watermark Olympic rings cut across both images. Gavin Slade was composed, erudite, in a well-fitted suit, entirely sure of himself. Neal sweated under the lights. He hadn't shaved and his shirt was creased. Infuriated by the direction of debate, his arguments

17

lost clarity. Max reran the last few minutes, starting with Slade: *'These people aren't in tune with what we're trying to do. The greatest show on earth is coming to their backyard next year and they're squandering the opportunity of a lifetime to make the most of it. It's good for Marlowe Estate and it's good for London—'*

Neal cut across: *'When you say that, you're talking about expansion, economic prosperity for you and people like you, not the people that actually live on Marlowe Estate. When I talk about it, I see obscene wealth, embezzlement, nameless investors; our people locked out of their own community and denied the right to live in the streets they've lived in all their lives. The council is selling publicly owned social housing to private developers, displacing vulnerable residents in the process. They've done it with Pepys House and they'll do it again with Jamaica Dock. We're being ripped off.'*

Slade smiled thinly, shaking his head throughout. Maitlis drew the piece to a close and moved on.

For the Jerome Standing demo, Neal was on more sympathetic territory. Outdoors on a cold spring morning with his people behind him, he found his voice: *'All we're saying here is Jerome Standing didn't deserve the treatment he received. It could be any one of us, but statistically it's way more likely to be you if you're a young black man. Jerome was stopped and searched five times in two weeks, arrested for no good reason by an officer who was joyriding and had no reason to be there. Jerome was beaten and left in a cell. He might have died. Think about that. We've been here before. A black man assaulted and left to die in a south London street, only this time the perpetrators wore uniforms. We're accountable for our actions, but the Met Police are accountable to us. We don't give our consent to racist violence in our name. We seek justice for Jerome and all other victims of stop and search used as an excuse for intimidation.'*

Max remembered the interview. It made for uncomfortable viewing then and now. Someone had needed to say the words, but not Fraser Neal in self-promotion mode.

He played the clip from the garden opening. Shaky handheld footage followed half a dozen excited kids running across the lawn and around a centrepiece water feature in a low, wide ceramic bowl. The shot cut to older folks seated on newly installed benches, drinking from plastic beakers, residents walking the paths between sensory beds, flowers in bloom, paper plates and the food table set up in a community centre. The camera turned on Neal, a rosy-cheeked grin, Hawaiian shirt, drink in hand. A woman's voice off camera asked him to explain what was happening: *'We're here to open the Clara James Community Garden. Clara was an inspirational woman who lived around here over a hundred years ago and she changed the lives of a lot of people living with deprivation and not much hope. Our garden in Clara's name shows there is hope, we have to come together. This is for all of us...'* He stood aside and let the camera take in the scene, the urban idyll.

Max sat back in his chair and clasped his hands behind his head. Less than a month after the video, parts of London went up in flames. Levels of street violence unprecedented for 30 years. Did he believe what Neal was selling? The cynic in him wasn't sure.

He called Conway for an update. Neal's sister was on her way from Edinburgh. Nothing more to add at this stage. He pressed Max for confirmation of Neal's status as a Special Operations source. Max said he'd be in touch as soon as Kilby cleared the release of information.

On cue, Kilby appeared in the doorway. 'I need some fresh air. So do you.'

It grew cold as dusk crept in. Kilby's stride lengthened as they crossed Queen Anne's Gate, slowing once they'd entered St James's Park. 'DI Conway released his press statement.'

'I heard. I'm guessing that's not why we're here.'

'It is not.'

'You want to know what I left out of our conversation this morning.'

'You might want to listen to this first.' Kilby took a voice recorder from his pocket and pressed 'play'.

The first voice was Fraser Neal at his most affable, the tone he used when he wanted something from you: *You know why I've come to you, because you're sound. I wouldn't be asking otherwise, but I need funds to make it happen. I can't get it for nothing.*

The second voice was Max: *Is this you getting yourself on the telly again?*

A change in register from Neal, altogether more urgent: *I'm asking you to be reasonable. I mean it. Christ, it's not even for me, but the risk you're asking us to take.*

Max heard his frustration: *I know and it's not taken for granted. But if you honestly want to do this, we'll need to work it better. You're not using the phone we gave you.*

It's run out of charge.

Not good enough. You call from this number, don't expect an answer.

I'm in the office. Your people said it was clean.

Three months ago, it was clean. Have you kept to the instructions we gave you? No. So it's not clean.

Will you get me the money or not? If you can this week, I'll get what you want, but I need the same as before. Soon.

What am I, a fucking cashpoint?

Laughter. *You asked me to find out and I've found out. You needed me to prove it and I'm proving it.*

If you can get me names, details, connections and proof they know where the money's coming from, we'll meet.

Can you get the cash, or not? Because if not...

I said we'll meet.

'That was a month ago,' said Max. 'If he'd come up with the goods, I'd have met with him and taken it from there, but he didn't.'

'And he called on Sunday?'

'Sunday morning, again in the evening. I didn't take either call. He left a voicemail. More of a rant, to be honest. He said his phone was tapped, his computer hacked, his mail opened. He claimed he was getting cold calls that were nothing of the sort, set up to sound like a call centre, but the *wrong kinds of voices*. He said he needed his home and office reswept. He wanted us to pay for it.'

'Tell me, why wouldn't he use the mobile we gave him?'

'He did at the start, but then inconsistently. He made the last call from the community centre office.'

Kilby said, 'And he recorded everything. You don't look surprised.'

'I assumed he would. We know some of what he says is attention seeking and the rest is a means to an end, usually a pitch for cash. But he was genuinely shaken. I had someone I trust audit his systems earlier in the year, an industry-standard safety evaluation of each device, all uses, software, passwords, the lot. My guy installed software on Neal's PC so he'd know if documents had been accessed or tampered with between each log-on.'

'This was the man I told you to distance us from.'

Max scratched his head. One way or another all their sources were liabilities. Kilby knew that. But the mood had changed since their morning meeting. If he knew about Sunday's call and had the recording, it came from Conway. 'I'd handled him, step by step. We didn't commit and we weren't exposed. And, for what it's worth, I think we were close to getting value from the association.'

'Between self-publicity, personal attacks on senior officials, and heaven only knows what press attention.'

'Apply pressure and if nothing comes of it, cut him adrift. That's what you asked me to do and that's what I was managing without blowing the house down. No one's arguing he wasn't difficult, least of all me.'

'You don't think his murder was connected with what he'd been doing for us?'

Max didn't answer.

They came to a standstill as the path turned towards the Mall, streetlights visible between the trees. Max buttoned his coat.

Kilby wasn't convinced they were clean.

'You and Conway, how well do you know each other?'

'Reputation only, until this morning.'

'But you know of his professional relationship with Commander Harding?'

Max was circumspect. 'He'd have reported to her as Borough Commander, South East. That's where she was before, wasn't it?'

They stepped off the path to allow a cyclist to pass. Kilby said, 'Conway was on duty the night Jerome Standing was picked up. It was his DS out cruising with the uniformed patrol who made the arrest. Conway has a responsibility for how this was handled before, during and after. He didn't come through the enquiry unscarred. My view is he should have gone.'

'But he didn't.'

'No, he didn't. Tessa Harding went to bat for him. Made sure the internal investigation focused attention elsewhere. If you want to be old-fashioned about it, Conway is in her debt. And full disclosure, I chaired the panel.'

Max sensed what was coming.

'If there's an outside chance Neal's murder had to do with information he attempted to acquire, was in the process of acquiring or had acquired at your request, we need to know.

I want you to shadow Conway's investigation. Talk to people, get a feel for the neighbourhood and see who picks up the pieces in his absence. If you can get a line on his sources, so much the better. And if Conway looks like getting his hands on material we'd rather he didn't, I want to hear it from you, not him or anyone else. I'll clear the secondment.'

'I can't see Commander Harding being keen.'

Kilby looked over his shoulder. 'Actually, it was her suggestion.'

There goes the neighbourhood, Max thought.

'Last thing, for avoidance of doubt, this is not a long game. Keep it tight. And regular updates, please. I'll be in touch.'

On his way home, Max picked up a bottle of Malbec and a pizza. The gloss was off the Friday night he'd planned. *Angel Heart* was next up on his rewatchable film session. Ten minutes in and his mind was wandering. He turned off the film with the pizza half-eaten and the bottle two glasses down. He dropped the needle on a Julie London LP. London's smoke-and-honey voice and Barney Kessel's simple, elegant guitar playing was timeless. He picked up his book, but couldn't concentrate. By the time the needle lifted on side one, the book was beside him on the sofa and he was mentally cataloguing conversations had with Neal.

For the second night running, it rained hard. He stared into the dark, sharing his thoughts with the walls. He'd grown used to the anonymity of Carteret Street and didn't relish leaving it for the ghosts waiting for him in south London. Of those, Fraser Neal's was the one he feared least.

3

Johnny

IT WAS LATE SATURDAY evening by the time Johnny Nunn crossed St Mark's Churchyard, a loosely packed rucksack over his shoulder, shaggy-haired and unshaven, the right side of his face bruised from a fight he'd had with a man who'd tried to steal his coat. The same coat was now heavy with rain. He should have let the bastard take it.

After walking all day, standing still was an effort. His calf muscles complained, his back ached. The last few miles he'd felt like he was walking on bone. His feet burned. As he joined the food queue, his belly gave a parched growl. A man he judged to be about his own age, maybe younger, eyed him warily and drew back. There was a chance they'd known each other in his former life, or he was someone Johnny had run into on the streets, but he doubted it. He'd have remembered.

St Mark's Church food kitchen was the same as every other place he queued, mainly young people washed up on a tide of addiction, abuse, poverty and shit luck. It was the same across London and the towns he'd passed through over the last five years. It didn't matter if you were a refugee in a country that didn't want you, or unwanted in your own, you came here because you were hungry. No one was searching for Jesus.

Johnny couldn't say for sure why he was here. The question had turned tricks since he'd woken up one morning a week or so ago and decided this was where he needed to be, somewhere he could name the streets without thinking. A counsellor he'd once backed against the wall called it 'doing a geographical'. A deep yearning for the familiar, a feeling he claimed came to everyone sooner or later.

Well, here he was, geographically wet through and thoroughly pissed off.

Conversation was scarce as they waited for the kitchen to start serving. A teenage lad pitched a line to two girls about an empty flat where they could bed down. Before tonight, Johnny had only ever seen the boy – he knew him as Stan – north of the river. Except here he was, bright and breezy in Deptford, chatting up two girls who clung to their backpacks as if they were lifebelts.

'It'll cost nowt,' said Stan. 'Belongs to a mate from home, he's away for a few nights. I've got the place to myself.' Johnny had heard it all before. If the girls had the price of a bed, they'd have had their heads down by now. Stan made it sound like the Hilton, reeling off pros (no cons) as though he was flogging a knock-off tea service: *You'll 'ave a roof over your 'ed. You'll be safe. One of you could stay here while your mate susses the place out. I've got a mate that runs a recruitment agency for the hotels, we can sort you out some work, off the books like.*

'We don't know, is too far to travel,' the girl's accent distinctly Eastern European. Johnny guessed Romanian. Desperation flickered across Stan's face, a sign he was shilling for someone. Neither girl trusted him, but the one with frightened eyes didn't fancy a night in the rain. Stan appealed to her. 'I'm tryin' to do you an' yer mate a favour. You want to spend the night gettin' pissed on, that's down to you. Seriously, it's a good place. A mile down the road. You know Lewisham, Lewisham Station?' They nodded without conviction. 'It's near there, Sedgefield House.' He caught Johnny's eye. *'What?'*

'Just waiting,' said Johnny.

'Well, wait somewhere else.'

'It's a queue, son. Waiting somewhere else defeats the object.'

'I know you,' he said.

'You don't and you don't want to.'

Stan thought about arguing but turned his attention to the girls hunched in sisterly conference with their backs to him. He danced into position to hear what they were saying. 'Come on, girls. Keep it English.'

A second incomer vied for their attention as the queue moved forward. Middle-aged and well dressed, doing the posh bloke's *excuse-me* through the queue, showing a photograph to anyone who'd spare a glance. Johnny picked up the words *'daughter'*, *'Bethany'*, *'fifteen'*. Nothing about him belonged in that place. Not his weekender's Berghaus, his suede brogues, or his good-school accent that pegged him as a tourist from the suburbs. He cornered the Romanian girls, aiming the light from his mobile phone at the photo. They shook their heads at the pictures. He forced the photo into Stan's hand. *Tell me if you've seen her. Take the photo. Show it to your friends. She's fifteen years old.* Stan, who couldn't have been much older himself, let the crumpled photo fall to the ground.

Bethany's dad's anxiety was contagious as he worked between huddled knots of kids. The more frantic he grew, the more they shrank from him. He'd reached the tail of the queue, insisting a terrified boy take a copy of Bethany's photograph, when a grey-haired priest put a hand on his shoulder. Father Sam Downey.

Johnny turned away. The last person he'd expected to see. Sam Downey still saving souls at St Mark's.

Bethany's dad was suddenly all business. 'My daughter hasn't been home for three nights. These people aren't taking any notice of my photograph. She's a child.' He choked back whatever he'd intended to say.

These people, thought Johnny.

Father Downey invited Bethany's dad inside the church. Someone would explain the process for registering Bethany's disappearance. They would make sure the right networks were aware. Downey spoke calmly about taking details, signposting websites and support agencies. Reassurance from a world Bethany's dad could comprehend, one that was organised and appeared rational. Downey stopped short of saying they'd help him find his daughter. Johnny knew too well, chances were they wouldn't.

Johnny picked up Bethany's photo and straightened the creases, angled under the light. On the reverse was a typed label: *Bethany Middleton Yr. 11, Coopers School, Chislehurst* next to a phone number, an email address and a handwritten note: *Please contact Keith and Rebecca with any information.* Johnny wiped the rain-spattered school portrait of a teenage rebel in an oversized black V-neck. Behind the home-dyed fringe, the look in her eyes said she was already lost.

Conversation picked up as church volunteers set up outside, making their rounds, bustling with hot drinks and good intentions. A woman bundled in a purple fleece made a beeline for Johnny, offering a beaker of soup and a clingfilm-wrapped cheese roll. 'My name's Shelly. There should be plenty to go round, so if you'd like more, let me know.' Her supervisor waved his encouragement from the church.

Johnny braced himself for well-rehearsed lines about living life in a good way and with the knowledge Jesus loved you even if you were lost, especially if you needed help with life's challenges. He was ready to explain he was no longer on speaking terms with Jesus, but what he got from Shelly was a shy, kind smile. 'I'm supposed to ask you some stuff about how you're doing,' she began. 'If you're unwell, if you need to see a doctor or anything? Sorry, I've only been doing this a few weeks. So, how are you?' She brushed a wisp of dark hair from her eyes.

'Cold, wet. You?'

'Yeah. Same. Is there anything you need I can help with practically? That cut's a bit nasty. We can get someone to clean it up. Niall's here tonight, he's a qualified nurse.'

He'd forgotten about the cut over his eye, another souvenir from the fight over the coat. He touched it with his finger. It had opened up and was bleeding.

'It's nothing,' he said.

'I could put some antiseptic on it if you like. No fuss or anything.'

'Soup and a cheese roll's fine for now, cheers. Thank you.'

Johnny took a half-step away, making it obvious the conversation was over. He pressed his coat sleeve hard against the cut.

Shelly made another nervous plea towards the supervisor, who waved her back. 'If there's nothing else, I probably ought to move on.'

She went to replenish supplies. The supervisor packed her up and sent her out a second time. She came past loaded up with hot-drinks beakers and a basket of Asda sandwiches. 'He says I need outreach training. Must remember to tell people about the podiatrist. How are your feet?'

Johnny found a quiet corner to eat. Others had taken their food back to doorways on Deptford Broadway or the High Street in the hope their mates would be holding places. Some found company and sat chatting with volunteers, sharing food and cigarettes in the shadows around the old church. He caught fragments of conversation. *Where was it safe to bed down? You know Karen, down Greenwich? Some pissed-up City tosser came out the Trafalgar, kicked the shit out of her where she'd bedded down. They've taken her dog to Battersea.*

Shelly buzzed about the place handing out food and hot drinks, quietly encouraging. She was with the Romanian girls when a shouting match broke out on the Coffey Street side of the churchyard. Stan was in trouble, his *fuck this* and *fuck you* protest singing out across the open space. He was cornered by two men. Johnny knew both by reputation. Tony Fitzpatrick and Pallo Gashi, who was growling like a scrapyard dog, his face two inches from Stan's. From the way they pushed him around, Stan was in hock to someone. Fitz had his hand in Stan's chest, pushing him towards the road. Stan motioned to where the two girls were standing. 'I'm there, man. Give me five minutes. What's five minutes?'

So that was the deal, pick up the girls for these two. In exchange for what? Fitz dropped his hands in a *what do I care?* gesture. Stan nipped between him and Pallo. Pallo reached out and caught Stan's hood, swinging him round. Stan's trainers slipped on the wet stone and Pallo let go, sending the lad skidding down the kerb on his back.

They laughed. Fitz bawled at him to get up.

Before Johnny realised what was happening, Shelly had run towards Stan, putting herself between him and the two men. She held up one hand, pleading, still with a cardboard tray of soup cups in the other. Whatever she said, Pallo wasn't listening. He grabbed her hair and punched her twice on the jaw. When he let go, she staggered forward, dropped and was still. Fitz gripped Stan's arm and dragged him, limping, to a dark-coloured Nissan at the kerb. He shoved him into the back seat and yelled at Pallo to stop pissing about and get in.

The churchyard emptied. Young people scattered. Father Downey strode down the path. Johnny fell in behind as the priest kneeled to place his coat under Shelly's head.

Johnny put a hand on his shoulder. 'Best not move her.'

She'd been unconscious before she hit the pavement.

'Of course, of course,' said Downey. 'Stupid, of course.' He held her hand. Blood oozed through her hair from a head wound.

Johnny walked away.

Downey called after him, 'Stay, please.'

He kept walking. The Romanian girls stood rooted at the roadside as if waiting for permission to leave. If they hadn't grasped what was going on before, they did now. 'You have to go,' said Johnny. The sirens sounded close. He asked one girl her name.

'Mira.'

'Okay, Mira, I'm telling you, it's not good for you to be here now. You have to move on.' He hustled them as far as the Salvation Army centre.

The girls were reluctant. Mira said, 'Where is Lewisham?'

'Come on, you *know* what happens, it won't be safe.'

'But where?'

He gave them directions along Deptford High Street, told them which streets to avoid. 'Mira, listen. Whatever it was Stan promised, I'm telling you it won't be safe. I know what he does and this isn't for you. It's bad for you, you understand?'

Johnny left with the intention of putting as much distance between himself and St Mark's as possible. But as he walked the backstreets, his route brought him back to the churchyard. Police made way for the ambulance, Father Downey still clutching his rolled-up coat. Shelly's supervisor was pacing, occasionally stopping to pick up rubbish. Johnny pulled up his hood and huddled in a doorway. Judging by the still warm cup in the corner, someone had left in a hurry. Much of what was happening around Shelly was obscured, but he had one glimpse. The paramedic pulled the scarf from her face, her mouth hanging open as they lifted her into the ambulance.

He told himself there was nothing he could have done. He'd been too far away; he was too slow, too old. But it didn't ring true. He should have done something. Alec Barnes used to say the only beaten man was one who'd stopped fighting. If that's what he'd become, he had no right being here.

4

Max

MAX WAS TEN MINUTES late for Conway's Sunday morning briefing. He was joining the team investigating Neal's murder, at least until Kilby was satisfied there was no connection with the ongoing Special Operations investigation. Conway had been given no choice. He'd phoned shortly before midnight. As far as he was concerned, he didn't owe Max a damn thing.

Finding a space that allowed him to see the screen DS Ferris was using to update the case status, Max made a note of the data collected at the scene and initial forensics analysis. Ferris rattled through a set of photographs. Neal pictured from all angles and in detail, from dirt on his palms, a scrape on his knuckles, a loose lace on his brown suede trainers and the blood and rain soaking through his shirt and his jeans, pooling around him. 'These are all the angles and perspectives we have,' said Ferris. The consensus was that it told them next to nothing. The same applied to CCTV. No camera covered the alleyway and street views were cheap and nasty with next to no definition.

Conway introduced Max. 'DS Lomax is with Special Operations, working for AC Kilby on whatever it is they're working on. I'm sure we'll be told in due course.' Conway gestured to each officer in turn. 'DS Ferris you met on Friday, DC Tolly, DC Cobb, DC Shannon Reed, family liaison. Shannon's been with us just over a year, promotion pending.

32

Missing is DS Ben Tait, who is currently working on a separate case which came in late last night. Lomax will be shadowing our investigation.'

Ferris puffed his cheeks and exhaled. 'For Christ's sake.'

'In case you were thinking,' Conway continued, 'that a senior officer would send his man to keep an eye on us, I'm assured that isn't the case. Rather an opportunity to broaden DS Lomax's experience. Give him a better concept of what it takes to be a working detective. Anything to add, DS Lomax?'

'One thing, you mentioned CCTV was hard to come by. Have we tried the night bus cameras?'

'We can do that, if you're willing to spend next week doing nothing else. To recap, our thinking, borne out by the investigation so far, is that the perpetrator was someone Neal knew and had dealings with in connection with his campaigning or...' He motioned towards Max. 'We've found a small amount of cannabis and cocaine at the scene in Flat C, top floor, not a majorly significant discovery, but it does suggest a selling operation. It may have been Neal's reason for being there, but according to his colleagues there's no suggestion he's a drug user. He may have come to this address in the past. We believe a first-floor flat was being used as a base for sex workers. Unlikely they had punters visiting, probably a pimp keeping them mobile.'

'Which flat?' Max asked.

Cobb piped up, 'The one not occupied by an eighty-year-old woman.'

Conway cut across the laughter. 'It's Flat A. We know the victim built a reputation for his campaigning work and we have a list of people he associates with regularly, as well as those he has opposed. DS Tait will assign those when he gets back from St Mark's.' He paused. 'However, we do have a blind spot with regard to Special Operations, in respect of which DS Lomax has a roving brief. Any questions, comments?'

Ferris wasn't satisfied. 'So what, is he running a shadow investigation?'

'Absolutely not. DS Lomax will have specific lines of enquiry, agreed with me in advance, and reporting either to me or to DS Tait.'

Reed said, 'No disrespect, but what experience has he got?' She turned to Max. 'I'm not doubting you, mate, but it'd be nice to know.'

They could have agreed the situation wasn't of their choosing, shaken hands on the terms of their working together, pooling knowledge as best they could. But Conway was determined to make his resentment known. 'He has insights we don't, though not for sharing at this time. Ben Tait will be on hand and I'll not be far away. Any issues let us know. Shannon, where are we with the Neal family?'

Reed updated them on conversations so far, afternoon arrival details of Fraser's sister – she'd be arriving at Stansted, flight due in at 13:08.

'Are we meeting her?'

'She says she'll make her own way.'

Conway wanted her brought to him first, a word before the formal ID. He worked the room giving each officer a two-minute slot. Unfailingly succinct and highly professional, given the absence of eyewitnesses, reliable CCTV, specific forensic evidence – any solid evidence at all for that matter, Max sensed a cold honesty seeping into the briefing.

DS Tait arrived in time to close the meeting. 'Confirmation, the victim was killed where the body was found. We still don't know why he was there.'

Since no one had asked, Max said, 'Do we know what happened to the alley gate? It was jammed open.'

Tait said, 'Give me five minutes, I'll find out.'

As the meeting broke up, Conway asked Max to join him at 491 New Cross Road, though he'd have to make his own way. Max suspected Conway was keen to avoid the intimacy of a drive, even one that wouldn't take more than 15 minutes. He left his car at Lewisham, blagged a lift with Reed as far as Deptford Broadway and walked.

New Cross as Max had known it was gone. You could mourn it, malign it, blame the council or the crash, but there was nothing you could do about it. Conway waited impatiently at the entrance to the alleyway. He repeated most of what Ferris said as if Max hadn't been there. The scene was used up in terms of forensics. It was over to them.

Conway unlocked the now functioning alley gate. Max followed. The alley was out of reach of full daylight, over-shadowed by the buildings either side. In through the side door of 491, a yellowish glow from a cracked plastic shade barely lit the hall. The stair carpet, worn to its fibres, shifted under his feet. They halted at the first-floor landing. Conway said, 'Flat A, unoccupied. Previously a crash pad for some individuals – we're assuming working girls, possibly trafficked – Mrs Archer in flat B thinks they were "foreign", but she's seventy-nine and has mid-stage dementia. She's not to be questioned without her daughter. Reed phoned her first thing, she's on her way from Eltham and taking her time about it.'

The second landing was brighter. A skylight from the third landing opened out into the roof. A uniformed officer stood at the door of Flat C. 'Another semi-furnished residential, currently unoccupied. Signs of recent use. Is the evidence bag still here, or did DS Tait take it in?'

The uniform brought out a clear plastic bag, sealed and tagged. Inside was a canvas duffel bag, a wad of banknotes, tens and twenties mostly, a set of scales and a dozen or so packs of grass. Someone had been dealing, but hardly big time. 'You think that's what Neal was doing here?'

'You're asking me what do *I* think?' Conway's mouth turned down at the corners. 'No, I'm sticking to my initial hypothesis.

He was killed for whatever dirty work you had him doing off the books. This place is a bonus. I wanted you to see for yourself we're considering all options and I'd be grateful if you'd mention that to Assistant Commissioner Kilby. In the meantime, make yourself useful and wait for Carol Archer. Speak to them both together, get what you can. And hang around until I get someone to relieve you. I don't want the place left unattended.' He lifted the evidence bag. 'The dickhead who left this might be stupid enough to come back for it. Wouldn't be the first time.' He called up from the bottom stair. 'Let me know when you're done.'

Max went to the top of the house, looking over the backyards at scraps of trees, untidy sheds and well-tended gardens. No different in his memory, though noticeably less well tended than his granddad's had been. He made his way down to the first floor and sat on the stairs. There was an audible shuffling on the other side of Mrs Archer's door. For a minute or more, he felt himself being watched. The door opened. A face appeared, blinking in the space the security chain would allow. Max kept a lightness in his voice. 'Mrs Archer, my name's Detective Sergeant Lomax. I'm a police officer. I'm waiting for your daughter, Carol, so's we can have a chat.'

The door closed and the chain dropped. When it opened again, Max showed his ID. 'That's me, Mrs Archer.'

'She's on her way over.'

'If you'd sooner wait, that's fine.'

The door swung open. Max followed Mrs Archer through the flat into the living room. Via a relay of steadying points on easy chairs, dining table and a sofa back, she arrived at her own chair in front of a silent television. He had a feeling this was where she spent her days. The chair and cushions moulded around her as she settled in. 'Do you want a cup of tea?'

Max took it as an invitation to do the making. 'Shall I put the kettle on?'

36

'Go on then, through there.' She waved towards the kitchen. 'I don't like it milky.'

Max set the tea down on the table within Mrs Archer's reach. A life-sized white Persian cat toy sat curled up on the spare easy chair. Blofeld's revenge, thought Max.

'Move that thing if you like. Carol bought it. I said, what do I want with a stuffed cat? She said I could stroke it. I said, how's stroking a stuffed cat s'posed to make me feel less lonely? People's what makes a difference.'

She sipped carefully. Clearly the tea passed muster.

On the shelf above the gas fire ran a gallery of framed photographs. Families, kids, grandkids. At the end a group of four women. 'May I?' Max picked up the photo.

'That's my lot, the Tuesday girls. We used to meet at the centre on Marlowe's Estate for lunch on a Tuesday. Known each other for years. Then they moved us out the flats and put me here temporary. I don't know where they are. Go on, then. What d'you want to know?'

'We should wait for Carol.'

'She weren't 'ere, I was. On me roof terrace.'

'That's nice, somewhere for a gin and tonic on a summer evening.'

'There's some brandy somewhere if you want a drink.'

'I'm fine, thank you.'

'Carol took the outside key. I found a spare. It's in the drawer if you want it.'

A door in the kitchen opened to a balcony. Beneath it a flat roof that must belong to the cab company. There was a single plastic garden chair and a pair of vests hanging from the washing line slung above the balcony railing.

She set the teacup back in its saucer on the side table and rested her hands on her knees. 'I go out there some nights when I can't sleep. Wrap myself up and look at the stars.'

He couldn't imagine Mrs Archer counting stars, but maybe she longed to. 'Were you out there Thursday night?'

'I couldn't tell you what night, but there was a racket. I thought it was to do with them two girls on the game opposite.' Another vague wave from the repertoire, this one towards the door and the landing beyond.

As if conjured by Mrs Archer, a key turned in the lock.

'And did you see who was out there?' said Max.

She shook her head. Either she hadn't seen or wouldn't say. It didn't matter, with Carol's arrival a shutter came down.

'You were supposed to wait,' she hissed, a more angular version of Mrs Archer. She bent down and kissed her mother's cheek and took the cup and saucer through to the kitchen.

Max followed. 'We've been chatting. Your mum was telling me she'd been sitting out on her balcony.' He motioned towards the locked door. 'She said she was there when the incident took place.'

'She wasn't. She can barely lift her leg over the doorframe, certainly not without help. And she hasn't got a key.'

'You might want to make sure of that. Can I ask, is this your mother's own flat?'

'Social. They pay a private landlord.'

'She says it's temporary.'

'I wish. You want to take it up, be my guest. There's a letting agent up New Cross Gate, Harry Shah. Talk to him, he deals with the landlord. I'd get her back to Marlowe Estate if I could. Council's useless.'

Mrs Archer was watching television, not inclined to continue the conversation. Max repeated the question about the row outside; could she remember what was said? Glassy-eyed, she barely acknowledged the question. Gently, he asked had she seen or heard anything unusual recently? Her eyes fixed on the screen. She said, 'This isn't my home. Tell them that, if they ask. Carol, I want the toilet.'

'Mrs Archer, when you say *them*, who do you mean?'

'Them up the ladders. Carol, toilet. Take me.'

Carol said, 'I'm sorry, I have no idea. She muddles things with the adverts.'

He gave Carol a card. 'If anything comes to light you think is worth passing on, give me a shout.'

Mrs Archer was repeating her request for the toilet as he left. Max closed the door on the beginnings of an argument.

The council waste bins had been pushed further into the alley since Friday morning. Judging by clean wheels and the absence of stale fat smell, they'd been hosed down. Max pushed at the end gate. It was locked. He called Conway, still at Marlowe Estate. The first interviews had taken longer than anticipated. He was heading back to meet Susan Neal. 'Unearth anything interesting with Mrs Archer?'

'I need to stop by the letting agent. I'll be with you afterwards.'

'Nothing there,' said Conway. 'Tait spoke to Harry Shah. He hasn't set foot in the place in months.'

'I want to know who owns it.'

'A company called Belmont Holdings, based offshore.'

'Do we have a name, other than Belmont Holdings?'

'It's complicated. We're trying to find out.'

'Let me know if I can help.'

'I think we can handle it. DS Tait's here putting together the timeline for Neal's movements over the last week. I assumed you want to be involved.'

'That would be a pleasure. You still want me to wait for a relief?'

'I'll send someone, then get over here.'

Max walked the boundaries of 489 and 491. He pulled back plastic sheeting attached to the scaffolding on 489. A sign at head height read, *This property is guarded by Kingsdale Developments Security 24/7*. Max took down the phone number. No cameras, but there were brackets fixed at each corner, trailing wires cable-tied to the cross poles.

It was early afternoon by the time the relief arrived. Max walked the route, New Cross to Deptford, he'd always taken as a kid. As he crossed Amersham Vale, he vividly remembered his mum and dad bundling him up the hill to the station in his pram. It should have meant something, but he felt no connection. They weren't here any more. It wasn't home, however much it tugged at his sleeve.

5

Johnny

WHEN HE WAS A kid, the doors of St Mark's refused to open without an almighty creak. You could oil the hinges until they oozed 3-IN-ONE, latecomers would still be shamed. That morning, Johnny leaned on the handle and slipped in without drawing attention. He stood in the doorway, unsure whether to take the next step, and was overwhelmed by the togetherness of voices, Father Downey's prayer and the congregation's response echoing around him.

The door closed with a low click. Johnny made his way to the rear of the church, eyes fixed on the flagstones. A bicycle leaned against the back wall, sit-up-and-beg handlebars, thick white grips, and a kid's seat on the back. A woman holding hands with a young girl in the rearmost pew moved along. Johnny kept his distance. The girl fidgeted, poking a finger down her sock and scratching her ankle. She yawned, staring thoughtfully as if about to open a conversation. The organist struck the first chord, they stood and prepared to sing. Johnny was silent for the entire hymn. He had no music in him. As the last chord died in the rafters, Sam Downey climbed the pulpit steps and adjusted the microphone.

He folded his notes and seemed to be weighing up how best to say what he had to say. 'Sometimes, because of who we are and what we believe, our faith and the reasons we come here, we see it as our duty to fix things, to fix people.

41

It's our place in this community to care about others who are marginalised and need a helping hand. Before coming here this morning, I was speaking with the police about Shelly Dowd, our volunteer who was attacked last night. She was working to help people.' He lost his train of thought, momentarily, then continued. 'So, do we stop volunteering? Do we stop helping those in need? Does God's work come to an end because it is difficult, because those in authority are not sufficiently moved to deal with the plight of the homeless? Of course not. We must come together, because that is our strength. In love and peace. The more difficult the challenge, the more this community needs us to rise to it and the more we need each other. Jesus suffered so that when we suffer, it makes us like Him. We must learn and we must not live in fear.'

With Downey at the church doors, blessing each member of the congregation as they left, there was no way of avoiding meeting. Johnny stayed seated. Downey came to him. 'You were here last night.'

Johnny said nothing.

'I've earned a cup of tea, want one?' He was already on his way. 'And toast. I'm having toast, lots of it.'

Downey might have recognised him from last night, but not, he thought, as the 14-year-old he'd counselled to lay off the fags and stop street fighting, keep to his training and box his way out of trouble. And definitely not as the lad who'd won regional titles and ignored his pleas to stay away from the syndicate of hard, ruthless men he'd fallen in with. They'd promised a career. Downey only had God on his side.

The tea came in white mugs, the toast in thick white buttered slices, just as it always had. Volunteers kept their distance behind the kitchen counter. Downey let him eat, then said, 'Tell me, why did you come back?'

'I'm not sure.'

'The police asked about you last night and again this morning. You're on our CCTV recording.'

'What did you say?'

'What could I say? I wasn't there, at least not at the beginning. You were. And now you're here.'

The kitchen volunteers chatted, preparing for the parents' and kids' lunch. One of the women called over, 'Sam, love, we need to start laying tables and brightening the place up a bit.'

'Of course,' said Downey, and to Johnny, 'let's walk.'

Late morning sun streamed through the trees. Dry leaves littered the path. Johnny felt the warmth on his back. Downey led them away from the place Shelly had been attacked. 'Did you know those men, the ones who assaulted Shelly Dowd?'

Johnny couldn't bring himself to lie. 'I've seen them around.'

'I see.' He waited for more.

Johnny said, 'I was in a hostel in north London last year. They had a scam going, there's not much else I can tell you.'

Downey said, 'Have you been on the streets long?'

'Long enough.' Johnny's stock answer. The rest he wouldn't repeat, not here.

They reached the end of the path. 'One more thing, I have to ask this, because the police have said they'll be back later and they'll want to know, will you speak to them?'

'Not a chance.'

Johnny expected an argument, an appeal to be a good neighbour. Somehow Downey's silent resignation was worse. Johnny wanted to give him something. 'If the police need to find anyone, it's the lad, Stan Moffatt. Everyone knows him. I'd be surprised if the police don't themselves.'

'And I wouldn't be betraying any confidences if I told them that?'

'Just not who said it.'

Downey lit a cigarette and offered the pack to Johnny.
He shook his head.

'Where are you staying?'

'Around,' said Johnny.

Downey took a buzzing mobile phone from his pocket. 'I have to go. But please stay and eat with us. I'll speak to someone about getting you a hostel place for a couple of nights if you need it.'

'No, you're all right.'

Downey said, 'Forgive me if I'm wrong in saying this – it wouldn't be the first time – but if you had got involved last night, you'd be in the same place Shelly is now, possibly worse. There was nothing you could have done.'

Downey broke into an old man's jog slower than his walk, stopped, turned back and put his hand in the air. 'You're Johnny Nunn!'

For an hour or two, it was warm enough for Johnny to take off his coat and spread it across the bench in the park in the hope it would dry. He closed his eyes, felt the sun on his face and tried to remember the last time someone called him by his name.

6

Slade

GAVIN SLADE WAS MAKING coffee for Sophie, still in bed on Sunday morning. They'd spent the night back to back. She wasn't best pleased he'd cut short their Edinburgh city break. A text from Martin Dyce the previous afternoon requested his return as a matter of urgency. She'd barely said a word since they'd arrived home in the early hours. Slade was aiming to make amends when Dyce called. Anxious not to discuss business over the phone, he suggested they meet. He'd be at the Moonstone Café in Greenwich Market around 11 o'clock.

Slade stepped out into Montpelier Road, instantly buoyed by his surroundings. This was his and Sophie's first autumn in their new home, a white-painted, double-fronted Georgian on a private estate on the fringes of Blackheath. He'd worked hard for his opportunities and considered himself the worthy inheritor of an ambition the merchants, brokers and traders who built these houses would have recognised.

Road-testing new boots as he strode across Mounts Pond Road onto the heath and through the gates at Greenwich Park, he felt awake. Bring on winter, he thought.

He made a beeline for the closed-off section of the park near the Naval College. Final-stage construction of the Olympic equestrian venue was under way. He leaned on the barriers, giving the site the once-over. An unsmiling security guard asked him discreetly, but firmly, to move along. The security guard's orange hi-vis bore the Kingsdale Security crown logo. He was about to meet his CEO. Slade introduced himself and the man straightened up. He liked that. All quiet overnight, he reported, more Western Front than Greenwich Park on the eve of the Olympics. But, of course, he meant the campaign. Locals had objected to being shut out of their park, threatening to protest. 'These things usually fizzle out,' said Slade. 'I wouldn't be overly worried. Just keep doing what you're doing.' He didn't mention he'd distributed complimentary tickets among the campaign ringleaders. Martin Dyce's well-placed negative social media had done the rest, easy when there was royalty due in town. Slade considered it a successful trial at handling stroppy neighbours.

He cut through to the Market, buying *The Sunday Times* on the way. Approaching lunchtime, the place was heaving. Shoppers and sightseers dawdled between stalls. A guy and girl uncased guitars and tuned up, starting into a set of easy-earner strum-along tunes for swinging tourists. The lad was a study in a beatnik brown corduroy jacket and turtleneck sweater. As for the girl, he'd never seen someone so desperate to be Joni Mitchell.

Martin Dyce sat outside the café, on the table in front of him a raisin pastry and a milky coffee in a long glass, topped with an elaborate mix of whipped cream and crumbled flake. Dyce was one of those men Slade's father would have called a rum chap. Initially his man inside City Hall, his role in Slade's business dealings had developed as the business grew. Flexible by necessity, he straddled public and private worlds with equal conviction.

Slade dropped his paper on the spare seat between them. 'Morning, Martin. That's interesting. A sort of anti-diet.'

'I asked for a latte,' said Dyce. 'I've ordered you an Americano.'

'That's a relief. What's this thing that's so important I had to piss off Sophie and ruin a perfectly good weekend?'

'There was one thing when I texted, now there are two. I sent Tony Fitzpatrick to bring in Stan Moffatt last night. It's as we thought, he was picking up women for George Laska, too scared to do otherwise in spite of what I told him. He took some persuading. A church volunteer got in the way and Pallo lost his rag. The woman's in hospital.'

'You picked Stan up at a *church*?'

'St Mark's is where they go to get a hot meal. We guessed he'd be there.'

The waitress set Slade's coffee down.

'Thank you.'

'Nothing to lose sleep over,' said Dyce. 'But I thought you'd want to be kept in the picture.'

Slade beckoned Dyce forward and edged his own chair closer to the table. 'I know I don't need to say this, because we had this conversation less than a week ago, but in case it's not clear, these are exactly the things I need you to fix of your own volition. I cannot be involved.'

'You're not *involved*. I just assumed you'd want to know.'

'I'd rather not sacrifice my Sundays worrying how your people spend their Saturday nights. Please, deal with it *quietly*. Second thing.'

'Fraser Neal was found dead early on Friday morning.'

Slade ran through the implications.

'Did you hear what I said?'

'*How?*'

'He was stabbed. They found him in the alleyway between 489 and 491 New Cross Road.'

Slade knew the addresses, two of their last buy-to-let renovations, taken on with the aim of a quick turnaround. An easy profit before the main event. He unbuttoned his coat, trying to quieten the advantage-seeking voice in his head. 'And it's definitely him, you're sure?'

'Named late on Friday. His face was across the news all day yesterday.'

'What was he doing there? Have the police arrested anyone?'

'First answer, we don't know. Second answer, not to my knowledge. I'm monitoring it.'

'Discreetly, please.'

It wasn't the first time Slade had been caught off guard by Fraser Neal. The man's persistence forced them to push the Pepys House project start date back three months, then Jamaica Dock three more. Pepys House had been vacant for weeks. Susceptible to decay and vandalism, this lessened the possibility of more disruption.

Dyce read his mind. 'You do realise this takes several problems off the table?'

Slade checked himself. 'Tell me, Martin, are we sure this had nothing to do with your people?'

'They're not my people, they're ours. And no, they weren't involved.'

Dyce stirred his latte, creating a brownish sludge. He drank a mouthful down with an audible gulp that made Slade feel queasy. There was no call for Fraser Neal to have been at New Cross Road.

'It's time they moved on, Laska, Fitz, Pallo.' Slade sipped his coffee.

'They're not officially on the books,' said Dyce.

'Tony Fitzpatrick has been, and your friend Pallo Gashi. They were on the payroll initially.'

'On and off, as casual labour. The paperwork says they're site workers, brickies' mates, painters and decorators, whatever. We must have used a ton of those.'

'I want them gone. If they can't do the job the way it needs doing, cut them loose. And find out who is taking over from

Neal on Marlowe Estate. We might get lucky and the campaign dies out.' He didn't expect it, but a period of grace while Neal's replacement learned the ropes would be sufficient time to close on the investment needed to move Jamaica Dock out of reach.

Dyce was straight-faced. 'I'll be in touch tomorrow. You want a pre-briefing for the meeting?'

'I don't think that's necessary, do you?'

Slade often wondered how he'd feel when a major scheme and the finance to deliver it matched his ambition. That was Jamaica Dock. Its time had come and it felt inevitable. Dyce needed to grasp the fact. Slade drank his coffee down to the grounds, weighing up whether to spit them back into the cup. He swallowed and leaned in close to Dyce, who recoiled as if he thought Slade might kiss him goodbye. He put his hand on Dyce's shoulder and whispered, 'I've had confirmation from the mayor's office. He's with us.'

Slade left Dyce to his coffee sludge and eased through the crowds cheering the buskers to an encore. As he walked into daylight, Joni and the Corduroy Kid were paving paradise and putting up a parking lot. If only it were so easy.

7

Max

MAX HALF EXPECTED SMOKE to be hanging in the air on Marlowe Estate, but all that remained of a summer of burned-out cars and looted shops was a good deal of bad feeling. Police questioning Fraser Neal's neighbours and associates wouldn't help, but generally it felt calm. A typically dreary Sunday.

By the time he walked through from Evelyn Street and reached the Clara James Garden, the shadow of Eddystone Tower had fallen over the community centre. Two men chatted to a third in the driver's seat of a parked BMW. They clocked him and went back to their conversation.

Marlowe Estate Community Centre was fixed on three sides by low-rise maisonettes. But the 1960s high-rise towers of Eddystone and Pepys dominated, giving an unimpeded view over the City of London, the river and beyond. Pepys House was empty now, its residents relocated. If Mrs Archer's experience was typical, they were scattered across the borough.

In the Centre café, men gathered around yesterday's football highlights on a wall-mounted TV screen. They barely acknowledged Max's presence. He scanned the noticeboard's patchwork of overlapping flyers: the Talking History Group obscured under exercise classes, Samba Drumming and Knit 'n' Natter sessions. Family Support Group hid local councillors' surgery times. Fully visible in the centre were laminated A4s of

Marlowe Estate Development team, headed by Fraser Neal. Under each photo was a job title and a list of that person's responsibilities. There was also a plain black and white notice inviting residents to a service remembering Fraser Neal. Anyone wishing to pay their respects was welcome to attend St Mark's on Friday evening at 6.30. A young girl, school age, appeared at the reception desk. 'They're in a meeting.'

'Thank you,' said Max. 'Do you mind if I wait?'

She sized him up. 'You can take a seat.'

Presumably Conway and Tait had moved on and would be back. He sent Conway a text to say he'd arrived.

The girl called over. 'They shouldn't be long. They've been in there for hours already. Café's open till three, unless Shana's gone home. If there's no one there, you can make your own drink and put fifty pence in the jar.'

'Thank you,' said Max.

A clatter of chairs from behind a closed door at the back of reception suggested the meeting was breaking up. The door opened, conversations carrying into the hall. Max caught the tail end of an argument, but couldn't gather the subject beyond not 'giving in without a fight'. An older man joined the girl behind the desk. He laid down a thick binder and put his arm around the girl's shoulder. 'Seems we both have homework before school tomorrow.'

Max's head turned at a voice, another unfinished debate carrying into reception, this one less serious. The speaker slung a rucksack over her shoulder, 'Well he would say that, he's never been to All Bar One on a Friday night.' She gave a husky laugh, the smile still in her eyes as she turned to him. 'Christ, another one. Are you lost?'

'Another what?'

'Another copper with dozy questions and no sensitivity. I'm going outside for a cig. Come with me if you've got something to ask.'

Max followed her through the doors. 'I'm with the investigating team.'

'Welcome to the humble neighbourhood.'

Quoting Strummer. The day just picked up.

She led them away from the centre in a slow circuit of the garden Max had seen on the YouTube footage. Shrubs opened onto a lawn bordered with hand-painted benches and heavyweight planters. The flowers had all but gone over.

'So, what do we call you, policeman?'

'It's Max. And according to the noticeboard photofit, you're Alison Barnes.'

'It's a terrible photo. The sickening thing is, everyone else looks amazing. I think Fraser liked seeing me cringe when I walked past it.' She stared at the grass, lost for a moment. 'When he bought the camera, he took one of each of us. We said it was so he could track us down if we ever tried to escape the Marlowe. It's a bit like that, you come for a day and never leave.'

She sparked up, offering Max a cigarette as an afterthought.

'No, thanks.'

'Seeing as Detective Inspector Conway, Detective Sergeant Tait and their merry men spent the morning interviewing the campaign committee, I'm not sure what more I have to say.'

'The committee?'

'Chris, Louis, whose granddaughter, Tamsin, you met at reception, Marco, Lukshana, Mo Duale, Mr Tousi, Mrs Ali, Mrs Stearns. I think that's it. Those are the ones who show up.'

'Can you tell me what you told them?'

'It wasn't much. They seemed to think I should have been more visibly upset. I don't really have the time. Enough on my plate holding together a community group that wants to roll over and go home. Bawling my eyes out in front of strangers isn't going to fix any of it, is it?'

Ali stopped to chat with an elderly couple dead-heading blooms in a planter before walking on. 'I can't give you more than a character reference and that's the same as we said on Friday. Fraser was the heartbeat of our community. I've no idea what we'll do without him. He organised the activities, got us the funding that made things happen – he knew where it was and he knew how to get it. He pulled us all together and fronted the Jamaica Dock campaign. No one knows what happened or why.' She stopped. 'It's been a long day, so can I be straight with you? We work with the local Old Bill and we walk a fine line. No one on this estate is going to tell you anything. You're the police and we don't trust you. There's already rumours your lot were behind it.'

'So why talk to us at all?'

'I didn't say it's what I thought, but someone needs to be up front.'

Max sensed she hadn't been with Conway and Tait. 'What are you doing now, your group?'

'That's what we've been talking about all afternoon. Short term, we're at a public meeting tomorrow evening. The council, the developers and their architects are laying out their latest proposals. A strategic planning briefing, they call it. We get to have our say. Fraser was representing the residents' group. Now it's me.' She ran her thumb down the lapel of a grey suit jacket. 'I'm all about business, can't you tell?'

Max said, 'Will they postpone – after what happened?'

Ali gave another husky laugh. 'Thoughts and prayers, mate. That's what we get.'

A light rain started to fall as they made their way back. They stood under the narrow awning at the main door. Ali lit another cigarette. 'If you're genuinely interested in what Fraser was about, come tomorrow evening and see what we're up against.'

'I will. Also, we need to put a timeline together, as DS Tait probably explained, covering Fraser's movements over the last week or so.'

'He mentioned it.'

She disappeared inside. Max called Conway, dialling up the diplomacy. They'd missed each other at the estate. Might it be an idea if they caught up the following morning? Conway insisted he was needed at Lewisham. Fraser Neal's sister had arrived from Edinburgh and wanted to talk to him. 'I'm not liaising on your behalf. You can tell her yourself what happened to her brother. Wait at the junction with Grove Road. Tait's on his way.'

Max killed time walking the estate, deserted in the gloomy afternoon. He dropped into the newsagent and bought a selection of Sunday morning papers. Kilby was right, they needed to keep the investigation moving. The longer Neal's murder remained unsolved, the more likely a combination of hacks and false friends would trash his reputation. What struck him was the speed at which the papers had drawn their conclusions and were running with them. Neal had been dead 48 hours and the *Mail on Sunday* was talking about the 'drugs den' on the second floor, describing the first-floor flat as a 'sex cell' for trafficked girls. They had details and they knew about the locks on the doors, the cash in the duffel and weighed-out bags of grass.

8

Johnny

THE ONLY WAY JOHNNY knew he'd gain access to St Thomas'
Hospital was through A&E. In the waiting area, a security
guard eyeballed him as if he'd enjoy nothing more than turning
him back into York Road. As Johnny approached the reception
desk, he could feel the guard's eyes on him.

The place was in chaos, patients crowding into seats or
taking up floor space. Some carried wounds from violent nights
on the streets. He knew the feeling well; Sunday comedowns
hit hardest. One poor soul moaned from a side room. Johnny
recognised a lad called Adie, deep in conversation with himself,
a space beside him in the line of chairs. He dropped in alongside him. 'All right, son, how you doing?'

The security guard clocked him. Clearly unconvinced, he
did at least keep his distance.

Adie gazed through red-rimmed eyes. 'I was kipping down
the Strand. Some cunt stamped on my hand.' He held up a
bulb of grubby bandage, which he began to unwrap.

'Leave it, mate, you don't need to show me,' said Johnny.
'Let the nurse do that.'

Adie wouldn't be deterred. 'See what they did?' His hand,
swollen, black and purple, fingers broken. 'It hurts, man. It
really hurts.' He started to cry.

'Have they given you anything?'

He held up a flimsy ticket with a number on it.

'For the pain.'

Adie shook his head.

'Wait here.'

Johnny caught the triage nurse's attention. She held up her hand. 'Not now. I'm busy.' She hustled a waiting patient into a wheelchair, shoved a cardboard kidney dish in his hands and gave instructions to a porter. She came back to Johnny. 'Waiting time is six hours minimum, depending on emergencies and patient welfare. That's the best I can do.'

'Have you seen this?' Adie held up the mess of his hand.

'He's been assessed. What do you want me to do? It's not urgent. He is, she is, they are and he is.' He followed her gaze along the row of patients: a frail elderly couple holding hands, as white-faced as Adie; an old man whose yellowing complexion and swollen feet in slippers told of grave illness; a child whimpering in his mother's arms. All sick and in need.

'Any chance he can have something for the pain?'

'What other medication has he taken?'

'Nothing, as far as I know.'

'Wrong answer.'

'He's clean.' Johnny took a chance he was clean enough.

The nurse looked Adie over and disappeared into a side room. She hustled back and put two codeine tablets from a blister pack in Johnny's hand. 'There's a water fountain over near the sluice room. Get him to take those and stay with him. He's in the queue, we'll see to him as soon as we can, but it won't be for a while.'

Johnny gave Adie the pills one at a time. He sipped and spilled water down his hoodie. 'Sorry.' He tried to wipe it away and spilled more.

'I'll hold that. You take it easy, son. They'll be with you shortly.'

'Thanks, man. It's good you came. I was wondering if you would.'

Johnny hadn't seen Adie since he'd last been in Tottenham. That was over a year ago. He let it pass.

Adie was quiet, lost somewhere. The triage nurse reappeared. What must it be like, a sea of desperate, drowning faces lifting towards you expectantly, day in day out? She dropped to her haunches and stroked the child's hair, spoke quietly to the mother and gently led them to a cubicle. A doctor followed them in. Adie pulled up his hood. His head fell forward. Whatever he'd been feeling, he wasn't feeling it so badly now.

Johnny said he'd be back and made his way through to the main reception. Ahead of him, an elderly man and his daughter were asking directions for the women's surgery ward. Johnny took a chance, stepping out of line and catching up with the pair at the lifts. He followed them in. 'Which floor?'

'Eight.' The father placed a reassuring hand on his daughter's shoulder. Johnny pressed the button and the one above. He got out on nine and took the stairs down. As he came through the double doors, a nurse stood in his way. What was he was doing?

'Visiting a friend,' he said.

'Your friend has a name?'

'Shelly Dowd. We volunteer at St Mark's Church. She was brought in last night. I want to know if she's all right.'

'You're not family, you shouldn't be walking around here. Go back to reception.'

A uniformed police officer came through the doors carrying a takeaway coffee. The nurse waved him over. 'Officer, this man is lost. Please can you accompany him to the exit.'

They entered the lift together, the officer trying and failing to get a phone signal. Johnny took a chance. 'How is she?'

'What?'

'Shelly Dowd. We work together.' Johnny filled the pause that followed. 'I was with her when it happened. They won't tell me how she is. I'm not family.'

'So, don't try it on with me.'

When the lift stopped at the ground floor, the policeman gripped Johnny's arm, scanning for assistance. The security guard's eyes lit up. He marched him out, warning if he came back, he'd be arrested. 'Now *piss off.*'

As Johnny walked across the paved concourse in front of St Thomas', he saw Stan Moffatt limping across York Road to a parked car. He had a few words at the driver's side window, then climbed in the back. As the car pulled into traffic, Johnny caught a glimpse of the driver. Heavyweight, square jaw, black leather jacket sleeve hung across the sill. *George Laska.*

He dropped down to the Embankment and followed the river under Waterloo Bridge, listening to the voice in his head telling him this business didn't concern him. He felt drained, tired of walking. There was only one reason Stan and George Laska were there and it concerned him whether he liked it or not.

Father Downey blessed the evening worshippers, the last making their way across the damp churchyard at dusk. He called the homeless drop-in volunteers together. He thought they should pray. Shelly was one of theirs, after all, and had fallen in the line of duty. He realised almost immediately he'd misread the mood. They didn't want speeches or prayers. There was work to be done. A collective will to push on and set last night's events behind them. After the Amen, he begged them to be vigilant, to care for each other. No one was to work alone. Chantelle had taken charge for the evening. Everyone was relieved. Downey asked to be told immediately if Johnny Nunn returned.

But it wasn't Johnny who interrupted Downey's writing that evening. Detective Sergeant Tait knocked and entered. Downey motioned to the chair.

Tait's tone was meant to be authoritative, but came across as whining. 'I've been calling on and off all day. Your mobile goes directly to voicemail.'

'What can I say, it's Sunday. I'm not difficult to find.'

'You didn't return the calls.'

'I'll make sure to check my messages more often while this is all going on.'

Downey felt bullied by Tait and was angry with himself. 'I made the appeal as we agreed. Both services.'

'And has anyone come forward?'

'Not so far. Give it time.'

'We don't have time.' Tait shifted in his seat.

He offered to have some tea brought in, but Tait was keen to hurry things along. St Mark's clearly didn't agree with him. Downey wasn't sure whether it was God's presence or his own hybrid mix of stoicism, socialism and Christianity that set the man on edge – he suspected all were beyond Tait's frame of reference.

Tait said, 'We want officers at the drop-in tonight and at the food bank from tomorrow. We'll be doing the same at the overnight shelter, they've been really helpful.'

'I don't care what they've been. Absolutely not.'

'Our people won't be in uniform.'

'They wouldn't need to be. People know who they are. It's intimidating.'

'Father Downey, this might yet become a murder investigation and it may well be linked to another.'

'Nevertheless.'

'We're dealing with serious assault, minimum. If these people who attacked Mrs Dowd are establishing themselves among the homeless community in your parish, it should concern you.'

'It does, deeply. All the more important for our people to have somewhere to come when they're in need, where they know they'll be welcome and not judged. We work hard to build trust within our community. It doesn't happen by accident and it wears very thin very quickly if we're too close to the authorities.'

Age had unearthed a capacity in Downey for animosity towards men with Tait's arrogance. It made him a terrible diplomat. He told himself he should be more sympathetic, acknowledge the man's burden of responsibility.

Tait leaned forward, both hands on the desk. 'It's your duty.'

'My duty and calling are to help the marginalised and vulnerable in our community.' He fought back his annoyance. 'How about this, I'll make sure we talk to everyone who comes tonight, tomorrow night, and for as long as it takes to give you the information you need. But it will be our people who do the asking. You'll get more that way, you must see.' The whisky bottle propping up Blake's *Songs of Innocence and Experience* was beckoning, along with the comforting prospect of pouring himself a large drink, if Tait would bloody get on with it.

Tait smoothed down his tie. 'The other option is we close down your out-of-hours activities until we're sure it's safe to re-open. Your people can find another venue in the meantime.'

'There is nowhere else and you know it.'

'So why not cooperate? It's not your people we're interested in, is it? It's those who put them in danger on the streets, but if you really want to know how much of a pain in the arse I can be—'

Downey didn't need convincing. 'Give me tonight, at least. I may be able to get you some names, but I need to speak with some people first. You'd be doing me a huge favour.'

'If there's information connected to the case—'

'You'll have it tomorrow.'

Tait drew a line under the notes he'd been taking and stood to leave. 'I'll be here first thing. I've asked Detective Inspector

Conway to come with me. We'll see if he can persuade you. My advice, don't waste his time.'

Tait strutted across the churchyard. Downey poured himself a whisky, drank it down and poured another. He was on his third when Chantelle knocked gently and told him Johnny Nunn was bedding down in the doorway across the road.

It was late by the time Johnny unrolled his sleeping bag. Father Downey appearing through the gloom with a mug of tea in each hand was the last sight he'd expected to see.

'There was another man who used to kip there,' said Downey. 'We used to talk philosophy. He'd read Rousseau. *There is no subjection so perfect as that which keeps the appearance of freedom.* I think that's right. Hold these, will you?' Johnny took both teas. Downey sat beside him. He produced a pack of Hobnobs from one pocket and a half bottle of Bell's from the other. He laced his tea, put the bottle with the biscuits between them and took the tea, cradling the mug between his hands. 'Thank you. Please do help yourself.'

There was already whisky on his breath.

'What happened to him, the bloke?'

'Went back to Sittingbourne, I think. Where his family were from. I know he'd been trying to get himself together to go back.'

Another tired body trying to find a way home. 'Did they take him back, his family?'

Downey's shrug said he had little faith he'd made it that far.

Johnny asked about the neighbourhood. Downey filled in details of comings and goings. He twice mentioned incomers knowing the price of everything and the value of nothing. 'Anyway, that's not what I wanted to speak to you about. I wanted you to see this.' He fished a black and white photograph from his inside pocket. A group of men in dinner jackets, pleat-fronted shirts and bow-ties, cheesy grins for the smudger, Hennessy and cigars all round. A men's night out. Behind them in the shadows, waitresses in uniform and restaurant tables with white cloths. Johnny scanned the faces left to right. Alec Barnes; Mick 'Ruby' Murray with his arm around Wally Patch, the two toughest men Johnny had ever met; Dave Price, ambitious, fearless and manipulative. Dave had ruled the roost for the years Johnny was making his name on the street and in the ring. Centre front, younger than the other by a few years, wearing a lounge suit, slim tie, pin-collar shirt, holding up a heavily decorated boxing belt, was a 19-year-old Johnny Nunn. Johnny with the men who put him in the ring. Dave was a long time dead. Ruby too. Wally, no one knew what happened to him. Alec, who'd trained him, if he was still alive, would be an old man.

'The cats that got the cream,' said Downey.

Johnny felt himself submerging, couldn't handle it. He gave the photograph back. 'It's not me.'

''Course it's you. I know it's you. I remember you.'

'Sorry to disappoint.' He sipped his tea, took a broken biscuit from the pack.

'In which case, you'll not be interested in the other reason I want to talk to you.'

Johnny's eyes fixed on the pavement in front of him.

'Lorraine Barnes was here a couple of weeks back, making arrangements. I see her at church once in a while, more recently. Alec isn't well and I know you were close. It seemed opportune you being here now. I thought it might be the reason you came back.'

Johnny hadn't known. He pulled his knees to his chest and held them.

'You've nothing to say?' Downey asked.

'It wasn't why I came back.'

'Have you been to see Alison?'

'I will. When I'm ready.'

'I'm sorry, son. It's my age. I'm trying to rush everything, all in your own time. It'll happen when it's meant to. I do have to ask, any news about Kerry?'

Johnny rested his chin on his knees. 'I tried, I really tried.'

'Always hope, though, eh?'

'If you say so.'

Downey twisted the biscuit wrapper tight. 'I've had several conversations with the detective dealing with what happened here last night. Detective Sergeant Tait thinks the two men who took the boy and beat up Shelly were part of an organised gang. There was a man murdered in New Cross a couple of nights ago. They think there might be a connection. I don't know.'

Johnny drank down the tea. 'It's a wonder they find the time.'

Downey went on. 'What a strange thing to say.'

'Why bother with Shelly if they've got a criminal empire to run?'

'The information you told me about them, I said I would drop it into the conversation, but I don't think I can. If I was willing to string out the notion of priestly confidentiality, which I'm not, Tait would still demand times, places, names. They're applying pressure on me personally, which I have no problem with, but threatening to close down the work our people are doing here, that's another matter entirely.' He faced Johnny. 'If those people target our community, something needs to be done before they do more damage. Will you speak to Tait and tell him what you know?'

Johnny said nothing.

Downey sat with his back braced against the doorway and poured more whisky into his cup.

The decision to come back and rebuild a life had weighed Johnny down for so long. He would see Ali, especially if her dad wasn't well. Him and Alec had been close, but he didn't kid himself it would be easy. Still, if he believed in finding a way back home, it was the right thing to do. 'Detective Sergeant Tait, do you trust him?'

'Not an inch. All I'm asking is that you pass on what you know.'

Downey had no idea what it meant. When they found out, they'd come for him. He looked up. The priest's face had fallen into shadow. 'I'll talk to him.'

9

Max

THEY MET IN THE hospital prayer room. All faiths and no
faiths. A pillar candle burned on an iron candlestick, set
centrally on a plain wooden table. Prayer mats, crosses, seven
candle-holders, Bible and Quran, stowed in separate cupboards,
each with a denominational sticker on the door to cause least
upset to anyone, not that Susan Neal was paying attention.
Max had the impression of someone low on reserves of
patience. Far from being able to return to Edinburgh with her
brother as hoped, she was in limbo. The body would not be
released. She'd asked to see him. Max pulled across a chair.
'Can I get you anything?'

'Your press statement said there was nothing to suggest my
brother's murder was because of his activism. Detective
Inspector Conway believes you were responsible, at least in
part. He said Fraser had been a source for your investigation
– not that he'd tell me what it was about – but you'd encouraged him to take greater risks than he should have.'

Max cursed inwardly, the candle flame flickering as if
disturbed by his thoughts. Conway's shit-stirring opinions were
damaging enough between colleagues, sharing them with
Susan Neal was a new level of shithouse behaviour. He met
her gaze. 'Fraser came to us because he believed he was
dealing with people acting unlawfully. But he wasn't an
informant or a source, as Mr Conway puts it. He might have

become one in due course – we'd had dialogue over some months, but he hadn't provided information to me. Truth be told, I thought his profile was too high, too public, to allow him to cooperate safely. You'll know better than anyone, he was very determined. If what happened was as a result of his campaigning on Marlowe Estate, or his offer to share information with us, we will find out. My aim is to help DI Conway find the people responsible. Anything else is conjecture and not helpful.'

'Do you not think you let Fraser down?'

He couldn't say categorically he hadn't. Or was the truth he had because everyone had? 'I don't think so.'

She tilted her head, close to tears. 'Thinking it's not good enough, is it?'

The tears came. She curled over, her jacket tight across her shoulders. She sobbed. Max let it pass. She sat up, eyed the box of tissues suspiciously, and took three, bunching them up to dry her eyes.

He said, 'Have you come to London alone?'

'Yes, short straw. Actually, I volunteered. My mother is in no state to travel and my father's alternating between blaming himself and everyone else. He's raging. I was with him when the news came. His legs went from under him. He…' She left the sentence hanging. 'I didn't think it would be good for either of us if he came down. Besides, the press are sniffing around and we'd prefer to maintain some dignity. Christ knows it's in short supply.' She went to the candle and broke off a line of wax from the base. 'It's Susan, by the way. I'm the family diplomat.'

'Where are you staying?' asked Max.

'They've put me up in a hotel. In Bromley, I think Shannon said. I came straight here, so I've no idea where that is. She said I could ring her if I needed anything. There's nothing more I can do until they let us take Fraser home.'

Max had checked in with the coroner's office. 'Most likely it'll be late this week, early next.'

'I might as well go home and make arrangements from there.'

'I can drive you to the hotel, if it would make things easier.'

He'd expected her to turn him down flat. He could only think that being alone in a place so intentionally emptied of faith at the close of an awful, godless day must have made him the least-worst option. 'Thank you, I'd be grateful.'

Max had known it as the Bromley Court Hotel several name changes ago. Susan hadn't said a word on the drive over, but as they pulled into the car park, she asked if he'd wait while she checked in and went upstairs to change. She'd promised her parents a call. Afterwards, he could buy her a drink if he didn't mind keeping her company.

He called Conway from the hotel bar, keeping the conversation professional. The standard two-minute update. 'I'll need access to Fraser Neal's flat and time with the case files first thing tomorrow, before I do anything else.'

As he hung up, Susan Neal joined him, scanning the bottles behind the bar. 'Large Glenfiddich, please. No ice.'

'Same,' said Max. 'How was home?'

She shook her head. 'Surreal. Desperate. Angry. At least I can make myself useful, sounding you out.'

They found an empty table, the only couple amidst family celebrations and pre-dinner drinks. To begin with, the conversation was self-consciously polite. Max asked about Fraser. 'I only know what he told me about himself, which wasn't much. I could never get my head around how he came to be doing the work he was doing.'

'On an estate in south east London? You're assuming it's out of character, because of where we're from, but it isn't, not in our family. He was supposed to follow my dad into the law, sailed through the first year at Edinburgh Law School and dropped out. My uncles' and my dad's legal firm has several specialisms. Fraser could have taken his pick, but he wanted to go his own way. You can read all sorts into it – throwing his education in our parents' faces if you really want to trot out the clichés, but he and my eldest brother were encouraged to experience the world. Fraser wanted to change it for the better. Idealistic, perhaps, but we knew he'd come home eventually.'

'You're very certain.'

'He was my brother.'

Max moved on, 'Did he tell you about his work?'

'I had no interest in it. That's not entirely true. The last time we spoke, he'd had second thoughts about coming home at Christmas. We had a standing joke, *shall I, or shan't I?* It was a wee bit tense, with mum especially. I assumed Fraser had met someone and wanted to stay in London, but he said not. Something to do with his campaign.' She sipped her whisky and thought carefully. 'He was definitely seeing someone.'

'Was it only your mum who found it difficult?'

She laughed at the thought. 'No, he and Dad had a time-limited truce for family get-togethers. You'd have a couple of days of peace and after that...' Susan mimed the explosion with her hands. 'You should know this about my dad – I told you he wants someone to blame, it won't be himself, not for long, my mother won't let him, nor will my brother and my uncles. Once Fraser is home, if there's any truth in what Detective Inspector Conway says, he'll ruin you. He knows your name.'

Good to know, thought Max. On another day, he might have defended himself. For now, he accepted it and wondered how much Fraser Neal and his father shared. Another day, he reminded himself.

He switched to coffee, staying with Susan Neal while she drank without getting drunk. They talked about Fraser growing up in Edinburgh, his commitment to doing the right thing, whatever the cost. The mates he brought home from football, the gigs they went to and the ridiculous parties at Highland castles. He asked, was she planning to visit Marlowe Estate to see where her brother lived and worked? She didn't think she could cope with it.

'If it helps, I'll come with you.'

'What purpose would it serve?'

Max said the offer was there if she changed her mind.

When it came time to leave, she was once again the Neal family advocate. 'I'll be going back to Edinburgh tomorrow. My family will want to know what progress is being made. I expect my father will contact your superiors when the time comes. Thank you for your company and for the drink.'

The evening left Max no closer to answers. Susan Neal was firm in her expectation that her brother would have completed the work on Marlowe Estate, then joined the family firm. But if Neal wasn't committed, why come to Max in the first place? Unless he was a fantasist after all, raising expectations on the estate before running for home. He wouldn't be the first or the last.

Back home, Max updated Kilby later as he made dinner. It didn't take long. The boss was unhappy that he hadn't yet searched Neal's flat. He said he was working on it. Half an hour later, he received a text from Conway; *Marlowe Estate. Tomorrow. 8 am.*

Next morning, Conway was brisker than usual, a walk and talk meeting. 'DS Tait's out with Ferris and Reed already. We've worked up the list of Neal's associates best we can, most known through his activities on the estate, a few socially, but not many. Or not that'll admit it. They'll have to account for their whereabouts. I want you with Tait this morning, see if the list rings any bells with your *dealings* with Neal. All right with you?'

Max's attention was drawn towards the dark blue Nissan, offside wheels parked on the kerb.

'You with us?'

'Sure.'

'Bloody switch on, then. I'm not wasting time covering ground because you miss the obvious. And I've got you clearance to access Neal's flat.' They stopped. 'First, we need to be clear on something. If I get another call from my boss telling me Assistant Commissioner Kilby says I *must* allow you access, to this or any other thing, you'll get nothing. And I mean nothing from me or my people. Secondly, we've been through the place. I supervised the search. There is nothing there that constitutes evidence as far as we're concerned. What there is will be on the file. I don't see any need for you to poke about to satisfy yourself, unless you have information that I don't.'

Max let him think it.

Conway dangled the key. 'Back at close of play. You find anything at all, you tell me.'

'Thank you.' He went to take the key, but Conway held on. 'Sir?'

'You need to remember, you joined the same police force as the rest of us.'

'Good job I've got you to remind me.'

Residents in the low-rises leaned on their balconies, following the detectives' progress door to door, block to block. Uniformed back-up was highly visible in three vans parked at the estate's edge. Whatever this was designed to achieve, it wouldn't be solid information. It was heavy-handed, too visible. Hardly surprising no one was talking. Max caught up with Tait, ran his eye over the list.

'Any names you'd like to add?' Tait rattled the change in his pocket.

'None worth repeating. Let's get on with it.'

As they walked to the first address, Tait said, 'I asked about the alley gate you were going on about. The team on site next door were supposed to lock it at close of play.'

'But they didn't.'

Kingsdale Security not living up to their PR.

'They reckon the manager at the Tennessee takeaway told them not to, said he'd do it when he locked up, but never did. We asked him. He said it's bollocks.' Another one to chalk up as inconclusive and likely to stay that way.

The list should have taken them at least half a day, longer if that's what it needed. But Tait was light on patience, heavy on notebook-tapping as soon as he felt the conversation had run its course. Give them time, Max thought. Responses, predictably, majored on blank denial of any knowledge of Neal beyond being 'that Scottish geezer at the community centre', or, as one elderly resident put it, 'the bloke in the papers – too much old chat.' Most had anticipated the knock at the door.

Tait was relentless, keeping up the pace between the blocks, insistent they keep to Conway's prepared brief. How did they know Neal? What was the connection with New Cross Road? Had there been any recent trouble? And account for their whereabouts between Thursday night and Friday morning.

'Keep knocking, keep asking, all we can do,' Tait said, walking away from another quickly closed door, this one belonging to a part-time care worker and volunteer who'd gone to some lengths to memorise last Thursday night's TV schedule. Conversation between door knocks was abrupt. As they took a shortcut through the community garden, Max insisted they take a break, slow the pace.

'Come and sit for five minutes. It won't kill you.'

The garden was calm, holding the outside at bay. Max asked Tait about his time on the job. It turned out he was a more recent addition to Conway's team than he'd assumed, arriving earlier in the year as replacement for DS Stratton, the officer who'd resigned as a result of the Jerome Standing enquiry. Conway brought him onside quickly, Tait said. 'He's been solid, taught me a lot in a short space of time. I had five years in Croydon before this, but the DI's another level of professional. This is the first case since I've been his DS that we've turned up nothing this far down the road. It's making me itch.'

Max read between the lines. Loyalty aside, Tait was bothered by Conway's approach.

Another hour into the interviews and the ratio of those not at home or not answering made it difficult to justify the manpower. Max left Tait, saying he'd be at Neal's flat if he was needed. They'd catch up later.

He approached the block with the expectation he was observed. A woman hung washing on a balcony-slung line, catching the late-morning sunlight. She knew exactly who he was and what he was there for.

The key slipped easily into the lock and turned. He paused before entering, a space where a prayer might have been, a thought for Fraser or his own chances of unearthing a worthwhile lead, he wasn't sure. On the hall radiator, last week's laundry. Two shirts dried stiff. A bottle-green polo shirt, long-sleeved. Into the living room, boxer shorts and socks.

Conway's team had searched and fingerprinted, evident from cushions scattered randomly, dusted door handles. Nothing in the place you'd expect it to be. In spite of her claim to the contrary, he didn't believe Susan Neal would stay away. There would be personal effects, gifts, the letters she'd sent. *What purpose would it serve?*

Max was drawn to the hi-fi, tilting his head to read the titles on a Jenga stack of CDs. It would have been easier to name Scots indie bands that weren't represented, at least those on the wistful, jangly '80s and '90s end of the spectrum. The lad needed some Jesus and Mary Chain in his life.

The eye-level bookshelves were taken up with science fiction. Below, a mix of supermarket crime novels and literature, and on the bottom shelf, Neal's undergraduate study books – a series of guides to public law, campaigning, volumes on activism and social justice. Second-hand bookshop labels, Bookmarks in Bloomsbury, Housmans on the Caledonian Road, the Quaker Bookshop on the Euston Road. All within walking distance of each other. He pulled out a yellowing edition of Ursula Le Guin's *Dispossessed*, Hochschild's *Bury the Chains*, Courtney Martin's *Do It Anyway*. None of his literature was overtly subversive. He had the hots for Naomi Klein. *No Logo, Fences and Windows* and *The Shock Doctrine* alongside. It amounted to a crash course in the language of activism from a privileged position. Max questioned whether this was Neal on his own initiative or someone fuelling the fire. The books didn't look well used. A very few had notes in margins or scuffed corners. The spines were bent, but not consistently, and not as obviously as the novels.

He held onto the thought as he worked around the room. Conway's people had removed photographs from their frames. One of Fraser with Susan, mid-giggle, alongside a frown-featured older boy he took to be the senior brother, was off-centre. At the opposite end Mum and Dad, windswept and outdoors, a backdrop of rolling waves. Most prominent was a group photo taken outside Marlowe Estate Community Centre, a banner across the top read MARLOWE *ACTION* – NO TO JAMAICA DOCK. Beneath, arm in arm, were Fraser Neal and Ali Barnes at the centre, laughs all round.

Into the bedroom. Clothes tossed from the wardrobe across

an unmade bed. Fraser had been an unfussy dresser, an excess of brewery freebie T-shirts – someone had done bar work and for more than one summer – jumpers, no-brand jeans, well-worn trainers. A pair of walking boots, expensive judging by the leather. A suit on the rail, its pockets empty. He felt through the lining and along the collar and lapels for papery inserts, stitches out of place, though he didn't imagine Neal was sufficiently skilled to unpick and invisibly mend a seam. He moved aside the clothes on the bed and sat on the edge. What had he expected? To know Neal better, to get a sense of what Conway might have missed, maybe a feel for what had been taken away or abandoned? There was always more.

Absently, he started to fold the jumpers, shaking each and laying it flat across the bed beside him. He arranged them on the shelf in the wardrobe and noticed a flake of chipped paint at the place where the doors met, just below handle height. A chair, wooden-backed, made do for Neal's bedside lamp, clock and bookstand. He set it next to the wardrobe. Its back met the chipped doors. He stood up carefully, keeping his weight over the legs – it seemed too flimsy to carry him, but it gave access to the top of the wardrobe. Enough to see the dust had been disturbed, something unhidden and taken.

By the time he'd worked his way through the flat and was on his way out, Neal's neighbour was bringing in her washing. 'You got the last sunshine,' said Max.

'We don't get much this time of year. I hate drying indoors, place feels like a sodding Chinese laundry.'

'Can I ask, did you know Fraser well?'

'He was a good neighbour. Him and Alison have done more for people around here than the council's done in years. I hope you find who did it, they want shooting.' She folded her pillowcases and laid them in her basket. 'I shouldn't say that, I know. He was someone you could talk to, didn't matter if he was busy. It's very sad.' She picked up her basket, turning her head away as a flurry of windblown rain came across the balcony. 'He was charming, so's his sister.'

'You've met her?'

'We had a chat yesterday morning. Lovely girl, so like her brother.'

10

Max

BY THE TIME MAX arrived at the Civic Suite at Lewisham Council, there was barely a seat spare. He picked up a glossy handout and made his way to the back of the room, casting an eye over the architects' drawings and digital impressions that lined the walls. A similar set of images, graphs, plans and statistics repeated on slides on a screen at the front. On a low stage, a panel of three men and one woman in suits faced an audience of residents. All simmering nicely. He slipped into a space unnoticed, recognising faces from Marlowe Estate, adding others from the group photograph in Neal's flat. He couldn't see anyone from Conway's investigation team.

A voice came over the PA, asking for quiet. Greg Walsham, elected member of the London Assembly, made his introduction and set out the meeting's aims: for the project team to talk through the next stage of the scheme, and for residents to ask questions, bearing in mind the project had already been discussed at length. He passed the microphone to Gavin Slade, introduced as a local business leader and the driving force behind the Jamaica Dock scheme. Max sensed a stiffening in the audience.

Slade paused for quiet. 'Before we begin, I want to offer my own and the project team's condolences to the Marlowe Estate community and the family of Fraser Neal following the sad news.' Slade was quite the performer, might have worked in the circles he mixed in, but here it stank the place out. He went on, 'We did not see eye to eye on many things. Nevertheless, I respected Fraser for his forthrightness, his passion for the issues that concern us all and his direct approach. We are deeply sorry for your loss and we hope this evening's proceedings can be carried out respectfully.'

From behind, Max heard a low voice: 'Only if you fuck off.'

Relieved to be getting down to business, Mr Hutchings, Strategic Director of Planning and Regeneration, summarised the scheme's status. He spoke plainly about its origins, its aims and objectives, a timeline for the development and, as an afterthought, acknowledged there were elements contested by the local community. It was, he concluded, their responsibility to seek solutions for the benefit of residents across the borough and London as a whole.

Ali stood. Max found himself willing her not to bite.

Hutchings opened his hand. 'Miss Barnes.'

Without the benefit of a microphone, it was an effort for Ali to make herself heard without sounding anxious. There was a quiver in her voice. 'The Jamaica Dock scheme is being done to the people of Deptford and the Marlowe Estate without our consent or support. Anyone reading your development proposal can see there isn't one single thing we asked for that you couldn't row back on.'

Slade interceded, 'But they are in the document, as Mr Neal asked.'

Ali responded, 'And for each one there's a loophole that means they'll disappear when it suits you.' She spoke to the room, 'They'll call it cost overruns, or whatever Mr Slade and his cronies cook up to add to their bottom line.'

Slade interrupted, 'You've no grounds to make that accusation – we have acted in good faith at every point. We wouldn't be here otherwise.'

A ripple of dissent through the audience.

One man caught Max's eye, standing diagonally opposite, closer to the stage and scanning the audience, noting the core of disagreement. He didn't carry himself as if he was security, but Max caught his gesture towards two men who certainly were. Ali was speaking. 'We know you have no intention of conducting a fair and objective consultation process. The clock is ticking and if you're to land the investment grants, the Olympic grants, and the shady foreign investment from wherever—'

Slade's voice rose highest. 'Miss Barnes, there's nothing new from you. It's one unfounded complaint after another. This is an important development for the whole of London. It has approval from the minister, support from City Hall, and the full backing of the councils whose residents and businesses will benefit.'

Ali's own people were drowning her out. She waved a sheaf of papers, shouting, 'You talk about respect, but you won't read our proposals. Why is there so little affordable housing? Why are facilities you promise will benefit the community, the parks, playgrounds and green spaces, only accessible to the occupants of your new flats? Will our children have to stand at the railings and watch? And the heritage, our heritage, that your scheme will destroy forever while you and your mates on the council line your pockets, how do you answer that?'

Slade was rattled, but not for long.

The man standing stage side right waited a few seconds before making his way to the rear exit, the other two falling in behind. As they passed, one caught Max's eye and instinctively turned his head away.

Greg Walsham belatedly joined the argument. 'What you're telling us, Miss Barnes, does not progress the debate. You asked for written reassurances, we've given them to you. You can't keep moving the goalposts, demanding we go further. Does anyone have anything new to say? If not, I suggest we move on.'

The Marlowe Estate contingent stood, angry voices calling out the meeting as a waste of time, wiping out any chance of further discussion, triggering anxious exchanges between the men on stage. All but Slade, whose satisfied expression didn't leave his face. What had they expected? For Gavin Slade, it was exactly this.

Ali headed for the car park, hoisting her bag onto her shoulder, keys in hand. Max hung back. Slade's senior floor-walker came from a side door and called her name. They spoke and she looked afraid at something he said. She saw Max watching. Something passed between them, a clear understanding. He made his presence known. Slade's man headed back the way he came, shielding his face from the CCTV cameras. Ali got into her car. Max walked across. She got out and offered the keys. You drive. I can't. Her hands were shaking.

Max drove through Lewisham, heading towards Greenwich. Best to avoid New Cross Road. Ali tuned the car radio to a late-night reggae station. Three tracks down and Max felt as if he'd time-travelled back 20 years. Same streets, same music. Ali turned up Gregory Isaacs's 'Night Nurse'.

By the time they were on Creek Road, heading for Deptford, he'd worked out Ali's random selection gearbox. The car had angry brakes. They rocked to a stop at a crossing. Ali's bag slid off the back seat.

'Jesus,' said Max.

'Sorry, I had the discs and pads replaced a couple of weeks back.'

'By a lunatic,' Max said. 'We're heading for Marlowe Estate, right?'

She shook her head. 'Not work, home.'

She didn't live on the estate. He waited.

'Sorry, it's Etta Street. Round the back of the park.'

He knew it.

Ali turned a cigarette between her fingers. 'Weird being driven in your own car. You don't mind if I smoke, do you?'

'It's your car.'

She lit up. 'I take it you're not local?'

'I'm the other side of the river, near Swiss Cottage.'

'Yet you drive as if you know your way around.' She opened the window enough to let the smoke out. 'We used to live on the Marlowe. Dad bought the house I live in from his Auntie Jean before house prices around here went north. She sold it to her favourite nephew to keep it out of my cousins' mitts. Still lived in it, but didn't have to worry about the bills and the upkeep. After she died, Dad said, Did I want to move in? I pay rent, cover Dad's mortgage. I don't know why I'm telling you this.'

Max recognised the need to justify how you'd 'got on' through a chance taken or an opportunity made. He'd kicked the habit long ago. It was no one else's business.

Ali's gaze fixed ahead. 'I screwed it up tonight. Slade set me up and I gave him what he wanted. We gained nothing other than making everyone angry.'

'It wasn't great, but it happens.'

'Yeah, but he's sussed out we're no good without Fraser. Next left and anywhere you can park is fine. I've got a resident's badge.'

Max pulled in and reverse-parked. Engine off, he handed back the keys.

'Do you want to come in, I've sort of marooned you here.'

'I'll get a cab back. Unless you want to drive me?'

'Very funny.'

She took the keys but didn't move, giving what she was

thinking a dry run before speaking. 'Slade thinks we can be bought off or kept out, but we're not ignorant people. We put time and effort into understanding their bullshit documents. Christ knows, they don't make it easy. I've sat in rooms and been talked at by council officers and consultants who get paid more for a day's work than I get in a month. But they don't live here. We do.'

'Sounds like you're up against it.'

'Never stops. So "it happens" isn't good enough.'

'Ali, tonight's gone.'

'You mean he's gone.'

'If you want to be brutal, yes, he has. But that doesn't mean you can't find a way.'

'Fraser made us *visible*. He got what it felt like to have your world turned over, built on and sold from under your feet with you powerless to do anything about it. Fraser made us feel we mattered. He made sure *they* felt it, Slade and Walsham. We had to be taken seriously.'

'Next time you'll be better.'

She turned to him, the shadow of an overhanging tree moving across her face. 'What are you doing here?'

'You asked me to drive you home, remember?'

'No, *here*. Part of this. We've had police crawling over the estate since Friday. Ask Shana in the café and she'll know how many sugars they have in their coffee. I don't like them being there, no one does, but they behave like police. You're never with them. You come on your own, you're here out of hours. You don't talk the way they do.'

Max wondered whether Conway had given his grubby opinions an airing. She had a right to ask. 'I want to find who murdered Fraser. That's all.'

'Right.' She wasn't buying it.

'I have a different background from DI Conway's people. You don't have to talk to me if you don't want to.'

'That's not what I meant. I meant you're more like one of us and that bothers me.'

Max said he'd wait outside for the cab. Ali invited him in, said she needed to know how many sugars he liked in his coffee. A scruffy black and tan mongrel met them in the hall, barking and frantically running around their feet. Ali dropped her bag and gave the dog a face to lick. 'This is Bobby Dog.' The dog raised its performance another level. Ali led them through to the kitchen, Bobby's claws scratched and slipped on the floor tiles. She opened the back door and he flew out, triggering the security light. Ali put a handful of biscuits in his bowl and Bobby was back, the food gone in seconds. Fussed and fed, he settled on a thick folded blanket by the radiator.

'Bobby.' Max shook his head.

Ali busied making coffee. 'Got him last year. A rescue. Named him after Bobby McGee, you know the Kris Kristofferson song – *freedom's just another word for nothing left to lose* – my dad's favourite. Him and Johnny Cash. "Honest men singing the truth," he used to say.'

He noted the past tense. Somewhere he didn't want to go. Ali saved him the trouble. 'Dad's still around, but I don't see as much of him as I should. You'd think after twenty years his wife would cut me some slack. Mind you, she doesn't like him listening to Johnny Cash either.'

They stood in the kitchen, a respectful distance between them.

Max said, 'What do you think you'll do now?'

'See you off, take Bobby for a walk. Drink a bottle of wine, stay up way too late and start again tomorrow. I'll get over it.'

Aside from the dog walking, Ali's routine sounded familiar.

She set her cup on the worktop and lit another cigarette. 'I need to find a different way to get through to them, or someone else can do it. I'm not Fraser. I say his words and they sound full of shit.'

'It wasn't a total write-off. What you said made sense.'

She pulled out a chair at the kitchen table and motioned for Max to do the same. 'I'm listening.'

'You didn't have a mic, so you couldn't be heard. Ask for one. You don't get one, go to the stage and speak from there. Say what you're saying on equal terms. Second, be more professional than they are. Think about what you need to say. If you can keep it to key points and back them up, it's better. If there are clauses in agreements they've reneged on, state them. Where were they agreed, when, who by? Last thing, if you make the fight dirty, they win.'

'They think we're toothless as it is.'

'The deck's stacked that way. You say investors are shady, you need to justify the allegation. Otherwise, it's dismissed as emotional blah!'

'Slade didn't deny it.'

'That's true, he didn't. But he didn't need to.'

She was quiet. 'What I said, most of it came from notes of meetings with Fraser.'

Max hadn't intended for the conversation to take this direction, but if that's what Fraser had planned to say, it stood to reason he'd have had details ready, names of investors he hadn't shared with Ali. He wondered what else they'd talked about in private. It was obvious they'd been close. He needed to ask the question. Ali didn't give him the chance. She picked up her phone. 'I have to answer Shana. She's asking how I am.'

'Before I go, I need your help. I won't get a proper sense of Fraser and what he was about unless I can spend time with local people, people who are connected. You knew him well...'

Ali raised a don't-go-there eyebrow. Max moved on. 'Who else should I speak to? More than these people we've been talking to. There's zero trust between us and residents.'

Nick Triplow

'When is there ever?'

'I still need to ask the question.'

'You've talked to your people, drug squad or the gang people, whatever they're called?'

'Nothing doing.'

'Speak to Muhammed, he heads up the youth work team. He'll have been at the maze over the weekend. Ask him if the kids have been talking. If they have, he'll know. You want me to have a word with him?'

'I'd be grateful.'

Ali walked him to the front door. An old brass artillery shell casing served as an umbrella and walking-stick stand. 'My granddad's, well, not his personally. He was an anti-aircraft gunner on Shooter's Hill.'

Her stories, her people. Max felt a rare sense of kinship. He'd lived without those connections in his life, but this felt different.

'Ali, can I ask about the man that spoke to you in the car park?'

'Martin Dyce. With a Y. He heads up the Jamaica Dock project for City Hall. Before that, he used to work for Lewisham Council. He's from the estate originally, believe it or not. He went to school round here. My ex knew him.'

'What did he say?'

'He said this business wasn't for me.'

'And that left you shaking?'

She inhaled deeply. 'He said I'd be better off spending time taking care of my dad, because he didn't have long left, rather than wasting it on lost causes.'

A car pulled up outside. Max's phone buzzed. 'That's me.'

Ali dropped the chain, opened the door and stood aside to let him pass. They hesitated. Only for a moment, but it was long enough.

11

Johnny

JOHNNY TURNED DOWN FATHER Downey's offer of a shower before meeting Detective Sergeant Tait. He'd missed the time they'd arranged on Monday. Downey rescheduled, insisting he stay at the hostel overnight. On Tuesday morning he sat in the parish office, tired, unshaven and hungry. He pressed his hands between his knees. Downey asked if he was okay. He stayed tight-lipped. It already felt like a mistake.

Tait was shown in and Downey made introductions. 'Mister Nunn was with us on Saturday night and has agreed to speak to you.'

Tait checked behind him before sitting down. 'We expected you yesterday.'

'I know.'

'I take it Father Downey explained we're investigating a serious assault leading to potentially life-threatening injuries for a volunteer worker.'

'I know what you're here for.'

'In that case, what can you tell me about that night, from your perspective? As much detail as you remember.'

'Two men were arguing with a lad from the food queue. When the argument got nasty, the volunteer, Shelly I think her name was, tried to get between them. One bloke punched her. She was out before she hit the ground. She hit her head. They dragged the boy into the back of a car and drove away.'

'Father Downey says you know the two men.'

'I've seen them around.'

'But you'd recognise them?'

Johnny wasn't ready to give ground. 'I can't say for certain.'

'We'll come back to that. The argument, what was it about?'

'I couldn't hear.'

'How far away were you?'

'Churchyard to the fence, however far that is.'

'But you could tell it was heated.' Tait repositioned his chair to face Johnny square on. 'So you saw the perpetrators but don't know them and can't be sure you'd recognise them. You knew they were arguing with the lad but not what it was about. Is that all of it, *really*?'

Not for the first time, Johnny was on the receiving end of Sam Downey's glare. The priest lowered his eyes. Any thoughts Johnny had of circling the answers evaporated. He said, 'One calls himself Fitzpatrick. The other's known as Pallo.'

'How do you know them?'

'Like I said, from around. From the streets.'

'You've had dealings before?'

'They do what they do and it means they're in places I'm in sometimes.'

'And what do they *do*?'

'What I've seen them do is supply drugs for people on the streets. What they do when people can't afford to pay is what happened at the weekend.'

'Tell me what you know about the younger man, the one they took away.'

'Stan Moffatt. They call him Adidas Stan.'

Tait raised an eyebrow.

'The story was he knocked off a black sack from outside a charity shop and came up with a load of designer sports gear. Samples or fakes someone chucked out. He sold some on and kept the rest himself.'

'What do you know about him?'

'He's from up north, on the coast. Yorkshire, I think.'

Tait opened his hands, expecting more.

'Last time I'd seen him before Saturday he was talking about going back home for his mum's birthday. But that was months ago.'

'And he's known to be an associate of the other two?' Tait made another note and flipped back a few pages. 'How long have you been coming here to St Mark's?'

Downey cut in, 'Mr Nunn's recently returned to the neighbourhood.'

'How recently?' said Tait.

'A couple of days,' said Johnny. 'I used to live not far from here.'

'Where are you living now?'

'Nowhere in particular.'

'You're homeless, I take it? Sleeping rough.'

'That's one way of putting it.'

'Before this visit, when was the last time you were in Deptford?'

'Some time ago. I couldn't say exactly.'

'So you weren't here, say, on Thursday or Friday night?'

Johnny shook his head.

'What about local connections, friends, family?'

'I haven't got round to finding out.'

Tait doubled back. 'Fitzpatrick and Pallo, can you remember where you've seen them previously, and when?'

'Last October, November time. I was staying in a hostel near Tottenham. One day they were there. They knew who had money, who didn't. They knew who was using and who wasn't. For a while, they turned up two or three times a week. Turned out they were dealing to half the residents.'

'Were they supplying you?'

'I don't use.'

87

'Have you ever used?'

Downey leaned in to protest, but Johnny held up a hand. 'I'm clean.'

'Two nights ago, describe to me exactly your movements.'

Johnny took his time, remembering what he'd said the first time around and explaining how he'd arrived and joined the queue in the rain, keeping himself to himself until Stan made his failed play for the two Romanian girls. He described how Shelly had approached him. She was kind, well-intentioned, not preachy, but nervous about talking to him and ticked off by her supervisor, who sent her back out, which meant she was closer to the argument when it happened.

'How long would you say the argument lasted?'

'Two or three minutes.'

'And when Miss Dowd put herself between Stan and Fitzpatrick and Pallo, how long was that?'

'Couple of minutes at most.'

'Did you witness the assault?'

'It was Pallo.'

'And how many times did you see Pallo hit Miss Dowd?'

'Twice. He had hold of her hair, the second he swung and connected and let go.'

'And because you'd had dealings with them before and knew them to be violent, you thought it best to keep your distance and not intervene to prevent Miss Dowd from being assaulted.'

'I hadn't had *dealings*. They were around, that's all.'

'But you were frightened?'

'It happened too quickly for anyone to stop it.'

'And you were closest, so you'd know. We'll leave it there. I need to make a call; can you hang on a little longer?'

'I'm sorry,' Johnny said when Tait had gone.

'Don't apologise, son.' Downey reached out over the desktop and gave Johnny's arm a squeeze. 'It's my fault. We should have dealt with this another way.'

Tait came back but didn't sit, directing his comments to Downey. 'I've spoken with Detective Inspector Conway and he agrees, given what Mr Nunn has told us so far, we need to do this properly. I want to carry on questioning Mr Nunn and take a formal statement at Lewisham Police Station.'

'When?' said Johnny.

'We'll go now. I have to inform you that you are entitled to additional support – that means you can have someone with you. Do you understand?'

He wasn't really sure he did. 'Are you arresting me?'

'No, but your statement needs to be on record and handled with due process. Nothing sinister.' Johnny didn't believe him. He opened the door. 'Shall we go?'

Downey was on his feet, taking his coat from the back of the door. Johnny waved him away. 'I'll be fine, it's okay.'

In the interview room, Tait took his jacket off, folded his shirtsleeves. A second plainclothes officer introduced himself as Detective Inspector Conway. Johnny took off his coat, took in the lights, the lead-grey walls and hairline cracks in the ceiling plaster that met in the corner where a CCTV camera light blinked.

Tait said, 'From this point onwards, what you tell us will form your witness statement. At the end, you'll be able to read it, correct it, and sign off as a true and accurate record of your version of events. Do you understand?'

Johnny's eye was drawn to the red light. 'Of course.'

'We're going to go over what you told us in Father Downey's office for Detective Inspector Conway's benefit and for the tape, but before we do, I want to run through the CCTV from Saturday night, see if we can jog your memory.'

Conway sat back, letting Tait take the lead. The senior man didn't seem interested. Tait tilted the laptop screen. A still image covered the churchyard and the path leading to the

89

kitchen entrance. The time code flickered 22.47. 'Can you see that; is that okay?'

He nodded.

Tait clicked 'play'. The scene unfolded soundlessly. Conway's eyes were on him. Stan came from the street to the food queue, directly to the girls, as if he'd already identified them as his marks. While he was talking, he jigged from foot to foot. By contrast, Johnny's arrival from Mary Ann Gardens minutes later was laboured and heavy. He stood apart with his shoulders hunched. Rain slanted in the church lights' arc.

Tait asked him to confirm this was him. 'And this?' It was Stan.

'Stan. You know that, I told you. He was chatting up the girls. He had a place where they could stay in Lewisham, so he said.'

'Where exactly?'

'I didn't hear him say.' He kept his eyes down to protect the lie. 'The girls weren't sure. One had him worked out. This one,' he identified Mira on screen. 'She sussed how desperate Stan was, way too needy. She didn't trust him.'

The footage ran on, Bethany's dad appearing from the street and working through the queue. 'This man, what do you know about him?'

'His daughter had gone missing. Father Downey spoke to him before he had a chance to speak to me. He'll have his name.' Johnny felt certain these were questions to which they already had answers. They were playing him.

Shelly Dowd and the volunteers fanned out into the church-yard. Johnny matched his memory to the events on screen and willed it to work out differently, but it played out as he knew it would. His too-quick dismissal of Shelly; Fitzpatrick calling Stan across and Pallo closing in from behind, unseen; Stan's lame resistance, then standing his ground when it was too late.

'What were you thinking?'

Johnny shook his head. Tait paused the recording, ran it back and pressed 'play'. 'At St Mark's, you told me Shelly was closest to the argument, which was why she responded first, but she comes from behind you. Something alarmed her, yet you didn't hear anything?'

'You learn not to.'

A sceptical glance between the detectives and Tait made another note.

'Let it run,' said Conway.

Tait insisted on a second viewing before they took a break, pausing to press for details Johnny couldn't possibly know. This Pallo, is that a nickname? Where's he from? Is Fitzpatrick Irish? Who do they work for? Where exactly had he met them before? When? How many times? Was he holding back because he was working with them?'

'*No.*'

'But you are holding back. If you knew these two were trouble and didn't want to get involved, you could still have warned Father Downey or the supervisor.'

'Or Shelly Dowd,' added Conway.

'I was exhausted. I'd been walking all day.' His excuses sounded thin and whiny so he stopped making them. 'I was too slow. Slow on the uptake, slow-thinking, slow-thick, just that.'

When they ran the final sequence a third time, Johnny counted 87 seconds between Shelly running past him to the Nissan disappearing out of shot. Whatever Fitzpatrick and Pallo intended – duping two girls back to Sedgefield House, coercing Stan into acting in a way he hadn't wanted and carting him off because he'd failed – was screwed because of what Shelly did in those 87 seconds. The number spun through Johnny's memory. At his peak, it was the time he'd taken to put Terry McAteer on the canvas and win his first professional fight. Now it was enough to shame him, seeing himself rooted to the spot while a woman was beaten unconscious.

Tait let the footage run until Johnny moved out of frame. 'This matters, doesn't it? This all *matters*.'

His silence said it did.

Tait pressed. 'They put her in hospital.'

Conway put his hand out for Tait to be quiet. He said, 'We can find these men, but the CCTV alone isn't enough for a conviction. I need witnesses who will go to court and convince a jury to believe them.'

Johnny gestured towards the screen. 'How is she, Shelly?'

'She has a severe head trauma and is still in St Thomas'. We haven't been able to trace Stan, although if he's still with these two I don't reckon his chances. If we do pick him up, it's unlikely he'll give us anything.'

Johnny's mind blurred as Sam Downey kneeled over Shelly's unconscious body. The churchyard bathed in monochrome flashes as the ambulance came to a stop and paramedics took over.

Conway spoke quietly. 'I want to avoid this ending badly for you. If you go back to the street, there is likely to be a chain of events which sees them finding you or you'll run into them. It's inevitable. If you choose to be positive about it, we can support you and make sure you have whatever you need to make things better, help find you somewhere to stay.' Conway gestured to Tait, who swung the laptop round for Johnny's benefit and clicked the first of a series of mugshots.

Johnny said, 'No.'

Tait clicked.

'No.'

Click by click by click, Tait's gaze intensified, searching for the flicker that his 'no' was a lie. A parade of faces showing blank resentment and hollow-eyed defiance passed by. Johnny identified Fitzpatrick and Pallo Gashi and thought they'd reached the end, but Tait scrolled back to a photo he'd already rejected. 'This man is known as George Laska.'

Conway came forward, showing an active interest. 'He takes underage girls to pubs, makes them feel all grown up. We've spoken to victims, teenage girls Laska recruited to sell weed to their mates, then coke and heroin to *his* mates, and who found themselves involved in other *activities*. He's controlling, he gets them in debt, invites them to parties, then demands they have sex with men and women for money. You know him?'

He was silent. He knew George Laska, everyone did.

Conway drove the point home. 'One fourteen-year-old girl our colleagues in north London spoke to refused to have oral sex with a man Laska introduced her to at a party. Later, he had her held down while he poured boiling water on her legs as a punishment.' He paused to let it sink in. 'Most people are too frightened to speak out, because they're young and vulnerable and they see no way out. But I can tell by your reaction to what we've shown you, that isn't you.'

Laska's face filled the screen. He thought about the Romanian girls, last seen heading for Lewisham. 'Sunday afternoon, I saw him driving Stan away from St Thomas' Hospital. Stan Moffatt is George Laska's boy.'

Tait indicated on the statement sheet where Johnny needed to sign. The pen felt fat between his fingers. His signature would most likely be a worthless scrawl he'd never be able to repeat. It wasn't his only reason for hesitating. Tait and Conway didn't know or care what his best interests were. They'd give him up if it suited their purpose. Tait tapped a slow rhythm, waiting for him to get on with it. He dropped pen to paper. The *J* was clear enough. The rest trailed into a loose, formless wave.

The tape was off, likewise the cameras. A courtesy while

Tait asked routine personal questions. Had he any history of mental health issues, drug use, problems with alcohol?

'No.'

'You've never had any kind of substance issues?'

A harder edge. 'Not since you last asked.'

Tait changed his tone. 'You were in Deptford on Saturday night. Where did you say you were before that?'

He hadn't said. 'I was in north London.'

'That's a bit vague, isn't it?'

'Finsbury Park, in a hostel.'

'What about Thursday night into Friday morning?'

'I wasn't in south London.'

'How can we verify that?'

'Ask the charity that runs the place. You have to do a drug test before they'll let you in, so they'll have a record.'

There was more Tait wanted to ask, but Conway held up his hand. He asked, Was there anything Johnny wanted to know?

'When do they get told I'm the witness?'

'That depends on who you talk to. My advice, let's not get ahead of ourselves. We need to put a case together first. After that, we'll see how it develops. If it does go to court, the CPS will give full disclosure. For now, though, with your situation as it is, it makes sense to find you a place to stay temporarily, somewhere out of harm's way.'

That meant a room in a box to sweat out nights, weeks, months until they took the case to court. 'But it'll be in London?'

'It'll be what we can find, where we can find it.' Tait gathered his things together, eyeing Johnny as if he expected him to do a runner as soon as they let him loose. He was narked about something.

Johnny felt a sense of dull, thudding panic at the thought of being sent away. He didn't know if he'd have the strength to find his way home again. He reached around the chair for his jacket. 'I'll be okay, I'll sort myself out.'

'I don't think so,' said Conway. 'Sit tight and we'll get you sorted. DS Tait can get someone to bring you a drink and something to eat.'

Johnny was too exhausted to argue. He rubbed his hands for warmth. Tait and Conway didn't trust him, but they didn't trust each other either. He'd be kept isolated until they decided whether he was worth bothering with. Doing the 'right thing' as the price for coming home was bullshit. He'd done this to himself.

12

Max

COPIES OF WITNESS STATEMENTS from the Neal investigation were on his desk. A covering note from Conway repeated the request for full disclosure of communications between Special Operations and Fraser Neal. Max set it aside.

Ali had been true to her word. A phone message from Muhammed said he could meet Max later in the afternoon. Max sent a text confirming he'd be there. He'd hoped to catch Kilby before heading off, but the boss was out of town for a conference, due back that evening. He spent the morning reading through statements. With each one, the lack of a substantive lead grew more concerning. It wasn't that Conway's team had overlooked anything obvious, but no one had given them anything beyond Neal's public persona. Conway's parameters for enquiry were hindering, rather than enabling, the process.

There was, at least, the semblance of a timeline. Neal had been home to Edinburgh the week prior to his murder, something Susan Neal hadn't mentioned. He'd shown up briefly at a community event on the Saturday afternoon, facilitated a meeting in Marlowe Estate Community Centre on Tuesday, had contact with Alison Barnes on Tuesday evening at his home and was found murdered in the small hours of Friday morning. Available CCTV from the cab office reviewed so far showed nothing. That included Neal's arrival. Conway declined to task his team to widen the scope of the search. Afridi, the Tennessee Fried Chicken shop manager, had been last to leave, but couldn't remember what time the rubbish had gone out. Tarkan, the lad who'd taken it, reckoned it was just after one o'clock, Friday morning. He didn't think there was a dead man in the alley at that time. 'I didn't hang about, *because it was raining*.' Max read the line again. He was sceptical, or maybe he just didn't want to believe Fraser had died in the dark alone, ignored. Post-mortem results stated cause of death as a single stab wound inflicted by a double-edged blade, approximately 9 cm in length. The pathologist noted it had been a weapon designed to kill. *And disappear without trace.*

Max set aside Conway's files and turned his attention to Gavin Slade. He'd had a nagging feeling that Slade's name cropped up in the Special Operations archive. Not a case he'd worked directly, but he found the entry. The officer they'd put into the firm's security team across an 18-month period, 2008–09, was a lad called Kevin Russell. According to the file, Russell hadn't come up with much, but it would be enough for Max to rattle Slade. He called Tait and said they'd catch up later.

Kingsdale Security's office was based in a row of business premises on a trading estate in Rotherhithe. Behind it, Jarrow Road backed onto the main railway line to and from the City. Neighbours to a hardware wholesaler on one side and an electrical supplier on the other, the place wasn't at its best on an overcast Tuesday morning, at odds with Slade's public persona, the urban pioneer and shining knight of new capital. Max stepped between uneven paving slabs puddled from last night's rain. His attention caught by movement behind the blinds at the first floor. Out front, two vans with this year's plates parked up in matching Kingsdale Developments' blue, white and red livery. On the rear doors, the London 2012 Olympics decal. Slade had been busy.

His assistant escorted Max to a first-floor waiting area. He sat on the edge of a grey leather sofa, one of a pair positioned either side of a low glass table, beneath a wall-sized blow-up of the Jamaica Dock Development site. Slade's PR would have you believe he was entirely self-made – it neglected to mention a sizeable inheritance from the sale of his father's industrial engineering firm. The biography skimmed early years at home in Chislehurst and a first job in insurance, followed by a lengthy spell in the City, most successfully with Credit Suisse, setting up residential real-estate development financing for the bank's clients, overseeing the purchase of prime central London sites for redevelopment. Little was made of his decision to leave the City to take overall control of Kingsdale Security. The family firm had lost its way under his cousin Stuart's management, notably through a badly planned move into the buy-to-let market, which Stuart was developing, alongside the firm's main site security business. Within a year of taking over, Gavin Slade had stabilised the company, winning lucrative contracts to maintain security of development sites across London.

In the aftermath of the financial crash, he bought out Dunton Homes, a once reputable building firm brought to the verge of bankruptcy. Slade wasn't interested in the name or the reputation. What interested him was the infrastructure, the knowhow and a willing workforce. He registered Kingsdale Developments, streamlined the company's management structure and appointed new board members, growing the company through a succession of commercial and residential development deals. Now he had his sights set on a grander prize.

The PA escorted Max through to Slade's office. Slade came from behind his desk and walked Max to two easy chairs in a well-lit corner. He gestured for Max to sit. Max declined the offer of coffee.

'Do you manage the Jamaica Dock project from here?'

Slade laughed. 'Good God, no. This place is a throwback, we'll be out of here next summer. We've run Kingsdale Security from this office for nine years, but that's winding down. Kingsdale Security will cease to exist as a separate entity, post 2012. The JD project team works out of City Hall. I have an office there. My own company offices are in the City.'

'Closer to the decision-making process.'

'Closer to finance, closer to civilisation if you want my honest opinion. I'm not sure what my investment clients would make of the backstreets of Bermondsey, though it has potential. I'm scoping one or two sites, nothing major. I'm thinking of investing in a pub in Rotherhithe, as a matter of fact. The China Hall, you know it?'

He did. The old dockers' pub on Lower Road was part of Lomax family folklore. The thought of it in Slade's hands was unsettling.

'Convincing investors of our vision for Marlowe Estate is a stretch, better to make the case from the City. It's where the cultural offer works best. Get them to see it from the river and it sells itself. Tell me, what did you make of the meeting?'

Slade wanted him to know he'd been seen and recognised.

'I thought it went exactly as you'd planned.'

'The sad truth is, these people are likely to be the beneficiaries when the scheme goes ahead. Property prices will rise, they'll be able to sell up and make a fortune. Go where they want. We're adding value at every stage, I just wish they'd see it that way.'

'And if they're council tenants moved out of their homes against their wishes?'

'It's a progressive scheme. I don't know how well you know this part of London, but it's been in dire need of wholesale regeneration for decades. We'll be maintaining social housing as far as we can, but when you have the opportunity to do something special, you have to grasp it, wouldn't you say?'

'I'll take your word for it. Can we talk about Fraser Neal?'

'I have had several conversations with Detective Sergeant Tait and Detective Inspector Conway since Friday. They were here yesterday and gave the impression they were satisfied with what we discussed.'

'You're working security on the building adjoining the alleyway where Neal was found.'

'Not just security. It's our development. There's a security team on site.'

'Presumably, DS Tait mentioned that the alley gate was open on the night of Neal's murder, giving access to anyone walking past.'

'At the request of the takeaway shop manager, as I understand.'

'I'd have thought site security was a priority.'

'I'll find out who was handling the job. You can speak to them.'

Max's eye was drawn to a framed *Telegraph* magazine front page. Slade in hard hat and hi-vis, behind him the Thames and Tower Bridge under the banner headline: LONDON CALLING: CITY SET TO CAPITALISE ON OLYMPIC DIVIDEND.

'What do you think?'

London Calling. Max knew it shouldn't have mattered, but it did. 'Last night, you spoke about Neal's forthrightness. Not seeing "eye-to-eye" was the phrase you used. What did that mean in practice, without the window dressing?'

'He was a pain in the arse. When it came to Jamaica Dock we disagreed on every level. His group don't want the scheme to go ahead, or at least they want a neutered version of it. We're not in a position to revisit minor clauses ad infinitum on the say-so of a community protest group. We'd never get the project off the ground. This is worth billions of pounds of investment, most already committed. The job is there to be done, and we're doing it.'

It sounded like a campaign speech.

'I guess, for a man with your background, a step into politics is the next move.'

Slade glared. 'I think I'm supposed to say "No comment."'

'In my experience, that never works for long. I couldn't help noticing the back-slapping from Mr Walsham last night.'

He laughed. 'Greg Walsham and I operate under a flag of convenience. We did agree on Fraser Neal, though.'

'Did you try to bring Neal onside at any time? A one-to-one away from the public arena.'

'*Mano a mano*. I never gave it a thought. Neal was never interested in constructive discussion. He was all about the collective, the big show. *Vive la communauté!*'

'And you don't believe – in community?'

'Not as a matter of faith. Not above progress, or achievement or ambition. All that passed between us was a matter of public record. Both of us preferred it that way. I did explain this to DI Conway.'

'There was mention at the public meeting about foreign investment. The word used was "shady". What do you make of it?'

'Last night, I put it down to someone out of their depth and clutching at straws. But you'd be better asking Alison Barnes. Foreign investment is inevitable, vital in fact. If she has proof that it's not legitimate, she should share it. Otherwise shut up. She's on very shaky ground.'

'The allegation doesn't bother you?'

'People have said worse. I am weary of these hackneyed arguments. Not because there's any truth in them, but they risk undermining confidence in the scheme. It's a stalling tactic, that's all.'

'You're not worried that your personal integrity takes a hit?'

'I might be, if the accusations came from a reliable source.'
Slade was resolutely unfazed.

Max said, 'Would I be right in thinking in the early days of Kingsdale Security there were concerns over the kind of people the company employed? Strong-arm rental practices. Overzealous site policing, specifically a spate of ABH and Assault charges in predominantly black or Asian neighbourhoods linked to members of a far-right organisation. One of which led to your cousin Stuart's conviction?'

'Our operational-decision making wasn't all it might have been in those days. Hiring and firing was never Stuart's forte, at least not the hiring part. We've moved on. The people we work with are all vetted. We have our own training programme and a code of conduct.'

'Your cousin glassed a young lad in a pub because he refused to sing the national anthem before a football match. The firm's co-founder and guiding influence did three years in Maidstone.'

'That's my cousin, not me. He wasn't in the best of mindsets at the time. He lives abroad now, in the US.'

'But he's on the payroll?'

'He's on the board in a non-executive capacity, for which he receives a fee.' Slade paused. 'It's no secret that security work is the reserve of people who can handle themselves. Stuart likes being around those kinds of people. The last time we spoke, he was looking at setting up a conduit for US contractors to work in the UK. I doubt anything will come of it. My focus is entirely on land and property, through acquisition or delivering the landmark residential developments London needs and which our friend Fraser Neal was so keen to disrupt.'

'Can we talk about Martin Dyce?'

'Martin's the GLA's lead project officer on Jamaica Dock. Highly experienced, very thorough, knows his stuff and knows the territory, does Martin. We've worked together to bring the scheme this far.'

'Effectively, he does your bidding.'

'As I said, he's employed by City Hall. The GLA pays his salary.'

'Does he usually take it on himself to intimidate your opponents, or would he need your permission to do that?'

Slade seemed amused. 'These are emotive issues, last night especially. Things are easily misunderstood. Martin's a big boy, he can speak for himself. If there's nothing more...'

Before Max left, Slade had his assistant confirm the site security supervisor for 489 New Cross Road, making the call himself. He confirmed that the alleyway had been used by site workers to carry materials to the back of the property during the afternoon and was kept open at the request of the takeaway manager. 'Good neighbour relations,' said Slade.

At the door Max said, 'Do you still see your cousin – presumably he visits?'

'We rarely get together.'

'What does he think about what you've done with his company?'

'Stuart sees, as I see, that only a fool turns away from an opportunity like Jamaica Dock. He offers his opinion when he feels he has something to contribute, or when I need his input.' He came close. 'Think what you like, Lomax. I really don't care, but do not think you can rile me into revealing anything I don't want you to know.'

The recording studio where Max was due to meet Muhammed was on the Marlowe Estate fringes, in an industrial area close to the river. He'd heard Alison call it 'maze', but had misunderstood. The facility was part of Marlowe Estate Youth Zone. Emphasising the point, a red, gold and green graffiti tag *MEYZ* covered one outside wall. Muhammed met him and led the way. 'Rosco runs the place, produces, engineers. I texted him so he's expecting us. The boys not so much. So go easy. It's sensitive.'

The studio control room was dominated by an old-school mixing desk, faders and LEDs blinking on open tracks, lined up according to Rosco's PC screen. Mounted left and right, a set of speakers click-tracked a count of four and cranked into a spaced-out dubstep bassline. The atmosphere in the place was smoke-thick and heavy. No one was smoking weed, but someone had been. Against one wall in the control room was a heavyweight leatherette couch, boulder burns on the arms and cushions. On the other side of the glass, a teenage boy in camo-combats and headphones played a five-note bassline to the drum groove his mate was putting down. In the chair, Rosco, greying dreads down his back, deepened the delay until it threatened to feedback. He swung around on the chair, acknowledging Muhammed and Max, paused the track and waved the boys through. 'Come an' listen.'

Muhammed named them as they entered the control room. Kieron, the bass player, and Kamal, drums. Max reckoned Kamal to be the eldest, by a year or two. Muhammed said, 'Sounds good.'

'We know,' said Rosco.

The boys sat back on the couch.

Muhammed said, 'I know you're busy so we won't keep you. This is Max. He's asking for some help. He needs to know about this man who was stabbed, Fraser Neal.'

Silence. Kieron shook his head.

'You know who Neal was, right?' said Max.

'Not our business to know.'

'I know you know he was murdered in New Cross last Friday morning.'

Kamal tilted his head towards Max, speaking to Muhammed. '*He* shouldn't be here. No police. Or we be in trouble.'

'With who?' said Max.

Kieron's amp gave a low hum through the speakers.

'It was my decision,' said Rosco. 'It's important.' He produced a half-smoked spliff from his waistcoat pocket and lit up.

'He's making a point,' said Max. 'He's telling you he can smoke whatever the fuck he wants in front of me. I'm not interested in anything other than what I'm asking. And I'm asking about Fraser Neal.'

Nothing.

'Do you know where the money came from to buy these decks and the desk and the amps and stuff?'

'It's clean,' said Kamal.

'I know it's clean and I know where it came from. I want to know if you do.'

'The project,' said Kamal.

'Who funded the project?'

'The council.'

'The government.'

They took turns, enjoying the game.

'Rosco's mum.'

'Nutty Linda.'

'The Queen.'

'Yeah,' said Max, 'they all had a hand in it. But who did the paperwork and got the cash? Answer, Fraser Neal. He got a youth music charity to part with thousands of pounds and got the council to match it, so this place was built and kitted out professionally. He blagged the desk from a mate in Fulham and bought the hardware, the software and amps, instruments, and handed the whole lot over to Muhammed and Rosco and MEYZ to run it. If you have any interest in doing the right thing and it doesn't cost you anything, what's to lose?'

'Talking to you? Everything, man.'

'So if you can't say, who do I talk to? Give me a name.'

Still nothing. It wasn't working. He thanked Rosco and Muhammed. 'Good luck with the track.' He'd have told them he liked the feel of it, raw like an old dubplate, only darker, heavier, grimier, but who'd want to hear it from him, a white cop coming over like he's *down with the kids*? But something must have connected. He was on his way back to Lewisham when Muhammed's text came through: *Dwight Payne. You did not get that name from us.*

13

Johnny

TAIT BROUGHT HIM INTO the main office. Finding somewhere to stay wasn't going to be as straightforward as Conway had said. Johnny hung around listening to Tait make calls. Conway had left instructions to track down a witness protection officer and get him somewhere to stay. Overwhelmed and under-staffed, there was nothing they could do. Conway came back around four o'clock and took over, pulling rank with the same result. There was no accommodation, not in London, not in any neighbouring force, nor further afield. Johnny's heart sank at the prospect of being shoved in an out-of-town B&B. As a last resort, Conway called in a favour. A mate of a mate selling a flat in Lee Green was waiting for builders to install a new kitchen. Johnny could stay there for a couple of nights.

Conway drove him. Johnny felt as he had on those first nights on the streets, powerless, carried along by circumstance. At the lights on Blackheath Hill, Conway reached behind and landed a Tesco shopping bag on Johnny's lap. 'DS Tait bought you some bits and pieces. Anything else, let one of us know. There's a phone in there. Our numbers are in the contacts. He's put twenty quid on it, so go easy. We'll have to account for it.'

'Thank you.' He took the phone out of its box and turned it over in his hand.

'The charger's in the box.'

They'd know who he called, but there was no one he wanted to speak to. Alison when he was ready, but that needed to be face to face.

'I can see why this isn't comfortable for you, but it's temporary. Keep it together now and we'll work out something better in the long term. See if we can get you a clean start. It's up to you. For now, just take a shower and get some sleep.'

Conway pulled into the kerb at the bottom of Belmont Hill. 'I won't come with you, best if we're not seen together. Go down the bottom, left into the main road, about twenty metres and you'll see a door set back from the road. Between the Tanning Shop and Aksaz Kebabs.'

Johnny got out, leaned down at the window.

Conway said, 'Any problems at all, give one of us a call. Stay low, keep the phone charged and I'll be in touch tomorrow. Don't do anything stupid.'

A bit late for that, he thought.

An ambulance sped down Lee High Road, siren wailing as Johnny closed the street door and walked up a narrow staircase to the third-floor landing and the reinforced door of Flat 5. The key stuck in the lock. Conway told him there was a knack, lift as you turn. Inside he found the wall switch and turned on the light, flooding the room in a 100-watt glare. He switched it off and gave his eyes time to adjust to the light bleeding in from the street.

He took in the room. From the slanted roof, it had been the attic, the lower end taken up with a two-seat sofa and chair. On a corner table stood a small-screen TV. Under the table crumpled Stella cans and Maccy D wrappers. The kitchen area had an electric kettle and a gas ring hooked up to a canister. The fridge door handle was held on with gaffer tape. In the opposite corner by the wall there was a bed with a pillow and a rolled sleeping bag. Something was underneath. Johnny used a crusty mop he found in the bathroom and dragged out a pair of grey panties. He carried them to the bathroom and dropped them in a corner by the shower stall. The toilet seat was cracked, cigarette burns dotted the plastic cistern lid. He pulled back the soap-stiffened shower curtain. A half-empty bleach bottle stood on the windowsill. Someone had made an effort, the smell said not recently. He sluiced what was left of the bleach around the toilet bowl, half-filled the bottle with water and ran it around the shower tray. He closed the door behind him. It was a place for those who had no place.

Charred meat smells from the Aksaz came up through the floor. He rinsed out a mug and made himself a brew. He switched on the TV and skipped between channels. The ads made his head spin. He emptied the contents of Conway's shopping bag onto the bed. Cereal, a pack of biscuits, milk, teabags and a jar of coffee, a wash bag and towel, a razor, spare blades and shaving gel, toothbrush and toothpaste, and a three-pack of boxer shorts.

Johnny shoved the shopping aside and sat back on the bed. There had been times he'd stayed somewhere for a spell, a cheap room paid for with a few quid from a week's casual labouring, which fed the idea he'd start out somewhere else, a place he might make a go of things, but every hostel and bedsit room he'd ever stayed in was haunted and this one was no different. With the door closed, his thoughts would turn to Kerry, his girl. He'd walked the streets to the point of exhaustion when Kerry went missing, night after night until there was nothing to go back to. That night, when he closed his eyes, she didn't come, but the Romanian girls at the church did. So did Bethany, another lost girl in a photograph. He felt hopeless.

14

Max

MAX BUTTONED HIS RAINCOAT as he crossed Tooley Street and headed for City Hall. Across the river in the City, a constellation of red crane lights shone through the drizzle. To the east, Docklands and Canary Wharf were barely visible. Another scheme that came good in the end for its investors, but it had been a painful process. The initial consortium withdrew; a second fell into bankruptcy. Max didn't question Slade's confidence in his grand plan for Jamaica Dock, but the precedents for a rough ride were there for anyone prepared to read the city's history.

The City Hall security guard cheerfully showed Max up to the Jamaica Dock project office on the fourth floor, where a lad in too-tight blue chinos and shoes with no socks showed him to reception. He was told 'Martin' would be with him shortly.

A pleasure boat made its way downstream, crossing with a police boat heading upstream at speed. The wake calmed and the river resumed its steady course. It was a wonder anyone got any work done. '*Sweet Thames, flow softly,*' he whispered to himself.

'Never get tired of it.' Greg Walsham spoke as if he'd arranged the view personally. He stretched out a hand, 'Greg Walsham, London Assembly member for Greenwich and Lewisham. We've not met.'

Max showed his ID. 'I'm with the investigation team investigating Fraser Neal's murder.'

'Yes, I know. With them, not *of* them. Gavin said you'd be heading my way. Incidentally, Martin will be along shortly. He's on a call.'

Max had a sense of team protocol coming into play. 'Mr Slade tells me you and he bonded over a shared frustration with Neal's opposition to the Jamaica Dock scheme.'

'Gavin, myself, and a host of others. We're bringing London into the twenty-first century, whether our opponents appreciate it or not. Fraser Neal was a buzzing in my ear. I've made it a principle not to lose sleep over people like him. They come and go.'

'Oh, he's definitely gone.'

Walsham spread his hands. 'Tragic, of course.'

'Can I ask, what do you stand to gain personally from Jamaica Dock?'

'Aside from the prestige of delivering it and the votes of a grateful public, not much.'

'Financially, I mean.'

'That's Neal's line of attack, that we're lining our pockets, embezzling the taxpayer. You were at the meeting on Monday, did you think there was substance to what those people were saying? There are responsibilities that come with public office. Apologies if it sounds pompous, but I firmly believe it and I've no time for anyone who doesn't.'

'Does Gavin Slade share your belief?'

'If he's got any sense he does.'

'Am I right in thinking he has his own political ambitions?'

'He said you'd mention that. There's not a great deal I can say. Gavin isn't one of us. We have a similar vision for south London, but please don't think we'd ever be on the same side of the chamber. He's never spoken to me about entering politics, why would he?'

'If he did, he'd be challenging you?'

Walsham shook his head. 'When the deserts freeze and the camels come sliding home, as they say. I'd still fancy my chances. He could land a seat somewhere safe. Bromley would be an option, though I can't see the current candidate moving over. More's the pity.' Walsham sucked his tongue distastefully. 'I'd say, with his network, Slade's likely to be given a London-wide brief on a closed party list.'

'The brief being?'

'He's the law-and-order man, isn't he?'

'When it suits him.'

'He'll be on your case if you're not careful.'

Martin Dyce joined them. Next to Walsham's made-to-measure, Dyce's suit, shoes and haircut were a study in ordinariness. He struck Max as an uninspiring conduit for the ambitions of men like Walsham and Slade.

'I'll leave you to it then,' said Walsham. 'Good to meet you, Lomax. I'll leave you in Martin's hands. Hope you're satisfied.'

Dyce greeted Max coldly, waving away his ID. Others were using his office for a meeting. They could talk in reception.

'We're aware Fraser Neal was in communication with this office and with you personally in the weeks leading up to his death. To help us create a complete picture, we need details of contacts. If you spoke, what was said? In correspondence, what was discussed? What degree of tension was there?'

'When you say *we'd like to create a picture*, who does the "we" refer to exactly?'

Max said, 'That would be the Metropolitan Police Service, you want me to show you the badge again?'

'It's a lot of work and the investigating team haven't asked for it. You don't belong to the investigating team, do you?'

This really wasn't the time for Dyce's rehearsed bemusement. 'Where were you last Thursday evening, into Friday morning?'

'I've been through this with Detective Sergeant Tait. I worked late, got back around nine, phoned my mum and stayed at home until I came to work the following morning.'

'Where's home?'

'A flat, I rent a place in Surrey Quays. It's handy for work.'

'On your own?'

'Yes, on my own. I'm married to the job, is it a problem?'

Max refused to be drawn. 'Monday evening, tell me about the public meeting.'

'You were there. What happened is what always happens – we set out a positive case for the scheme and they shoot it down.' Dyce was starting to fluster. His accent slipping revealed more Surrey Docks than Surrey Quays.

'I got the feeling you enjoyed it.'

'I'd rather they accept we're all in it together and support the scheme, it would save time, effort and paper.'

'I meant the intimidation aspect. Cornering women in car parks, is that a perk of the job?'

Dyce was ready to defend himself, but decided better of it. 'I don't think there's any advantage in my answering, is there? We know who you've been talking to and they've got a track record for shit stirring.'

'Fraser Neal walked into an alley in New Cross and didn't come out. He bled to death in the street, alone. A violent, unexplained death. He was a vocal and effective opponent of your scheme. This office – you personally – tangled with him on a weekly basis and came out on the wrong side more than once, otherwise you'd have bulldozers on the estate right now. Want me to go on?'

'I'm just unclear—'

'No, you're not. What you are is obstructive. I need to see any and all communications between this office and the

Marlowe Estate Community Action Group and Fraser Neal, specifically.' He handed Dyce his card. 'Detail covering the last month to start with. Work back from today. Include records of phone conversations, emails, direct messages, social media, written requests for info, Freedom of Information requests. I gather he was fond of those.'

'That'll take some time.'

'The first batch by Friday would be good. Email is fine, I don't need hard copies at this stage. My address is on the card.'

Persuading himself a beer with his new colleagues would be worth the grief took some doing, but Max knew if he didn't go, it meant one more line in Conway's black book and another excuse to keep him in the cold. But as he pushed open the door of the Lewisham Tavern and heard Tait greeting the barman with a fraternal 'Aye-aye, Alf, usual for me and Mister Conway', his heart sank.

Tait reeled off the remaining drinks in the round, 'Tolly's the same, Shannon's on Diet Coke, Cobbo's a Guinness and the bloke getting ready for his ball and chain, he'll have a double vodka and tonic. You made it then,' he said to Max. 'The boss didn't reckon you would. We're over in the corner.'

Max bought himself a gin and tonic and joined them.

First couple of rounds they avoided talking about the job. Ferris was the butt of as many life-sentence digs as Reed and Tolly could think of. Max kept quiet and listened. Inevitably, the conversation turned to work. Conway and Tait had spent the early part of the evening at St Thomas' Hospital, interviewing the victim in the church assault. She'd given them nothing. Tait complained about interruptions from overprotective medical staff.

Tolly mentioned they'd tracked down and arrested a ringleader from the August riots. 'You remember, boss, Flatscreen Brandon, that twat that did the shops at Rushey Green?'

Conway smiled, in spite of his sour mood.

They'd all been involved in the riots at street level. Conway's unit faced down violent crowds at Stone Lake Retail Park before being brought back to shut down Lewisham Town Centre. His officers contained rioters on Lee High Road, who smashed their way into the Dirty South bar, laying waste to the place. Tait had been in Woolwich. In the thick of some of the worst violence, looting and burning seen south of the river. That night, they'd all but lost the streets. It wouldn't happen again.

'Maintain order by any and all means. Zero tolerance,' said Conway. 'You know what that is? I don't s'pose you've ever seen a riot, not up close.'

Max sidestepped. 'Not recently.'

He got the next round in and had hardly put the drinks on the table before Tait railed against 'shit intelligence' on radicals and gangs.

'That's why connections with people like Neal are fundamental.'

'Fundamental to *me*?' said Conway. 'Thank you for your advice, I'll bear it in mind.'

'If we'd had a better sense of the scale of the unrest, there's a chance it might have been contained. At least we'd have been better organised.'

Conway regarded Max warily, 'You say that as if we're on the same side.'

Tait chimed in, 'We had our hands full enough keeping those fucking animals from torching the city.'

Max's head dropped. He didn't mind that Conway thought he was on the wrong side, whatever that meant. He minded them doubting his integrity, but he'd live with it. What pissed him off was how wilfully they misread recent history to suit themselves, the same racist tabloid bullshit. Max had been on the street in Tottenham at the start; he'd carried out detailed analysis for Kilby in the aftermath. It wasn't 'the city' that went up in smoke; it burned in places where people had no hope their lives could ever be different.

A handful of hard-drinking souls nursed their pints, but by 9 o'clock Conway's team had the place to themselves. They were flagging, the evening drawing to a close. Max had the feeling Conway preset the curfew for his people. Tolly was first to leave. Ferris called the future Mrs Ferris to pick him up at 10 o'clock. Max was ready to head off too until Conway held out a hand, 'You can hang on a bit longer.'

It turned out Reed was driving Tait home – both lived on the other side of the water, Tait in Romford and Reed further out at Brentwood. 'That's a hell of a commute,' said Max.

Reed said, 'You get used to it. I wouldn't want to do it forever, but I wanted this posting.'

Conway cut in. 'It's called dedication to the job.'

Reed checked her phone. 'Ben, we're off in ten minutes, all right?'

Max and Conway would be last to leave.

Conway said, 'So the time has come. You going to let us in on how your private investigation is going? Are you planning to follow up with every potential witness we speak to?'

Max said, 'What do you know about Dwight Payne?'

The atmosphere turned a degree cooler.

Tait said, 'We know he's king of the dealers in London SE8. Marlowe Estate's merchant class in a nutshell. Class A and B mainly. Has half the Estate scared shitless of him; the other half haven't met him yet. An army of hustlers on the streets, kids fallen through the net. Anything from ten-year-olds upwards. Keeping tabs on the general populace. Who talks to who—'

A look from Conway and he shut up.

'Has he done time?'

'Cautioned for possession. Did a six-month stretch for

carrying a knife with intent three years ago. We've not been able to touch him since.'

Conway cut in. 'If Neal was involved with Dwight Payne, we would know. I guarantee he is too busy building his dirty little empire to waste time on Fraser Neal.'

'But you haven't spoken to him.'

'Not since Friday morning and we're not going to. Neither are you.'

'But he'd know what goes on if anyone does. And the gear you found in the top flat at 491.'

Tait laughed. 'It's beneath him. He'd be offended.'

'You know him well enough to know?'

Conway stood up. 'That's enough. It's a no, Max. Find another way.'

Max sensed a blind spot, a prohibited grid square at the heart of Conway's territory. Odds were, if Conway and Tait were under orders to back off, another unit had it covered. He'd make his own enquiries, see if a word in the right place could save time.

Reed tried to catch Tait's attention. Tait lifted his half-full glass in response. He was pissed, looking to score points at Max's expense. 'It's not real police work what you do, is it? Not much pride in it. Nothing to show at the end of the day. The dog-work's eighty per cent of an investigation like this. You're too busy arse-covering, doing more harm than good.'

Max held himself together. He'd put up with worse from better men than Tait. He looked to Conway. 'Is that what you think?'

'Ben's opinions are his own,' said Conway. 'He's free to express them.'

As long as they don't contradict the boss.

'Now you've analysed the case files,' said Conway, 'in your expert opinion, would you say there's evidence that Neal was other than who he presented himself to be? According to the post-mortem, the weapon used steers to this being a professional piece of work, rather than an opportunist act. Lack of DNA and witnesses says the same. It wasn't a random attack. Someone planned it. What that says to me, in the absence of solid evidence to the contrary, is that your link is the one. Your case. Your boy.'

Knowing Conway had made his mind up made no difference. Max was giving him nothing.

Conway changed tack. 'You get anything useful from Alison Barnes?'

'If I do, I'll let you know.'

Tait chipped in. 'We'll know when we want to know. We're bringing her in. She's taken evidence from Neal's flat.'

'Says who?'

'Paperwork was removed from Neal's flat before we arrived on Friday,' said Conway. 'Photographs and personal effects weren't where they should have been. We know Alison Barnes was there late on Thursday evening. I want you to bring her in and I want you there when we interview her.'

Max thought about the dust scraped off the wardrobe top. Ali was tall enough to have reached it without the chair. Susan Neal was not.

Chewing it through as he made his way back to the car, Max had the distinct impression that Tait giving him a hard time bothered Conway, not for what he'd said, which was mainly drunk talk, but for what he might let slip. Maybe about Dwight Payne, maybe something else. It reaffirmed Conway's determination to palm responsibility for Neal's death onto Special Operations, Max specifically.

Ali's house was in darkness. He drove to Marlowe Estate on the off-chance she was still working. He needed a conversation before Conway's ham-fisted intervention undid his efforts. As he drove around the estate, he thought about how he'd never be more than a stranger to these people. It didn't usually matter that he entered lives, worked a case and was gone. The waters would close over and you expected nothing more. But here, he felt different.

Searching for a parking space, he noticed a dark-coloured Nissan parked up close to Grove Street shops. Two men in the front. No one in the back. He kept driving, pulled in around the corner and dialled the community centre office number. Ali answered on the fifth ring. 'Ali, it's Max. Where's your car parked?'

'At home, I walked this morning. I was just locking up, what do you want?'

'Keep the place locked and stay there. I'll give you a lift.'

'I'll be out shortly. Where are you?'

'Stay put. I'll come to you.'

Max reversed as far as the junction, then turned into Grove Street, parking in full view of the Nissan. He crossed the road, hands deep in his pockets, and stopped at the Nissan's front bumper, showing his ID to the occupants for a full ten seconds before heading into the estate.

He took a shortcut through the Clara James Garden. A patch of light fell across the lawn. There was movement in the shadows. He took an instinctive step away, into a batted blow across his belly. He stumbled, winded, to the path. A second blow came down across his back. A third struck behind his knees put him face to face with the turf. He covered his head. They hit him three more times across his side and back. A hand grabbed a fistful of his hair and pulled him up. 'This is not your business. Neither is Slade.'

The voice was grit and vinegar, an accent borrowed for the occasion. He should have been able to place it, but couldn't. In the darkness, two men in masks stood off, hoods up and caps pulled low.

He tried to get up, but couldn't, making it as far as a bench on his knees, fearful he'd piss himself involuntarily if he tried standing, not daring to move further. He was cold. Something didn't feel right deep in his guts.

Ali found him there. 'I thought it was you. What are you doing? Shit. Where's your car?'

'Grove Street, outside the chemist.'

'Can you get up?' She took his arm and walked him to the car. She helped him into the passenger seat. 'My turn – give us the keys.'

His focus drifted as she drove the short distance to Etta Street. Each time he moved one part of his body, a new pain announced itself.

He needed the toilet desperately. Thinking he might be able to make it up the stairs on his own, he twisted to lever himself up and his back went into spasm. He fell against the banister and sat, dropping his head between his knees at another wave of cold nausea. No chance he'd make it without help. 'This is not good,' he said, clinging to the understatement.

Ali stood in front of him, crouched, knees bent. 'Right, we do this one move at a time. Put your arms around my neck and on three...' They rose together. 'Okay, now catch your breath.'

He steadied himself. She came beside him. 'Which side hurts the worst?'

'Left,' he said. In truth, it made no difference.

She moved to his right side. They took one step at a time. At the top, the stairs were too narrow to climb side by side. He made it up, half crawling on his knees with Ali behind him. She helped him as far as the toilet and left him. He pissed and life was bearable.

Max let his head roll back on the sofa, Ali's vodka neutralising what the paracetamol had missed. 'Ali, the blokes that did this didn't know I would be there tonight. They were waiting.'

'You were unlucky. There's not as much of this kind of thing going on as people think. Did they take anything?'

'No, they didn't. I think you're missing the point.'

Ali came and sat on the floor by him, resting her head against his knee. 'I'm not. I'd just rather not think about it.'

They were silent for a time. He liked her being close. 'Did I tell you we used to live on Etta Street, up the other end?'

'No, you never said. When?'

'Years ago, first house I ever remember. My grandparents in the downstairs flat, Mum and Dad, my brother and me upstairs. I used to come back and visit regularly until Nan died.'

'This hasn't been much of a homecoming.'

'Ali, I have to ask, did you know some stuff was taken from Fraser's flat?'

'What do you mean *stuff*?'

'Paperwork, I'm guessing. Maybe some personal things. I haven't been told what exactly.'

'Are you asking me, as in formally asking?'

'Not yet, but I probably will be in a day or so.'

He lay awake on Ali's sofa, running through the night's sequence of events. It must have been a two-minute walk from where he'd parked to the community centre. Time enough for the men in the car to warn their mates waiting. Unless their phones were turned off and they'd acted on the spur of the moment. But why name Slade?

Wednesday morning, dawn came in grey smudges. Max stiffened at the pain hardening in his body and rolled himself off the sofa. He pulled on his trousers and shirt and made it to the toilet on his own, taking a mental pain inventory. By the end, he was worn out.

He was emptying coffee-pot grounds down the sink when Ali appeared. Daylight now. She drew close and put her arms around him. They held each other without speaking. Max listened to her breathing. She moved her head and he thought she would pull away, but she nestled in and held him longer, then went to get ready for work.

Something should have been said. They spent the next half hour not saying it. After she'd gone to work, he made himself believe it didn't matter. Sometimes the right moment didn't come.

He called Conway and told him he wouldn't be around. He was needed back at Carteret Street. He didn't mention the beating.

'Take your time,' said Conway, 'I'm sure we'll manage.'

Max ended the call. He filled Bobby's water bowl and put down a handful of biscuits. The dog seemed disappointed and retired to his blanket.

Max's head was clearer by the time he arrived home later that morning. He wrote and sent Kilby's update email, leaving out the beating and the night on Alison Barnes's sofa. As expected, the call came in soon after.

'You think this man Payne is worth pursuing.'

'He's worth talking to.'

'But you think he's already a target.'

'My guess would be Trident Command, which is why Conway's itching to keep us well away. If he can't make a play, he doesn't want us making one either.'

'You'd need Commander Harding's approval for an approach. She'll find out anyway.'

Max had hoped Kilby would clear his path. He didn't seem inclined.

'There is, however, a former colleague of yours currently kicking her heels with Trident.'

Max had to think. The majority of his former colleagues were dead or pensioned off. A few he could name were drinking themselves into oblivion. One DS he'd trained with had fathered a child and expected to be named in a Sunday newspaper spy-cop exposé. Realistically, it could only be one. 'Maggie?'

'Detective Constable Denny was note-taking in a meeting I attended last week. Woefully underused. I take it you weren't aware. Keep it away from the office – hers and ours. No pressure and no promises, but you never know. If she can help us with this, it might be in our shared interests in the longer term.'

Five years on from a working partnership that ended with Max narrowly avoiding dismissal and Maggie Denny assigned to HM Customs liaison in Dover, he wasn't optimistic. She'd been Kilby's protégée, well-versed in those methodical chops Conway and Tait bleated about. Except Denny had greater insight and was smarter. Max hadn't known she was back in London and he should have done. Denny had backed him when it mattered. He'd make the call.

15

Slade

SLADE KNEW FROM THE outset, for Jamaica Dock to succeed – not least guarantee City Hall's backing – he'd need key people in his corner. He'd wasted no time winning over elected members on the council's key decision-making committees. Within six months of the scheme's first mention, Martin Dyce had ferreted out the vulnerabilities of leaders and decision-makers on planning and scrutiny committees. That was his strength, find the angles and make the play for their loyalty. For the chair of planning, a petty shrimp of a man called Pendennis who made Slade's skin crawl, he promised Section 106 funds from Jamaica Dock would deliver the new-build project a constituent of his had been failing to deliver for the last three years. A straightforward proposition once Dyce confirmed the amount Pendennis owed the man in gambling debts. Vice-chair, Miss Henrietta Osime-Bennet, whose brother-in-law was struggling to keep his import business afloat, was in no position to turn down the promise of a supply chain contract on his behalf. In the case of Councillor Baskin, a pending harassment case was made to go away after a late-night visit to the complainant from Dyce and George Laska. One by one, he brought them in line.

In his quiet way, Dyce had done well. Slade was satisfied his own involvement was deniable. They'd never know their benefactor until it suited him.

Dyce's next task was to draw the sting from public opposition. These were his people, after all. Marlowe Estate close to the place he'd spent his formative years. But over coffee at the back table of Santini's Café, he was hedging, telling Slade, 'Maybe it won't be so easy, maybe Neal's death will bring them together.'

Slade was impatient. 'They believe there's a negotiation, Martin. Which is to say there is ground to be gained and lost. *That* is the illusion you need to maintain and use.'

'It isn't that simple.'

'I think it is.'

Dyce argued. 'The security fences are up around Pepys House; the scaffolders are in and you've put boots on the ground. You can't expect them not to notice.'

'You think so?' He raised an eyebrow. 'They need to know it can't be stopped, that's all. Once they realise it's happening, they'll accept it and cut their losses. Your job is to present the scheme as though everybody wins if they play. Or loses if they don't.'

'And you think they'll come round.'

'I have no idea whether they'll come round. You're the one with the feel for the community. I do know the noise at the last meeting will be hard to maintain without Neal's banner-waving. You need to remind...' He wafted a hand, feeling for the name.

'Alison Barnes.'

'...if she is the one to pick up the reins—'

'She is.'

'Then she needs to know what the stakes are, personally and professionally. But this time, please, some control.'

'I did speak to her. Afterwards.'

Dyce's got-at expression irritated Slade. They had momentum, couldn't he feel it? This needed a dynamic approach and a shrewd application of pressure. He seemed increasingly unsure, provincial in his ambition. Not the man he'd have selected, given the choice, but needs must for the time being. 'We know they're divided. Fraser's death will fragment them. Persuade them. If some dig their heels in, it won't be for long. Find out who's amenable and take the waverers one at a time.'

'And George Laska and the others, last time we spoke you told me we had no further use?'

'Serving notice. A few weeks more, that's all. It'll be over by Christmas.' Dyce didn't get the joke.

16

Johnny

CONWAY CALLED IT A safe house. Johnny sat on the bed with his back against the wall and felt the vibration from a passing bus. He didn't feel safe. He covered himself with the sleeping bag as best he could, pulling his hood over his eyes and rolling into sleep. Some time after he was woken by a fist hammering on a door downstairs. Raised voices, then a sick wailing as if an animal was in pain. He sat up and checked the phone. Three o'clock. He'd slept for less than an hour. He put on his shoes, picturing the door kicked off its hinges. He wedged the chair under the handle, then shoved the sofa over on its end against the chair. He sat with the sleeping bag around his shoulders, feeling the walls and windows vibrate down to his bones each time the night bus passed by. He closed his eyes and fell asleep a second time.

At 5 o'clock he ate Weetabix. At 6 o'clock he made tea and turned on the television. At 7 o'clock he took a shower, shampooing his hair until the water ran clean. He scrubbed dirt from under his fingernails. He shaved for the first time in a week, having to switch to a new blade part way through. The end result was that he barely recognised himself. He washed with clean hot water and towelled dry. When he came out, there was a text from Conway: *Hope all's okay. I'll be in touch later, setting up meeting with CPS.*

The sense of losing control turned over in his belly. He tidied the flat, rerolled the sleeping bag and deconstructed the barricade. He took the phone and door key, not knowing if he'd be back.

Along Lee High Road towards Lee Green, most shops were shuttered. Of those that weren't, he counted three takeaways and five Turkish barbers in the space of half a mile. Lee Road stretched out imposingly in front of him. As a kid, he remembered it went on forever, but at the end was the Heath. An open space, somewhere to clear his head. An hour later, he reached the top entrance to Greenwich Park and sat, exhausted, on the first empty bench he came to. He folded his coat over his arm and felt the breeze coming off the river. If it all ended here and now, it would be fine by him.

The phone buzzed in his pocket. Tait calling, 'Boss says it's all set for tomorrow afternoon at four. I'll swing by and pick you up around three.'

'Sure.'

'Are you outside?'

'I needed some air, that place was doing my head in. I'll go back soon.'

'Stay away from St Mark's. Stay away from Deptford and Lewisham full stop.' Tait said he'd call later and rang off.

High in Greenwich Park, London unfolded before him. Fifteen years ago, he'd walked a seven-year-old Kerry up to the same viewing point. She'd complained all the way. That time it was the two of them together. Another time they'd taken a kite up there with Alison. In those days they were trying to be a family. Kerry had been 13, too grown-up for kite-flying. Johnny blocked out the memory. Across the river, rain clouds hung over the City. He should head back. He made his way back through Blackheath Village. Saturday night's events played out in his head. He remembered the looks on the faces of the two girls. Stan telling them they'd be safe. At

Lee Road, when he could have gone back to the flat, he carried on towards Lewisham.

Three young lads kicked a ball against a low wall. Young mums guarded buggies, chatting with one eye on their pre-schoolers running around in the playground. Johnny kept moving. He knew the prospect of coming across Tony Fitzpatrick's blue Nissan in the streets around Sedgefield House was a slim one – the smart move would be to ditch it. But it was Fitz's car and, if he was true to form, stubborn trumped smart every time.

If the car was a long shot, spotting Pallo Gashi up ahead was like finding a fat needle in a haystack. Pallo was fully intent on his phone, holding it in front of him like he was auditioning for *Star Trek*. Still playing that god-awful Albanian death metal, whatever it was, tinny as shit through his phone speaker.

Johnny made a snap decision to follow, keeping a safe distance behind Pallo as far as the Tesco Extra. He waited outside. There was another buzz in his pocket. Tait's text: *Where are you?* Johnny guessed he'd driven to the flat and found him absent. He should call, but wanted to keep this to himself, for now at least.

As he waited by the trolley park, he could see the Tesco security guard, a moon-faced heavyweight in a stab vest, working himself up to move him on. Pallo saved him the job, coming through the exit with two full bags. Someone's errand boy, Johnny thought. He kept his distance, assuming they'd be retracing the route back to Sedgefield House, but was caught off guard when Pallo stopped to light a cigarette. He thumbed the spark wheel of his lighter, turning his back on the breeze as Johnny passed. The lighter sparked. He picked up his bags. They walked in sync, Johnny a pace or two ahead, before peeling away. Pallo kept walking. He circled behind in time to see him cross the parking bays at the front of Sedgefield House. By the time Johnny reached the doors, Pallo was inside and gone.

He found a place to wait where he could see comings and goings, but that didn't leave him exposed. Ten minutes passed, 20, half an hour. The longer he stayed, the greater the risk. He had no way of knowing who was in the flat, or which flat they were in. He promised himself another five minutes, then another and another. His fingers felt numb. It started to rain. He began to think he'd be better letting Tait deal with it, weighing the options as he turned towards Lewisham High Road. One last look back at Sedgefield House. Stan came out onto a second-floor balcony. Johnny knew he'd been clocked.

He wanted off the estate and quickly. He walked past the medical centre with a menu of classes, courses and activities posted outside. He was on Merrill Street, where the houses had tidy gardens and clean cars parked outside. He'd known a girl who lived there and was trying to remember her name when a black Mercedes pulled up in front of him and two men got out. George Laska and Tony Fitzpatrick. Laska asked what he was doing.

'Walking home.'

'I live round here and I've never seen you. You don't live here.' He stopped, took a step back. 'Fitz, do we know him from before?'

'I was at the dentist.' Johnny thumbed towards the medical centre.

Fitz pulled out his phone, took a picture of Johnny, sent it and made a call. 'Stan, is this him?' From the wait, it seemed Stan wasn't sure either. 'Well, is it or isn't it?'

Laska said, 'You were hanging round just now. You wanna come in and see, yeah? You wanna score, you want a girl? You got cash?' He patted down Johnny's pockets. All the time Fitz kept his phone to his ear, sizing him up.

Johnny took a step back, sensing the conversation stage was over. 'I've come from the dentist in the medical centre, go ask if you don't believe me. See, I had a filling.' He came up close to Fitzpatrick and set himself. He hit Fitz hard. An uppercut that 20 years ago would have lifted him off his feet. It rocked him backwards, sent his phone spinning across the pavement. He threw a second at Laska, this one not so effective. Laska came at him, throwing him to the ground. Johnny rolled away under a parked car. Gravel and windscreen glass dug into his knees. Fitz shouted at him to come out, it'd be worse if he made them drag him out. Their feet moved around the car. Fitz was unsteady, Laska pacing while they worked out what to do next. They came either side of him and Fitz made a grab under the car. Johnny gripped his hand and jerked it towards him. Fitz's head smacked the bodywork. He bent back his fingers until Fitz yelled and he let go. For a while it was quiet. Johnny tried to see out from under the car. The chassis started rocking, bouncing so the exhaust manifold punched him in the back of his head on each dip, forcing the right side of his face into the tarmac. Flecks of rust rained down the back of his neck. Then it stopped. Fitz shouted at him to come out. Laska was ringing doorbells, shouting down the street for the car's owner. Johnny stayed put and it went quiet. The Merc's engine turned over and revved hard. He had a vision of the car shunted from over him, ripping along his back as it dragged him down the street. The Mercedes took off. Johnny stiffened, expecting the impact. It accelerated, tyres squealing, and took the turning, racing until it was an echo, streets away.

There were more voices, people coming out to see what the fuss was about. A pair of brown brogues came to the kerb. A familiar voice. 'You staying under there all day or what, you twat?'

*

Tait drove. Johnny sat in the back, quietly. Conway asked if he needed a doctor. He said he didn't. No one spoke again until they got to the flat in Lee Green. Conway took him upstairs to collect his things. The furniture was back in place and there was a fresh bag of food and some clothes on the bed, labels attached. Johnny took the clothes to the bathroom. He brushed the grit and rust flakes out of his hair. The side of his face was grazed and bleeding, the cut above his eye had opened up. He washed it clean, feeling the soap sting. He stripped off and showered down, dressed and brushed his teeth.

Conway waited on the sofa. He motioned to Johnny to sit. 'Feel better?'

Johnny gave a nod. He moved the groceries aside and sat on the bed, anticipating the lecture. Conway didn't disappoint.

'Getting involved with a police investigation takes some bottle, I get that. But it does come with a responsibility to keep clean and do the right thing.'

Johnny noted the emphasis, *clean.*

'So I need to know, is there anything we can do to help? Is there something you need? I can probably get it easier than you can right now.'

'You think I was there to score? *Jesus Christ.* I've got no deals to make, nothing to offer, other than what I saw on Saturday night. That means George Laska and the animals that work for him get to know who I am in court. What do you think my chances are? Seriously, put a number on it.'

'That's not how it works.'

'Because you don't know. You talk as if because you want something, it'll be that way. And it isn't that way. The minute I step out, they find me and mess me up. I don't do drugs, because I can't handle it and I don't want to die. I don't drink because it makes it harder to stay alive. You'll finish this case and move on. And if it doesn't work out, you'll have a pint with your mates and say: *Fuck it, we gave it a go.*' Johnny bundled the clothes he'd discarded into a bag. 'So what now? Do I stay here or am I back on the streets?'

'Father Downey has an idea.'

Tait waited at the kerb by the car. 'Church then?'

Johnny got in the back seat. Tait lifted a hand to the cab driver who'd stopped to let them in the traffic. Johnny closed his eyes as Conway made a call, heard him say, 'He's fine. We're on our way.'

The elderly man in Sam Downey's office stood to greet him, stepping forward stiffly with his hand out. The grip was firm, the other hand enclosing Johnny's. 'Hello, son. You all right?' Alec Barnes had been his father-in-law-to-be and, before that, the man who'd mentored and trained him for the ring.

Johnny fought to hide the shock of recognition. Downey had mentioned Alec hadn't been in the best of health, but the loose skin under his jawline and hollows under his eyes told their own story. Tait ushered Conway into the room and Downey bustled, taking books and orders of service off chairs to make space. Johnny clocked Alec eyeing Conway as if recalling a past encounter.

Downey settled behind his desk. 'I have what I think is a solution to our shared dilemma. Mr Barnes has suggested Johnny stay with him and his family for a short time, at least until alternative arrangements can be found and Johnny's status as a witness confirmed, with the benefit of the support that would be available as a result.' He motioned to Johnny. 'This is entirely up to you.'

Tait held up a hand. 'I don't think so. I've applied to the Protected Persons Service. They're treating Mr Nunn's case as a priority. With all due respect, I don't know this man and I'm not sure either of you have thought through the consequences.'

Downey was undaunted. 'How long will it take to put in place?'

'A few days, no longer.'

It was a lie. Tait hadn't the first idea.

'But until then,' said Downey, 'given the risk he is taking for you, for all of *us,* in fact, we share the responsibility of seeing he's properly supported.'

Tait shook his head. 'That's our job.'

'What do you want, John?' Alec's voice cut through. A deeper growl than he remembered, it had lost none of its quiet authority.

He was reluctant, but what choice did he have? 'I'll be okay with you for a while, thanks, Alec, if it's all right?'

Tait said, 'I'm sorry to repeat myself—'

'Then don't,' said Alec.

'Mr Barnes, you're one of Father Downey's parishioners, is that right?'

Conway cut in. 'I doubt religion plays much of a part in Mr Barnes's life. Mr Barnes is retired – I'm assuming you've retired – a former associate of David Price. Price used to run a significant criminal enterprise here in his corner of paradise.'

Tait raised his eyebrows.

Alec said, 'Johnny was a fighter. I knew him well as a kid. Some friends of mine supported him when he turned professional. Mr Price was a businessman. He was one of them.'

Johnny's eyes dropped, the word *friends* doing some heavy lifting. Those men in Downey's photo had been a successful criminal firm. One of a handful in south east London to prosper into the early 1980s, mixing in the legitimate world until Dave Price died of cancer. Alec's friends, Johnny's sponsors, were ruthless men.

Downey cut in. 'Let's be clear, we know who those people were and they aren't with us any longer. In the here and now, what matters is John's security. If you can't guarantee his safety, he can stay with Mr Barnes. No one outside of this room will know where he is and you'll have the space to make whatever enquiries and arrangements you need to make.'

Conway was wavering. One less problem to think about. 'DS Tait?'

Tait took the hint. 'We won't stand in your way if that's what you want to do. Just be aware these people aren't likely to piss about, so stay low.'

There was no further discussion. Alec wrote down his address and phone number. Tait held out his hand to take it. Alec gave it to Downey.

Johnny and Alec gave the police a five-minute start before making their way out through the church. Alec's walking stick clicked and echoed on the stone, beating slow time. Downey stopped to give instructions about the evening order of service to a young priest, who was fretting over a list of incoming calls he'd missed. 'They'll wait until later. I'm seeing my guests out. This is important.'

Johnny walked at Alec's shoulder as they followed the broken churchyard path. As they approached the waiting taxi, he heard music and assumed it was the cab driver's radio, but as Downey and Alec Barnes were shaking hands and saying their thanks and goodbyes, Alec puffing his cheeks and panting a little now, he scanned the street and there was Pallo, phone in hand, stony-faced, playing that shitty music. Wanting to be seen. He did his best not to panic. He settled Alec in the front passenger seat and went to thank Downey. As the priest embraced him, he slipped a folded £20 note in the palm of Johnny's hand.

17

Johnny

JOHNNY SAT AT ALEC'S kitchen table, reading the faces in Sam Downey's fight-night photograph and tried to feel something good. What he wanted was a solid memory of what there was between them; what he got instead was lost in the separation between how much they'd meant to him and how things turned out. He'd been a scrap of raw talent with instinct and a willingness to learn. That's all he'd had as a fighter. Same as a dozen other kids his age he could name. Roy Kinsley, Leo Moore, Stevie O'Brien, either of the Cardale brothers. He'd been nowhere near ready to turn pro. Alec knew it, but Dave Price had treated him like his own son and Dave wanted it done, so it got done.

Johnny had barely spoken since they got back to Alec's. Alec's wife, Lorraine, made herself scarce. A previously arranged visit with Denise and her kids at Downham, said as if Johnny had the first idea who Denise was. Lorraine's disapproval was obvious. He'd done his best to smother Alec's attempts at conversation. Memory lane was a dark place. They sat, quietly, in the kitchen. Alec sipped a glass of whisky. Johnny left his untouched.

'Have you seen Alison since you got back?'

Johnny shook his head. 'Not had much of a chance with all this.'

'You should. I haven't told her about you staying. It's down to you.'

136

Alec didn't say she'd missed him. Alison, his only daughter, the woman Johnny abandoned when she most needed him. He didn't say he'd gone by the house on the way to St Mark's on Saturday night. He'd planned to walk straight up and ring the bell, until the moment he was staring at the front door, unable to make himself take the final dozen steps. What would he say – *Sorry I went off for five years, it all got a bit hard to handle*? That much was bloody obvious. Kerry's disappearance hollowed out their lives. He slid the photo across the table. 'You lot loved all that game, didn't you? Big nights out, smart suit, black tie, fat cigar.'

Alec studied in silence.

Johnny ran his hand through his hair. 'Christ, we were full of ourselves.'

'You were a prospect.'

'If you say so.'

'Not only me, son. All sorts of people who knew more than I did thought so.'

'I did all right against blokes you picked who knew how to make me look better than I was and not get stopped, but when it got real...' He flexed his right hand and held it up for Alec to see scarred knuckles, the little finger and ring finger repeatedly broken, twisted inwards. 'It was Price's money behind those fights when I turned pro. Easy wins.'

'You did all right, more than all right.'

Johnny surprised himself how much he remembered, recalling each beaten-up face in the opposite corner. 'I chose my moments. Mickey Jarrett and Terry McAteer, both on the way down. I should have beat them and I did. That Dutch geezer, Jimmy van Klaveren. He was all right. Then Dave brought Mickey Grant down the gym to look me over, all that talk about the next level, the road to a regional title and a national. Next time out you put me up against Lenny Kincaid. You remember?'

'I remember the name,' said Alec.

'Big angry Geordie. Never took a backward step in his life. He put my lights out, you remember? Dave coming in the changing room afterwards, talking rubbish about learning more from a loss, being game, and getting me a rematch, remember that?' Course he did, thought Johnny. He could see it all over his face. He took a moment to remind himself where he was and who he was sitting with. Alec was helping him out. He was a guest in the man's home. The kitchen clock ticked round another ten minutes before he spoke. 'I'm sorry, mate.'

'Say what you want to say. I'd rather that than sit in silence.'

'Do you remember the Italian feller, Franco? He came to the gym a couple of weeks after Kincaid. I thought you and Dave sent him. He said he could train me, but you told me he'd decided not to take me on. Mum said call him, so I did. He spent an hour taking me through what he'd seen with Kincaid and how he could straighten it out. Then he goes, "You got to be careful, boy. Find someone you trust." I came back to you and passed on what he said. Next thing, Dave's slagging me off in front of everyone for going behind his back, telling me I was disloyal, couldn't be trusted. That I was nothing special. You said nothing.'

The old man's eyes were glazed, colour draining from him. 'Honestly, son, you might be right, but I can't remember one way or another. I'm sorry. Really, from here.' Alec put his hand over his heart. He winced, obviously in pain. He went to the sink, ran the cold tap and filled a mug of water, washing down two pills from a blister pack. He supported himself, leaning over the sink until the worst passed and his breathing became more even. He straightened, speaking with a firmer tone. 'What you're doing and what you've been through, I can't do bugger all about it and I'm certainly not trying to make up for it. I want to help. You tell me what you need and we'll see if we can sort it out.' He came back to the table and poured himself another drink. 'One bit of advice, don't for Christ's sake say any of this in front of Lorraine.'

'I know she's not keen on me being here.'

'It's not her decision to make.' Alec ran his hand through his hair, starting to sweat. 'I need to talk to you about something. Not now, tomorrow's fine. I don't mind putting you up, but I'll be honest, there's a couple of things I need you to help me with. I should have done it before, but I don't want it left to Lorraine.'

For a while after his medicine, Alec's conversation grew vague. He knew it and made light of losing his thread, saying he didn't have the stamina for an all-nighter, not like the old days. He sipped water. 'I suppose I ought to show you where you're sleeping.'

Johnny followed Alec upstairs with his carrier bag, not wanting to put it down. The room was compact, no more than a box room. Clean carpet, coordinated curtains, very pink.

'Will this be all right?' Alec picked up Lorraine's night clothes, draped over a chair, and took her bathrobe from the hook on the door. They'd been sleeping in separate rooms. Now it made sense.

'Of course. Thanks, Alec, and please thank Lorraine, I appreciate it. And sorry for what I said earlier. It's past, forgotten.'

Alec waved away the apology. 'The bathroom's across the landing. Don't worry about the flush. It's noisy, but needs must. Kettle in the kitchen, tea in the caddy, milk in the fridge. Help yourself. Any cup you like, except my Millwall mug.' He hung back. Something he had to work himself up to say. 'Son, so we're clear, I'm no one's keeper. I haven't got the time or the energy. You come and go as you want. I don't trust the Old Bill any more than you do, so if it goes bad and you feel you have to move on, I'd be grateful if you'd let me know first. This time I won't come looking. Just promise me you'll see Alison sooner rather than later. You owe her that.'

He owed her a lot more besides.

Johnny lay awake listening to the traffic on the South Circular. Alec's basement-level expectations of him staying around were reasonable given his track record. The clock on the bedside table showed 12.20 when Lorraine came home. He thought about what he would say to Ali. The old man wasn't well and Johnny couldn't let him down. When he slept, there were no dreams. Only Alec's phrase repeating: *This time I won't come looking*.

18

Max

'IS THAT ALL YOU'VE got?' DS Tait's Tuesday night trash talk in the pub stood in stark contrast to the evidence in front of him. Maybe his hangover was taking a long time to clear. Max tossed the file on Tait's desk. 'Go with this and you're a fool.'

The papers Alison Barnes had allegedly removed from Fraser Neal's flat – Conway's justification for bringing her in for questioning under caution – turned out to be notes she and Neal had worked on together in the lead-up to the public meeting. Nothing confidential and, from Max's reading, in no way did they relate to the case. The personal effects Tait mentioned were a photograph borrowed to scan for the Marlowe Estate newsletter. There was no cause, unless there was something they weren't telling him. 'You need to learn to hold your beer or be less of a yes-man.'

Tait dug in. 'It's all we need. She could have told us she'd been in there when we interviewed her, either on Friday or Saturday, but she chose not to. Why did we have to find out from the neighbour? She could have taken other paperwork, anything.'

'So that's it, you want to ask, did you take any other documents from Neal's flat? By the way, did this neighbour tell you Susan Neal was at the flat on Sunday morning?' His expression said she hadn't. 'If you don't want my advice, that's up to you. But if you alienate sympathetic witnesses on the basis Conway thinks he can embarrass me, we won't get beyond *this*. And, for what it's worth, I'm not easily embarrassed.' He brought the flat of his hand down gently on the file. 'Alison Barnes ruffled feathers on the estate, Martin Dyce has it in for her and you know there are some that don't appreciate her stepping into Neal's shoes. How were you planning to handle it? *Miss Barnes, you took papers from Fraser Neal's flat on Friday morning, why was that?* She'll say: *I needed them to prepare for Monday's meeting.* Your counter: *You didn't tell us you'd been there.* She'll say: *Why would I? Nothing strange about it. I didn't know Fraser had been murdered until later.* Or words to that effect. Come on, Ben, wake up. You're sharper than this, I know you are.'

Tait was almost apologetic. 'DI Conway says you're holding back information, stopping us seeing the connection between you and Neal. You were seen driving Alison Barnes away from Lewisham Civic on Monday night. Several Marlowe Estate group members mentioned it. They thought it strange that she hadn't hung around.'

'So what, he's dragging her down here because he thinks it'll wind me up?' Conway's determination to turn the case into a pissing contest had been tiresome from the off, but it was starting to offend Max on a deeper level.

'The boss takes the view we apply pressure and see what we can draw out.'

'Let's assume for a minute he doesn't have you by the nuts, what do *you* think?'

'Neal's murder and the attack on Shelly Dowd. I think there's a connection.'

'And you plan to prove it by intimidating Ali Barnes. Or trying to. What am I missing, where's the sense in it?'

'It's so bloody easy for you. We're not used to...' He didn't finish.

'We're not used to what?' Conway had joined them.

'Doesn't matter.'

Max said, 'I don't want Alison Barnes brought in. I'll talk to her on the estate, in her own space and report back.'

'Of course, she's part of your personal agenda.' He turned to Tait. 'And he's persuaded you, as well?'

Max interrupted before Tait could defend himself. Having less to lose had its advantages. 'Why alienate the one person connected with the community who's shown some inclination to help, who might actually *know* something?'

'There are others.'

'But she's the key. She's the person other people confide in. At least admit you've realised that much. And don't expect me to shovel shit on your behalf.'

Conway pointed to Tait. 'You go with him. You ask our questions. Don't come back without answers and, if you're not satisfied, bring her in.'

Ali Barnes was on her way out of the community centre when they arrived. Max stood back and waved Tait forward. Tait explained they needed to go over her statement. 'Is there somewhere private we can go?'

'Café's fine by me,' said Ali.

'Somewhere private would be better.'

'Yeah, for you.' She stopped at the reception desk on the way through. 'Can you call Muhammed and tell him I'll bring the posters over later. Something I need to deal with here.' She chose a table close to the serving hatch, pulled out a seat and motioned for them to join her. Tait stalled.

Max said, 'Sit down, Ben. No one's near enough to hear.'

Tait composed himself. 'Miss Barnes, we've been reviewing your statement. You failed to mention that you went into Fraser Neal's flat last Friday morning and you took away papers relating to a forthcoming meeting. Ordinarily, we'd be conducting this interview under caution in a more formal

143

setting. We're giving you the opportunity to expand on the answers you've given us so far and we'll decide what happens from there.'

'This is you doing me a favour? Thanks.'

'You said the last time you were with Fraser Neal was late Tuesday afternoon at his flat. You were there to "talk tactics" for the meeting scheduled for the following Monday evening. Is that correct?'

'That's what I said.'

'But you didn't mention you'd gone back on Friday morning.'

'And Thursday evening.'

'Thursday?'

'The first time I went back for the documents was Thursday evening. Fraser wasn't there, so I went back the following morning.'

'You went twice?'

She leaned forward conspiratorially. 'I have a key, but I didn't have it with me on Thursday.'

Tait thought he was onto something. 'Why did you have a key?'

'Because he asked me to hold a key for him – you ever locked yourself out? And in case I needed to get in any time he wasn't there.'

'Such as?'

'Such as if he'd taken home documents I needed for a meeting, which I did. It's not a big deal. There is a core group of around five people sharing the Jamaica Dock file. One of their tactics is to overwhelm us with paperwork, so we don't print out every report and memo and set of minutes five times. We can't afford it for a start. Of the core group, two don't have email. I know, shocking, isn't it? But they don't. I do. I also have a scanner and a decent printer in the office. Fraser does not. See where I'm going with this?'

'That doesn't alter the fact you didn't tell us you'd visited the flat and you didn't mention you'd taken important documents away. How do you explain that?'

'You didn't ask. Your boss didn't ask. No other police officers I spoke to then or since asked the question. I don't know how to make it clearer, it wasn't unusual. Can I ask where this information came from?'

'I can't disclose. It's confidential.'

Max cut in, 'Did Fraser keep his work on view at home? Was it spread out across the table, order in chaos, kind of thing? Or was he tidy?'

'We have a folder. A lever arch file marked Jamaica Dock on the spine. It was on the kitchen worktop, which was where we'd been working on Tuesday evening. There was nothing missing as far as I could see and all I did was pick it up, make sure our notes for Monday were on the file and left. I locked the door behind me. That's it.'

The fight looked to have gone out of Tait. He gathered his notes. 'One last thing, I wonder, would you be able to help ID a couple of suspects?' He lay a photograph face up on the table, a screenshot CCTV image. 'Do you recognise any of these?'

'You want me to do this here? You've got to be kidding.'

'Please, it's important.' The second photograph.

She hardly looked. 'No.'

Third.

'No.'

Fourth, a younger man.

'No.'

'What about this one?'

A hesitation. 'No.'

It was a lie. Max knew it. Tait must have had an idea. But it was her reaction to the fifth image that struck him, she was barely able to take her eyes away. Tait collected the photographs and put them back in his coat pocket.

On the way back to Lewisham, Max asked about the faces in the photos.

'First three we believe are connected. Suspects for trafficking, intimidation, drugs offences. The fact they're here on our patch is a concern. The fourth is Stan Moffat, the lad at the centre of Shelly Dowd's assault at St Mark's, the fifth...' He stopped himself.

'Come on, Ben, say it. He's not here.'

'I don't want the DI to know I showed her the photos.'

Max helped him out. 'Because you think there's a connection with Neal and Conway doesn't.'

Tait frowned.

'Or put it another way,' said Max, 'you think it's worth considering. He disagrees because he's fixated on laying this at my door to the exclusion of any other avenue of enquiry, because he's got the arse that Fraser Neal nearly lost him his job after Jerome Standing? Or that my boss thinks he should have done? I know he resents the fact I was talking to Neal on his turf and didn't consult. Plus, he's mates with Tessa Harding and they cover each other's backs and whatever... I get all those things. But what do you want me to do, perm any two from that lot to get my job done? You tell me.'

Tait kept his eyes on the road ahead. 'I don't think he rates you.'

They drove into the car park at Lewisham. Max said, 'You want a beer?'

'It's lunchtime.'

'Fine, have a Coke and a bag of crisps, I'll get you a straw if you want. Give me half an hour and we'll sort some way of working this out between us.'

The bar was quiet. Daylight drained it of atmosphere. Tait was subdued, mulling something over. Max put the beers down in front of them. 'Tell me about the fifth photo.'

'His name is Johnny Nunn. He's a witness to the assault that put Shelly Dowd in hospital at the weekend. Formerly homeless, he's been on the streets getting on for five years, we think. He knows our suspects. He says because he's seen them around, but I think he knows more than he's admitting. I'd go so far as to say it's an even bet he's involved in some way – that's my personal view. He's given us a positive ID of the other faces and a statement that's a master class in bullshit by omission.'

'Can I see him?'

'He's staying at a house in Grove Park. Apparently, he used to box and was pro for a short time. The bloke he's lodging with was his trainer and, so I'm told, his prospective father-in-law before he took to the streets, Alec Barnes.'

'And you showed Alison Barnes the photo with a date and time code on it. She didn't know by the way.'

'You don't think so?'

'I know so.'

'Okay, that's good.'

'Because if Nunn came back from his wandering, found Neal with his ex and lost it, that makes him a suspect.'

Tait lowered his voice. 'I don't know what your connection with Fraser Neal is, that's your business. But Neal was at that address for a reason. It could have been a stash house; we know there were sex workers staying there. That's faces one, two and three and Nunn admits to the connection. So, if you say it's nothing to do with you, why not this?'

'That's your job to find out.'

'But I can't go after it the way I want to. You can.'

Max went to the gents, still finding it difficult to piss without pain after Tuesday night's batting practice. Bringing Tait onside was one thing, moving on Conway's territory was another. Back at the table, Tait was ready to leave. 'The boss called. He wants me back.'

Max finished his pint standing up. 'You think I've got nothing to lose because DI Conway's dead set on pinning it on me anyway, and he thinks I'm useless.'

Tait ushered him through the street door. 'We both do, remember?'

19

Johnny

DAYLIGHT HARDLY BROKE THROUGH the curtains. Johnny lay in bed listening to Alec struggle through getting washed and dressed, lungs rattling and gasping. The routine he must have practised every day of his adult lifetime almost beyond his physical reach. Alec had sent Lorraine downstairs. It didn't sound as though he was coping. Johnny tapped quietly on the bedroom door. 'You all right?'

There was a long pause while he found the breath to speak. 'Right as rain, son. You sleep all right?'

'Yes, thanks. Just shout if you need anything.'

'Will do.'

Johnny washed himself, avoiding the mirror. There'd be time for a shave later. As he came out of the bathroom, he startled Lorraine coming the other way with two mugs of tea. 'I'm sorry, I didn't mean to make you jump.'

'He's had a bad night,' she said. 'He shouldn't have been drinking, it upsets his medication.'

It hadn't been Johnny's idea, nor had he provided the booze, but it was going to be his fault.

Later, they sat at the kitchen table while Alec dozed. Lorraine topped up his coffee. 'Do you want some toast?

'Please, if that's okay.'

She was working up to saying something important. She waited until he'd finished eating, frayed nerves from a sleepless night playing across her face. 'So what was it last night, old times and goodbyes?'

'Something like that. A lot to catch up on.'

'He'll fight it his own way, you know that, right?'

Johnny said nothing.

Lorraine opened her purse and held out a wad of notes. 'I want you to take it.'

'What for?'

'I know some of what Alec did. I know he's got his secrets. I was there for more of it than he realises. Word gets around and people were only too ready to tell me things in those days. What I don't want is him spending his time going over it all with you. You're not family and you're not a part of our lives. You haven't been for years and I don't see why you should be now. Take it and go.' She pushed the money towards him.

Johnny wiped his hands on his trousers. 'If Alec wants me to help sort things out and bring him some peace of mind, I'll do it. I won't get in the way.'

'I've got news for you, boy.'

'I'm not taking your money.'

She went to the cooker, lit a cigarette and put on the extractor fan. Smoke curled upwards into the vent. 'Did he tell you he's refused treatment?' She didn't wait for an answer. 'I bet he didn't mention it. The oncologist said he could have another course of chemotherapy. It could give him a bit more time, but he won't have it. He thinks he's being brave. I don't want brave. I want my husband for as long as I can keep him.'

Alec called from the living room. Lorraine's cigarette hit the sink and hissed. She stood over him as if she had more to say, but thought better of it.

'I'm going out in a bit. I'll get some more milk,' said Johnny.

Lorraine put her key on the table. 'Let yourself back in quietly.'

*

It took him a while to get his bearings. The streets looked different. He walked the length of Geraint Road as far as the shops near Grove Park Station, realising he'd missed the cut through that might have saved time. He'd come out without his coat, in too much of a hurry to be away from the house. The hooded sweatshirt from DS Tait's sympathy parcel gave little protection against the wind rattling across Downham Way. His phone buzzed. Conway calling. He felt like a bloody yoyo. Every move he made; someone tugged his string. *Was he still where he was supposed to be?* 'Of course,' Johnny said. 'Like old times.'

'Alec's a good man,' said Conway.

Johnny didn't need to be told by someone who didn't know what a good man was. He's a better man than you, he thought. 'Let me know if there's news.'

He bought a sliced white and a two-pint semi-skimmed from Sam Downey's money, replacing what he'd had last night and for breakfast. The flimsy bag handles strained at the weight.

When he got back, Alec was settled in his recliner with his eyes closed, breathing through an oxygen mask. Lorraine sat at the kitchen table doing a word-search puzzle. Johnny put the shopping away and took himself upstairs. He kicked off his trainers and chose a book from the stack in the bedside cabinet. Lorraine was a lover of wartime sagas. He read the blurb and picked out a paperback, *The Moonlight Girls*, a good girl led astray in wartime, a fly-boy on last leave, reported missing on the big mission. The heart-sick girl volunteers as a nurse, saved by the friendship of her plucky fellow nurses, all from the blacked-out streets of south east London. He read the first 30 or so pages. It didn't sound the way his old mum described it, flashers in the blackout and dirty deals on the docks.

He woke to the sound of voices with no sense of how long

he'd slept. He sat up and swung his legs round. There were light footsteps on the stairs, a soft knock, a pause, and the door opened. Alison stood in the doorway.

All the times he'd seen her in his dreams since they were last together, she'd been angry with him. For weeks and months before he left, they'd battered each other with blame and resentment. It suited them to put it down to the whisky or the wine, or the weed she'd smoked to deaden their evenings. In dreams her eyes blazed. She accused him wordlessly and walked out, leaving him desperate and alone. In the real world, Johnny had done the walking.

This wasn't how he wanted it. In borrowed clothes in a room painted in pinks and unicorns to keep Lorraine's granddaughters happy. Rain dripped off Ali's coat onto the carpet.

'Lorraine phoned me at work. She said you were in trouble with the police. She said I needed to come over. So I've come. Obviously.'

Johnny was unable to find words.

'I had a visit from the police earlier. Detective Sergeant Tait showed me photographs, one was you. They're investigating the murder of a friend of mine.'

'That's nothing to do with me. I witnessed an assault on Saturday night. A woman was beaten up outside St Mark's Church.'

She didn't believe him. 'You were at St Mark's on Saturday?'

'I can identify the men that put this woman in hospital. I'm here because the police don't want me on the streets and I've got nowhere else to go.'

'Lorraine's on my case to let you stay with me. I'm telling you right now, it can't happen. Your timing is shit, by the way,' said Ali.

'I didn't know Alec wasn't well. Not like this.'

'And now you do.' She took in the room, the stupid kids' duvet cover and the plastic carrier with his things in it, as if for the first time. 'John, what am I doing here, what do you want?'

He couldn't answer. But he knew it wasn't this.

When they went downstairs, Lorraine made tea. Ali and Johnny sat at opposite ends of the living-room sofa like a couple of kids meeting the other half's disapproving parents. The sheepish expression on Ali's face said she was thinking the same. Alec spoke first. 'You're welcome to stay as long as you need. That's what I told Father Downey and that's what I want.' Then to Lorraine. 'We'll be all right, love.'

'Is that right?' Lorraine hadn't stopped chucking daggers in Johnny's direction. Now Ali was getting her share. 'Anyone want to tell me how, exactly?'

'Because I said so,' said Alec. 'It's a few days, a week at most. Please, love. I need John's help to sort things out.'

She sighed heavily, close to tears. 'But you won't tell me what.'

For the first time, Johnny understood how frightened they both were. Christ, you could waste years learning there are things that can't be made right. Ali asked, *what did he want?* Right now, he wanted out. He'd take his chances somewhere else. Beyond that, he had no answer.

20

Max

MAX ARRIVED LATE. HE shook off his raincoat and made his way upstairs. Early Thursday evening in the Warwick was quieter than expected. Pimlico had been Denny's choice. Far enough from Scotland Yard to avoid inquisitive co-workers, sufficiently close to Victoria Station for the getaway if it went horribly wrong. She sat at a table by the window, gazing into the street. She'd poured him a drink. Old colleagues meeting. Purely social.

'The raincoat's a nice touch.' She'd been observing him along Warwick Way.

'Good to see you.' Max made a hash of folding his raincoat across the adjacent chair.

Denny was amused. 'You do realise there's a coat rack in the corner? You're ten minutes late, by the way.'

'I know, I'm sorry. It took longer to get across than I thought.' He settled in and raised his glass. 'Cheers, Maggie. It's been a while."

'Yeah, a while.'

'How's it working out?'

'Today, it's fine. Tomorrow, who knows? I've convinced myself it's the step in the right direction I hoped it would be, but you know how it goes, one dogsbody assignment's pretty much as thrilling as the next. And you?'

'I'm okay.'

'Max, I appreciate the call, but you didn't say much on the phone and now I'm here. There's no need for us to play this out over three courses and coffee; just say what you want, then I can decide whether I make the next train, or finish the bottle and enjoy myself making you feel shite for crashing my career.'

The waitress appeared by the table, asked if they were ready to order.

'Give us a few minutes. My friend arrived late.'

When he was certain the waitress was out of earshot, Max took out his phone. He scrolled to a photo of Dwight Payne and showed Denny. 'Name's Dwight Payne. I need some intel on him, because I think he might know about what happened to this guy...' He scrolled to Fraser Neal's tribute page and picture, a screenshot from the Jerome Standing footage. 'He's my case, the first probably a target for someone in your team. I've been told not to speak to Payne by the senior officer locally, DI Andrew Conway, former colleague of Commander Tessa Harding. I don't want to make a formal approach to your boss, so I'm asking if you'd find out what the deal is.'

'Ask DI Sewell. He'll tell you.'

'He's not the issue.'

'Jesus, Max. It's straightforward, why complicate it? You want me to ask Sewell, put in an information request and I will. You want me to go through our database, no problem, but it'll be with his permission. He's my boss, Max. I can't afford to mess up another opportunity and it's not fair of you to ask.' She dipped into her bag, took her debit card from her wallet. 'Split the bill for the wine, okay?'

Max topped up their glasses. Out of the corner of his eye, he noticed the waitress poised for a second attempt at a food order. It was getting busier. 'The second guy is a community activist called Fraser Neal. He was murdered in New Cross in the early hours of last Friday morning. I don't think it's a random attack. He'd been making strides against a major land deal and property development called Jamaica Dock that he claimed was laundering and receiving dark money.'

'And is it?'

'That's what I'm trying to find out. I do know he's brought disparate groups together to campaign around that single issue. He made a difference. That's what Trident's about, right, working at street level to marginalise the bad guys?' He fingered the photo of Payne. 'His record isn't good, that's not in question, but he must know what goes on and I can't believe he and Neal didn't connect somewhere down the line. I can't go directly to Mick Sewell. It puts him in an awkward position if I ask and he doesn't report it to Harding and I don't want her involved because... Still with me?'

'You'd rather put my arse on the line than DI Sewell's.'

Back to the photos. 'All I need to know is, is Dwight Payne under investigation by Operation Trident? If he is and I approach him directly, am I risking a significant piece of work? If you can find out without landing yourself or anyone else in the crap, we'd be grateful.'

'*We* being you and Assistant Commissioner Kilby. The two people responsible for my last five years of arse-freezing mornings on Dover Docks.'

'Is this you making me feel shite for what happened?'

'I'm warming up.' Denny called the waitress over. 'I'll have the fish and chips. Max?'

'Same, please.'

They spoke little as they ate. Max was grateful for the din of conversation from the neighbouring tables, all now occupied. Before ordering the second bottle, he leaned forward. 'This one is strictly social. Catch up properly.'

'If you say so.'

They started with Denny's relationship. She and Graham,

her long-term partner, had parted a year ago. 'He got a call – a series of calls – from a former colleague back home. His old PSNI boss dangled a job offer and Graham accepted. Went back to Lisburn and expected me to wrap things up here and follow.'

'You didn't want to go?'

'Couldn't do it, Max. The thought of it turned me over.'

She didn't offer details and Max wasn't digging. From what he knew of her past and the domestic pressures Graham had imposed, Max caught the drift. She'd had a rough time. 'I thought going back there was a no-no for him.'

'So it was, but he had assurances he'd be safe. Apparently, he's no longer a target.'

'You don't buy it?'

'Course, I do. We're all pals now. No more reprisals. Let's put the flags out. Oh, they already are, on every lamppost in the street like they've always been. I couldn't do it, Max. I couldn't. Took me a few drinks, mind, to tell him I was staying.'

Max winced.

'Aye, exactly. Didn't go down too well. But it means I get to make the decisions about what's best for me without being made to feel guilty. I don't think I'd ever have come back to London otherwise. I needed to do *something*. I got word a task force was being put together to work through the Trident database, evidence gathering after the riots, cross-matching CCTV with known faces. I thought it might be interesting.'

'And you applied, presumably with a good reference from a senior officer.'

She avoided the question. Kilby must have helped.

'It's a temporary posting. The initial work they needed me to do is finished and signed off. And I don't exactly fit in. You know me, I get in a cold sweat if I forget to shine my loafers in the morning. I turn my hand to whatever DI Sewell needs doing. Fetcher and carrier. I'm on duty roster as designated housekeeper on a place we use near Finchley. Witness interviews away from the neighbourhood. Sometimes over a couple of days, extolling the benefits of cooperation with us and a life worth living, weighed against the deep shite of being dead in the street.'

As the evening wore on, the Warwick emptied out. The music, a mix of 1940s swing and 1950s Rhythm 'n' Blues, had been virtually inaudible until now. *Rocket 88* sounded fresh to Max's ears. He did his best to drink slowly, in no rush to return to the question of Dwight Payne. Denny's company was easier than he'd any right to expect, but eventually he had to ask. 'Maggie, it's been really good to see you.'

She raised her glass. 'Good, because you're paying.'

'Dwight Payne. Yes or no?'

She reached into her bag and took out an A5 envelope. 'That's all I could get. But take it from me, you can't go near him. He's not your man for Fraser Neal.'

The realisation that he'd been played dawned slowly. Kilby had made the request and Denny obliged. Max put his hand on the envelope. 'I don't want to drop you in it.'

'It's been okayed by a senior officer.'

The envelope stayed in Max's raincoat pocket as he rode the underground home. He brewed coffee, laced it with Bushmills, closed the curtains and flicked on the desk light.

Dwight Payne was a key target for Trident Command. A significant dealer and importer of class A drugs with connections across south east London and into the north Kent suburbs, his control of the drug trade on Marlowe Estate was absolute and unchallenged since 2008. The last crew that tried, headed by an ex-con, Liam Cross, was outthought and outgunned. Cross was shot dead at a party in Streatham along with his kid sister. She was nine years old. Trident intel led them to believe Payne carried out the job himself. He was said to have boasted about it subsequently and Cross's killing was mentioned in a grime track first aired on pirate radio later the same year. When the track was played at a second party at a club in Woolwich in early 2009, it triggered a full-scale gang fight that spilled into the street. Three teenage boys received knife wounds. A lad named Freeze, thought to be Payne's closest friend, died in hospital of wounds sustained in the chaos.

Max turned the page and went to top up the coffee, reading in the kitchen as he waited for the kettle to boil. Denny had made her own notes alongside the main text: *Inconceivable Neal operates on Marlowe Estate without Payne's approval and/or support. Some thought DP has invested significant cash in community activity, possibly persuaded by Neal.*

Corporate Social Responsibility. Good for business, thought Max.

On the second page, Denny listed some half-dozen occasions when Neal visited Payne's flat. Dates, times, length of visit and assessment of mood and gait before and after each meeting. The conclusion was that he'd developed an association with Payne to their mutual benefit. The disclosure made Max shiver. The last date had been two weeks earlier. Neal leaving his shoes on a mat on the balcony outside Payne's front door – Payne insisted all visitors did the same. The surveillance team believed it had to do with transference of DNA and Payne's paranoia over the potential for a stitch-up. Neal was inside for just under four minutes. On the way out, he chatted to Payne's bodyguards by the stairwell. Audio surveillance and lip-reads suggested the conversation was around the forthcoming Hallowe'en party for kids on the estate. Neal wanted it safe for youngsters to trick or treat.

Denny: *There is no record of Neal meeting Payne subsequently. He was at home at the time of Neal's murder. Though he could have given the order, we have no reason to believe*

*he did or would. Payne remains a key Trident target. He is
not to be approached under any circumstances.*

Max realised this was Kilby's way of telling him his time
working alone was coming to an end. An audition Denny had
passed. Right now, he was more concerned with her note about
Neal. That he'd do business with Dwight Payne if it got him
what he wanted was hard to handle, but what would make
him take the risk? If Max couldn't approach Payne directly,
he'd work around it. Equally disconcerting was the realisation
that Alison Barnes must have known about their relationship
and said nothing. Protecting her man, at least that's how it
looked.

21

Downey

SAM DOWNEY HAD CONDUCTED memorial services and funerals every working week of his life. He'd developed a finely tuned sensitivity towards his office and the reassurance it could bring, balanced with the secular lives most people lived. But in describing the life and violent death of Fraser Neal, he was confronted by the inadequacy of the little he knew. Words crumbled in his mouth. He skipped over a good deal of what he'd planned to say, hoping others would say it better.

After the service, the congregation hastened into the darkness. He told himself the numbers weren't important, certain there were at least 50 people. It was a decent turnout on a cold, wet night. He prayed for their safety and comfort. He returned to the office to pick up his book bag containing the paperwork he'd promised Sheila Okenia he would read before the morning. It was unlikely he'd stay awake to fulfil the promise. Another parish meeting beckoned where he'd suffer Sheila's periodic tutting and come across as a doddering fool. She was right, of course. He vowed to make the effort as he locked the office door behind him, telling himself effective administration was as central to keeping the church running efficiently as his ministry. Serving God and the community demanded it, now more than ever.

He carried this pep-talk with him on the short walk to the

rectory. Two men waited at the gate by his car. 'Evening, gents. Cold night.'

'Father,' said the first. This man was dressed for a business meeting. A suit jacket, clean shoes. Not someone Downey recognised, though he felt he should.

The second man, the one blocking his path to the gate, had been one of two men in the churchyard on Saturday night. Too late, he realised they were there for him. 'Excuse me, I need to pass.'

The first man spoke. 'Where's Johnny Nunn?'

Downey put his bag down, freeing up his hands. 'I don't know the name.'

The second man said, 'He was here with you and the police two days ago.'

'Oh, *him*. Quite right. Had you asked me then, I could have told you. Clearly, that is no longer the case.' He gambled they hadn't seen Alec, or had assumed he was with the police.

'See him again, you can tell him he needs to think carefully before interfering.'

'That's a fairly meaningless threat—'

'Tell him it's from Martin Dyce. I'm sure he'll get the gist.'

'Good grief, man,' said Downey, 'say what you have to say, but don't dress it up. You demean yourself. I'll tell him no such thing. If you do not leave now, I will go inside and call the police.'

The second man came forward, taking a fistful of Downey's jacket and propelling him backwards. Downey lost his footing and slipped as the man pushed him back against a parked car. Dyce shook his head. 'I don't believe in God. And I don't believe in pisshead priests.' He moved in closer. 'Johnny Nunn is not an angel, whatever you think. You don't want to get involved. Rumours spread. They don't have to be true.'

They left him at the gate.

Downey sat at the dining table, cradling in both hands the glass of whisky he raised to his lips. His eyes fixed beyond darkness into nothing and nowhere. He called Conway and left a message, shocked at the tremor in his voice.

22

Max

TAIT WAS WAITING OUTSIDE Michelle Dowd's block on Marlowe Estate's southern edge. Max had insisted on joining him for the ride, earning an irritated sniff from Conway back at the office. 'Clutching at straws, so soon, Lomax? I gave you at least another week.'

One week since Neal's body had been discovered; two days since Shelly Dowd's discharge from St Thomas'. So far, she'd been unable or unwilling to cooperate. Tait thought it was the latter. He led them up to the fourth-floor flat and rang the bell.

The river view was obscured by Pepys House. For the last week, scaffolders had been at work constructing the exoskeleton of tubular steel and planks around the lower floors, now enclosed in the same plastic sheeting Max found at 489 New Cross Road. Refurbish or demolish, stick or twist. They'd know soon enough. Shelly Dowd opened the door and Tait made the introductions. She led them into the kitchen-diner. 'I'm a bit on the slow side since I discharged myself. I don't know if I'm coming or going.'

Tait took one of two chairs around a small square dining table, turning to face Shelly. Max stood by the door, listening as Tait tried to generate conversation. Shelly made a point of repeating she'd been discharged early and was suffering with headaches. They'd needed the bed and the doctor didn't take

164

much convincing when she said she had family to take care of her. She wanted to be in her own home.

Tait missed the inference, that whatever she told them now would be deniable later. She'd say she was concussed, confused. On he went, the official line as dictated by Conway. 'So that you're aware, Shelly, Detective Sergeant Lomax is working with us on another case. He's here to observe, but he does have a couple of questions first. Is that okay with you?'

'Whatever.' She stared towards the hallway as if expecting someone to arrive.

'The people that run the community centre—'

'I don't have time for what they do.'

'But you know who they are?'

'You mean Fraser Neal. He's a local hero, except we don't really have them around here.'

'Were you aware he was the victim of a violent attack?'

'It was on the news. But I didn't know him.'

Before Max had a chance to follow up, Tait had moved them on. 'When we spoke at St Thomas' you mentioned you'd started to remember some of what happened before you were assaulted.'

The memory played across Shelly's face. 'I remember it was a normal night. Mainly kids wanting to eat, one or two wanting to talk, but not many. Most are in their own world. There's a lot of pain, but you get past it, the best you can. One feller came looking for his daughter, which was a bit upsetting – for all of us, really. I remember this shouting match started and I tried to settle things down. That's about it.'

'You said you weren't sure if you'd seen the men before. Will you try to help us identify them?'

'I don't think I could. You're better off asking Father Downey.'

'He and your supervisor, Richard, is that right? They got the impression you knew the young lad you were protecting from these men.'

'Did they?'

'Are you saying you don't know him?'

'You see a lot of young people. You're supposed to keep a professional distance, put the barriers in an' that. I do try, but it's hard. They all matter.'

'So, to be clear,' said Tait, 'you don't have a personal connection with the young man you were shielding. You've not seen him before and you're not sure about the men who assaulted you. If we showed you some photographs, would that help?'

Her shrug said it was unlikely.

Tait laid out half a dozen photographs. Shelly shook her head. He laid out six more. She scanned longer with the same result. From over Tait's shoulder, Max recognised the images he'd shown Ali Barnes. She put a finger on one photo, went back and placed a finger on another. 'Those two, I think.'

Tait took a harder tone. 'You *think*. Be clear, Mrs Dowd. Would you recognise these men?'

'You're asking a lot.'

'Because?'

'Because if it's them, they've already put me in hospital and they'll do worse, and if I'm wrong, that doesn't bear thinking about.'

'But if we could protect you.'

'That's not a chance you'd take if you was me.'

Tait placed the photo of Stan Moffatt down. 'Is this him, the boy?' Stan stared out, grinning defiantly.

Max wandered to the window at the view back into the estate, workers crossing the Pepys House site, moving tools and setting up machinery. In the corner, beside the TV, stood a low, teak-stained wooden bookcase. Home to a dozen or so DVDs, 90s rom-coms, some paperbacks and magazines. Ranged across the top shelf were photographs of elderly relatives. A sun-bleached line separated light from dark where a photo frame had been removed.

Tait was laying it on thick. 'You took a risk intervening, Mrs Dowd. These men were threatening violence. Why would you take that chance for someone you don't know?'

'I didn't think about it. If I had I might not have been so stupid. Can we stop now? I've got a banging headache.'

One last question, 'What can you remember about the man you were speaking to before the two men arrived?'

'He had a cut over his eye, and he had words with this one.' Her finger settled on Stan's photo.

'You think he knew him?'

'I got that impression.'

'What about the men who assaulted you, did he know them?'

'He might have, I really don't know.'

'Of course, Shelly, we realise. You've been very helpful.'

From where Max was standing, it was hard to see how. She'd evaded the most important question, why she'd put herself in harm's way. Her identification of Tait's suspects was shaky at best, besides which she'd given herself an easy out. As Tait stood to leave, Max said, 'Shelly, do you mind me asking what you do for a living?'

She pondered the question, 'I'm a care worker. Keaton's House Care Home on Lamerton Street, if I've still got a job.'

'Have you been there long?'

'A few months, why?'

'And before Keaton's House?'

'I did some bookkeeping. Admin work. I worked at the hairdresser on the estate, Justine's, before it closed.'

'You mentioned you were allowed home early. Is anyone helping with your basic needs, shopping and stuff?'

'I can manage.'

'Of course, but better if there's someone to help. Any family?'

'I've got good neighbours. I'll be fine.'

As they were leaving, Max hung back. 'It's impressive what

you're doing. Care work must take it out of you, then finding the energy to volunteer at night at St Mark's.'

'I do it for them.'

'It's hard keeping young people out of trouble, isn't it?'

Close to tears, she couldn't wait to shut the door behind him.

Tait waited at the entrance to the flats. 'If you want a social-work job, apply for one. I'll get the boss to write you a reference. We were interviewing a witness. She was the victim of an assault and she can identify her attackers. We've established she didn't know Neal, so she's not a connection.'

'On that showing, of course not. But if you treat a conversation with a witness like a fucking sprint, we'll never know.'

Max had sensed a deeper concern, something to do with the kids at the church she wasn't saying. She was hanging onto something.

23

Ali

'THIS IS SUPPOSED TO be your job,' said Chris.

He was switching on the community centre's lights as Ali arrived. She was late and he'd opened up in her absence. Ali managed a polite good morning. Chris carried on as if she wasn't there, unlocking the café shutter and hitting the kitchen light switch, pausing as the bulb flickered ominously. In the main room he ran his hands over the radiators. He bent down to feel around the pipes at the base. Rust showed through the paint. 'These'll need sorting soon.'

'Of course.'

'They need to be replaced. Have we got the budget for it?'

She didn't know. Other things on her mind. 'We'll find it.'

'Where?'

'I've got some funding bulletins to go through.'

He moved through the room, rattling the security grills. A chunk of plaster dropped to the floor. He picked it up. 'Damp, Ali. The roof needs doing. The walls need proofing. The boiler replacing—'

'I get it.'

'You reckon? I don't. No more than Fraser did. Campaigning for this, that and the other doesn't get people a place to come to when they need it. It doesn't fix this.' He tossed the plaster in the metal waste bin, an angry, tuneless clang. 'You need to make up your mind what's important. I've had enough of

169

call-outs at three in the morning when the alarm goes off, scraping a few quid in donations to buy parts for the boiler or raiding me shed for bits of wire and tools to keep the poxy lights on. We won't last the winter, not like this.'

Ali said she'd do what she could, but it was to an empty room.

She went through to the office. It was cold. She wrapped a navy-blue and green shemagh scarf around her neck. Money for radiators was one thing, but for all she knew, the council or the developers would close the place down after next week. Slade certainly wouldn't let it rest after they stepped up their campaign as she intended.

As the morning wore on, the place filled up. Old men in the café with mugs of tea and toasted teacakes and later the old loves that came for lunch. From the office, Ali listened to notes of conversation and laughter ringing through the place. The prayer group finished in the back room. Mums and toddlers took over the messy play corner, sharing their exhaustion with wants and needs and too many decibels. Periodically throughout the day, she stood at the office door and observed the comings and goings. Chris was right, as much as she loved the people, she didn't care about the heating or plastering, not if it meant letting Slade walk all over them, making a fortune from the deal and leaving them marooned, marginalised and broke. Whatever he promised, it would be worthless. They'd be gone in five years, Fraser had shown her the plans that proved it, laid out in an unabridged feasibility study that made a mockery of the sanitised version they'd been given. The document was marked 'Personal, For Named Recipients Only', stamped with Kingsdale Developments' logo on the first and last pages. Fraser had refused to name his source, saying only that they were inside City Hall. Ali's first instinct had been to share the plan with the estate committee. Fraser was adamant they keep its existence between them. He thought they'd lose hope.

The scale was staggering. Jamaica Dock Development, starting with Pepys House, envisaged wholesale destruction of the estate as they knew it. The community would disappear, effectively wiped off the map. 'They couldn't do that, could they?' she'd said.

'They'll do whatever they can get away with.'

Getting his hands on the study had been the trigger for Fraser. Ali had taken a risk retrieving them on Friday morning.

There was no formal agenda for the afternoon meeting and only one item for discussion. Chris was complaining to Marco and Mr Tousi about the community centre's poor state of repair and Ali's failure to take it seriously. Ali let the room quieten before speaking. 'We've been invited to a consultation event at City Hall. This will be the first time the full council ratifies the deal with GLA officials and the investors invited, and the mayor will also be there. The catch is the invitation is for me and one other. I think we should all go, or at least as many as can make it. We'll take our petition and the community plan and present it to the developers in front of Slade, Walsham, Hutchings and their friends. Give the investors something to think about.'

She hadn't expected a round of applause, but the dead space was deafening.

Mr Tousi said, 'You think they'll let us, that they won't try to stop us?'

'I'm sure they will. That's why it's important whoever goes knows what we're doing.'

The penny dropped. Ali was talking about a public protest.

Chris piped up. 'This is Fraser talking. All that student shit about direct action – 'scuse my language. It does nothing. Gives them an excuse to treat us like children. They won't give in, Ali, you do know that?'

'It's a reasonable request for independent consultation on the existing plans and our proposal.'

171

Chris said, 'You think this is how we make them take notice?'

'I think it's how we show them we have a voice.'

'That they'll ignore.'

Ali met him eye to eye. 'Which is why the day after, we'll occupy the Jamaica Dock site.'

Chris did the money thing. Chris always did the money thing. He wanted Mo Oni there with their accounts before he'd agree to anything. But Mo was at work. Ali agreed to call and they'd come together later if he was available, how did that sound? But they'd need to make a decision.

Ali didn't blame them for their reluctance to take action. They hadn't lived with the knowledge of what was at stake as she had, but a time was coming when she'd have to let them see. Carrying the weight would become unbearable. She explained as much to Johnny later in her dad's kitchen. He listened while she set out her course of action.

'I'll come with you.'

'To City Hall?'

'To the meeting this evening and City Hall, if it's what you want.' He finished rolling her cigarette and passed it across the table. Always more adept than she was.

Ali lit the roll-up. 'On top of the wardrobe in the bedroom at Etta Street is a suitcase. It's what I kept that's yours. Some of it went to the Red Cross shop.' She paused. 'I don't want you to get involved in this, thinking it makes up for what you did.'

'It's a start though, eh?' Johnny tucked his hands into his pockets and leaned back in the chair. He scanned the paperwork spread across the table and eased out an architect's plan, tracing the estate's outline with his finger.

Alec didn't take it well. He tried to lift himself, but couldn't make it out of the chair. When Ali tried to help, he waved her away. 'You're out of your mind, girl. And you, what the hell are you doing? None of this is your concern.'

Johnny said nothing.

Alec sniffed, 'Alison, you need to think it through properly. Both of you. You're supposed to be keeping your head down. What about Father Downey? He put himself out for you. No offence, Ali, but John chucking his all in with your lot makes no sense.'

Johnny fidgeted, still a guest in the man's home.

Ali did her best to keep calm. 'Dad, I won't be told what's right and what isn't. You've seen what they want to do. If we still lived on the estate we'd be up in arms. It's John's choice if he wants to be a part of what we're doing.' She bent down and kissed Alec's cheek. 'See you later, Dad. I've got a meeting to get ready for.'

The front door closed more quietly than either of them expected.

'Help me up, son, will you?' said Alec. 'I'm going for a kip.'

24

Johnny

ALI HELD HER OWN at the meeting. Johnny listened quietly, struggling to get his head around arguments that flared up and were talked to a standstill without reaching agreement. Chris acknowledged him with a look a couple of times. He was a good man, Chris, they'd known each other since school. A lot of what he said seemed to make sense. After two hours, they were repeating themselves. Ali called a halt and the group agreed to meet the following evening.

A few people stayed, but they weren't there for long. Ali locked up, going through a routine that was second nature. All those nights, all that repetition. Windows locked. *Check.* Cabinets locked. *Check.* Doors locked. *Check.* Shutters bolted. *Check.* Alarm key in, code ready. He would have offered to help, but it was the same as all the other changes he couldn't get his head around; he didn't know how.

She sat by him. 'You fit? We should go soon.'

'You've got it all down pat, this place. Locks and lights.'

'It's practice. Even when Fraser was here, it was usually me last out.'

'I went by the shops this morning. Justine's place is a Turkish barber.'

Ali picked up her bag, keen to get moving.

'So how come you left Justine's and stopped hairdressing?'

'That's ancient history.'

'Not to me it isn't.'

'It was more a case of Justine leaving me.'

'Thought you were mates.'

'We were.' She set the bag down between her feet. 'You know what she was like. If she bought a car, it was new. If she bought a bag, it was uptown designer. Soon as she got together with Rich, they lost any thought of living within their means. The business wasn't doing well. We both knew. I'd had the same clients since I was eighteen, same as she did. They got old. A lot were moved off the estate and went elsewhere. Some passed away. It must have been the same for Justine. There were rumours about what was coming and the shops getting refurbed for the Olympics. One morning I got to the salon and it was locked up. Notice on the door. *We are sorry to say Justine's is closing from 21st November. Thank you to all our loyal customers.*'

'She never said anything?'

'Not a word. I was locked out. All my things were in there. When they gutted the place, they repossessed every piece of kit that wasn't nailed down. I persuaded the bloke to let me get a few bits and pieces, my scissors and clippers, a few bottles of shampoo and towels. Whatever I could chuck in a laundry bag. It turned out Rich owed some serious people a lot of money. No chance of paying it back, so they did a moonlight flit.'

Johnny laughed.

'It wasn't funny.'

'It is a bit.'

'There were a few old dears I went to see around the flats, but it wasn't a living. By then, Fraser had arrived and taken this place over. There was a move to get people together, so I volunteered and got stuck in. People knew me, so it was easy. He talked about *engaging the community*. I was chatting with people I'd known for years, same as I'd always done.

After a few months, he offered me a job as a development worker. He got the money and created the job he wanted me to do.'

The times Johnny dared to imagine Ali living her own life while he was on the streets, she had been the woman he'd left, doing the same work, seeing the same friends. He'd got used to not being able to see her face, but the thought of her was real, only it wasn't this person he couldn't reach, who spoke in a voice he knew but with words that didn't belong to her. What wasn't she telling him about Fraser Neal? *Ask, don't ask.* No sense being jealous of a dead man, but sense didn't come into it. Johnny said, 'You talk about Fraser a lot.'

'We worked together. He taught me loads. If he'd stayed…' She tailed off.

'And?'

'And what? Jesus, he died a week ago. He was a mate, we worked together. I've spent the last week either panicking about how to hold this together without him or answering questions from the police.'

'They're doing their job.'

'Getting in the way of me doing mine. Which reminds me, I owe Max a call.'

'Max?'

'DS Lomax. He's working with the local police on Fraser's case. He gave me the heads up about a problem he didn't have to.' She hopped down from the table. Conversation over. She ushered him out and punched in the alarm code.

It had been raining, the street was empty. The sound of beats from the MEYZ carried across the open spaces. Ali offered him a lift back to her dad's. They drove in silence. *Ask, don't ask.* But you had to be up front with each other, didn't you?

9 November 1993
New Scotland Yard SW1

The disciplinary board convened at 10 o'clock sharp. Max was advised by his Federation rep the chances of keeping his job were slim to none. Half an hour into the session, that's how it was playing out. Whitley's first ten minutes were a lecture, serving no purpose Max could see. His uniform shirt collar cut into his neck. Sweat ran down his back. As far as he was concerned, the sooner it was over the better. He was under no illusion the Board had already made up their mind.

Whitley was a scratched record. 'Are you maintaining what you did was justified?'

Max remembered his rep's instructions, speak clearly, show due deference but don't be pathetic. Try to avoid saying sorry more than once, you'll sound like a fool. 'No, sir. Clearly, events meant I was unable to follow your orders to the letter. Once mounted section came through the demonstration, I was concerned for vulnerable members of the public I felt had no intention of being involved in violent action.'

'You felt. What insight were you able to employ that your senior officers and colleagues could not? They were all able to follow my orders. These people were to be regarded as

extremists and not permitted to leave the demonstration until we released them in an orderly and safe way.'

'Some were elderly, some brought their kids.'

'These are the people we're dealing with, no sense of responsibility.' Whitley peered along the line for support. On his right, Colwill, a bespectacled arse-kisser from the Home Office, then Chief Inspector Blenkin. He'd turned Max over without a second thought. And on Blenkin's left, Chief Superintendent Kilby, whose crew of undercover screw-ups delivered the intelligence that justified this whole shit show. There were acquiescent mutterings from two out of three Board members. Whitley was intent on drawing a response from the third. 'We had intelligence, didn't we, Chief Superintendent Kilby?'

Kilby looked up. 'Yes, you did.'

Max wondered how many times Whitley would get away with repeating himself. 'These people were intent on disruption and it was my decision, the Commissioner's decision, we would choose the ground. We would control the demonstration and it would be funnelled away from the bookshop area and held until we decided it was safe to allow people to leave. I thought I'd made it explicit.'

'Sir.'

'That was the purpose of the news briefings and media appearances myself, the Commissioner and the Home Secretary made in the days running up to the event. These people were warned what to expect.'

They hadn't been warned what happens when the word 'Hillsborough' sends panic through a penned-in crowd, though, had they? No one warned them about that. And no one warned that poor sod in a wheelchair he'd find himself trapped with horses on one side and a riot on the other. My mates, your officers, the ones following your shit-brained orders, told him it was his own fault and pushed him back into the crowd, laughing.

'Anything to add before we go on, Lomax?'

Max's Federation rep remained blank-faced, silent.

He was on his own. 'I was aware of your orders, sir, but in my defence, this was the first time this has happened. My record is clean. As I said, there were vulnerable members of the public, war veterans, pensioners, mothers and babies, and the risk assessment had not accounted for the collapse of a 150-year-old cemetery wall.'

'I'm not sure anyone could have foreseen it, PC Lomax. That hardly excuses – what was it PC McFarland told us? You "aided and abetted violent demonstrators to make a swift exit" and were "handing out rubble to extremists intent on causing chaos."'

'That's not how I'd describe it, sir.'

One more rhetorical flourish from Whitley, Max thought, and he'd have him, have them all.

Kilby chewed on a pen lid, making notes as if he'd worked out nine across on The Times cryptic. He seemed bored.

Blenkin, chairing, brought the hearing to a close. 'Do you have anything to say, Lomax, before we conclude our deliberations in private?'

He swallowed hard, thought about the first words and brought them to the tip of his tongue. No expletives deleted. P45 guaranteed. Go down in a blaze of self-righteous glory. Tell these stuffed-shirt arseholes it was a miracle they hadn't killed someone. Then he caught Kilby's expression.

In the years to come he'd reflect on the fallout from Saturday, 16 October in Welling, the day he realised policing by consent – that guiding principle of policing in London the brass guffed on about at Hendon speech days – was consigned to history. He'd remember his disciplinary panel, Whitley grandstanding like the arsehole he was, and the subsequent discovery that the father of the Scottish lad and his sister he'd helped across the wall had been sufficiently influential to write a letter that *ensured he kept his job. But no matter how many times he ran it through, he could not reconcile how, in the instant he was ready to blow it all apart, Kilby conveyed an entire series of detailed instructions with one glance and an almost imperceptible shake of the head.*

Max took a measured breath. 'I assure you this was an error of judgement on my part, in many ways down to my inexperience in this kind of situation. It won't happen again, sir.'

'Wait outside. We'll send for you when we're ready.'

'Sir.'

A week later, when the call came from Kilby's office, his answer was always going to be yes.

Part Two

November 2011

25

Max

FOR AS LONG AS Max had known Kilby, he'd been suspicious of networks and social hierarchies a man in his position was expected to hold in high regard. His patience with university drinking club alumni, Inns of Court councillors, and worshipful masters of discreet lodges could be measured in single-digit minutes. Approached by a colleague for a favour, invariably one of those men who meet in high-ceilinged dining rooms in St James's Square, where friendship is settled over Cognac and a word in the right ear makes an inconvenient truth disappear without trace, Kilby would decline. He wanted nothing the clubbable types offered, relying instead on making the right strategic, operational and political calls and making them early.

Anticipating disbandment of the Special Duties Squad in 2008, he'd called on Max to establish alternative sources of intelligence. The brief was for sources to come to him, making the most of networks and organisations Max had infiltrated and drawn intelligence from for the best part of 15 years in the SDS. He'd been marking time and needed a way back. If 'Research and Archives Officer' sounded dull, it suited him fine. What was going on underneath the job title certainly wasn't.

One by one, he'd scanned and coded the most sensitive case files. These were mainly cases he continued to work on with Kilby's knowledge, though whether he'd admit to knowing was another matter. Then there were emerging interests, which brought them back to Fraser Neal.

They'd agreed there was something in Neal's original approach, a genuine alarm at public funding finding its way into the pockets of private developers and back to public officers in key committee posts. He could prove it, he said, claiming they were ripe for exploitation. Max had noted his words, *They didn't even try to hide it, being on the take was the only Olympic sport that wouldn't win you a medal.* But it was payment coming the other way that interested Kilby. Criminal or foreign state capital that pumped up political coffers and set the tone for policy change. *That* was another matter entirely and there were already signs of influence from the far reaches of Europe and beyond. Potentially subversive, certainly of interest. London property deals were a by-product. What they were actually buying was political influence.

Neal had agreed money was going both ways. Could he name names, obtain proof? Ask him who and how? Kilby said, never convinced, and tell him to keep his mouth shut. When nothing came, other than requests for cash and more extreme public pronouncements on Jamaica Dock, Max was ordered to end contact.

At his desk, Max spread the file in front of him. The words clouded. Sometimes, the dead find a way to set you back on track, but so far Neal wasn't leading him anywhere.

Kilby's suitcase was parked in the corner of his office. His uniform in its suit carrier hung on the door. He was brisk, gesturing to Max to take a seat. 'I'm away for what I hope will only be a few days, though it's threatening to be open-ended. I'll be in contact as and when, but you won't be able to reach me directly. Commander Harding will take responsibility for my urgent work.'

There was no need to say more. Max would be vulnerable. He brushed it off. 'Before you go, you were going to update me about Denny.'

'I hoped she'd tell you herself. You need reliable back-up and I'd rather it was someone I appointed and who I knew you could work with. It reduces the risk of interference in the process.' He meant Harding.

Kilby wasn't wrong; he did need help. Intelligence gathering, analysis, making best use of existing contacts and networks to capture narrow fields of information was achievable solo up to a point. Patently, the Fraser Neal case was not.

'She'll stay on DI Sewell's books until the formalities are dealt with. He's aware, but sensitive to not losing a member of his team off the roster – he doesn't think she'd be replaced if she was to come over now. You'll need to brief her as soon as possible. I'll be in touch in a few days.'

That afternoon, Max retraced his steps, anticipating Denny's lines of enquiry. He called Carol Archer. Her mother had moved out of the flat. Carol had found her sitting undressed on the bed one afternoon, hands over her ears, crying at the phone ringing and the knocks on the door. Carol moved in for a short time, but couldn't cope with her mother's care needs. Mrs Archer now lived in Pear Tree Court Care Home in Sidcup. She had no use for memories of the time before, other than of bombs and big bands, and the girls at the jam factory she'd worked at 60 years ago.

Max did a trawl of media reporting going back to the discovery of Neal's body. Tait had posed the question at one early briefing – on a morning when the *Guardian* speculated Neal had been murdered to silence him over revelations connected to the Jerome Standing case – was someone talking to the press? He'd thrown Max a glance for Conway's benefit. A shitty thing to do, in line with all the other shitty things.

He had his own suspicions. If someone from the team was speaking to journalists off the record, they were doing so with Conway's knowledge and tacit agreement. Conway was slow to make any kind of comment. He'd recently held a press conference announcing a new appeal for witnesses. But the damage had been done and the tabloid stories stuck. Neal was discredited. He was a drug user, except he wasn't; he had sex with under-age Romanian girls in locked-room apartments, except he hadn't. There was no evidence to suggest he'd been inside the building.

Conway's press conference signalled a shift in strategy, effectively downgrading the case's priority. It was still open, but there was a backlog of work and he'd allocate officer time accordingly.

Denny called late in the afternoon. Kilby had given her the hurry-up before he left. What was Max doing that evening? It would have to be his place – no way was she letting him see where she lived. She followed him home, arriving ten minutes after he'd arrived. Max felt an overwhelming sense of relief and, for the first time since Neal's murder, he was confident.

Denny settled in and demanded coffee. 'Right, where are we?'

26

Downey

FATHER DOWNEY WAS FINDING the climb to the pulpit more difficult as the weather grew damp. He dreaded his knee giving way, as it did on occasion, sending him sprawling. That Sunday, he took each step carefully, determinedly. At the final step, he told himself the Lord was with him. He was not alone.

'It doesn't do to speculate. We are, by our faith and our beliefs, committed to seeing the good in all. We are taught not to wish harm on any man, but to offer brotherhood and blessing in Christ's name. But that does not mean where we see injustice and wrongdoing, we close our eyes and say nothing. This weekend marks one month since our volunteer, Shelly, became the target of people in our community who'd abuse God's love. One month since a leader in our community, Fraser Neal, was murdered. Young people walk the streets in fear of violence. We do not have to accept the illicit and immoral way of life, peddling this drug or that drug, trafficking in human beings, dismissing the rest of us or using violence on us should we stand in the way. The Psalms tell us, *"The Lord examines the righteous, but the wicked, those who love violence, he hates with a passion."* Their day will pass and it is up to us to hasten that day. We know who they are, we see them. And yet they walk freely to cause pain and suffering. It must stop now.'

*

'You're not seeing me now, you old cunt.'

Martin Dyce assumed Downey wasn't aware he was among the congregation. Attending the Sunday morning family service had become a weekly ritual since Downey failed to recognise him when he'd visited with Pallo Gashi. He made sure there was no sightline and did not take communion. Had the priest been aware of his presence, might he have tempered his lesson, taken a more conciliatory tone, appealed to his conscience or shone a light along a different path? Probably he'd have said what he wanted anyway. Dyce ran a finger around his shirt collar, offended that the priest would call him out. He took the threat personally. Who was he to do that, and in God's name? Wasn't very Christian, was it? He took several deep breaths, storing the hurt until it was needed.

27

Max

MARCIA STANDING OCCUPIED HER doorstep with the same
defiant refusal to be coerced Max had seen in the news reports.
'It's simple,' she said, 'you're the police, you hurt my boy.
Put him in hospital for six months and lied to cover up what
you'd done. Now he can't walk further than the shops. He has
to use a stick. The doctor doesn't know for sure what healing
can happen. And they say he's entitled to nothing.' She tapped
the side of her head, 'You broke him here. The people that
investigated it said the police done nothing wrong, that it was
regrettable, that Jerome was in a gang threatening them. It's
a lie. I've got nothing to say to any of you.'

Max cut in. 'How can I help?'

'You waste my time. Forget it. I talk about justice and
people like you turn up. You don't know what justice is. I do.'
Tears came to her eyes. It made her angrier. 'You know, I'll
tell you. I am sick of sad white faces on the television. White
boys coming into my home and making promises. Soon as
the cameras go, they're gone. Using my boy getting killed to
make yourself a career.'

'There aren't any cameras here, Mrs Standing, and I haven't
promised anything. I'm sorry you've been let down.' It was
getting late in the day, deep November cold, the last light
dipping over the low-rises.

'Why do you want to help? Tell me that and I'll listen.'

'Can I see Jerome?'

'I said, *why*?'

'I'm investigating the death of Fraser Neal.'

She shot him a look. 'You serious? Hope the man rest in peace, but his ghost isn't welcome here either.'

'I want to talk to you and Jerome about Fraser. In return, I will go back to Jerome's case files and, if there is any information that I think will get you the help you're asking for, it will find its way to your solicitor.'

'My solicitor did nothing. They talked to me *once*.'

'Find a better one. Your choice, Mrs Standing. The risk is mine. You're already convinced I'm wasting your time. What's another five minutes? Ask Jerome. If he doesn't want to see me, I'll go.'

The garish purple and blue set of a daytime quiz programme filled the screen. Slouched in his armchair, right eye semi-closed, Jerome Standing. A broad crescent scar curved under his hairline, a memento of the surgery that saved his life, but left him with headaches, reduced mobility and difficulty speaking. Marcia introduced Max. 'Sit up, Jerome, and turn off the TV. Another policeman wanting to know about Fraser.'

She motioned to Max to take a seat.

'Thanks for agreeing to see me,' said Max.

'I've said all I'm saying.'

'To who?'

Marcia spoke up. 'Detective Sergeant Tait.'

'Out of interest, what was he asking?'

She was ready to tell him to ask Tait himself, but thought better of it. 'He wanted to know when we'd last met Fraser, what his interest had been in Jerome's case, any other connections we might have known about and did we know about what had happened to him?'

Tait's usual combination of banal and pointless. Max turned his attention to Jerome. 'When did you last see Fraser?'

Jerome sighed.

'I want to satisfy myself nothing has been missed, that's all.'

'A couple of months back, he came to see if we were coming to the meeting about Jamaica Dock, that's what he said.'

'You think there was another reason?'

Jerome gave a lopsided 'Dunno'.

Marcia shifted uneasily in the doorway, making it clear Max was on the clock.

'When Fraser approached you, after all you'd been through, can you tell me what persuaded you to let him help?'

Jerome said, 'I thought people would listen to him. He did stuff for people on the estate. I thought he'd help us.' Jerome struggled to marshal his thoughts and turn them into language. He wiped his mouth on his sweatshirt sleeve to see if it was wet. 'It feels like I've got drool on my chin. I don't know I'm doing it. Fraser said he knew people would be on our side and he could get us help.'

'What did he tell you about the campaign? I mean at the beginning, what was the plan?'

Marcia said, 'He didn't tell us, that's the problem. First thing we know is a poster at the community centre and people coming up to me at church accusing me of making a profit from what happened to my son, like I was asking for charity. It made me feel ashamed.'

'We didn't want his money, did we, Mum?'

'No, love, we said we'd get by and we will.' She turned to Max. 'See, when Fraser Neal made us feel we were out of our depth, and God knows we weren't in a good place, then he says, "We can sort this for you, Mrs Standing" and "Don't worry, you focus on getting better, Jerome." I believed him, because I wanted to – you would, right? But he didn't ask us.'

Jerome sniffed, cuffed at his nose. 'The campaign was trouble. People thought we was rakin' it in. That's when the leaflets come out.'

'What leaflets?'

Marcia went to the bookcase and pulled out a cardboard folder. She handed Max an A5 flyer. 'These were all over the estate.'

Glossy paper, third-rate design and print job, the leaflet was a takedown of Fraser Neal, stating he'd personally profited from Jerome Standing's campaign fund, that the accounts for the fund proved it. An image of Neal, lifted from the internet and never intended for print, was set alongside the text:

FRASER NEAL is lining his pockets with YOUR dona-
   tions.
FRASER NEAL is a tourist on the Marlowe Estate.
FRASER NEAL is out to make a name for himself and
   doesn't care about you.
WHAT IS FRASER NEAL'S GAME? What does he want
   from YOU?

Max put his glasses on to read the fine print at the foot of the flyer: *An urgent bulletin from South East London Futures Group.* 'Can I keep this?'

'We have spares. I went round picking them up wherever I came across them. There was more after that, one a week for a month, then it stopped.'

Jerome said, 'Y'know, when Fraser trash-talked the police, it made things worse for me and everyone else, and then they think what's in the paper is right, that I was in a gang and it was my fault. And then this...'

'But did Fraser bringing your case to a wider audience make any difference? Either of you?'

'People know my name. They know I'm a *victim*.' He spat

the word. 'But it didn't make me walk better or stop crying from headaches.'

'We didn't get justice,' said Marcia.

Jerome said, 'End of the day, I was walking home with my mates and I got pulled up by the police. The only reason I know is because that's what my mates tell me. I can't remember, not what happened in the van, in the cells, not that day, the next day or the three weeks I was in a coma after the operation. Everyone tell us what we have to do, the police, the doctors, the solicitors, the people at the community centre. I thought I was going to die. He said he'd help, but he never helped, did he? We're still here, like… *this*.'

Max was under no illusions, Neal's motive for helping the Standing family went beyond his community work and being a good neighbour. He'd been a frequent visitor, more often than they'd admitted. It didn't alter the fact any one of half a dozen people could have written articles as Neal had and none would have got a sniff of a *Guardian* campaign or a think-piece in the *New Statesman*. Fewer still would have been given licence to rekindle arguments about sus laws and victimised black youth in London's streets on regional TV. The white middle-class boy had taken on Jerome's case, because it worked for *him*. The flyer was proof he'd rattled someone's cage.

Max caught the train back into town, walking against the tide of people leaving work on his way back to Carteret Street. Half an hour with his files would be useful. He picked up messages, among them Conway's demand for an update on his enquiries, which he ignored, and a handwritten note from Janice Wetherall, Kilby's PA, telling him the boss was likely to be away for longer than anticipated.

Max went back to the case notes. The half-hour became two as he worked through legal arguments made by the solicitor representing the Standing family in their private prosecution.

Actioned before the dust settled on the Met's internal enquiry, the judgement found insufficient evidence, a conclusion the solicitor should have drawn before taking the case to court, unless its purpose was solely to maintain media attention. Digging through the case history, Max found the prosecution had been initiated by Adamson's, a Lewisham-based firm, but was transferred in the later stages to Gladwin, Pascoe and Rae, head office in Wimpole Street.

He took the work home, needing his own space and time to think.

He worked into the night, piecing together the timeline of Neal's campaign and the momentum triggered by the *Guardian* article. Neal had appeared alongside Marcia Standing on BBC2's *Newsnight* and *Channel 4 News*. Through several viewings, Max watched loaded arguments put forward by seasoned law-enforcement campaigners. A notoriously outspoken Greater London Authority Crime and Policing committee member, Oliver Beresford, made the most of Marcia's unease in front of camera. It was uncomfortable viewing. Camera angles, lighting choices, adversarial questions, and bad make-up didn't do them any favours. Neal was passionate, but came across as naïve. Marcia was monosyllabic, mistrust written across her face. In the space of a few weeks, Neal frittered away the public support he'd created. No wonder Marcia Standing was angry.

It was close to midnight when he turned off the laptop, the room quiet and the angle-poise casting low light over his notes. It had grown cold as he worked, the last CD finished over an hour ago. He pressed 'play'. *Disintegration*, as if Phil Spector produced a goth album. Max let it wash over him while he drank the last glass of wine from the bottle. As he was gathering his papers together, a thought struck him. It should have waited until morning, but not if he wanted to sleep. He rebooted the laptop and typed in a single search request: *Solicitors, Marlowe Estate Action Group*. He scrolled down the results

and clicked on the third entry, an article in the South London
Press, dated July 2010, in which application for planning
consent on the site had been subject to an objection lodged
by solicitors acting for Marlowe Estate Community Action
Group, *'Mr James Rae of Gladwin, Pascoe and Rae, Wimpole
Street, London W1'*. He visited the firm's entry on the
Companies House register. Address, nature of business, last
set of accounts. GPR was an established family firm, judging
by the names of the majority of its directors, but two names
stood out. The first was Kenneth David Neal, Fraser Neal's
father, and the second Jonathan Coles, senior partner of
Delaney and Coles's legal practice, a notable human rights
solicitor with a prestigious track record. There was a link. Max
sensed the presence of another ghost. Fraser Neal giving him
a nudge after all.

28

Max

COMMANDER HARDING WASN'T HANGING about. The summons to a meeting at ten o'clock sharp was waiting on his desk. He'd done well to keep dry on the way in, but was caught in a shower on his way over to Scotland Yard, shaking off drips when he knocked.

Conway was at her side, pleased with himself. 'You made it then, no prior social work commitments on the Marlowe?'

Conway's cheap shot and Tessa Harding wasn't impressed.

Since Max was last in Harding's office, a collection of photographs had been mounted along the wall, either side of her Commissioner's commendation and Criminology Masters certificate. Max recognised faces in the cricket team. Harding in whites front and centre, a sweater loose around her shoulders, surrounded by senior officers. The muddied faces in the women's hockey team were more difficult to pick, college years perhaps, dishevelled and victorious, a decent-sized trophy on the ground before them. Harding, in oversized pads, had been minding goal. Over her left shoulder, photographs testified to political associations: cabinet ministers; the Home Secretary and the mayor of London, glass in hand. She was connected, no question.

'Thanks for coming over at short notice, Lomax. I thought it was time the three of us had a conversation. A couple of things. Firstly, we've received a letter from the Neal family,

196

demanding a full explanation of Fraser Neal's association with Special Operations. You are named in the letter. I'll draft a holding response, but we will need to provide substantive answers to their questions. Secondly, as you're aware, I have concerns of my own, mainly to do with how you've handled the case and the events leading up to Mr Neal's death. DI Conway has updated me and he believes you and he have taken this as far as you can collectively.'

Conway sniffed, but said nothing.

'My officers need to work together, or accept the consequences of not doing so. To put it another way, you simply cannot continue to follow DI Conway's team across the patch, undermining their investigation. You need to choose a side.'

Someone had seen him visit Jerome Standing.

'I thought I already had. Working alongside DS Tait, as requested.'

Conway really should have brought popcorn. He was clearly entertained.

'It's time you gave full disclosure. I accept there are confidentiality issues, so in this case I will make the decision as to what we can and cannot release. I want a full progress report. All you have on Fraser Neal. Every detail going back to his initial approach. I want to know where and when you met, what was discussed. I want an explanation of your strategy for dealing with him, the intelligence he proffered, your assessment of the intelligence, or its potential value; a list of payments made and how you accounted for them. And I want a blow-by-blow of your thinking and decision-making at each stage.'

There were times, Max knew from bitter experience, when being reasonable beyond expectation was the only course open. Give them what they want, or a version of it. If nothing else, it would give him time to think. 'I have an appointment later this morning out of town. I'll put the report together when I get back.'

Conway chipped in, keen to twist the blade. 'Cancel the appointment.'

'Is that what you want, ma'am?' Max directed the question to Harding.

She gave an irritated shake of the head. 'Later will do.'

'Thank you, much appreciated.' They'd expected more of a protest. He realised the politics of it was infantile, but it's where they were heading.

Calling Jonathon Coles in advance was a risk. Max ducked into an empty shop doorway on Victoria Street to make the call. Coles's office number diverted to voicemail. He took a chance and left a message he was on his way.

Mid-afternoon on an almost empty train from King's Cross, he revisited Neal's history of activism. Initially arriving in London to study in the early 1990s, he'd finished his first degree and gone back to Scotland. Returning a decade later with a point to prove, he'd applied to Lewisham Council and been given the job of supporting the community on Marlowe Estate. Within six months, he'd found himself battling his bosses, claiming publicly they were scamming the people they'd been elected to serve. Neal wrote letters and fronted protests as the council floated the idea of selling public housing stock to private property developers for luxury flats. Max read the extract from minutes of a public meeting – the first time Neal accused councillors of social cleansing. He'd repeated the accusation for a BBC documentary crew some weeks later – the interview was subsequently pulled from the edit on the insistence of the council's legal team. Undeterred, he'd used any and all means to make his voice heard. Some elderly residents were rehoused out of area, separated from friends, their health suffering as a result.

The callousness struck Max as it must have done Neal. If Mrs Archer's story was typical, and he suspected it was, it was easy to see how Neal was radicalised by the experience. He'd continued to call out council officers and elected members, appealing directly to any authority that would give him the opportunity, all the while building his media profile.

The train sped through north London suburbs, the backs and gardens of Victorian terraces giving way to post-war semi-detached, embankments rising as they passed through the tunnel at Enfield Chase. Max took a text from Jonathon Coles, confirming he'd be at the station to pick him up, what time was he arriving?

He read on. The council wasted no time in disestablishing Neal's post, burying the decision in a round of funding cuts at the subsequent spending review. Any expectation on the council's part that Neal would clear out proved optimistic. He'd approached a smallish Edinburgh-based funder, Marchmont Charitable Trust. As far as Max could see, the trust was inclined to support health and education projects, but Fraser persuaded them to fund his work, initially for three years. Max sensed a helping hand, a family connection or old school alumni.

Jonathon Coles waited on the platform at Cuffley Station. He led Max across the car park, apologising for the working-from-home dress code. The dark orange Puffa jacket, jeans and tan boots told him he'd crossed the line.

'We're not in London any more,' said Max.

'No, we are most definitely not, thank God.' Coles bleeped the central locking on a silver Range Rover.

He was exactly as Max remembered. Still the energy of a younger man, relentlessly interesting and interested. The successful campaigning lawyer, cash in the bank and fighting the good fight for society's beaten and oppressed.

The lights were coming on in the Hertfordshire villages they passed through. Glimpsed over hedges across open fields, in the distance a string of stationary red tail lights on the M25.

'Happens two or three times a week, morning and evening. Complete misery. That's why I sold the place in St Albans and we moved here, brought Liz's caseload from Turnpike Lane. We keep an office in Covent Garden, hot-desking in an accountancy firm of one of my better-paying clients.'

'Liz is here, too?'

'Yep.' Coles smiled.

Max's history with Delaney and Coles, more accurately and personally with Liz Delaney, had stalled since the death of a journalist and activist, Phil Mercer, some years before, for which neither or both were responsible, depending on whom you spoke to and how much they'd had to drink. Sober, Max would tell you it was out of his hands. Three drinks down on a bad night, he'd admit he'd taken a risk with Mercer that backfired. Keep drinking and, at some point in the small hours, he'd tell you Liz backed him into a corner and he'd made a terrible decision, one he'd regret until the last. Either way, they were off each other's Christmas-card list.

'How is she?' said Max

'Eager to see you.' Coles kept his eyes firmly on the road, just about keeping a straight face.

The house stood in its own grounds at the end of a rutted track. Coles pulled up alongside a modest off-roader, a Suzuki. A semi-circle of mature trees ringed the house to the rear. A fast-flowing stream nearby caught his ear. Max breathed deeply and filled his lungs. 'Jesus, fresh air's a bit of a shock to the system.'

Coles led the way, throwing his jacket on a hook in the hall. 'Can I take your coat? Drink?'

'I'm fine. Just as soon get down to it.'

'Later then.'

Max followed Coles through the dining room to a low-ceilinged lounge with a fire, laid but not lit, and into an extension converted into an office at the rear. A wide window framed a broad expanse of lawn, punctuated by spindly shrubs, leafless trees and a few evergreens. Liz put down her paperwork and took off her glasses. 'Did you wipe your feet?'

Coles said, 'I'll put the kettle on and leave you to it.'

'Coward,' said Max.

Coles's hosting instincts were so conditioned, he didn't risk leaving them while the kettle boiled and coffee brewed. He returned with a bottle and three glasses. No questions asked, he poured them each a drink. They were far from their inner-city roots, the days when their successes proved eye-wateringly expensive for the Home Office, the GLA, and several London councils. In the heart of rural Hertfordshire, they were a world away from Marlowe Estate and an alley in New Cross Road.

Liz set a digital recorder on the desk between them. 'If you don't mind. Not that I don't trust you.'

'Whatever. Which of you had the idea to put Fraser Neal my way?'

Coles gave Liz a knowing nod, 'It's the Michael Corleone play. Present a fait accompli, that it had to be one of us. Next line is we're insulting his intelligence if we lie, which makes him angry.'

Max took out an A4 notebook, loose sheets of notepaper bulldog-clipped between the pages. 'You studied law with Kenneth Neal, Fraser Neal's father, at All Souls College, Oxford, graduating in 1976. From there, you went your separate ways: you into practice in London; Neal to Edinburgh Law School. You're a director of Gladwin, Pascoe and Rae, the firm of solicitors that brought the failed private prosecution in the case of Jerome Standing and who acted on behalf of Marlowe Estate Community Action Group in respect of Jamaica Dock. You also sit on the board of trustees of the Marchmont Charitable Trust, which took over paying Fraser

Neal's salary when Lewisham Council withdrew funding. Marchmont Trust's holding address in London is the one you share with your accountant in Henrietta Street, WC1. All of this is a matter of public record. It doesn't insult my intelligence, but it does waste my time. I'm trying to find out who put a knife between Fraser Neal's ribs and let him bleed to death in an alley.' He raised the glass. 'So, *con rispetto*, balls to your *Godfather* analogy and tell me why you sent Fraser Neal to me.'

Coles turned off the voice recorder. 'Of course, you're right. Ken Neal and I were friends at Oxford, but our careers took very different paths. This you know. Fraser moving to London and doing community work was him accomplishing something for himself. As I understand it, the expectation had been he'd travel for a while, do some growing up, and enter the family business. But Fraser wanted life experience. Let's not sugarcoat it, he lived a very privileged existence. It wasn't as if he didn't know that. But there's a difference, isn't there, between knowing people have decisions made about their lives with zero right of reply and being one of them. Fraser didn't cope. He drank too much. Ken thought he was smoking dope as well. Then Jerome Standing happened, a uniformed street crime with a DS on hand who shouldn't have been anywhere near it. It's a miscarriage of justice, call it what you like, it's actionable. Fraser went to his father for help. Ken Neal is not of that world. We are.'

'But you didn't bring the case.'

'No, we didn't. We probably should.'

Max appealed to Liz for more.

'We were reducing our caseload,' she said.

'That was your only reason?'

'It was a case we'd have taken on a year, six months before,' said Coles, 'but I'd made the decision to draw back, publicly at least, from the kind of work that brought us into the spotlight. It was becoming counterproductive if I became the story. I'll be honest, I didn't want to do it any more. Damned if you do, damned if you don't, so it seems.' He stood. 'This room gets cold after the sun goes down. Do you mind if I get the fire lit now?'

Coles busied himself, getting the fire going. He was practised, resetting kindling and firelighters, building with logs until it was throwing out warmth and light. He held up his hands. 'Just going to wash.'

With Jonathon out of earshot, Liz said, 'We did discuss it. I offered to take it on pro bono to save Jonathon having to turn the Neals down. Fraser was on a trip, that was my take on it, along with the daddy issues, but you'll have sussed that already. He misjudged Jerome's case badly, behaved like a missionary and brought in Adamson. I spent three days briefing him. Nice man, but he wasn't right. Jonathon convinced James Rae to take it on and acted as consultant, using his media contacts to get Fraser the coverage, but he was out of his depth.'

'I've seen the tapes.'

'He made it about himself. And the *Guardian* article…' She motioned towards the door. 'Jonathon wrote it.'

Liz moved around the room, putting the lamps on. She centred the clock on the mantelpiece. Coles rejoined them and refilled their glasses. Max wondered whether their partnership had moved beyond professional. As if reading the thought, Liz asked, 'What time's Theresa back from town?'

'Soon, I expect. Though if Aimee gets her way, they'll more than likely finish up in The Boot for a pint.'

She picked up the thread. 'Fraser was well-meaning and, in some ways, very good at riding his luck. When he came back to us with claims about the Jamaica Dock Development and proceeds of crime, it was a step up. Pepys House was a shameful way to treat people, but it didn't look as though anyone had broken the law. Fraser said differently. That public officials were openly taking cash for pushing through property deals that wouldn't stand a chance otherwise. We said he needed to go to the police. He said he couldn't.'

Coles added, 'When he started dropping names, high-profile names, people he said were on the take, dark-money payments, my suggestion, rather than go to the police locally, was for him to find a back-channel. Someone we knew would take the investigation to the places it needed to go. *If* there was a case to answer.'

'And you thought there was.'

'We'd had dealings with these people before,' said Liz. 'They run the GLA and the local authorities and now they have friends in higher places and there are billions at stake, with more to come. They have the wind in their sails, all the more with the Olympics as a shop window.'

Max leafed through the notes and closed the book. 'Can I throw some names at you, then we'll call it a day? I need to get my head around this.'

'Go on.'

'Detective Inspector Andrew Conway.'

'I would be very surprised if he's not on a fast track to somewhere extremely lucrative and not in the public sector.'

'We believe he's on a promise,' Liz added.

'From?'

'Can't say.'

'Or won't say?'

'Same thing.'

Max waited, then said, 'Gavin Slade'.

Coles lowered his voice. '...is the reason we can't say.'

'But that's who Fraser Neal was trying to get information about, to prove his complicity. Dark money, political payments, bribes.'

'All of those. Add intimidation and extortion.'

'Gavin Slade?'

'The people around him, I don't know.'

It was fully dark by the time Liz drove him to the station. He'd had more surreal afternoons, but this one had given him an odd, dislocated sense of having been here before. Homely and familiar yet now, with Liz negotiating the lanes under a clearing moonlit sky, he'd rarely felt more out of place.

She opened the conversation. 'You know how we felt about Phil Mercer, how we had to accept we'd gone down a very wrong path; whatever the reasons were for doing it, we made decisions we shouldn't have made. Jonathon's feeling that and a whole lot more about Fraser. He'd pleaded with Kenneth to do something that would persuade Fraser back to Edinburgh. Set him up with a community project closer to home, if that's where his heart was, but they wouldn't have it. Makes no sense.'

It surprised him how easily Mercer's name tripped off Liz's tongue. She slowed to a stop for a car coming in the opposite direction, too late to lower its full beam. 'All the time, these people. So thoughtless.'

'See, you're a city girl at heart.'

She laughed. 'Jonathon tells me you get used to it.'

'Except you haven't.'

'No, not really.' She picked up speed as they approached the lights of town.

There was no sound, except for the tyres on the wet road and the steady engine note. He felt warm, insulated. She pulled into the station car park, drawing to a halt in the drop-off zone.

'It's been good to see you, Liz.'

'Don't get soppy, will you?'

'I didn't want to say in front of Jonathon, but if you get the chance, it'd be useful to know why the Neals are so intent on stringing me up for what happened to Fraser. I know they want to make sense of it, so do I. But believe me, they won't get answers from Conway.'

A beat while she worked out something. 'I need to say this and it needs to be between us. There is something about Fraser Neal, about his family, I can't work out. We thought we knew what we were dealing with, but we didn't. Neither do you. Watch yourself and if you want to come back on this, call me. I'll speak to Jonathon about the complaint. And if you need a lawyer…'

Walking home, Max called Denny. A favour, could she cast an eye over Gavin Slade and the people around him? Track record, political ambitions. Any obvious sponsors.

By the time he'd finished typing the case report and emailed it to Harding, it was gone 2 am. He'd been circumspect, omitting what he could get away with, including information he'd discussed with Liz and Jonathon that afternoon. They'd given him the first genuine lead – a thread that Coles and the Neal family had wound tight, but until he'd had a chance to verify and make sense of it, there was nothing to be gained by sharing.

He was ready to close down his laptop and go to bed when two emails dropped in quick succession. The first was from Harding: *Better late than never, I'll read in the morning and get back to you.* The second from Alison Barnes: *Please can we meet urgently.*

The sensible response would be to log off and go to bed. There was no way she'd expect an answer this late. He typed: *How urgent?*

The answer came almost immediately. *Now.*

29

Max

'I'M COMING IN.'

Ali's front door was wide open. He found her in the kitchen, head on her arm, curled around an empty vodka bottle.

She lifted her head, brushed the hair out of her eyes. 'Don't worry, there was only an eyeful. I'm relatively sober. Mainly, I'm knackered.'

'You know the front door is open?'

'I couldn't get it to shut.'

Max had to lift the door on its hinges before it would drop into place. He managed to work the latch and lock it, but whether it would unlock was another matter. She met him in the hall and threw her arms around him. He gently stroked her back. 'What's this about, Ali?'

'Thank you.' She broke away, went to the fridge and took out a second bottle of Absolut. She returned to her seat, poured herself a drink and pushed the bottle towards him. 'Emergencies only.'

'That bad?'

'Fraser used to say they'd take everything you've got and not think twice. *Your home, your past, your future.* I thought he was overdoing it, but he really wasn't.' The pitch of her voice rose.

'Ali, you need to explain. Otherwise, I can drive back across town and make it home in time for a healthy two hours' sleep.'

'I found out this evening that half the group, all the men

207

and at least two faithful sisters, held a meeting. I wasn't invited. The person who told me said it was a "no confidence" meeting. I mean, not everyone agrees on everything, they never did before, but not like this.'

'As fascinating as Marlowe Estate politics is, I think I'd rather get some kip.'

She held his gaze. His conscience pricked by her plea for patience. 'Just give me a minute. Fraser kept the cash rolling in, which meant they got their pet projects and all the friends you can buy. Now they think it'll dry up, so we have to change our approach. Now *I* need to not rock the boat. Be more pragmatic. Or I'll be out and someone takes over. Apparently, they've said they're happy for me to be the Centre Administrator. If I'd wanted to push paper, I'd have gone for the sodding job Fraser wanted. At least it paid well.'

'I'm not with you. Which job?'

'Project administrator at City Hall.'

'When?'

'Earlier this year. He got the forms without telling me, cheeky sod, and said he'd help fill them in. I told him I wouldn't leave the estate.'

'You didn't apply.'

'For a job working on Jamaica Dock? Martin Dyce would've seen the name on page one and binned it, after he got up off the floor. That's typical of Fraser. His ideas were always game-changers, until they weren't.'

'Let me get this straight, he wanted you to work in the Jamaica Dock project office?'

'Cor-rect.'

'To what purpose?'

'What do you think, Detective Sergeant Lomax?'

'I think you dodged a bullet.' If there was an end to Neal's recklessness, Max hadn't reached it yet. It left the question of who might have been persuaded to take the job.

'And if that wasn't enough to deal with, my ex has turned up out of the blue and he wants to come back, how about that?'

'Johnny, right?'

'Not back five minutes and he's involved with your lot.' She reached across the table for the bottle. 'I'd written him off. His timing's useless, always was. And my dad's not very well and he's not getting better. And I'm on my stepmum's shit list for not having Johnny back in my life like nothing happened, and now my dad's.'

They moved into the living room. Ali directed the lamp away from the room into the corner. She took her time, told him about Johnny, how they'd been mates since they were at school. How he'd married Tanya Moss young, barely 18 when she had Kerry. As a kid, Kerry confided in Ali like a big sister. 'She used to tell me who her mum was seeing when Johnny was away. He was away a lot in those days.' Her voice grew distant. 'Nothing changes. When Tanya left, we just fell into doing the family thing. Kerry had a tough time at school. Johnny never handled it very well. When she was sixteen, she walked out and we haven't heard from her since. Johnny went out to find her, that's what he told me, then he stopped coming home. He's not a bad person, just lost.'

'Ali, there must be better people than me to talk to.'

'Oh, that's small talk. I haven't got to your bit yet. You ready? Martin Dyce was waiting when I got home tonight. He says if I don't back off campaigning about Jamaica Dock, I can kiss goodbye to the community centre. And if I carry on after that, things will get *difficult*. This rough-arsed gimp he had backing him up said what happened to Fraser would happen to me.'

'What did Dyce say to that?'

'He didn't say anything. I know they pulled this shit on Fraser, the close-down threats and watch-where-you-walk-home rubbish, but nothing ever happened, except those crappy leaflets.'

'You didn't mention those before.'

'He said it was nothing, some bitter old racist with a laptop and a printer. Words, that's all it was. The difference here is I'm on my own. I know I should have told you. I can handle most of it. I'm trying so hard to fill Fraser's shoes, but I don't have what he had. I don't have his money or a family to go back to if it all goes wrong.'

'Did he talk about them much, the family?'

'He said his old man kicked him out. He hardly ever went back.'

'As far as you know.'

She bristled. 'He made sure I knew when he was going home, not that he needed to tell me, it was obvious the way he was afterwards. Barely spoke to anyone else for a week, but he'd talk to me.'

'And the last time?'

'They called a couple of weeks before he died. He bought a ticket straight after. I thought something must've happened.'

'And when he got back?'

'As flat as I've seen him. He stayed a couple of hours at the community get-together and hardly said a word. We had a five-minute conversation and he was talking compromise, said we couldn't go on expecting everyone to support what we were doing, which he'd never done before. It was like he was beaten.'

'Did you go round to see him?'

'No, I was pissed off.' She held her arms across her body at the memory. 'Some things were said and I wish they hadn't been. We had our scheduled get-together on Tuesday, then carried on at his place, but it was different. He was there, but not there. I don't know what he wanted from me.'

'Ali, I need to ask about Dwight Payne. I know there's no way Fraser could operate without keeping him onside. I know he used to visit Payne's flat.'

'Is this it, I get one thing off my back and now it's back to Detective Sergeant Lomax? Fraser didn't tell me everything.'

He hadn't meant it that way, but was too tired to argue. 'I'll talk to Dyce and warn him off, but I need to speak to Payne.'

Ali was worn out. 'Dwight's mum goes to St Mark's, speak to Downey. That's what Fraser did. That's all you get from me.'

She gave him the sofa and fetched a blanket. He fell asleep with a draft across his back, Bobby snoring contentedly in the corner.

30

Max

SHELLY DOWD KEPT MAX on the doorstep for as long as she could. He made light of the visit, explaining there were one or two things he needed to clear up from their earlier conversation, mainly to satisfy his curiosity. She went inside and sat at the kitchen table, fretting over her cuffs, turning and unturning. She'd had a tough week, she said. There was nothing to add to what she'd told them the first time. Besides, Detective Sergeant Tait told her that he had nothing to do with going after the people who beat her up.

Max said, 'That's not strictly true. I have a special interest in Fraser Neal's murder. I think what you went through might be connected.'

She stared through him, the words not fully registering.

'I take it you knew Fraser?'

'I told them before, I didn't.'

'You've lived on the estate for twelve years, worked in the area most of that time, but never had any association with the community centre, and never met Fraser Neal?'

'I don't believe in all that community business. Might have done once, but not any more.'

'You're a care worker and you volunteer at the church drop-in. That's more community-minded than most people, wouldn't you say?'

'No, I wouldn't.'

'Mrs Dowd, I need to know what you know.'

She was fragile, traumatised beyond the physical effects of her beating.

'You can't protect me from people like that.'

'Which people?'

'The people who put me in hospital.'

'Come on, Shelly, you live here. If you think saying nothing to me gets you a pass with them, it doesn't. You've seen what happens enough times.'

She took in what he'd said, looking around her as if the walls had answers.

'Last time we were here, you'd taken a photograph off the shelf unit over there. Who didn't you want us to see?'

She was wavering, ready to lie, but then reached behind her in the kitchen drawer and took out a photograph of a younger, less obviously world-weary version of herself, cheek to cheek with a sweet-featured boy, maybe 12 years old, certainly his mother's son, both bathed in the same ethereal sunlight in an outdoor café. The backdrop, a beach and a clear Mediterranean sky.

'Last holiday we had together, in Turkey, five years ago. His name's Nathan. He's in Wandsworth on remand. He's not very well.' She held her arms around herself.

'What's he in for?'

'The police said he was carrying a knife. They said they'd had a tip-off he was going to stab this other boy at college, but that's rubbish. All his life he's stayed away from them people. You know how hard it is to do that round here?' Tears came to her eyes; she fumbled for the photograph.

'Talk to me about Nathan.'

'He went in clean. He'd never done more than have a bit of puff, but he's in pain. This man turned up on my doorstep one morning. I thought he was from the council or probation. He knew Nathan was inside, then he started talking about him being vulnerable, needing help. He said he has friends in prison that'll watch Nathan's back. They'll get this other lot that are giving him shit to leave him alone and make sure he gets what he needs.'

'Did he give you a name?'

'George Laska.'

Max gave no sign of acknowledgement. 'And you paid him how much?'

'A hundred pounds the first time. I couldn't keep up. I was working all hours, backwards and forwards to Tooley Street, doing eight- or nine-hour days and most of what I was earning went to them people. I started getting into work late, making mistakes. I kept getting panic attacks.' She put her hand to her chest.

'Take your time. Shelly, you said Tooley Street.'

'I was working at City Hall. They said I had to leave.'

'Who said?'

Her expression said she realised there was no way back.

'My boss, Martin Dyce. I had no money and I missed a payment. The next time I visited Nathan, he'd been beaten up in his room. They broke two of his fingers. He pulls up his T-shirt and there's bruises all up his back. He said, "I can't cope, Mum. It hurts when I breathe." I tried to get a meeting with the bloke in charge, but he wouldn't see me, so I went to see Fraser.'

Here she became quiet.

'It's all right, go on.'

'It was Fraser who'd persuaded me to get the job at City Hall. He helped me with the application form. It should have been easy really. I'd worked at Lewisham Council doing admin and bookkeeping from when I left school, but I couldn't do the hours when I had Nathan, so I did care work part-time and kept my mate's books for her business. I was chuffed to get back to an office job. Your confidence goes. Fraser gave me a bit of a boost.'

'What did he ask in return?'

'Jamaica Dock.'

'What about it?'

'Stuff was everywhere. I didn't know what was useful and what wasn't. I got him this report, like a feasibility study on the whole development. I made a copy, all ninety-six pages. Martin spent hundreds of thousands on consultants to put it together, then the one we gave out to the public was... well, it was nothing. An eight-page summary, enough to raise an argument and give a bit of ground. He's clever, Martin. But I got Fraser the real one with the plan showing what they were really looking to do.'

'Was there any information to do with the finances, the money, investors, that kind of thing?'

'I didn't have much to do with figures on that side. Martin kept it to himself.'

'At no time did you give Fraser any information about the financial side, no figures, no investors, no names or amounts?'

She shook her head. 'No, but that was always his first question when we got together, "Did we get the money, Shelly? Did we get the money?" I'm in the shit, aren't I?'

'Not with me, Shelly. Absolutely not. Tell me, in your time there, did you ever come across Gavin Slade?'

'Of course. He never spoke to me, except at the Christmas party, when he was sloshed. They all were. His cousin, Stuart and Martin Dyce were taking the pee out of him for trying to get his own office before he was elected. To be honest, I was trying to get away. It was getting to that stage where you could see it was nasty. Not funny, you know?'

'Was Stuart Slade often around?'

'On and off. He was around *last* Christmas.'

'Did you tell Fraser?'

'He knew already. He definitely knew about Mr Slade going into politics. I didn't think it was much of a secret. Everyone knew who his friends were.'

There was a sharp noise outside on the landing, raised voices. Shelly went back to tugging at her cuffs. 'Just kids,' she said, 'that's all it is.'

'Can we talk about St Mark's; the argument wasn't about Stan Moffatt, was it?'

'I didn't know the boy's name until they told me. It was about money. I owed Laska two hundred quid. I couldn't pay and he was doubling it every few days. I just wanted them to leave Nathan alone.'

'Does anyone else know about this?'

'Father Downey knew. He said he'd give me the money from his own pocket, but I couldn't take it. God help me, I thought about pinching a bit of jewellery from an old lady at the care home. She kept offering me things anyway. I thought I'd take something that wouldn't be missed, a shameful thing.'

'Who's paying Laska now?'

'After this week, I don't know. He reckons I owe him three hundred quid. I sold my mum's engagement ring three weeks ago. That was the last thing I had worth anything.' She bit back the tears. 'I know what he wants me to do. He asked me to have sex with him. And he wants me to keep his stuff here.'

'Will you make a statement to the effect of what you've told me?'

'Not while Nathan's inside. I'll find a way to pay him.'

'Shelly, I can't promise, but if you don't mind me sharing your details, I'll talk to some people and see if we can help.'

'Whatever.' She wasn't hopeful.

Max left, but was back an hour later. When Shelly opened the door, he put a thick envelope in her hand. 'This is between us, no strings, no debt. I'll be in touch.'

Dropping in on Commander Harding unannounced wasn't ideal, but Max had no choice. He went in hoping she'd see the sense in what he was asking. She gestured for him to sit.

He explained he'd conducted a second interview with a potential witness, Shelly Dowd. 'I believe she's being pressured, directly and through threats made to her son – he's on remand in Wandsworth. It's a sensitive situation, I realise, but she believes he's being abused and I think, if we were able to have her son moved—'

She didn't allow him to finish. 'You're not telling me anything. What's the connection with your work?'

'She was attacked at St Mark's Church. DI Conway's team has one or two individuals in the frame, but have made no arrests as yet. They believe she was assaulted because she came to the aid of a young homeless man.'

'And she can help Conway identify her attackers, so why won't she? I repeat, what has any of this to do with you or Fraser Neal?'

'I don't know the extent of what she knows, but there is more to gain. She's obviously vulnerable. But if we relieve the worry she has about her son, there will be more to come.'

'Sets a precedent, intervening in a case at this level. I'm not sure I'm willing to do that. What does DI Conway think?'

'I brought it to you directly.'

'You know what I'm going to say.'

'I realise, but it's important as few people know as possible.'

'I'll think about it. Put your request through DI Conway.'

'I've got no guarantee she'll be there tomorrow at this rate. We need to get the boy moved somewhere safe and take it from there.'

'I'm ordering you to speak with DI Conway. Let his people deal with it.'

A peculiar quiet descended as Max walked back to Carteret Street. He'd been around for enough years to recall evacuations, either as a drill or for the real thing, but that afternoon the traffic had stopped at a distance. The streets were emptying of people and those who walked did so with their heads down, intent on being elsewhere, as if they knew something he didn't.

Liz Delaney was in a client meeting when he called.

Nothing Harding said surprised him. Since Jerome Standing, she was patron saint of the risk-averse. She certainly wasn't going to act on speculation in Kilby's absence and Conway wouldn't authorise it. It wasn't good enough. Shelly Dowd was Neal's source inside City Hall. He'd gambled on her delivering sufficient evidence to convince Max there was a case to make.

Liz returned his call. Judging by her tone of voice, the meeting hadn't gone well. Max asked, 'Are you in the market for some pro bono work? It's nothing complicated and it comes with the bonus of pissing off the kind of people you enjoy pissing off.'

'I'm listening.' She sounded grateful for the excuse to sack off the remainder of the afternoon. 'Does this mean you're buying me dinner?'

Max hadn't expected the memory jolt that hit him when he drove into the King and Tinker's car park. Hidden in a country lane north of Enfield in what was once a hunting ground for Tudor kings, the pub had been a private meeting place for the relationship that wasn't meant to be. Max remembered underlining the section in his covert operations training manual about relationships while working under cover. They were, it stated, to be *fleeting and disastrous*. The one he'd had with Liz had been meaningful, enduring, but still, ultimately, disastrous. He parked and went inside.

Liz was in the process of unwinding her scarf. 'I didn't know what you'd want. It feels furtive, doesn't it? Being here?'

'It's good. I like it. Read this while I get a drink.' Max handed Liz the thin file he'd put together with Shelly and Nathan Dowd's details. By the time he came back from the bar, she'd read enough to make up her mind.

'Can I keep this?'

'Between us, yes.'

'First thoughts, he shouldn't be in Wandsworth. He should be in a Young Offender Institution. At his age, there's a chance we can get him into a secure training centre, but I'll make a more considered assessment when I've got the case file. My feeling is we can pick this off and get him out altogether. If you take into account time served, the fact he's a vulnerable young man with no record of any criminal activity, no gang association, I see no reason to hold him. The evidence is patchy. The body search wasn't properly conducted. If we add Shelly's own situation into the mix—'

Max had forgotten the reassurance that came from having Liz Delaney on your side. 'I don't want to make the association with Neal until there's more to work with. As far as we're concerned, her situation can only be that she's recently been the victim of a violent assault.'

'That's enough on its own, Max. She must be terrified. Has she had medical help?'

'In hospital, but since then, probably not.'

'Leave it with me.'

'Thank you, on Shelly's behalf.'

'Fraser left a trail of wounded disciples, didn't he?'

'I'm really not sure he knew what he was doing. He didn't know what he was taking on with Slade and Jamaica Dock. Investment opportunity on that scale brings the ghouls out to play and they're not likely to get rinsed by Ali Barnes and her crew, are they?'

'They might, with the right advice.'

'Come on, Liz, they're harmless. You've got the Jamaica Dock scheme – investor-loaded, PR-savvy, and politically backed – up against Marlowe Estate Community Action Group – fragmented and underfunded, trying to stand in the way. What?'

She turned her head, a professional enquiry. 'What's your investment?'

'Fraser. Who killed him and why? That's it.'

Liz read him better than anyone. 'If you say so.'

If Max was going to tell anyone, it would only be Liz. 'I knew him, briefly, a long time ago. Before I worked for Kilby. I helped him out of a tight spot, which landed me in trouble and Kenneth Neal acted to get me out in return.'

'Shit, I didn't know. And we told him to talk to you. Did he remember you?'

Max didn't answer. Outside the sleet was coming down. They were reflected in the window, ghosts of their former selves. Max caught himself, lost in thought and memory. 'Are we going to order?'

31

Ali

IT WASN'T THE FIRST time a meeting had fallen flat, especially when confidence was in short supply. A couple of times it happened to Fraser, in spite of the energy he poured into the campaign, but tonight was a new low. Faced with deciding the most effective way to oppose Jamaica Dock, Ali invited each group member to speak in turn. Their views were met with scowls from Chris and Marco, muttering at how things were being handled, arguing to a standstill. As far as they were concerned, it was a lost cause, not worth fighting for.

Chris had often been Fraser's voice of reason, but tonight he was relentless, bullying Lukshana and Geesi who stared at their papers in silence. Mrs Stearns was subdued, Mr Tousi mystified. Ali asked for constructive suggestions, any suggestion at all other than *do nothing*. She tried once more, 'This is how I see it.'

Chris cut in, 'We know how you see it. We've had it rammed down our throats. They think we're nothing, shit on their shoes.'

'What's your alternative? They're launching the final plan for Jamaica Dock with or without us there.'

'Don't give them the satisfaction.'

She lifted herself. 'But this is how they do things. It's a process. Not how we want it, but while we work out how we carry on without Fraser, we have to deal with it. They won't wait, Chris.'

'You know that, do you?' said Marco. 'Have you asked them to put it back, like a mark of respect?'

'The launch event is in two days' time.'

'But have you asked?'

'Yes, I asked. Of course I asked.'

He shook his head, disbelieving. Ali ignored him.

'We must be visible.' Around the table, seven blank expressions showed only the desire to be somewhere else, trusting their lives and homes to Gavin Slade's assurances the developers would take community interests into account. Their views would be considered *at the appropriate time*. No one truly believed it. 'We asked to be included and they've invited us to the event. If we give up the chance to present our case in front of everyone else, we'll have shot ourselves in the foot.'

Another disapproving shake of the head from Chris.

Mr Tousi said, 'You think Mr Slade will listen?'

'It's not about him. We have a voice, we can talk to people and persuade them, or find out they're not persuadable. You can't make an offer if no one knows who you are. Thanks to Fraser, they know who we are. We shouldn't back down before we've stated our opposition and put the alternative on the table. We have to decide tonight. I'll go on my own if need be.'

Her dad's house was quiet. Only Johnny was still up. She thought he'd been drinking. When she told him how the evening had degenerated, he gave nothing away. Ali said, 'Things are different now. After what's happened, I don't think it would be right for you to come to City Hall.'

The four representatives of Marlowe Estate who made their way to City Hall for the formal launch of the Jamaica Dock scheme came through security into a grand atrium. Lukshana, Mrs Stearns and Mr Tousi loitered nervously near the entrance, reluctant to commit to the gathering, populated overwhelmingly by men in suits. Ali encouraged them to move into the room. Badged delegates nursed flutes of champagne. A waitress approached and offered them a drink. To Ali's knowledge, neither Mr Tousi nor Shana drank alcohol. She didn't know about Mrs Stearns, but on past performance she was more likely to fill her handbag from the buffet. Ali took a glass and sipped, overcoming the temptation to empty the glass in one. She needed to keep a clear head or risk saying something they'd all regret.

A pint-sized photographer appeared from behind a display stand. Ali turned her back. A few seconds later he reappeared in her eyeline. She mouthed 'fuck off' and he went to bother someone else. She scanned for familiar faces, seeing Martin Dyce deep in conversation with the man she'd seen before. Heavy stubble, no stranger to a Turkish barber, white V-neck T-shirt under his suit jacket. She moved away, at first not noticing Greg Walsham in conversation with a quartet of senior council officers. Ali picked up scraps, comments about 'keeping the natives onside', 'Section 106 funds' and 'queueing up for handouts'.

'Excuse me, were you talking about us?'

Heads turned.

'No offence, Miss Barnes.' Walsham rocked on his heels. 'Throwaway comments between colleagues. Just a joke.'

'Not to us.'

'In which case, I'm sorry you're offended.'

Lukshana squeezed her arm and she turned away, but he hadn't finished.

'Though I would say, if you're genuinely so thin-skinned, you're in the wrong business.'

Lukshana squeezed tighter.

Walsham said his farewells to the group and headed towards a raised, roped-off area where Gavin Slade entertained VIPs. Ins and outs were supervised by a man in uniform, buttoned breast pockets and epaulettes on his shirt. Ali recognised the Kingsdale logo across the sleeve. He unlocked the rope and waved Walsham through.

Ali scanned the room. On similar occasions, she'd been undaunted by the presence of wealth and privilege. People had money, so what? But invariably, Fraser took the lead, working the room as she trailed in his wake. He was fluent in their language, effortlessly reasonable, as if these people were his true tribe. Now she carried the responsibility, the weight made heavier by the unholy, corrupt stink of the place.

She visualised the route to Gavin Slade. She'd present the alternative proposals on the community's behalf in front of witnesses. If Slade refused, she'd make it loud. She went to move and Martin Dyce stood in her way. 'Wait your turn, Alison. Mister Slade knows you're here.'

'I need to speak to him.'

'And you will, but you might want to reserve judgement until you've seen the presentations.'

'Who are those people with Slade?'

'Can't you tell, they're the money. Most of our key investors leave this kind of work to their financial advisors and there are a few we've yet to settle on, but there are Chinese, Eastern European and Indian representatives with us. The gentleman in the grey silk suit represents a major Brazilian bank, resident in the UK.'

The Brazilian banker was deep in conversation with someone who looked like private security. 'Does he always wear a bodyguard as an accessory?'

Dyce laughed. 'That's Stuart Slade, Mr Slade's cousin.'

'So that's him. Who's she?' Ali motioned towards a young blonde woman in a red suit jacket, prominently placed.

'She works in the mayor's private office.'

'Doing what?'

'We're not totally sure. Here we go...'

Gavin Slade made his way forward to the lectern. Lights dimmed and the room fell quiet. Ali realised Dyce's intervention was coordinated to ensure she didn't make herself a nuisance before Slade's opening address. He kept the welcome brief, handing over to the mayor, a caricature of the mess of a man Ali had seen at a distance. He stumbled through a prepared speech, amused by his own jokes and distracted by the cinema-sized screen lowered into place behind him. He mumbled about blue movies, but seemed unsure whether to stay at the lectern. The red-jacketed assistant stepped in and led him to the side, accompanied by stuttering applause.

The screen filled with images. A street-level fly-through of the proposed Jamaica Dock Development, artist and architect impressions, commentary supplied by an actor whose voice she recognised. Ali's face froze. Streets that she knew fell away to new-build and tree-lined mews terraces. The famous actor's voiceover announced the scheme had consulted and secured support from the local community. Cue a montage of multiracial images: kids and old folks; scenes from last year's summer holiday activities; the Samba drummers who'd led the procession around the estate; the singers and dancers from midsummer night; the neighbourhood picnic celebrating the opening of Clara James Gardens. The sequence concluded with a photograph of Fraser at the gardens, an immense ice-cream cone held up for the camera and a sweet, proud smile across his face. The image held for what seemed an eternity before the presentation moved on. A celebration of Deptford's heritage, claims that it would be maintained in street names of new residential areas, throughout the cultural quarter close to the river where MEYZ currently stood. Ali couldn't see for the tears in her eyes.

The film stirred to a climax with swelling orchestral strings. Corporate logos framed the screen: the scheme's architects, Bronson and Kean; Kingsdale Developments; the south east London councils; the GLA and City Hall. The symbols faded and were replaced by a single image, the new logo of the Jamaica Dock Development Corporation.

The lights came up as applause spread through the room and fell into an echoing babble of conversation. Dyce said, 'What did you think?'

Ali couldn't speak.

By the time Dyce escorted the Marlowe Estate delegation behind the rope, the mayor, his entourage and the majority of investors had left. Ali walked towards Gavin Slade, unbuckling her bag. The photographer darted through her peripheral vision as she produced the Marlowe Estate proposal. Slade's guests witnessed him welcome the community representatives. If they registered the chill in the greeting, they were too polite to acknowledge it, preferring to witness Slade's magnanimity.

Ali kept her voice steady. 'You can put what you want in your video, you lying prick. We won't go away. I'll make your life a misery and if you send Dyce and his morons to intimidate us, I'll report you and them to the police, the press, whatever it takes.'

Slade handed the proposal off to Dyce, speaking to make sure those around them took notice. 'This is the beginning, Alison. Here's where we sell the concept. There will be plenty of time to engage the community and make sure needs are met. We want to work with you. We will read your proposals carefully and be in touch. And, of course, we have next week's public meeting in the diary, so ample opportunity for us all to consider our views over the weekend.'

Ali brought the Marlowe Estate party together ready to leave, all except Lukshana, who hadn't returned from the restrooms. She went in search, following signs along a series of corridors and was met by a terrified Lukshana, close behind came the man she'd seen Dyce talking to earlier. Ali was ready to stand her ground. Shana pulled her away. 'Please, can we go?'

Mr Tousi and Mrs Stearns waited outside. Lukshana dragged Ali by her sleeve, Mr Tousi and Mrs Stearns fell in behind. Dyce's man came through the doors, his white T-shirt dazzled among the office-worker lunch crowd. They hurried along Queen's Walk, Shana wailing all the way, 'Don't leave me, don't leave me.'

Within sight of London Bridge Station entrance, Dyce's man was on their tail and gaining. As they prepared to cross Tooley Street, Ali caught sight of a familiar figure leaning against the railings. Johnny registered the panicked expression and walked towards her. He looked beyond her and kept going, calling out as if he'd run into an old friend, 'Hey, hey, George Laska! Long time no see.'

Ali didn't dare stop. She stepped up the pace, keeping Lukshana moving forward with an arm round her waist. At one point she swore Lukshana's feet lifted from the pavement and she was carrying her along. Mrs Stearns and Mr Tousi were well ahead. She chanced one more glance behind. As Johnny came within touching distance of Dyce's man, he stalled, turned on his heel and headed back towards City Hall.

Later, they walked Bobby round the park.

Ali said, 'You knew him. You called him Laska.'

'I knew his name.'

'He legged it as soon as he clocked you.'

'Nah, he just wasn't taking chances.'

Ali had arranged to meet Johnny at the park gates, not wanting him at the house. 'You knew him and you knew he was giving us grief.'

He kicked up leaves. 'One look at you and your friend's faces told me that.'

'Of all those hundreds of people on the street, you picked him out.'

'What did he do?'

'Shana wouldn't tell me.' Ali had done her best to keep her calm on the train. She'd been steadier once they were back on the estate, hugging herself as she walked, eyes fixed on the pavement. Ali accompanied her as close to her home as she'd allow. Shana kissed her on the cheek and thanked her. Ali didn't expect to see her any time soon.

'What do you do now?' said Johnny.

'Now Slade's presented his vision for Jamaica Dock and the estate like Pontins for bankers and oligarchs, only without us scummy locals.'

'There's not much more you can do, is there?'

'It's easy in your world, isn't it? Try something and if it doesn't work, pack your bags and do one.'

They were quiet for a time, walking in step without touching. Johnny said, 'By the way, I spoke to Chris. Someone did pay him a visit.'

'Go on, then.'

'Chris described a white bloke, mid-thirties, cheap leather coat, bit of a belly. Marco got a visit as well. He reckoned they were Polish or Russian. He wouldn't know the difference. He means foreign. Chris says he had his mate with him, heavy, in his words, "a knock you about and not think twice" sort of geezer. Which sounds a lot like Laska.'

'And Chris told you this?'

'If you want to know something, it's best to ask. If he hadn't wanted to say, fair enough.'

'You didn't hassle him?'

'I *asked* the man. He told me. So what next?'

'I don't know. It's not a straight fight, not like one of yours

228

anyway. You don't win with the referee lifting up your arm and the other bloke not knowing his own name. Lomax reckons if you play dirty, they win. But they pull these stunts and get away with it.' She thought about the Jamaica Dock presentation video and the gut punch as Fraser's image filled the screen in front of all those people. 'Fraser said—'

'Here we go.'

'He said, if we ever got to the stage where it looked like there was nothing to lose, don't back down, even if you win back an inch, just an inch, do it. We have to toughen up.'

32

Max

DOWNEY CAME OUTSIDE TO meet him. The morning was warm enough, but it had rained. Heavy skies threatened more to come. The priest spread a plastic shopping bag on the bench in the churchyard before sitting. 'Need to keep my trousers dry.'

Max smoothed down his raincoat and sat beside him. 'Thanks for seeing me.'

'I won't say you're welcome, because you're not. Frankly, I've had enough of the police being a nuisance, but Alison believes you're someone I should listen to, so here we are.'

'I take it she told you I'm investigating Fraser Neal's murder. What she probably didn't say is that I want to speak with Dwight Payne.'

'I know who Dwight Payne is and what he does for a living. I also know his reputation.' He opened his hands.

'I can't approach him directly.'

'And why would that be?'

Max ignored the twinkle in Downey's eyes. 'As far as some people are concerned, having Payne as a source would undermine any information he gave me. Plus, he wouldn't speak to me if it was out in the open.'

'I very much doubt he'll speak to you at all.'

'But you could approach Mrs Payne, as you did for Fraser.'

'You think he listens to his mother when it comes to dealing with the police?'

'I think his mother listens to her priest. I'm guessing her priest is as keen as I am to find out what happened to Neal and, to coin a phrase, get the heat off the street.'

'Thank you, Mister Serpico.'

'There are other reasons why this is best handled sensitively, those I can't go into, but it's important for you to realise what I'm trying to do has risks.'

'Go on.'

'It might screw up future relations with the local police.'

'I tend to leave the future in God's hands. He'll take it anyway.'

Downey gazed across the churchyard, lost in thought. 'See that spot over there by the fence, one of our volunteers was beaten unconscious a few weeks ago. She was giving her time to help young people feel safe. We've always had challenges, malicious policies that punish the vulnerable or stupid ones that do it by default. We deal with violent and abusive people, the kind that put Shelly in hospital. The question is, how do you stand up to it? Do you desire the knowledge to understand it? Have you the courage to resolve it, front up if necessary?'

In the silence that followed, Max realised the priest was asking himself.

Downey shook his head. 'It's a difficult question. One the authorities in my line of work would rather we skirted around. I daresay it's the same for you.'

It began to rain, a fine drizzle blown across the churchyard.

'I want to do the right thing by Neal,' said Max.

Downey got to his feet and picked up his plastic bag. 'The police have not been our friends. I'll make no promises. Frankly, I think it unlikely Dwight will talk to you, but I will speak to Lorna Payne. We'll take it from there.'

Sunday morning and Dwight Payne accompanied his mother to church for the first time since her birthday in June. He'd missed his brother's commemoration service in August, a Sunday when the cars smouldered on the High Street.

Dwight guided his mother to the pew closest to the altar. He joined her for prayers. As they rose for the first hymn, he slipped away and through a side door to the vestry.

Max put his finger to his lips until the organ rolled through its introduction and the congregation began to sing. 'Father Downey says we've got about five minutes. He's added a couple of extra verses.'

Payne leaned against a table and folded his arms. 'You've got some front, asking me to do this. You know I'm watched, right?'

For a man under surveillance and knowing it, Payne appeared entirely at ease. 'No one's watching you in here, unless...' Max raised a finger skywards.

'What is it you want?'

'Fraser Neal.'

He stood tall, squared up to Max. 'Not me. Do not go there.'

'But you knew him. Knew him well, from what I've been told. No way he'd have been able to work the estate and set up that studio without your help and your word. Someone tells me you also put your own cash into it. Anonymous private donation.'

'What I do with my money is my business. I'm into music that only people like me can make. I'd say the lines myself if I could, but others do it better. If I see potential, I'll help it along.'

'For a cut.'

'Yes, for a cut. That's how the thing turns.'

'Fraser Neal was a regular visitor to your flat, the last time was a couple of weeks before he was killed. I don't think he'd have done that unless you invited him. Or he had business with you. And we know what your business is, which means I have to ask, what was he buying?'

Payne snorted. 'You people do my head in. Do me down and come to me for help.'

Max wasn't interested. 'Let's assume it was gear and not protection. Why come to you direct? Why not one of the kids you have peddling on the street, or any of a dozen places?'

'I don't think you'd get it. It was different.'

'Try me. I'm trying to find out who knifed the bloke and left him in an alley to die. You're saying it wasn't you.'

'It wasn't. You want me to swear on the Bible, must be one around here somewhere?'

'You've got eyes and ears in all those shady corners on the estate. New Cross is a different postcode, but I know you know what goes on there, so tell me what you came here to tell me, or go and sing with Mother.'

'He bought drugs, mainly weed. But he didn't have to pay. This we kept between us. His buyer, his *end user*, also didn't have to pay. It's medicinal. A family thing. Someone I owe. Someone Fraser owed.'

'You've lost me.'

'Jerome Standing is my cousin. Marcia is my mum's sister. They don't talk.'

'Because of you.'

'Fraser made a big mistake when he put Jerome in the papers. He doesn't need that kind of attention. You've seen him. It'll be a long time before he gets healthy, maybe never. But Marcia has a bit of weed, a puff for herself, and she makes a Saturday broth for Jerome. When he come out of hospital, he wasn't eating. He has a little of Auntie Marcia's soup and gets an appetite for real food. They get some peace and no pain for a while.'

'But you stopped supplying him?'

'Had to. Fraser was warned off. That last time he came round, he told me your man Conway was on his back straight after. *What was he doing, consorting with a man like me?*

233

After that, I didn't see him for a long time. He sent word he wanted to get together, but it never happened.'

'And you don't know what it was about?'

'It wasn't grass.'

'You trusted him?'

Payne's chin dropped, thinking it over. 'He tried to do right by me. And he definitely did good things for people, but he was mad to keep going at the council for selling off Pepys House, the Jamaica Dock thing. That's only going one way. But did I trust him? I don't trust anyone who talks that much or likes a drink that much.'

'Who might he have scored off, if not you?'

'No one on the estate.'

'No one close?'

'He could've gone anywhere.'

The organ's descending cadence told Max the hymn was drawing to its close. 'And that's it?'

'That's it. Now we have to sort out what you're doing for me, your side of this thing. Father Downey reckoned you'd help me out with something.'

'That's thoughtful of him, but it's not how this works.'

Payne had his hand on the door. 'I think it is. You owe me.'

Max watched through the door crack until Payne was back at his mother's side. Downey's voice rang out, 'The heavens declare the glory of God, and the firmament proclaims his handiwork. Day pours out the word to day, and night to night imparts knowledge.'

Congregation voices rose in response: *Their message goes out through all the earth.*

33

Ali

THE COUNCIL MEETING ROOM was quieter than usual as Rod Hutchings dealt with the introductions. Greg Walsham outlined progress since the last meeting, making extravagant claims for the City Hall event as if he'd arranged it personally and paid the bar tab. Ali was thinking through what she intended to say when a voice from the audience called out, interrupting Walsham in mid-flow. She didn't know the man and could only see the back of his head. He wasn't one of their people, though he spoke as if he was.

'You keep talking about regeneration. Who says we want to be regenerated?'

The question was planted. Ali knew it.

Martin Dyce rifled through papers and passed Gavin Slade a single page. Slade took the microphone. 'Forgive me, I don't think we've spoken before. But it's a fair question you ask. For those who may not have caught it, this gentleman is asking "Who says we want to be regenerated?" The answer is at least a thousand Marlowe Estate residents. You'll remember our consultation events in the summer, the main one at your community centre, at which more than two hundred local people expressed their support for the Jamaica Dock proposal.'

Ali had been at the event. She and Fraser head-counted somewhere between 93 and 107 people. A few had dropped in to see what the fuss was about, took a turn at the buffet and made tracks. Slade's phantom 1,000 had been repeated over and over and was written into the paperwork. At the time, Fraser brushed it off. At the next meeting, he'd loaded the room with estate residents and manoeuvred Slade into taking a straw poll. A show of hands went overwhelmingly against. He followed up by producing the event signing-in sheet. Giving Slade the benefit of rounding up, the actual number had been vastly exaggerated. Slade had been caught in the lie.

Now the 1,000 were back. Slade and Dyce weren't wasting time. Ali felt increasingly she was wasting hers. She felt sick and angry, filled with the urge to stop putting herself through nights like these or take action to make them listen.

Dyce's planted 'residents' led the applause as Slade finished speaking. They were still cheering when Ali stood to respond. The enthusiastic clapping and whistling turned to a chorus of jeers and demands that someone *shut that bitch up* before she'd said a word. Father Downey stood up at her side and pointed to the gobshite-in-chief, a thick-bellied middle-aged man, demanding he show respect. The others quietened. Downey's raised finger hovered over the audience, his gaze settling on the loudest and most profane. 'Do not think Mister Slade and Mister Dyce's bullying tactics will work here. Stop your noise or meet me outside.'

A hush came across the audience. Had the priest really offered to fight them? Downey held onto the seat in front. Ali put her hand on his shoulder.

'I'm fine,' he said. 'Say your words.'

Ali made her way to the stage and asked for a microphone. One was handed down to her. 'I want to make sure this is heard by all of you.' She picked out Johnny, Chris and Marco in the audience and darted a look back at Slade. 'He tells us Jamaica Dock is the beginning of an Olympic dividend. Promises it. But nothing is more overstated than the benefit to us, the existing community. He describes it as the opportunity of a lifetime. Those of us who are old enough recognise those words. The same words that persuaded residents to evacuate Docklands so they could tear the guts of the old East End. We will not stand by and allow it to happen here.'

The response was muted, no jeering, but no support either. She continued. 'We gave you our proposals at City Hall last week. You said you'd read them. You said you'd respond. We think they're reasonable. What is your response?'

Slade stood. 'Exactly who do you speak for Miss Barnes? From what we're told you don't have the confidence of your own group, let alone the community. Where are they? Yours seems to be the only voice we hear and my God, we're sick of it.'

Slade returned to his seat, the taunts and insults from his supporters raised a level.

Ali climbed onto the stage. 'These people have no intention of honouring any promise made to the people of Marlowe Estate. We've seen the plans, the real plans, not the bullshit summary they gave us. We know they intend to build 144 luxury flats on the site of Pepys House with underground parking and 24-hour concierge and uniformed security. We know it'll be behind fences and gates. We've spoken to their agents; in fact we tried to put in an offer and were told they've all been sold in advance. How many of those are bought by shady offshore funds, how many are bought with dirty money? He wants you to believe there's benefit for you. How?' Ali looked into the faces ranged against her, using their aggression to feed her anger. She fronted up to Slade. 'You want to kick our people out of their homes for your wealthy criminal friends. Think again. You want to money-launder your way to a seat in City Hall and sacrifice our neighbourhood in the name of profit. Think again. And if you think I can't prove it, try me. You want to bully and intimidate us into submission. Think again. It's a lie that a thousand people on Marlowe Estate support what you're doing, Mr Slade. No one does. Leave Marlowe Estate alone.'

34

Slade

USUALLY, SLADE STAYED TO bathe in the admiration that followed a performance. That night he was away with Dyce following, before Hutchings formally closed the meeting. A conversation was needed, one that needed guaranteed deniability. It couldn't be put off any longer.

Wisely, Dyce said nothing.

They reached the underground car park. Slade unlocked his BMW. 'Get in.'

Dyce didn't take his eyes off the security light blinking above the number painted on the wall. 'I didn't know the priest was coming, must have been a last-minute decision.'

'It's done, Martin. Over. Please make sure there's no repeat.'

'We've warned him off once.'

'Am I supposed to take comfort from that?' Slade tapped the steering wheel. 'It's the business at the church, it's drawn him out of his shell. Do you think you could put him back in it?'

'Certainly, if it's what you want.'

'Yes, Martin. At your earliest convenience. And if we could find out what Alison Barnes has in her possession to make her so damn sure of herself, that would be helpful.'

Dyce had his hand on the door. 'There's one other thing, a name and a face that keeps appearing where we'd rather it didn't. Someone who worked for us a while back.'

'Deal with it. I'm going to go back up and have a chat with Walsham and limit the damage. I'll see if we can move things along more quickly. We need to make sure Father Downey doesn't make a habit of waving the revolutionary flag. His own pulpit's bad enough, but not in my meetings, that needs to be nipped hard.'

35

Johnny

FOR THE THIRD NIGHT running, Johnny kept one eye on the luminous hands of the bedside clock. Its daytime tick was too loud in the dark. He went downstairs. Alec was awake in his recliner. A low side light cast heavy shadows across the carpet. They talked, but not for long. The old man's throat was dry. Johnny put the water bottle straw to his lips.

'Thanks, son.'

He put his feet up on the sofa, listening to the old man's rasping breath. He must have dropped off. He was asleep when his phone buzzed in his pocket.

He took the call in the kitchen. Father Downey's tone of voice told him there was a problem. 'I've a young man here. He says he knows you. Says he needs to speak to you. He has something to tell you. He says his name is…'

Johnny heard the voice in the background. 'Stan, tell him it's Stan.'

'You get that, John?'

'I heard.' Only one reason to rock up at church right now. They'd be waiting for him.

'He needs to meet you. Doesn't want to talk over the phone, but he's very keen that you have this conversation soon.'

He caught Stan's backstage whisper. 'Tonight, tell him he has to come tonight.'

This was a set-up all day long. He told Downey he'd be there in an hour.

He called Ali. She didn't take the call at first, then texted back: *Free now*.

She listened while he explained. 'I think you should call Lomax. Want me to give you the number?'

Downey was in bother. If that wasn't bad enough, it was Johnny's fault. The plain truth was he didn't trust Lomax. No, that wasn't it. He didn't want to be beholden and have Ali thinking he'd had to run to him for help.

'I'll deal with it.'

'I'll call him.'

'No, it's down to me.'

Johnny's mouth was dry. Nerves rolled in his belly as he circled the church, attempting a crude surveillance. What did he expect, some dickhead sitting in a parked car in full view? Laska would have it covered. He ducked down, waiting in churchyard shadows. They must think him dim enough to walk in knowing he had zero chance of walking out. Downey called a second time, two hours since the first call. Was he coming?

'I'm on my way.'

'Only your friend is rather on edge.'

'I'll be there shortly, Father. We'll say a prayer together.'

Johnny hadn't said his prayers since his mother stopped making him when he was nine years old, a point of contention that had vexed Downey since their first meeting. He'd sent his message, but what now?

He sent Ali a text: *Call Lomax. No one else.*

36

Max

'NICE NIGHT FOR IT,' said Max.

Johnny was crouched, hood up, hugging the dark corner on the Albury Street side of the church, his hands shoved in his pockets.

Max said, 'I got the shout from Alison. She says you know this kid Stan. What can you tell me?'

'Not much. I seemed to draw these kids to me. He's had his problems, tough times an' that on the streets. A bit unpredictable, but someone's put him up to this.'

'Your best guess is *someone*?'

'The people who beat up that woman, that's what this is about, isn't it?'

You tell me, thought Max. 'We'll go with what we know and work the rest out on the way. Tell me about the layout. How I get to where your man Stan is now?'

'Father Downey has a small office at the rear. There's a side door that's usually locked from the inside, but they're expecting me to come in that way, so it should be open.'

'That's fine, I don't want to be rattling around once I'm in.' Max started towards the church.

'You want me to come with you?'

'It's you he wants to see.'

Johnny caught up. They reached the side door together. As expected, it was unlocked. Max opened it carefully and led them into a closed hallway lit by a single overhead light. There were two doors facing, one to the left, one straight ahead. Max indicated the left and Johnny gave him a thumbs-up. There was a barely audible murmur of conversation from inside. Max sensed movement. He held up a hand. Someone was there. Johnny nodded that he'd understood. He showed Max his phone screen. He had a call coming in. Max put his hand to Downey's door and turned the handle.

Downey was sitting at his desk, telephone in hand, as Max came in. Stan stood by the window, clenching and unclenching his fists. The kid was wired, addled, blinking, chewing. 'Who are you?'

Johnny followed in behind.

'It's him, he's the one. I don't know who you are, but you have to go. Seriously, mate, piss off now.'

Downey was shaking. 'Are you okay?' said Max.

'Better now. I don't think we're alone.'

Johnny said, 'You had something to tell me.'

'You, not him. You've got to come with me, I've to show you something.'

'That's not happening,' said Max.

'It has to, has to.' The boy gnawed hard on his knuckle, staring between the window bars into darkness.

'Who's out there, son? Who's with you?'

Stan didn't answer.

'Listen to me,' said Max. 'You listening? It's good that you came here. This is a safe place. Sanctuary, they call it. Take a couple of deep breaths and we'll talk about what you want to say to Johnny and what we do to sort this out and make it safe. We'll sort it, right?'

'He's got to come, that's all.' Tears welled up in his eyes. He pushed up the sleeves of his hoodie and pulled them down. Max glimpsed slash scars, recent cigarette burns.

'Okay, we'll come with you.'

'It has to be him on his own.'

'We'll both come and I'll see you out. Father Downey will stay here and Johnny and me, we'll go outside with you. Get some air, is that okay? You and Johnny can go off and deal with whatever you need to deal with.' He turned to Downey. 'Can we get into the church and outside from there? I don't want to go back the way we came in.'

Downey reached into his pocket for a set of keys, isolated three. 'That one gets you into the nave, those two the door on the other side. Should I?' He moved his hand towards the phone.

'DS Tait, soon as we're gone. But tell him quietly. Where are the lights?'

'Right side, as you enter.'

'You ready, then, Stan?'

As they came into the main body of the church, Max flicked the switches on the wall panel. The lights came up over rows of empty pews. George Laska and Tony Fitzpatrick waited at the rear door. As they came forward, Max held up his ID. 'DS Lomax. You need to leave now.'

He sensed Downey arriving at his shoulder. 'You people, leave my church. You can go out that way.'

Fitzpatrick didn't take his eyes off Max. 'I'll see you later, cunt. Old Bill or not. And you, Johnny Nunn, I owe you. You be careful what you say, very careful. Come on, Stan, we're going.'

'He stays,' said Max.

Laska stood his ground, 'No, no, no. Stan, you leave with me, or it will be worse. You know this. Come. You can't keep him, no way.' He stepped towards Max, hand beckoning Stan to join him.

Max locked one handcuff around Stan's wrist, the second cuff around his own. 'He stays.'

37

Max

'ON WHOSE AUTHORITY DID you set up a meeting with Dwight Payne?'

Conway repeated his question for Harding's benefit, in case its significance had escaped her the first time he'd asked it.

Max was growing sick of Commander Harding's office. It never came out well. He did his best to swerve the question. 'Our leads have come to nothing. Maybe they will in time, but it's too slow. The one person with a handle on the estate comings and goings is Dwight Payne. I needed to talk to him.'

Conway said, 'He claims you gave him assurances, immunity from arrest.'

It would have been laughable if his arse hadn't been on the line. The longer Kilby was side-tracked by whatever was keeping him out of London, the more vulnerable Max's position was becoming. He fixed Conway, 'You know that's not what happened. He wouldn't ask and I wouldn't give it, but let's say this hot take of yours is a misinterpretation of what was said. A misreading of me telling Payne our meeting had sweet FA to do with his business, nor any ongoing investigations he's connected with, and everything to do with Fraser Neal, because he and Fraser Neal had some kind of confidence-and-supply arrangement. At the very least a mutual understanding to leave each other alone.'

Harding was interested. 'And did they have an arrangement?'

245

'Ma'am, Neal wouldn't have been able to do the work he was doing without it. We're close to having a firm insight into what he was trying to give us and how he went about getting it. If, as Detective Inspector Conway insists, Neal's death was connected to my work, I need to work the leads as I find them.'

She gave it some thought. For a moment, Max thought she might be swayed, not exactly sympathetic to his view, but not hostile towards it, either. She tracked back. 'Did the fact Detective Inspector Conway ordered you to stay away from Payne enter your thinking at all?'

Conway chipped in. 'I made it abundantly clear.'

'You did and I disagreed. You were wrong.'

Conway did well to keep his mouth shut.

Harding said, 'That's not your decision to make. It's DI Conway's investigation and he gave you an order, which you ignored. In fact, you did the opposite. He has the right to demand you return to your main duties and allow his team to investigate Neal's murder unhindered.'

Harding and Conway were trading favours. Eventually, the credit would be used up. Max had a feeling that time was closer than he'd realised. Conway was pushing to have him removed, but if she'd wanted to reel him in, she'd have done it already. It could be that Kilby's absence made her cautious, or she had doubts of her own.

'I think DI Conway is correct, we've reached the end of the road. I'll book a call with Assistant Commissioner Kilby later today. We're not having this continue. My officers respect the chain of command.' She closed the file, meeting over. Conway walked past him in the corridor and didn't say another word. He'd wanted more of a show and a firmer resolution.

38

Max

THIS WAS THE FIRST time Max had known Denny kick off her shoes and look as though she wasn't working. She'd brought an oversized grey hooded sweatshirt, which she pulled over her head. She saw him watching, 'Just getting comfy.'

'Good. Can I get you a drink?'

'D'you have whiskey?' She settled into Max's armchair, kicked off her shoes off and put her feet up.

He went to the kitchen and came back brandishing a bottle of Bushmills in one hand and two glasses in the other. 'See the effort I've gone to in case you dropped by.'

'You knew I was coming. Or have you been converted?'

'I wouldn't go that far. Talk to me about Gavin Slade.'

'You want my professional opinion?'

'We'll get to that, your take on the man.'

'He thinks he can't be wrong. Has no self-awareness, no empathy, incapable of accepting the smallest wee criticism, so he insulates himself against it. If any blame gets through, he reacts badly. There was a minor outcry over the way they went about sectioning off Greenwich Park after some pretty aggressive treatment from his people. He called the protestors a bunch of "yummy mummies" and "pussy-whipped Charlies".'

'He said that?'

'It's on film. Black-tie affair at the Grosvenor. Any attack is an unfair attack. Regards himself as above such things. He'd steal your wallet and play the victim, because *you* made him feel bad. If he feels anything, it'll never be shame or guilt, not that you and I would recognise.' She sipped her whiskey. Light hit the glass.

'What about professionally?'

'He's having his day and he's handling it well. That's the commercial stuff. The business is expanding. The dirty work, which is effectively the business plan set up by his cousin – site security, limited-scale acquisition and buy-to-lets – that's drying up. He made his moves and he made them early. Pepys House, Jamaica Dock, the Olympic Park, at least one other investment in the pipeline. Similar council sell-off in Enfield pending. Branching into politics, that's harder to get a handle on without stirring too much muck. But it's as much a business calculation as a commitment to any political principle. Do I believe he's capable of murdering Fraser Neal? Question is, why would he?'

'He's forty-six years old and he's never been king.'

'And you think he wants it that much?'

'Men like him always do. Exposing him puts it all at risk. But track back, you said he was insulated.'

She sat up. 'They all are. They pay people to handle the shit. Assume Ben Tait is right and the connection is with George Laska, Tony Fitzgerald, Pallo Gashi, all of whom have a track record of violent, criminal behaviour'

'Add Martin Dyce to the list. He's involved.'

'If they found out Neal was in contact with you, looking to trigger a full investigation into company finances, promising you information, even if nothing came out of it, that doesn't matter. You're paying him and he's behaving as if you owe him for more than you're letting on. People like that would finish him on a rumour. And he told you he was hacked, didn't he?'

'It doesn't need to be that complicated. A few drinks down

and he'd spill it to the barmaid. Meanwhile, the Neal family are calling me out and Conway and Harding want me back in my box.'

'Our box.' She held out her glass for a refill. 'I could be persuaded.'

Max tipped the bottle, ready to pour. 'Could you give me the next couple of days? I can get Kilby to clear it with DI Sewell if I can get hold of him, but I'd rather not wait. I called Susan Neal this afternoon. I'm going to Edinburgh to meet Kenneth Neal.'

'And he's agreed to it?'

'I told Susan I had questions for her dad it wouldn't be right to ask at a distance. I don't expect much of a welcome. Kenneth Neal's started proceedings. According to Susan, I'll gain nothing by trying to change his mind.'

'But you want to give it a go?'

'I want a conversation. It's not unreasonable.'

They left shortly after 5 am, Max easing through early traffic on the North Circular. They hit the M1 and headed north with Denny sleeping off the whiskey. She'd had the best of the sleeping arrangements, a decent six hours crashed out in Max's bed while he dozed on the sofa. At Leicester Forest East, they walked off the stiffness and ate breakfast. Denny took the next shift into Yorkshire. Max found himself measuring distance in trees clinging to sparse verges. Rain spattered the windscreen. A grubby bedsheet slung from a bridge, spray-painted *Happy 60th SEAN*.

Denny broke the spell; had he thought about what he wanted from the meeting?

'A dialogue. So far, all the feedback I've had has been third-hand, via Conway and Tait. If the family have something to say, let them say it to my face. I want a line on why they've not been straight. Fraser was home shortly before he died.

Alison Barnes reckons that's a once-in-a-blue-moon occurrence. I want to know what was serious enough to call him back and what changed while he was there, because something did.'

With Max driving from Scotch Corner, Denny worked through the Special Operations case file for Fraser Neal. Max's additional notes were spare, no more than an observation, or a coded reference to a space in his memory. She said, 'You've got lazy. Many bad habits.'

Denny picked up the stretch that took them along the coast from Berwick. By the time Max drove into Edinburgh city centre, it was growing dark, rush-hour traffic building.

If the boardroom walls at Gilchrist Neal were any indication, the Neals leaned hard on their heritage. Founders' portraits graced the wood-panelling, a family resemblance evident in formal photographs and team presentations. Less apparent in Susan Neal, Max thought. Max and Denny stood as she led her father and Uncle Calum, introduced as Fraser's godfather, into the room. Kenneth Neal was a leaner, neater version of his late son. Uncle Calum hid behind an expensive suit, a beard and a permanent scowl.

Max opened. 'Thank you for seeing us, Mr Neal. Detective Constable Denny is here at Assistant Commissioner Kilby's request. I hope that's okay?'

Denny didn't flinch.

'Let's get on with it, shall we?'

'You're aware I'm with the team investigating Fraser's death.'

Kenneth Neal met his gaze for the first time. 'You can say the word *murder*, Lomax. We're living with the consequences.'

'I had limited contact with Fraser in the weeks before he was murdered. I can tell you he approached us and suggested he could access information we'd be interested in, relating to criminal activity – corruption, fraud, illegal payments. We instigated enquiries, based on what he told us, but they didn't amount to a substantive basis for a case, not that we could act on. You'll also be aware, apart from Fraser's work on Marlowe Estate, his media profile put him front and centre of highly contentious campaigns.'

Calum Neal groaned. 'Come on, man. Get to the point.'

Max didn't deviate. 'Fraser wasn't what you'd call a frequent visitor home in recent years, would that be fair?'

'His work was important. His mother and I were proud of his achievements, his commitment to others. We encourage community-mindedness, as we've done with all our children.'

'He'd been back home how many times since he moved down, roughly?'

'A dozen or so,' said Susan. 'We don't tend to keep count.'

'Christmas, New Year, family gatherings, that kind of thing?'

A flicker from Susan towards her uncle, words unsaid.

'Can you tell me the reason for his final visit?'

Uncle Calum cut across, 'He came to visit his family. The why of it is none of your concern.'

'Nothing to do with business, then, his work or yours?'

'They are unconnected,' said Calum. 'What is the point of this?'

Kenneth Neal lifted his chin. 'Let me ask you something, why do you think my son was murdered?'

'Truth is, I don't know. I can say he was unlucky, that he could have walked along the same street a thousand times and been safe, but I don't believe it. Fraser took risks by exposing what he considered unjust in a very public way. He was standing in the path of a juggernaut investment and doing his damnedest to make sure it didn't happen, at least not the way the people behind it wanted. I can tell you he pissed off as many people as he won over.'

Susan touched her father's arm. 'Dad, tell him what Fraser said. He should know.'

251

Kenneth Neal spread his fingers on a blotter in front of him. His eyes stayed down. 'We didn't know much about my son's work, not the blow-by-blow detail of it, only what made the papers as a rule. But he did confide there was untoward activity in financial arrangements between the council, people at City Hall and the development company he was up against, the *juggernaut* as you put it. For our part, we told him he needed to take care of himself. If he was unsure, he should go to the police.' He paused before continuing. 'My wife, inevitably, begged him to come home, but Fraser told her she wasn't to worry, because he had a friend. A police officer who was helping him stay safe, guiding him in how best to deal with what he'd uncovered. It was you, Detective Sergeant, he named you. He trusted you.'

Max booked them into the Premier Inn at Waverley Station, rather than face the night drive home. He'd half expected Harding to have hauled them in. Silence from London told him word of the visit had yet to find its way back. When he came downstairs to meet Denny, the receptionist called him over. A message from Mr Neal, asking to meet first thing in the morning.

'Kenneth Neal?' Max asked.

She checked the computer, 'No, it's Mr Calum Neal.'

Denny found him at the bar. He passed her the note.

'I don't think he took his eyes off you once. You touched a nerve.'

Max sensed it too. The meeting had been tense, but as much between the brothers as directed at him.

'Do you fancy a drink before we eat? Pub, not here.'

They made their way out into the city, collars up against the cold. Max felt a long way from home.

Calum Neal was waiting alone in the boardroom the following morning. He poured coffee and set a basket of pastries between them on the table. 'Please, help yourselves. You've a fair old drive ahead of you.'

'That's very kind.' Denny picked off a croissant and broke a piece from the end.

'We get them delivered each morning, the bakery on Hanover Street takes care of us. Saves the early shift having to stop on the way in.'

'Thank you.' Max was feeling the energy drain from yesterday's drive.

Calum was breezy. 'I wanted to share some context with you. Thought it might help to make yourselves familiar with what we're about. Our family firm specialises in private clients, many with high net worth. We guarantee discretion and we are extremely careful in how we advise, encourage and support our clients.'

'We've read your website. It's impressive.' Max was tempted to ask him to get to the point, but let it pass.

'Some of Scotland's most notable families come to us and, in the last few years, especially emerging from the crash, our reputation has extended internationally.'

'As far as the City of London?'

'We have close links with corporate finance specialists across Europe and we're a market leader in real estate, commercial, construction, ports and marine developments. A central tenet of our investment client work is that we minimise risk.'

Max cut in, 'This is the business you and your brother hoped Fraser would come into?'

'He'd have come in time.' He paused. 'What I'm going to say now is sensitive for all of us, but it needs saying. You have to forgive my brother right now. He's carrying the weight of this pretty much on his own. He's always had that capacity, has Kenneth. Craig – he's my younger brother – him and me, we make mistakes, but Ken doesn't permit himself the latitude. In part, that's why he gave Fraser the freedom to express himself. But there comes a time when you have to stand on your own two feet and earn a living.'

'Which he was doing, wasn't he?'

'His visit, the one you asked about, was at our request. A family issue we needed to discuss face to face. The company had been paying Fraser an allowance which allowed him to continue his work. Since the local authority had ceased funding his post, we'd supplemented his income.'

'I was told he'd sourced funds from grant applications.'

'Marchmont Charitable Trust. We set it up some years ago to support the arts and education in Scotland, helping those from rundown communities to complete their education. We allowed Fraser access to the fund on the understanding he'd bring the knowledge and experience he gained in London back into the business.'

'And was it pre-agreed when that would happen?'

'End of the next financial year. We gave him until March to sort himself out.'

'You're telling me this now because?'

'He was coming home to his family. Makes it even sadder, don't you think? But as you say, important you have a full picture.'

Max knew he had nothing like it. 'Is Detective Inspector Conway aware of this?'

Calum thought before answering. 'He is, yes.'

The boardroom door opened and a face appeared. Unmistakably another Neal. Max recognised the dour expression of Fraser's elder brother from the holiday photo. 'Ah, you're in here, we've got the conference call.' Noticing Max and Denny, he corrected himself. 'It's in fifteen. We're ready to pre-brief.'

'I'll be along. Couple of minutes.'

The door closed. Calum spread his hands and pushed away from the table. 'I supported my brother in his decision to help

Fraser find his own way. There was merit in what he'd decided to do. We admired his social conscience and hoped he'd bring his learning to our public law department or our cross-border work. I had no say in how he spent the grant we provided; but as treasurer of the trust, it was my view it couldn't be an indefinite arrangement. I hope you find the people that murdered my nephew, and soon. He deserves justice and we'd like to see progress.'

'If you and your brothers have me removed from the case, as Conway has no doubt advised, I guarantee you never will.' Max got to his feet, wanting to be on the road. 'I have a question, Calum, then we must go.'

'Please be brief.'

'Have you advised clients to invest in the Jamaica Dock Development scheme?'

Calum's face darkened, then broke into a smile. 'Safe journey.'

39

Max

MAX AND DENNY ARRIVED at the Jamaica Dock project office in City Hall to be told Gavin Slade was in a meeting. Martin Dyce had left for home and no other senior officers were available to see them. 'In that case, we'll hang on for Slade,' said Max.

The PA hid behind her computer screen. Frantic typing told Max she'd let the boss know they were there. Not long after, the door opened. Gavin Slade emerged alone, deep in thought. A meeting of one, it seemed. The PA caught his attention, but Slade had already seen them.

'How many times do you have to be told?'

'Excuse me?' said Max.

'I have another meeting to get to. We can do this another time.'

Denny offered her ID. 'No sense putting it off. Better here than somewhere more public.'

Slade waved them through to the room he'd left, a bare-walled meeting space.

Max pulled out a chair and sat. 'Simple question. Detective Constable Denny and I have just come from a meeting with Fraser Neal's father and uncle. Their family law firm, Gilchrist Neal, provides investment services as part of their commercial practice. They're dealmakers, Mr Slade. It occurred to me you might have come across them in that capacity?'

Slade dipped his head, as if working through a complex calculation. 'Not aware of that, no.'

'Can you confirm whether they have a role in the Jamaica Dock scheme?'

Slade rolled his eyes, 'Again, no.'

'But you would know, wouldn't you, if you'd been canvassing for potential investment partners and made an approach to Gilchrist Neal?'

The colour went out of Slade's cheeks. 'I have my own networks, my own brokers, my own people. Due diligence is done by them as I've explained to you before. I don't need to go hawking the scheme around the country. This is London, Lomax. People come to us.'

40

Slade

SLADE CORNERED MARTIN DYCE in the Kings Arms in Tooley
Street as the after-work crowd was building. They'd be
standing shoulder to shoulder in half an hour. Dyce looked to
be waiting for someone and, from his sour expression, wasn't
pleased at the intrusion. 'Tracey said I'd find you in here. Do
you tell her everything?'

'My whereabouts in work hours, standard practice. You're
flustered.'

'I've just come from the JD office. That man Lomax was
there, asking about goings-on in Scotland and what did we
know about Fraser Neal's family involvement in Jamaica Dock
investments?'

'To which you said?'

'I wasn't aware there was one. You should have bloody
been there.'

Dyce peered over his shoulder as the door opened. 'Do you
mind if we get a drink and sit down, I'm meeting someone
and you're probably not going to want to be seen with them,
or them with you come to think of it. Best if I've got a clean
view and head them off.' He was too late. At that moment,
Conway walked through the door. He noticed Dyce first. Seeing
Slade, he grinned and joined them at the bar.

'Gentlemen, what can I get you both?' He caught the attention of a barmaid pouring a pint. 'When you're ready.'

'Rude not to,' said Slade. 'I'll have a large Bombay Sapphire and tonic, ice and lime, please.'

'Mr Dyce, your usual port and lemon?'

Slade gave Dyce a pat on the arm. He was blown. It didn't need Conway taking the piss to prove it. 'Have a drink Martin, no harm in it.'

They found themselves a recently vacated table. Conway moved the empty glasses to one side and raised his pint. 'Are we drinking to *the project*?'

Dyce seemed to shrink in his chair. 'Not so loud.'

'It's not a secret, is it?' He waved a discreet finger at Slade. 'Your boss has been all over the telly giving it the big 'un and you're his loyal... whatever it is you are. What else would we be talking about?'

Slade put an end to Conway's performance. 'Martin and I were discussing an issue we thought had been addressed, a colleague of yours, one whose way of working is still causing a few problems. Call it duplication of effort, if you like.'

Conway put his glass down. 'Lomax?'

'Better if you use your influence, I think, rather than us. Apparently, just back from an unscheduled trip to Edinburgh.'

'Explains one thing, at least. Word came through this afternoon; the family are withdrawing their complaint against him. They have *reconsidered in the light of new information and are no longer seeking redress.*' There were too many punters within range to say more.

'We'll leave it with you.' Slade sipped his drink. 'Come on then, Martin. Mr Conway didn't give up his evening to visit me, did he? Don't let me stop you, or is it a secret?'

Dyce hesitated, then downed his lager and left.

Conway raised his glass. 'Well, wasn't that a coincidence?'

Slade sucked on a lime wedge and tossed the rind in the empty glass. 'Have you thought about the proposal?'

'The timing's not the best, but if you're serious, I'll consider an offer.'

Slade deliberately looked him in the eye. 'I won't ask twice, Andrew. I have a seat on the Assembly assured. Committee chairmanship will follow. Your post will be established in a matter of weeks. The offer is the offer. What you do with that on the side, is up to you. I don't need to know. But I want Lomax off my back.'

41

Johnny

'YOU GOT A MINUTE, son?'

Alec was dressed, coat on, standing at the bedroom door. Johnny put down *The Moonlight Girls* and grabbed his jacket off the chair. They went downstairs, Alec taking one step at a time. He stopped at the bottom, holding onto the banister. 'It's not far, a walk round the corner.'

It would be a stretch. The night before, Lorraine had been getting onto him about buying a wheelchair – *it would do you good to be out in the fresh air instead of cooped up in this house.* She wasn't wrong, but Alec didn't want it.

'When the time comes – not yet.'

Alec led them down a path at the end of the row of terrace houses. A wide alley ran alongside the last house, leading to a cracked, uneven road running behind the houses. Alec took Johnny's arm to steady himself. At the end of each garden, a garage door opened onto the access road. 'Most of 'em park in the street and use these for sheds and garden crap.'

As they arrived at the back of his house, Alec handed Johnny a set of keys. 'It's the green ones. Do the lock in the middle first, then the one at the bottom.'

He slipped the key in the central lock. It turned with a hefty clunk. Evidently, it needed to be heavy-duty for whatever Alec kept inside. The up-and-over door lifted with some encouragement. It, too, was heavier than he'd expected. Covered under a patchwork of canvas tarpaulins was a vehicle. 'You want those off?' asked Johnny.

'Yeah, go on. Ta, son.'

Johnny had never learned to drive. As a kid, there was no-where he wanted to go that you couldn't get to by tube or bus easily enough. At 16 he'd had the first in a series of 125 cc bitzers that got him around. When he came of age and was boxing across London and the south east, there was always someone to give him a lift. His task was to be right for the ring. Dave Price had promised, when the money came in, they'd sort him out with decent wheels. Something else that never happened. He pulled away the tarpaulins in Alec's garage, revealing a spanking clean, pale blue Rover.

A smile came across the old man's face. 'It's a Rover 45. Top of the range – they call it the Connoisseur. Two litre V6, not that it means bugger all to you. Leather seats and walnut dash, all the extras. Go on, get in.'

'You know I can't drive, right?'

'You're talking to the bloke who ferried you across half of England. Go the other side. I want to sit behind the wheel.'

Alec put the key in the ignition and ran his hands around the steering wheel. 'Bloody hell, I love this car. I'd wanted a Rover forever. Couldn't tell you why, except it feels like a classic. I only wish I'd done it sooner. This one came with a couple of grand on the clock. Me and Lorraine used to go out driving on Saturday nights, bowling down Hastings for a bag of chips.' He paused, lost in thought. 'There's something I need to explain.'

'You want me to wash your car?'

'Shut up and listen, will you?' Alec choked up, tapped the wheel with his fingertips. 'Sorry, son, this has hit me in a way I wasn't expecting. It's hard.'

'You're all right, take your time.'

'That's the problem.' He pulled himself together. 'Things happened when Dave died. Things you probably didn't realise.

People I thought were my mates did a bunk. The grudges people had against Dave turned up on my doorstep. Wally Patch and Ruby and them lot had problems of their own. Ruby went away, never told anyone where. Frank Neaves was inside and missed most of it. Wally had his hands full keeping Rose and Carl and Terry out of bother. I was an easy target, so they came after me. Ah, sod it.' Alec turned the key. The engine purred smoothly into life. He slipped into first gear and edged forward until the car was over the garage threshold. He pulled on the handbrake. 'Come with me.'

Underneath an old rug at the back of the garage, a Burton floor safe had been cemented into a half-metre square recess. Alec gave Johnny the keys. 'The red keys. You'll need both.'

Inside the safe was an olive-green metal file box. It had a military look to it. 'Bring the box and lock up,' said Alec.

He reversed the car back into the garage and turned off the engine, gesturing to Johnny to give him the box. He opened the lid and took out a brown zip-up wash bag. 'I need you to mind this for me. Lorraine mustn't know.'

Johnny knew from the weight what was inside.

'It's a Browning. One mag, thirteen rounds. Wally got it for me. It's not been needed for a while, but it's clean and it's looked after.' He went back to the box and produced an A5-size plastic zip-lock wallet. 'Car docs and five grand cash. When I'm gone, lose the gun. Take it apart and dump the bits somewhere safe. The car and the cash are yours. I'll tell Lorraine.'

He started to sweat, ran his hand through his hair. 'I'm not apologising for this, but my God, son, we waste so much time.'

42

Max

CONWAY'S TEAM WERE TALKING among themselves as Max entered the room. The buzz of post-weekend catchups for those that hadn't been working. Shannon had taken a couple of days for her kid's birthday, a trip to Alton Towers and a second mortgage to pay for it. Max dropped into an empty chair. The atmosphere was noticeably chilly. 'Am I okay here, no one's special personal seat?'

Conway came in soon after, Tait behind him, chastened. 'Lomax, you're leaving. Pack your stuff and get out.'

'Do I get a why?'

Conway stood back from the door and waved Max through. 'You're covering your arse, no interest in doing the work properly or allowing us to do the same. Either Neal was your source, in which case you put him at risk and he was killed for it. Or he wasn't, in which case you didn't handle him effectively and left him hanging. It makes you a bad judge of people and a worse one of police work. Either way, you should have asked permission to speak to the Neal family, same as you should Dwight Payne, same as Shelly Dowd, same as Gavin Slade.'

'You'd have denied it.'

'With good reason. It undermines our work.'

This wasn't about Max's professional reputation. Conway didn't think he had one. It was about Conway's failure to justify what had happened to Neal. He'd screwed the case from the off and had his scapegoat.

'Can we talk,' said Max, 'in private?'

'Say it here.'

'It's irrelevant whether he was a registered informer, an occasional source, or a bloke chatting in a pub. He was murdered and you don't know by who or why. It's not about what I did or didn't do. That's not your call.'

'It's Commander Harding's. She'll have my report by close tomorrow. You don't have the requisite skills or training to work with this or any other murder investigation team. You've contributed nothing of use.'

'Pleasure working with you too.'

Max collected his things. He might buy himself two or three days, but unless he had an alternative and rock-solid line of enquiry with the evidence to support it, it was unlikely he'd get more. If Tessa Harding was behind Conway's efforts to discredit him, he'd find the reason for that too.

Max leaned against his car, parked up at the back of Deptford High Street.

Johnny came towards him from the Broadway. More of a swagger than he'd seen before. 'Ali said you needed to see me, so I'm here.'

Max was not in a conciliatory mood. 'You deal with me now. Otherwise, Conway and Tait will drag you through a pointless court case for Shelly Dowd and all the shit you don't want to come out will come out.'

'I don't think Shelly sees it as pointless.'

'Yes, she does. They're pressuring her into making the complaint. It's odds on to fail. Slade will buy those thugs' lawyers, who, in turn, will bury you. Conway will hold you responsible for his case dying on its arse and one or more of Laska, Fitzpatrick or Pallo Gashi will come after you and whoever you care about.'

'Ali says you went to see her. At home.'

'That's your answer?'

'She says you came on to her.'

'Not me, mate. I'd have remembered.' Max spun through their conversations. He couldn't see how she'd read it that way. 'We talked about Fraser Neal and we talked about you.'

'What did she say?'

'That's between us. But you need to tell me why you came back here. You told me and Tait it was coincidental you were at the church when Fitzpatrick and Gashi picked up Stan. That's bollocks. You knew they'd be there.'

Johnny tried to speak and turned away, coughing uncontrollably. His hand went to his chest, obviously in pain. He held up his hand for Max to wait. They made their way to St Mark's Churchyard and sat on a bench. Screwed to the back was a brass dedication plate:

Irene and Patrick Miller
Together in the Lord
July 1997

'Last winter was the worst.' Johnny kept his hand pressed to his breastbone as if holding back another spasm. 'Fifteen-hour days demolishing a disused care home in Southend in January and February. Not much fun.'

'Off the books?'

'What do you think? No safety gear, no waterproofs, nothing. I got ill, but I wasn't getting paid unless I kept working. I collapsed on the job. The bloke in charge dropped me at the roadside. Someone must have called an ambulance. They kept me in. Chest infection, they said, could have been pleurisy. I had a course of antibiotics, but it's never really gone away.'

He inhaled and coughed hard once, rigid again until the

pain passed. 'There's a bloke who used to hang around with me and my mates. His name was Martin Dyce. You know that line comedians trot out, *I used to make my mates laugh at school and that's how I started out as a comic.* Dyce was a dickhead who thought he was funny. He stopped himself.'

'What we say here is between us,' said Max. 'If what you say goes further than that, I'll tell you.'

'Some years ago, I had a spell working in a hotel round the back of Oxford Street as night porter, barman, chief chucker-out, whatever the boss needed.'

'Was this after your daughter went missing?'

Johnny's eyes flashed. 'She told you.'

'I asked.'

Max was aware it could have gone either way at that point, but Johnny wanted to talk. 'One night, Dyce came in the bar with a bunch of blokes. Proper chaps, you know what I mean? Out for a taste of the seedier side, like they knew they were where they shouldn't be. Dyce was pissed. I don't think he recognised me or, if he did, he didn't say so. We hadn't seen each other in years. Different worlds, an' that. They'd been there about half an hour. He was sitting at the bar, far end from me, talking to this pimp they called Marku as if they knew each other. My boss kept a corner room on the third floor, right at the back. The cleaners' duty roster had it down as a store room, but they never went near it. He'd done it out like a standard hotel bedroom. Him and Marku worked it out on an hourly rate. My boss took a slice and management knew nothing. The deal with Marku's girls was they were young.'

'Under age?'

'He wasn't bothered either way. That night he was near as I am to you, looking through photos on his phone. Dyce thought he was buying a night with this kid who looked sixteen years old. For all I know, she might have been younger. But it was a scam.'

'You thought Kerry had been through there?'

'I don't know what I was thinking. I'd made one bad choice after the other. I was chasing scraps, anything that might give me hope.'

'Tell me about Dyce.'

'I went for my break and when Marku brought the girl upstairs, I was waiting. I caught him cold, one punch and straight down. I gave the girl the cash I found on him and told her to wait for me outside. I went in the room and there's Dyce, halfway out of his strides. I told him he was about to be stitched up. He thought it was a joke. I took down the mirror and let him see the spyhole. Nothing. No shame. I still don't think he knew me. I told him if he turned up there again, I'd batter the life out of him. Next time I saw him, he was standing next to Gavin Slade on the teatime news, slick as you like, talking up Jamaica Dock.'

15 December 1993
Grafton Arms, Strutton Ground SW1

For once, Max didn't mind the television being on in the pub. An announcement from Downing Street was expected during the evening. The Met were on full alert in anticipation of a backlash: an action to reassure the boys back home no ground would be given, either towards a United Ireland or to No Surrender. London didn't need reminding after October's bombing campaign, this wasn't over. But it was a first step.

The signing of the Downing Street Declaration dominated Special Operations' agenda. As a result, since joining Kilby's branch of SDS at the beginning of December, Max had been mainly reader and observer. It would stay that way until he'd completed training. In the meantime, lesson one: how to stay alive when a loose word or gesture could get you killed. The lesson encompassed lying for a living. Be contained. Be thoughtful, observe, minimise risk. Live close to the truth.

The decision to assign him to the field belonged to Kilby alone. There wouldn't be many more nights to feel as free as this.

Fraser Neal balanced two pints and two whiskies on a London Pride tin tray. His attention was drawn to the screen and he just missed walking into the table. Susan, his sister, *wouldn't be joining them after all. She had to finish packing before heading back to Scotland, at least until the New Year.*

'Are you going home for Christmas?' said Max.

'Eventually, if they'll have me. I'm not in my parents' good books just now. Susan's my advance party.' He picked up the whisky. 'Slanj-a-var.'

'Cheers.'

'My dad wants me to switch courses – Law and Economics at Queen Mary and Westfield isn't up to his expectations. He wants me to do Law, straight and true. He dines with Professor Andrew Cairns, Head of Edinburgh Law School. Christ, it's an awful thing to admit, we're a terrible bunch of social climbers.'

Max was taken aback by Neal's openness. He'd got in touch the previous week and asked for an informal meeting. Kilby okayed it on the assumption, reasonable enough, that mutual thanks were in order. The Neal family's intervention in his favour had saved Max's career. But this familiarity was unexpected. Fraser spoke as if they were old friends. Or perhaps he needed someone to drink with?

'They'll work on Susan, but she's only here until June and she's finished. Then she'll go back and marry Murdo or Hamish or some rugger arse.'

Max suspected Neal had got himself a cheeky one in while he was waiting at the bar.

'She'll do fine, my sister, as long as she doesn't follow me into the mean streets of Welling too many more times, metaphorically speaking.'

Fraser was watery-eyed, slurring. Max needed to get on and say what he'd come to say. 'Fraser, I wanted to thank you and your dad for going out on a limb on my behalf. They'd have kicked me out otherwise.'

'For disobeying orders.'

'Along those lines.'

'Well, I'm glad you did. Susan was in a bad way that day. I should never have persuaded her to come.'

'You couldn't have known.'

'Yes, I could. Still, lessons will be learned, as they say. But thank you.'

'What I'm saying is you couldn't have known, because I didn't know. I didn't know what it would feel like. I didn't know until the last minute they'd change the route, change tactics. Seeing people panicking and doing nothing goes against, I dunno, human instinct.'

'You're in the wrong job, pal.'

'I was. D'you want another?'

'No, they're on me, I told you.' He went for his wallet and patted himself down, every inch the music-hall gentleman Scot. 'It appears I am financially embarrassed, I'm terribly sorry.'

'I'll get them,' said Max.

As he stood, the TV in the pub cut to a newsflash direct from Downing Street and the pub fell quiet.

Part Three

December 2011

43

Max

MAX KNEW HE WAS close. City Hall wanted a piece of what Gavin Slade was selling, as did the South London councils. The Jamaica Dock Development was driven by him, whether personally on decision-making boards at City Hall or through associates motivated to do his bidding. His assets, Max now knew, belonged primarily to Belmont Homes, registered offshore. He stood to make a fortune in landmark residential property developments south of the river over the next decade.

This time Max was buying the drinks. Kilby had returned to a summons from Commander Harding and was not happy. 'You're saying for certain that Slade was the target for Neal's claims of dark money. Any criminal associations?'

'Deniable, so far.'

'But he has them?'

'Our records verify he was linked with active criminal networks up until 2009. You remember a few years back, Kev Russell got close to those ultra-right offshoots, old-school BNP and British Movement types? Kingsdale Developments, specifically Kingsdale Security – call it what you like, they're one and the same – was employing those people across Essex and Kent. Slade would have you believe it was down to his cousin and not him, a hangover from the past. Neither of those things are true.'

'You don't think so?'

'Martin Dyce is City Hall's Jamaica Dock project lead. Slade refers any task not directly needing his attention to him. Dyce, in turn, has links with the sale of drugs, prostitution, possibly trafficking. I don't think cousin Stuart is the silent partner Gavin Slade claims, either.'

'Any closer to Neal's source?'

'Shelly Dowd. Dyce fired her, but I think she was blown well before. She's vulnerable. Her son is on remand. They pulled him for looting a month after the riots. Charged with possession of a knife and threatening the arresting officer. Same time Shelly was fired from City Hall. He has a drug problem that he didn't have before he went into Wandsworth and Mrs Dowd is paying a man called George Laska to keep him supplied. It's money she doesn't have. He's asked her to store drugs at her flat as part payment, and is trying to coerce her into sex work. I want the son moved. If he's safe, I think she'll talk to us. Not before.'

'What are we doing about it?'

'Her case has been taken up by a legal firm specialising in that kind of work. You should be aware, I arranged it privately behind Commander Harding's back. The proper channels weren't available. I tried.'

Kilby was impassive. 'Commander Harding says you're more interested in settling scores on behalf of people on Marlowe Estate. Specifically, this woman who worked with Neal.'

'If anything, Alison Barnes clarified my thinking, not clouded it. Slade's people are organised and hostile.'

It didn't matter to Max whether Kilby kept him working the case or bumped him as Harding wanted, he'd made the commitment. 'Slade has built his power base incrementally. He's an ambitious operator. Neal should have been no more than a minor irritation. Alison Barnes the same, but everything about it says Slade is heading down a dark road.'

'And DI Conway?'

'Impossible to keep onside. His team resented me being there. He sets the agenda and they follow to the letter. Tait's concerned Conway sidelined viable lines of investigation, because he's intent on laying the responsibility with us, me personally. I've gone at it straight and with an open mind, but since I met with the Neal family, he's flipped. My sources suggest a connection with Slade. And here's the other thing, Slade has been promised a seat in the GLA through the closed-party scheme. He has friends in the mayor's office. He's their man, no question. His oppo in Lewisham, Greg Walsham, has been putting it about that he'll be fast-tracked into the post of Deputy Mayor for Policing and Crime.'

'And you know this how?'

'Read through his media in the last six months. He's edging towards it. There was an article in the *FT* which set out his campaigning position. Denny spoke to people in City Hall and it's out in the open. Shelly Dowd knew it, which means Neal knew. This is politics, deal-fixing, intimidation and they come back to the same thing: Slade, Jamaica Dock, and dark money, exactly as Neal claimed. But what I have so far isn't enough to tie Slade or Dyce or Laska to Fraser's murder. I'll get it but I need Conway and Commander Harding off my back.'

'Make the case against Slade and his people. Pass it to the CPS for charging advice and hand it over. Let Conway's team see it through. We need to stand back.'

'It won't happen. Conway will find a way to kill it before it gets to court.'

He pushed his glass aside and folded his arms across the table. 'I choose my words carefully and so should you. Use your judgement and do it better than you have so far. Do not make an enemy of Tessa Harding.'

44

Max

ACROSS THE RIVER, THE Shell Centre, the London Eye and
the old County Hall were lit like Dreamland. The night chill
hadn't deterred tourists along the Embankment. Office lights
burned late in the MoD Main Building. A group of lads, already
well oiled, staggered up the gangway onto the Tattershall
Castle. A man, late thirties and unshaven, sat alone on a bench,
taking in the spectacle. He settled a compact grey rucksack
in his lap. Dominik Saski.

Max took the other end of the bench. 'Don't mind, do you?'

Saski said, 'You know how you tell real Londoners – they
always trying not to see each other. People are invisible. Except
children, they see everything.'

Max knew not to encourage Saski in this kind of mood. It
generally took a dark turn. 'Some work I need doing.'

'I guess that much. Am I working for risk?'

Their infrequent conversations – half a dozen since their
first, brought about as Max tried to retrieve the parts of his
identity Saski had stolen to order and for cash – usually began
with Saski complaining he was being ripped off.

'Zero risk,' said Max. 'The rate is what the rate always is.'

A graduate of his home country's security services, now
granted British citizenship with help from Kilby's Home Office
contacts, Max had helped Saski out from under a noxious
relationship with a north London gangster named Andre

Connor. Now he had a well-paying gig and a list of regular clients. His speciality was the discreet dip into the electronic lives of his subjects – he refused to call them targets. That was the kind of word people in Max's world used, he said. It belonged in his old life. This was their dance. Saski made himself useful.

'Straight answer please, Dominik, what are the chances you get caught out?'

Saski pinched a thumb and forefinger. 'Same zero as your zero.'

Max hoped not. 'You remember the search and find you did for me earlier this year?'

'Sure. Scottish boy, Fraser. I liked him.'

'I need to know whether his system is still secure. And I need details of any contacts between his account and these people.' He pressed 'send' on a text with the details. 'And I need you to follow up the first two names on the list. Bank accounts, cash not from an obvious source, one-off payments. Same for close relatives. One is a man called Gavin Slade; the other is Detective Inspector Andrew Conway.'

'You go after one of your own?'

'I wouldn't put it that way. Some information I need without making it obvious.' Max met Saski's gaze directly for the first time. 'I wouldn't be asking if I thought there was another way. Don't wait until you've got everything. I need what you have by the end of the week, sooner if you can.'

That night, after he'd picked up the rest of his things from Lewisham, Max drove to the estate. He parked and walked by Fraser Neal's flat. He went up the stairs quietly, stepping past the curtained glow of neighbours' windows. In Neal's flat the curtains were open. Susan Neal was boxing up books, carefully flicking through each one, making sure nothing had been slipped between the pages, before allocating storage crate, cardboard or black bin bag. Curating her brother's memory. Max rang the bell. She invited him in. 'It's chaos, mind where you're walking. My brother held onto pretty much everything, it seems.'

'I was passing.'

'On the third floor?'

'You can see the light from the street. Do you want me to go?'

'Eventually. I was coming to see you tomorrow.'

'You'd have a job finding me. I'm no longer working the case. Officially, at least.'

She was taken aback. 'You know that's not our doing. What about unofficially?'

'That's how I do my best work.'

She picked the next book from the pile, Jerzy Kosiński's *Being There*. 'I bought him this. We saw the film at the Cameo, years ago. The Festival ran a retro season. Funny men in serious suits or something. Fraser loved it, so...' She flicked through the book. 'Have you read it?'

'Not for a while. It got trashed with some other stuff when my flat was turned over a few years back.'

She offered him the book. 'Take it. This lot are most likely to finish up at Oxfam. I'm only holding onto things that belong to us.' She fumbled for the words. 'Most of it doesn't mean anything, other than he owned it. Books, DVDs, T-shirts, they're just things, but they'd break your heart if you let them.'

Max took the book. 'Thank you. If you ever want it back.'

'I won't. Will you stay for a cup of tea, though? Something I need to ask.'

Plans had been made. She was taking Fraser's things home the following day and had come to London early. 'Being at home is unbearable. Dad's ranting, mum dissolves in fits of weeping if anyone mentions Fraser's name. My brother's bustling about, being all stiff upper lip about everything, which confuses and upsets me in ways you can't possibly imagine. I need to get things done alone. All this is a useful distraction.' She passed him the mug. He fished the teabag out and dropped it in the bin.

They made space, sofa and easy chair, facing each other. Max rested his cup on his knee. 'There's not much I can tell you about the case, less from Conway's side. It's slow. Slower than I'd expected.'

She held up a hand. 'I don't want your progress report, save it for my dad. Max, would you meet with my dad and my uncles early next week? There's been some soul-searching, which, for them, is a minor miracle. Your visit made more of an impact than you think. More than I realised, to tell you the truth. Also, and this is why I wanted to see you, we can't talk or discuss any of this over the phone or in emails. No means of communication that isn't certified secure. New family rule.'

'What's caused this?'

'Our phones have been hacked. We think home and office.'

'You're certain?' Max hoped Saski hadn't gone to work straight away.

'You know what our business involves, the clients they handle. There's a responsibility that comes with it. Our cyber and phone security is handled by serious people. The hack came up in a system scan last week. So yes, I'm certain.'

'Do they know by whom?'

'That's above my family pay grade.' She sipped her tea. 'There'll be no more of an invitation than this. Call the office the day before and tell them you're coming. On your own this time.'

He rinsed the cups before he left. Susan was ready to pack it in for the night. She'd get an early start and box up the rest in the morning, before heading north the next afternoon. He slipped the book into his pocket with another thank you. She led him to the door and said goodbye. Before heading down the stairs, Max glanced back along the landing. Susan was leaning over the balcony, wondering how he'd managed to see light in Fraser's flat from three floors down.

45

Ali

IT WAS A LOT to take in, Conway hanging around in reception as Ali arrived at work with that worried look on his face, arms folded, as if waiting for permission to enter the building proper. She noticed his shoes, how scuffed and unpolished they were compared with every other time he'd been there. There was a crumpled uncertainty about him. He's got bad news and doesn't know how to tell it, she thought; something to do with Fraser. 'You coming in or signing up for knit and natter?'

A vague toss of the head, otherwise not a flicker.

'It's better if we speak privately, Miss Barnes. And informally.'

'Not under caution then.'

'I don't think so.' He followed her in and waited while she unlocked the office.

Ali hung her jacket on the door and flicked down the Post-it Notes lined up on her desk. Conway couldn't take his eyes off her, sizing her up.

'Reason I've come, some things you need to be made aware of concerning DS Lomax. I've had him removed from the case.'

46

Max

MAX FOUND ALI WALKING Bobby in Deptford Park. He caught up with her on a circuit and walked alongside. As she strode out, her hand came up. She slapped the last leaf from a low branch. Max said, 'Okay if I walk with you?'

She didn't answer.

'No problem,' he said. 'We can talk another time.'

Her stride shortened. 'What do you want?'

'I spent last Friday with Fraser's family. I thought you'd be interested.'

'His sister couldn't spare two words for us when she came down. Fraser always said his family had a superiority complex.'

'I got the impression Fraser found it hard to settle in at the beginning. Bit of a culture shock.'

She stopped and lit a cigarette, let the smoke rise to the trees. 'If you're trying to tell me he wasn't the working-class hero we all thought he was, we never did. He didn't hide where he was from. Not many of us are *from* here.'

'But you are. It's not a career move.'

'And it was for Fraser, that's what you're saying?'

'He came to make a name for himself. To prove something. Kicking against his rosy-cheeked middle-class Edinburgh upbringing. He needed a cause. This was it.'

She made a slow circle of what Max had said before settling

on one thing. They came to the park gate. 'He was committed to us. To all of *this*. I don't care what you think.'

Max weighed his options. 'Tell you what, we'll have this conversation another time.'

'No, we'll have it now.' The strain of carrying the campaign showed in her eyes. 'I want to know what you want from us. Never mind what Fraser did and what he wanted – what do you want?'

'I want to know who killed Fraser and why.'

'Conway came to see me. I don't think he likes you a whole lot. He said you were "a user of people", that's what you've been trained to do. He said you come across like you believe in what we're doing but it's bullshit. You set Fraser up. He said he was telling me because he thought I liked you and because that's something else you do. That's your game. Which is why he's had you removed from the case.'

'Conway knows what I want him to know.' It started to rain. 'But if you're choosing to go along with his opinions all of a sudden, you're welcome. It's not up to me to change your mind.'

'He told me you worked under cover. Special Duties, or whatever it's called. Fraser warned us someone like you would turn up if we made enough of a fuss, but he said we'd notice.'

'I haven't had an undercover job in eight years. You knew who I was, I told you.'

'What I wanted to hear.' She gave Bobby's lead a tug. Reluctantly, he came to her side.

'Ali, you have to know Conway told you this because he knows this is how you'll react. Which means he's shitting himself about your fiver and my fiver making a tenner. I don't think he's doing it off his own back.'

Bobby walked to heel obediently, glancing back at Max as he followed Ali across the street.

*

Max had endured dark nights of the soul before. They went with the territory. Liz taught him to steer away from the shady corners in his past, but there were times he couldn't manage it. His lie, the one that cut deepest, had been to her and to others he'd come to call friends. He regretted it still. Ali was different. If she wanted a share of his remorse because Conway told her she had a right to it, they'd both be disappointed.

Fraser had sold them a version of himself. Max could see how compelling it must have been, having someone on your side with the charisma and confidence to make Gavin Slade and the people backing him think twice. But Slade had staked his reputation on delivering. For his investors, there was no reversing their commitment to Jamaica Dock or to Slade as the scheme's figurehead. They had that in common with Alison Barnes and the residents of Marlowe Estate: once they'd invested their futures in Neal, there was no going back. But he'd found himself chasing down dirty money, rubbing against people in Max's world. The odds were narrowing that he was murdered because of it.

47

Max

MAX WAS STARTING TO question whether Johnny Nunn knew
or remembered what happened in the years he'd drifted. He
didn't seem punchy or hollowed out, but he was elusive. His
story, assembled from fragments, was a patchwork of unver-
ifiable detail. Max could relate, to a point. It took time to learn
to be yourself when you'd been someone else. The news he
received that morning shed some light, but as he walked to
Alec Barnes's front door, he knew he'd have his work cut out
persuading him to let his guard down.

Johnny kept him on the doorstep. 'What do you want?'

'Can we talk about Stan Moffatt?'

'Yeah, go on.'

'He's been moved to a secure mental health unit in
Beckenham. I got a call from his key worker. It's not the first
time he's been an inpatient.'

'Doesn't surprise me.'

'Well, it wouldn't, would it? He was in Chase Farm Hospital
two years ago, the same time you were there, which is where
you met. He asked us to pass on a message that he's sorry, I
assumed he meant for our church social. Can I come in? I'd
rather not talk about this on the street.'

Johnny showed him through to the kitchen.

Max picked up the thread. 'The medical team found cigarette
burns and scarring on intimate parts of Stan's body. They're

working on the assumption he's been subjected to abuse over an extended period, which amounts to major trauma. He's not able to talk about it, not yet. And he's certainly not in a fit state for me to question, but the reality is he was with Laska and his people and you know more about them than you've told me so far.'

Johnny's head dropped. 'Jesus, those people.'

'I know you did off-book house clearances and labouring. It was for them, right?'

'Yes.'

'And we both know they're desperate to shut you up over an iffy assault charge on Shelly Dowd.'

Johnny ran his hand over a patch of scalded wood on the kitchen table. 'Martin Dyce did recognise me at the hotel. He came back a couple of nights after. That's when he got me work labouring. He didn't know about Kerry and I didn't tell him. I'd kidded myself I was still trying to find her, but the site work led to other things. "Johnny, can you mind this place for so and so," and I'd end up in a weed factory for a week. Or "Can you help Fitz empty this flat?" and we'd go round and put the shits up a load of dopeheads and move them on. Another job turned out to be a place Laska was running girls from.'

'And they were all involved, Laska, Pallo, Fitzpatrick, Martin Dyce. What about Gavin Slade?'

'I don't remember seeing him, but we knew who we were working for.'

'What about Stuart Slade?'

He hesitated, leaving something unsaid. 'I wasn't around all the time. Talk to Martin Dyce.'

'Can you remember addresses, any other names?'

'They're long gone.'

'I realise, but can you?'

Johnny talked about flats and houses, often in leafier suburbs, and the work he'd done at each one, the comings and goings of George Laska's cousins and brothers. Max was conscious of time. 'We'll need to debrief properly, get the details so they're admissible. You okay if I set it up?'

'Go ahead.'

Max readied to leave.

Johnny said, 'Before you go, something I want to show you.'

Max followed into the hall. From the cupboard under the stairs, Johnny dragged out a storage box and unclicked the lid. Setting aside a photo album labelled FAMILY PHOTOS in faded felt tip, circled by a little girl's flower decorations, he unpacked fight-night programmes and press cuttings, an amateur championship trophy, then found what he was looking for. A short wooden rod the thickness of a broom handle, around six inches long, carved in a dumbbell shape with a flattish disc half an inch thick at either end. 'You know what that is?'

He handed it to Max.

'It's a yawara stick, right?' The last time Max had seen a yawara was an off-syllabus self-defence course Kilby arranged as part of his induction. He'd been introduced to a quietly spoken man named Stamford. The former Hong Kong police instructor had set up a makeshift dojo in a scout hut behind Hither Green Station. Stamford taught him the rudiments. Strike the right pressure point and your opponent was unlikely to still be standing, but it took practice.

Johnny's yawara fitted Max's hand snugly, the raised waist nestling between his second and third fingers. He switched hands. It felt more comfortable in his left, the ends extending from either end of his fist. 'I used to train with a bloke. His was darker than this, dirt and sweat in the grain. He was lethal with it.'

'Did he show you how to use it?'

'It was a long time ago.'

'I made this one,' said Johnny. 'I turned it at Foleys when I worked there one summer. Made from a single piece of crab apple.'

Max ran this thumb across the warm, coffee-toned grain.

'Keep it.'

'No, you're all right, it's too precious. But thank you.'

'You might need it.'

He weighed it in his hand. 'Are you sure?'

Johnny was tight-lipped. Max took it as an offering given in good faith and not to be questioned.

'But I do want to ask you something.' He faltered.

'Go on.'

'I never got much help from the police when Kerry went away. I always thought it was down to me. Who I was, all that history. I know they never took her disappearance seriously. If it's because of me, I'd rather know.'

Max weighed it up. 'If I get the chance, I'll call up the file. I don't have the resources to do much, but I'll give it the once-over and I will tell you straight what I think, good or bad.' He tucked the yawara in his coat pocket and headed down the path. It felt good in his hand.

48

Johnny

JOHNNY WAS SOAKED BY the time he arrived at Etta Street. Alec had called Alison in advance with the hospital update, but she'd heard only what she wanted: there was a new drug and a chance Alec would be involved in the final medical trial. His condition was no better, no worse. She'd latched onto *no worse*. She closed the door behind her and sat him down. Her mood was different; the news had taken a load off her mind. They sat with their knees touching and she took his hands in hers. Something she'd been burning to say. 'Please don't speak, I've been thinking about this. We've always had to struggle through shit times. There's always some bastard chucking his weight around, Slade and Martin Dyce for me and Dave Price in the old days for you. When you say you want us to be together, how badly do you mean what you say?'

'Oh, I mean it. I don't know how.'

'Because you want it perfect, but that's not how it happens. We've got what we've got and it goes really quickly. You do know that?'

'That's what your dad said.'

There was light in her eyes, an excitement. 'We can have this together. If it's what you want, but not if it means I have to sell myself short. I'm seeing it through.'

Johnny listened to the night noises from outside. He thought about those times he waited up, desperate for Kerry to come home, knowing she wouldn't, dying over and over. He thought about the haunted bedsits, the men who ripped him off and laughed while they did it. Tears came into his eyes. 'So it's down to me.'

Ali squeezed his hand. She didn't need to say more.

49

Ali

LORRAINE PUT A FINGER to her lips to hush Alec. Ali was on
a call, trying to keep calm. 'Never mind, give me the details.'
She mimed for pen and paper. Lorraine fetched the shopping
pad from the kitchen. Ali made notes across three sheets of
narrow notepaper and finished the call.

'What's up, love?' said Alec.

She took her time before answering. 'That was Chris. We've
been given notice at the community centre. The council made
a snap inspection this afternoon and we've failed to maintain
the building to the required standard, which contravenes the
terms of our lease. They've given us a month to vacate.'

Lorraine spoke first. 'You'll argue against it though, won't
you? They're chucking their weight around. You said before,
happens all the time.'

She placed her hands, palms down, on the table. If she
hadn't, they would have shaken. 'That isn't all. He said we'd
been sent an email from the council informing us that a
special meeting of the Planning and Economic Regeneration
committee was convened earlier this evening and they've
given final approval for Jamaica Dock.' She read from her
notes. 'The land is an initial parcel, sold to the Jamaica Dock
Development Corporation for £100. Confirmed as of tonight.
The council will grant a further sum – as yet unspecified – to
undertake full site remediation. They've given it away, Dad.

You realise this means we're all paying. Your council tax, mine.'

'We don't know all the names, love,' said Lorraine. 'Who's the Corporation?'

'A partnership between the council, the GLA, and Gavin Slade's development consortium led by him and Kingsdale Developments. They've screwed us, Dad.'

'Take your time, think it through. You might want to talk to someone at the council. It doesn't sound right.'

'Doesn't sound legal,' Lorraine added.

'Well, they've done it. Chris got the email half an hour ago. That was part of the official press release. Their vision for a new London, the *Olympic legacy*. It's Slade. Him and Dyce and Greg Walsham and the rest. Thieving bastards.'

Alec rubbed his chest. Whatever he'd had for tea wasn't agreeing with him.

'Dad—'

'If you need to go, please go. Don't worry, we can do this another time.' That earned a frown from Lorraine.

'Do what another time?'

Alec cut in before Lorraine had a chance to speak, 'Catch up, have tea, whatever. We'll do it another time.'

'As long as you don't mind?'

'No, you need to. It's important.'

It was only as she was driving back to the estate the realisation dawned. Dad had wanted to talk and Lorraine didn't think it could wait. Her mind raced. It was his treatment, had to be good news. The alternative didn't bear thinking about. 'Not now, please not now.'

For the rest of the evening she made calls from the office. Chris had pre-empted most of them. They'd all heard. What was that song Fraser used to play over and over, 'The Last to Know'. Said it all.

Ali was measured on the phone, calmness personified as

she asked each member of the group to come together to discuss how they deal with the closure notice, and agree their response to the Jamaica Dock press release. She refused to be drawn, saying only that she needed to sleep on the news. Any more strident opinion risked spooking them before she'd had a chance to make the case for direct action. By the time she got home it was nearly midnight and Bobby was waiting for a late walk. She kept it short and was within sight of home when a car pulled up beside her and Martin Dyce got out. George Laska glared from behind the wheel.

'I've told him to stay put,' said Dyce. 'This is between us.'

'Hello, Martin. What do you want?'

'A chat.'

'Say what you want to say and go.'

'You're up with the news, I take it?'

'You know Slade thinks you're not fit to lick the piss off his shoes, don't you?'

Dyce's face formed a faux-perplexed expression.

'I give it a month at the outside, you'll be cracking out the CVs and scouring the *Guardian* for an admin post in some shithole council up north. Time for a career change.' Bobby tugged at the lead, eager to be out of the cold. 'I do know you won't be sipping fizz in Greenwich Park with Princess Anne and the kids next summer. He might let you shovel up horse shit for his garden.'

Dyce didn't take his eyes off Bobby as he spoke. 'It is changing, Alison. Whether you accept it or ignore it, or whinge about it with your mates, that's up to you, but it really is. You can keep crusading, but your people, they'll get bored. They want a quiet life, everyone does. Let it go. This is the last chance. It's dog eat dog.' He eyed Bobby, shook his head and walked back to the car.

'You're threatening a dog, seriously?'

Laska was grinning. He started the car.

Ali shouted after him. 'That's who you are, a man who threatens a dog. You wanker.'

Lights came on in the neighbours' upstairs windows. They could fuck off as well.

50

Ali

THEY ARRIVED EARLY FOR the 10 o'clock meeting. Chris was last in. He circled the table, placing an identical flyer in front of each member of the group, without taking his eyes off Ali. 'These are all over the estate. People I don't know stopped me on the way in wanting to know what we're playing at.'

THE BIGGEST THREAT TO YOUR COMMUNITY'S FUTURE

THE TRUTH ABOUT ALISON BARNES AND MARLOWE ESTATE

Fact. Alison Barnes couldn't wait to get away from Marlowe Estate

Fact. Alison Barnes promotes her own private agenda over yours

Fact. Alison Barnes spends your Council Tax on youth projects that feed violence

Next to the text was the second most unflattering photo of herself she'd ever seen, taken at the City Hall launch, champagne glass in hand, scowling at the camera. The flyer was credited to a group calling themselves Concerned Citizens for Deptford's Future, their address, 491 New Cross Road.

Ali had hoped for positive defiance and would have settled for grimly resolute, but their faces told her they were resigned to losing. She barely registered Chris rereading the council's notice to vacate and the Jamaica Dock confirmation. He gave the impression they were already beaten and seemed relaxed about it.

Ali let him finish. She'd thought carefully about how to say what needed saying to argue the case for keeping going, but now it came to it, she hadn't the energy. 'Two things I want to ask,' she laid her hand on the flyer. 'Firstly, aside from this piece of shit, which any idiot can see is rubbish, it sounds like you're ready to give it up. Or do we want to challenge either or both of these decisions? Which is it, carry on or give up? I want a show of hands and I want it recorded.'

Ali got a whiff of shabby deceit as they went round the table, each giving their reasoning for backing down. They had their show of hands. It was over.

'What was the second thing?' said Chris.

'What's Dyce promised you? It'll be worth nothing, but I'd like to know for my own sanity.'

Ali took Bobby over to her dad's place that evening. Lorraine was pleased to have company. She and Bobby had an understanding. He did the sad eyes and she fed him freshly cooked chicken and rice. 'It won't be for long,' Ali said. 'The next few days I need to be out and about and it's not fair to leave him.'

'That's okay. Me and Bobs can please ourselves. Have you spoken to your dad?'

The nagging anxiety rolled in. 'Is Johnny here?'

'He's taken himself out, didn't say where. I don't think he wanted to be around.'

'Because of me?'

'Speak to your dad.'

Alec was dozing, Millwall deep into the second half against Coventry City. He opened his eyes. 'Is it over?'

'Two–nil up, ten minutes to go.' She kneeled beside his chair.

'Good.' He sat upright. 'Bobby settled in?'

'He's in the kitchen with Lorraine, playing mind games with the biscuit tin.'

'Don't leave him too long. He'll be the Fat Boy of Peckham by the time he comes back.'

Distracted by Millwall's third, they gave the match their full attention. Alec reached for Ali's hand and held it. The gesture was absent-minded, but it floored her. His skin was warm, dry, rough around her hand. 'They're not sure I'm well enough to have the new drug. They told us yesterday.'

'Not sure meaning?'

'Meaning they've not said a flat no, but that's what it is. They said I can have another course of chemotherapy, but I don't want it.'

'Oh, Dad.'

'I'm fine with it, well, not fine obviously. But I'm not scared, so don't you be either.'

'We can remortgage Etta Street, pay for the drugs ourselves.'

He touched her cheek. They were quiet for a time, then he said, 'You remember when you were little, me and you used to go for walks in the City on a Sunday, get the boat from Greenwich down Tower Pier, walk through all those secret squares and alleys and end up in Bloom's on Whitechapel High Street.'

'Salt beef sandwich. Half each. I remember the time you gave me your half, covered in mustard.'

Alec smiled at the memory. 'I was thinking about Sidney Bloom the other day. A lovely man. I used to go in for a bowl of soup when I worked up in the City. I told him I liked his tie once, next time I went in he'd bought me one the same, burgundy silk. Set it down on the table in its wrapper. A gift for a loyal customer, he said.'

Alec seemed to drift and Ali thought he'd lost the thread of the story, but that's all it was, remembering a kindness, a time, a place.

He let go of her hand. 'One thing Ali, over the next few months, we have to be honest. Me and you and Lorraine, and John as well. No keeping things from each other. If something needs saying, say it.'

'That's easier said than done.'

'I know. But it is important, same as afterwards. And don't put off doing what you'd normally do. I've got business of my own to sort out, make sure nothing gets left along the way. We're not waiting, we're living.'

He was seeing the end, planning for it.

It wasn't until she was home that the tears came. The hollowness made worse without Bobby there to lay his head on her knee. The feeling was a long time passing. She needed to do something and grabbed her keys, locking the door behind her.

Someone, she guessed the sister, had given Fraser's flat a comprehensive going-over. Most of what was packed up and labelled had a clear destination. Suitcases, black bin bags, cardboard boxes. Some going home, some to charity, some to the council tip. How painful would it have been to sort through it all? She would have helped if they'd asked. But maybe this was a job you did alone, to feel the loss and make it real.

She peeled back the tape from a cardboard box marked BOOKS OXFAM, lifted the lid, scanned the titles and sealed it. What she was searching for wasn't here.

51

Max

MAX RECOGNISED A MAN at the end of his tether. DS Tait made it to Carteret Street, but from the way he dropped in the chair and dragged off his tie, he'd be hard pushed to go much further.

'You're not on the run, are you?' said Max.

Tait shook his head. 'What have you said?'

'Oh Christ, loads of terrible stuff.'

'About Conway?'

'Still loads. Awful things.'

'I'm serious. Since he sent you packing, he's sent us after pointless leads, going over evidence we've binned three times over. You were a pain in the arse when you were there, you're an even bigger one now.'

Tait hadn't made the journey into town to let off steam. Interesting that Conway was racking up the pressure to get a result. 'Ben, if you want to hold me responsible for what your DI does, it's generous of you to share, but I don't need it.'

Tait slapped a copy of a flyer on Max's desk. 'These are all over the estate, as of this morning.'

Max took in Ali's unflattering photo. He scanned the text. Tait leaned over and put his finger on the address.

'I see it,' said Max.

'That's not all. You know you said we needed to check the CCTV on the night buses?'

'I've a vague memory. Too resource-intensive, or words to that effect.'

'Want to guess what I've spent the last three days doing?'

Max couldn't help himself. 'Rather you than me.'

Tait reached into his pocket and handed Max a memory stick. 'You need to see this. It's off the N21 night bus.'

The video was time-stamped 1.36 am on the morning of Friday 15 October. The route took them past Lewisham Station towards Loampit Vale. As they approached New Cross Road, Tait slowed the video to half time. The bus slowed, anticipating the traffic lights near the Star and Garter. On the corner of Wilshaw Street, a figure walked alongside for half a dozen paces before the bus accelerated towards New Cross Station. No question, it was Johnny Nunn.

'You want to run it through again?' said Tait.

'I know who it is. It says he was there, no more.'

'Having claimed he didn't get back until Saturday night at St Mark's. Come on, Max, it's got to be followed up.'

'Has Conway seen it?'

'Not yet. I missed it earlier in the week, went back and found it this afternoon.'

'I know you've got suspicions, but I don't think this is right. You take this to Conway and he'll have Nunn arrested and charged within twenty-four hours. He'll say Nunn was jealous of the relationship between Fraser Neal and Alison Barnes, you know that's what'll happen, right?'

'It's a reasonable assumption, Max. And it gets you off the hook with the DI. It's got nothing to do with you or this place. We have to at least ask the questions.'

'Yeah, we do. But not now. I realise this is difficult for you to handle, but I need you to hold on. Don't show anyone. I want the right people for this and I don't think that's Johnny

Nunn. I don't care if it ends up at my door, it is anyway. Keep it to yourself. Give me a chance to interview Nunn. He knows, Ben, he *knows*.'

'Monday, no later.'

'If that's the best you can do.'

52

Johnny

IT WAS ONE OF those December mornings you got the feeling
the sun might not come up at all. Ali called, asking him to
come to Etta Street. He expected a conversation about Alec,
but she didn't mention him, instead she talked about Pepys
House. The quiet anger in her voice had him worried.

'Work starts on Monday. Rolled into the first phase of
Jamaica Dock. Slade builds his high-end residential. Luxury
flats and gated communities.'

Johnny thought she'd said it was over. 'And your lot are
chucking it in.'

'They are, I'm not. Not without a protest. They can put
their shitty leaflets round the estate, I'll get the biggest banner
I can make and hang it across the top of Pepys House.'

'Then what?'

'Stay until the police come. They'll charge us with trespass
and we'll have got people's attention.'

'Who's "we"?'

'People on the ground who can make sure we get our
message across. I'm not asking anyone to go up with me,
there's no need. It takes one person to make the statement.
Slade will shit his pants at the negative press.'

'They'll say you're a danger to the public and yourself.'

She laughed, 'They can say what they like. It's a peaceful
protest at what's being done to our community. I want to make

a point. I can go in the back and get up the stairs before they know I'm there. It's action that'll get attention. If I delay the work by a day—'

'They'll never let you get close enough.'

'If this was a demo outside the stock exchange over global capitalism, or knackering the environment, or a student fees protest – Christ, I'm not chucking a fire extinguisher off the roof.'

'You won't get to the roof. You won't get twenty yards through the gates, *if* you're really quick and really lucky. Your biggest worry is you get in, they lock the gates behind you and the police let them do it. Ali, the people guarding the site are who you should be worried about. I've been down there. It's not a couple of old geezers in flat caps drinking tea in a hut.'

'Thanks for that, no really. Where d'you think I've been the last five years, fucking fairyland?'

'You're not listening. Have you been down there recently, since yesterday?'

She shook her head. 'I went past on Wednesday.'

'They've changed the site security staff. These people are one step away from being hired mercenaries. I've worked for Martin Dyce and Gavin Slade.'

'I know, you told me. You did labouring.'

'I did. When Kerry went missing, I did what I thought would get me close. Martin Dyce offered me security work on the houses they buy, steal or take in payment for debts. Between taking possession, doing them up, and tenants coming in, I guarded drugs for Tony Fitzpatrick and Pallo Gashi and his family. I did door security for George Laska on a place where trafficked women got locked in a room with a bed and enough gear to keep numb between punters. You know who's down at Pepys House? The same men who answer to Laska. Trust me, they'll be waiting.'

She turned away, struggling to take it in.

'I'm sitting down with Lomax day after tomorrow to give a formal statement, names, dates, whatever I can remember that ties these people to what they are, for real. I'll go to court if I have to. You said it was down to me to back you up. That's what I'm doing. Don't be reckless because they lied about you in a crappy leaflet.'

'That's what you think? Fraser was murdered, John.'

'And it's on my conscience. All of it. Kerry leaving, me and you losing our way, Tanya's shitty marriage, letting Alec down, that lad, Stan Moffatt, Shelly Dowd at the church and Fraser.'

'How is Fraser on your conscience?'

He turned his head away. The world would be stuck as it was unless he made it change. He just wasn't sure he had the courage.

'How, John?'

He looked up. 'I was there.'

53

Max

MAX'S SECOND VISIT TO the Gilchrist Neal boardroom was almost over before it started. He wasn't surprised to see Jonathon Coles alongside Kenneth Neal, his younger brother, Craig, and Susan. Liz had forewarned him. Jonathon wouldn't be drawn on the detail, though she'd tried; all she could tell him was that Kenneth Neal felt the need for guidance from outside the family. When Calum arrived late, red-faced, obviously dissenting, Max realised why. Calum insisted Max leave while they had a preliminary conversation. He felt he'd entered a dream: the closer he came to his destination, the further it receded. Driving solo overnight from London wasn't helping. He moved his chair away from the table. 'When you people have made up your minds, I'll be in the café down the street.'

'Susan, you go with him.' Kenneth touched his daughter's elbow.

Susan was reluctant to leave.

'Go, it'll be fine. I promise.'

London had been cold enough. Edinburgh was chillier still. They crossed Lothian Street under a sky about ready to unload. 'Remind me why I'm here.'

'I'm sorry.'

'Uncle Calum singing a different song from your dad. But you don't think your dad is totally sold on whatever *it* is, either.'

307

Max ordered coffees. Susan checked her phone. 'Shouldn't be long.'

'Waiting for a verdict goes with the job. Some say it's underrated.'

'I've said I'm sorry.' Another fruitless flick at the screen. 'And your analogy is wrong. We know what the verdict is. At least Dad does, so does Craig, unless Calum persuades him otherwise.'

'And Jonathon?'

'He's advising on our legal standing with what we're disclosing and sticking up for your integrity.'

Max was glad someone was.

The phone buzzed. 'Here we go.'

They resumed their places. Kenneth put a reassuring hand on Susan's arm. Calum's expression could have been smug or stoic, hard to tell behind the beard. Craig appeared ready to burst into tears. Jonathon Coles edged his chair from the table very slightly. This was family business.

Kenneth Neal began, 'The last time you were here, you asked about the visit Fraser had with us shortly before he was murdered. Some information has come to light we feel we need to share with you. But in sharing, we risk compromising the integrity of our business and one, if not several, of our clients.'

'Hence you stacking the odds.'

'Oh, you're not to be trusted. We're well aware of it.' That was Calum.

'That's not true, Cal.' Kenneth Neal's voice was calm, searching for conciliation. 'We are not able to breach client confidentiality, Detective Sergeant. We can play games with Chinese walls and we can use back-channels, but it amounts to the same and the courts will make no exception if we disclose client information without permission. We can go to court to override it, or you can, but given the time it would take and the nature of our business, it would cost us a significant proportion of our business and give notice to this particular client that we are assisting in his investigation. I'm guessing you'd rather we didn't do that. Effectively, unless a client informs us that they are about to commit a crime, we're powerless to act.'

'You told me you'd been supporting Fraser in his work through the Marchmont Trust,' said Max. 'You said he'd expressed concerns about criminal payments going into the Jamaica Dock scheme.' He turned to Calum. 'I asked whether you'd directed investment clients to Jamaica Dock. I left with the impression that's exactly what was happening.'

Calum went to speak. Max held up a hand. 'Who told Fraser?'

Silence.

'Fuck it, I'll get a court order. You're wasting time. This is your son we're talking about. Your nephew, your brother.'

Craig couldn't hold it in any longer. 'He came to me first at the beginning of summer to ask my advice. He thought the scheme was a conduit for money laundering. At that time, we hadn't been instructed by any investor clients, we'd made no deals with anyone, but we were getting enquiries.'

Calum cut in. 'Several, in fact. These were high-net-worth individuals, primarily overseas, private-equity-backed buyers, institutional investors and fund managers wanting us to put them together with opportunities in south London. London is the great attraction, now especially. Pepys House and Jamaica Dock are by far the best prospect for a quick turnaround, but we held back and held back.' He stopped himself.

'And?'

'We were approached by someone at the London end and offered favourable terms for a limited period.'

'Who approached you?'

'We can't say. But we did background investigation. The scheme was in some trouble. One or two investors whose post-crash recovery had flattered to deceive. The opportunity was too good to turn down.'

'So you called Fraser back here and told him his family company was investing in Jamaica Dock.'

'We thought he'd want to know,' said Craig.

'The project that threatened to destroy his community and his *home*, that he dedicated himself to opposing, was being held up by his own family. Too right he'd want to know. Did he still claim the scheme was funded by criminal capital?'

Max waited for an answer, a flicker of understanding. None came. 'Okay, let's assume he did. Given what he'd told you, you must have gone back to those high-net-worth clients and carried out additional assessments. If you suspected the money flooding the system was fraudulent or criminal or being used to destabilise the state in some way, you'd investigate, right? You'd make sure. Safeguard yourselves, if nothing else. Because Fraser being Fraser, there's no way he'd be quiet about it. He'd go out of his way to expose it, which would leave him at risk from some serious people.'

Only Kenneth Neal appeared to grasp the reality of Max's synopsis. 'We couldn't risk the conflict of interests... so we decided to get Fraser out. We withdrew the funding for the post.' He looked briefly at Calum. 'It was a bloody stupid idea. Craig diverted potential new clients to other investments in the meantime, mainly here in Scotland.'

Calum tapped the table. 'Ken, enough.'

'Shut up, Calum. A major client, who we redirected, informed the Jamaica Dock Consortium that Gilchrist Neal warned them off investing.'

'Excuse me, but they didn't tell the *Consortium*, did they? They told a person. Give me a name.'

'Our client was at a dinner with Gavin Slade and his

associates. He mentioned it in passing. Slade assumed we had reneged on our agreement. He called Calum and was apoplectic.'

'He had every right to be,' said Calum.

'We reassured him that wasn't the case.'

'Was pulling Fraser central to the agreement? Is that what Slade wanted?'

Kenneth Neal bowed his head. 'It was.'

Susan's complexion grew paler as the conversation dragged through the morning. On several occasions, Kenneth Neal lost focus, shaking his head, telling him their hands were tied. Whatever Max asked, however sensitive or blunt his questions, they allowed him only so far before the shutters fell. In frustration, he called them out. 'I don't get it. You're his family. What is wrong with you?'

Susan placed both hands over her heart. 'Fraser didn't know for sure where the money going into Jamaica Dock was coming from, but he knew we did. It was the money those people used to trash his work, to tear him down in public, pay off newspaper editors, journalists, media people, to ruin his reputation. You're right, Max, we did betray him and he knew it.'

'Can I see the list of investors?'

Jonathon Coles raised a finger. 'I'm sorry, Max, for that you'll have to go to court.'

Snow at the borders turned to sleet by North Yorkshire. Spray hampered visibility. By 4 o'clock in the afternoon, he was staring into darkness at Doncaster. An hour's kip in a service station car park hardly made up for the sleep he'd missed, but it would do.

Through the outskirts of London and down the home stretch of Finchley Road, sleet turned to rain. Max pictured Neal striding out on New Cross Road that night in October, streetlights and shop lights reflecting in the wet pavement. On

Nick Triplow

his way to a meeting, thinking… thinking what? Thinking he was buying 50 quids' worth of weed for Jerome and Marcia? Paying the next instalment to keep Shelly Dowd out of Laska's hands? Or fronting up to Gavin Slade and Martin Dyce over Jamaica Dock, threatening to bring their world down around them? Untrained, unaware, betrayed. Already lost. Max told himself, *You should have taken him on: you should have found a way, schooled him, protected him from himself.*

312

54

Max

MAX SHOWERED AND POURED a large whisky. He opened the bedroom window to the sound of rain and sat in the dark, the drink warming in his hand. Liz called, was he okay? Still processing the day's events, he said, and promised he'd call her soon. He sat back against the pillows, closing his eyes momentarily. The phone rang. Dominik Saski had come across a link between the two subjects he'd asked about.

'There's no record of contact, until *your* man sets up a new email address and they have regular exchange two, three times a day. Sometimes more.'

'Starting when?'

Saski gave him the date. The day he'd been to see Harding and Conway to answer for meeting Dwight Payne. 'Anything else?'

'The other client, not your man, sporadic traffic from a heavily encrypted account in the States, but goes quiet mid-October. I've got more, but not for now. You sound like you're asleep.'

Max turned off the phone. He tried to work through the significance of the date, how it fell in with Conway's shifting priorities, but rational thought was beyond him. He set the whisky on the side table without taking a sip.

313

55

Ali

In Ali's mind, it would have been a bright day marching to the gates, the collective power of residents in their hundreds demanding their rights and gathering support, carrying banners and placards. Rattling the gates while she edged between the gap in the fence panels and made it to Pepys House entrance unseen, through the hallway to the staircase, a fast climb to the top floor and out onto the roof to unfurl the banner. She'd padlock it to balcony railings on the land-side top and bottom, keeping it taut, so the words were clear and direct:

JAMAICA DOCK DEVELOPMENT
ILLEGAL AND CORRUPT
FULL ENQUIRY NOW

Delivery lorries had been coming and going through the site gates all morning.

The protestors made for a dignified procession as they approached. Father Sam Downey linked arms with Marcia Standing and the others from St Mark's, including Dwight Payne's mother, Lorna, whom Downey had tried to dissuade from coming along, but she insisted she'd lived on the estate most of her life and had as much right to protest as anyone. Downey must have known this was the first time Lorna and Marcia had breathed the same air since Dwight caused the rift between them. Lukshana and Mr Tousi, the only two from the Marlowe Estate Community Action Group who'd joined them, were alongside with activists from Southwark. These were good people Fraser had come to know through protesting against new-build on the site of their community park and playground. Ali had asked for help and they'd shown up in solidarity.

Ali felt dreadful, waiting for her moment to break off from the main group. She made it just before they strolled, too easily, through the open gates and formed a tight line, refusing to move. As she made her way to the rear of the site, she prayed her nerves wouldn't get the better of her. The workers downed tools, coming to see what the fuss was about. She'd reached the loose fence panel before she heard the first sirens. As she squeezed through what looked an easy route in, Lukshana ran towards the front of Pepys House, caught by a Belmont Homes security guard who tripped her up. He kicked her backside as she sprawled on the ground. 'Get up, bitch.'

Father Downey arrived at Shana's side, so did Marcia Standing and Lorna Payne. Between them, they helped Shana to her feet. Fitzpatrick hurled clods of earth, urging others to join him. Pallo Gashi turned on the fire hose. Martin Dyce directed the jet at Downey and the women as they huddled together for protection, exposed on open ground.

Ali kept going, staying low and running for Pepys House. She'd barely gone ten metres when she felt herself dragged back and thrown to the ground, the breath belted from her lungs. George Laska hauled her into the now empty ground-floor hallway of Pepys House. She registered the blur of graffitied walls and cracked, smashed tiles. Laska punched her and flung her into a corner by the stairwell. He lifted her by her coat, forcing her up against the wall. She felt his hand by her crotch, unbuckling his belt. His hold on her loosened fractionally and she managed to turn herself away. She grabbed a broken tile, tearing it from the wall, raking the raw edge across Laska's face, ripping the skin from his forehead to his mouth; he put his hand to his cheek as the line of blood opened to a gash. She kicked out and scrambled to the doorway, making it out the way she'd come. She reached open ground before Laska caught up and kicked her legs away. She looked up, blood ran from his face as he raised his boot.

That was the photograph splashed across social media by the evening, printed in the *South London Press* the following morning, gaining traction in the *Guardian* online later the same day and in the print edition the day after. Others ran with the photo of the priest as he shielded Shana, Lorna Payne and Marcia Standing, lashed and slammed into the mud, his arm raised in pitiful defence. Photographs taken by Shelly Dowd from her balcony, with Fraser Neal's camera.

Whatever you do, get pictures, Fraser said. *Make people see them for what they are.*

56

Max

MONDAY MORNING, MAX WAS still struggling to hold it together. Minimising the risk to Johnny Nunn meant a change of venue. He tracked down Denny. She swapped a shift and secured the safe house in Finchley for a day, longer if necessary. With Nunn's statement on record, he'd move quickly. Better he was safely away from south London.

The two-bedroom maisonette on the junction of Ballard's Lane and Regent's Park Road took the first floor above a money exchange. Close to Finchley Central Station, access was via the gate and staircase at the rear. Max and Denny were waiting when Johnny arrived.

Max made introductions over coffee. Denny had been in since early morning and given the place an airing. She closed the windows. Triple-glazing reduced traffic noise to a muffled hum. The flat had a lived-in feel, freshly laundered curtains, well-tended house plants, a half-decent TV and hi-fi system. Max explained to Johnny all the rooms were wired. Everything they said would be recorded. They chose their places. Johnny was nervous as he settled into the easy chair facing the door. Max and Denny took the sofa.

'Must be unsettling to come this side of London,' said Max.

'Would have been once,' said Johnny. 'I've travelled a bit since then.'

'Of course, you said. Places change, though. You think you

317

know somewhere, head back a year later and hardly recognise it. Five years must feel like a lifetime.'

Insecurity played across Johnny's face. 'You've got no idea.'

'So tell me. What's it been like?'

'I don't want to talk about it.'

Max was careful not to rush to a resolution.

'I was over this way before,' said Johnny, 'We did up some retirement flats. Might have been the last legit job I did for them.'

'Them being?'

'Is this how it works, then, we're havin' a chat. Then what?'

'To start with, I want to get my head around your involvement with these people, how it worked, what you did.'

'Tony Fitzpatrick pulled the crew together. Laska and Pallo Gashi arrived later. Martin Dyce was there from the start, giving his orders. He offered me work on a refurb of some flats in Kilburn. The client was away and we had three months to do a job he reckoned could be done in six weeks. We got it done in five and for the rest of the time it was a shop. Stash kept in one flat, selling from another. Pallo kept an eye out downstairs, me as extra security in the stash flat. Easy money.'

Denny said, 'Who got paid?'

'Laska took the cash. He paid Dyce and Dyce put it through Gavin Slade's books. They took their cut as consultancy or used it to pay the site team, unskilled, off-book labour.'

'You know this how?' said Max.

'They talked about it openly. It didn't matter if I was there.'

'Were you ever recognised?'

'What, from me boxing? Dyce knew, but I'd gone to shit by then. That's why he liked having me on a string. He was never one of us when we were kids, but this was his business and he made sure I knew where I stood. He talks a lot. I'm not saying these were all Slade's places, but I knew the ones that were. Buy-to-let conversions. Get the refurb done quick and cheap, give the owners as little reason to get involved as possible, which is what they want anyway.'

'You mentioned before that it wasn't always dope.'

'I still had this vision of finding Kerry and bringing her home. Some nights I'd go back to Ali, some nights I'd wander places asking the same question a hundred times. No one knew anything. If they did, they wouldn't tell me.'

They worked on through the morning, going over the scheme as it developed in time, breaking for lunch around midday. The food perked Johnny up. 'That's the healthiest I've eaten in weeks. I used to eat proper healthy stuff all the time when I was in training.'

'Would you go back to it?'

'Too old, mate.'

'What about training youngsters? They'd take advice from someone who knows the game, especially someone like yourself.'

'What, someone who had it and chucked it away?'

Denny brought them back. 'Could you put a figure on the number of jobs you worked for Dyce and Laska?'

Johnny ran down his mental index. 'There's about a dozen I can remember. There will be others. They didn't come south of the river much. Any jobs close to home, I stayed away. And I have a kind of block at times. I wasn't around.' He nodded to Max. 'He probably told you. I wasn't well.'

What Johnny did remember was detailed, down to streets and house numbers. A list of properties that fitted the grid of London neighbourhoods: Edmonton Green; Wood Green; Bruce Grove; Southgate; Barnet; Barkingside; Neasden; Wembley Central; Wandsworth; Streatham…

When they broke mid-afternoon, Johnny went to get his head down for a couple of hours. Denny went to the spare bedroom and hooked up her PC. She spent an hour cross-referencing Johnny's location data with the SOCA database and discovered at least eight sites he'd worked on had been raided, in connection with either a suspected drugs haul, prostitution or people trafficking. In all but one case, the raids were the result of anonymous information.

Before logging off, she clicked on her newsfeed. The violence at Pepys House headed the London bulletin. She called Max. 'What do you think?'

Max weighed the options and called Tait. Alison Barnes was in hospital, not life-threatening, but she'd been badly beaten. Three women had been admitted as a precaution and would be kept in overnight, Marcia Standing, Lorna Payne and Lukshana Dahir. They'd arrested Father Downey.

'What for?'

'Conway's orders. And he wants Nunn brought in for questioning in connection with Neal's murder.'

'You gave him the CCTV?'

'Not me. Shannon went back to the footage. It was a matter of time, Max. You can't stop it.'

They reconvened in the evening. A couple of Coronas and a pizza down, Max signalled Denny to continue. Denny asked, 'When you knew what the score was, how come you kept going back?'

'They paid me. There was a roof over my head when I couldn't handle the street.'

'And Kerry?'

'I told myself I was getting closer. I'll be saying it when they stick me in the ground.'

'So when it came to using the houses and flats that you refurbed or did security on for young women who were forced to be there?'

He wiped his mouth with the back of his hand. 'That was different.'

'What made you decide to start informing the authorities?'

He turned away. 'You know what it's like. You ignore it for so long, then you can't. It wasn't one thing. All those times George Laska turned up with frightened women in tow, it was just wrong. I remember him driving this girl, Anya, from punter to punter. She was 17, come in from Kosovo or some place and he set her up in Edmonton with another girl. I called social services. I didn't think they'd bring the police in, but they did. The place got raided. Dyce thought the neighbours sussed out what was going on. Worked once, so I thought I'd keep doing it.'

'That's some serious risk.'

Nunn smiled for the first time since he'd arrived. 'It felt right.'

They talked deep into the evening. By the time they were ready to call it a day, Max had full disclosure of Dyce's criminal activities. Insufficient to prove Slade must have known what was happening, but enough to go back through his books and source payments. 'Talk to me about Stuart Slade.'

'He was around a handful of times before he went inside. When he was there, they answered to him. Then America, so we didn't see him so much. He'd come back, a few weeks at a time to collect his cut, according to Martin Dyce. You know he's hooked up with some home security mob in the States. Like home protection, armed to the teeth, them lot.'

'When was the last time you saw him?'

'That place in Southend I told you about, before I got ill.' He looked away. 'Can I have another beer?'

'Nearly there,' said Max. 'Gavin Slade?'

'I don't know the man, but when he won the Olympic Park contract and Jamaica Dock started to be talked about seriously, Dyce was pushing to clean the business up on Slade's instructions. Laska wasn't having it.'

Johnny was silent for a time, raking over the memory as if there was something precious in the ashes.

Denny said, 'Why were you at St Mark's on the night Shelly Dowd was beaten up?'

'I wanted to come home.'

Max kept his voice low. 'No, John. That's not true. It wasn't chance you turned up in time to see Pallo Gashi and Fitzpatrick pick up Stan Moffatt. You followed them across the river. You knew they were making permanent moves to be somewhere you knew well.'

He shook his head. 'Doesn't matter if Downey calls them out in church. Doesn't matter if Ali protests Jamaica Dock. Doesn't matter if I call in a stash house. They won't shit themselves and go away. They'll do what they need to do.'

'There's something you should see.'

Denny brought the laptop through. The late evening news reports included images, a shaky camera-phone clip of Sam Downey's hosing and the photograph of Ali Barnes with Laska's raised boot above her.

'I've spoken with Detective Sergeant Tait,' said Max. 'Alison is being cared for in hospital overnight. She's going to be fine. She's protected. John, you need to know, it's a question of when, not if, this is taken out of my hands. I wish we could take our time, but it's inevitable. What were you doing in New Cross on the night Fraser Neal was murdered?'

'I need to get back.'

'Tell me what happened.'

'I saw what I saw. I have to go.'

'Who killed Fraser Neal?'

'I said I need to go.'

57

Max

SOME PEOPLE HAVE A knack of looking the other way when it matters. Max was about to find out whether Ben Tait was one of them. They met, at Tait's insistence, away from the office in a café off Rotherhithe New Road. Max took Tait through the findings from the Neal family and Johnny Nunn.

'After you said what we had on Ali Barnes was straw-clutching, *this* is your case? I'll stick twenty quid on the table now, this case never gets to court. If that's all you've got, you've got nothing.'

'I didn't say it was all. On the night Fraser Neal was murdered, we now know that Stuart Slade was at 491 New Cross Road.'

'Stuart?'

'So was George Laska, and Pallo Gashi, and Tony Fitzpatrick. Martin Dyce came later. Nunn was across the street. He saw Fraser Neal arrive.'

Tait raised his eyebrows. 'He's flaky, unreliable.'

'Step into his shoes for a minute. Your life's gone to shit, relationships are a mess, no roof over your head, no money, a daughter you haven't seen in five years who could as easily be round the next corner or in a flat like Slade's place on New Cross Road, or the one in Edmonton, or wherever. You've been on the streets, you're tired and you want to come home. *How?* How do you handle a thing like that? You say he's flaky. If that's what you see, I won't argue, but the man survived.'

'You said Slade's place?'

Max unfolded the list in front of him. 'Two columns: on the left, property addresses where Johnny Nunn worked for Martin Dyce and George Laska; on the right the companies listed as the property's registered owners. Those highlighted have been raided in the last three years, either on anonymous tip-offs, or because someone connected with them has gone to the police, usually someone who managed to get out. You know where the inside info came from?'

'You're saying it's Nunn.'

'Cross-check the registered owners against the raided properties and the names on the Companies House info.'

Tait scanned the list.

'See it? Which name comes up more than once, three times if you're counting?'

'Kingsdale Developments.'

'Slade's either corrupt or an idiot. These are proceeds of crime and my money's on them going through Slade's accounts. He still getting your vote? Nunn came back here because he contacted Dyce for work. Dyce told him 489 New Cross Road. He knew what it was. The girls in the flat. Same two girls in the churchyard. Stan Moffatt wasn't trying to pick them up, he was trying to get them back.'

'So what are you doing about it?'

'Apply some pressure and see what happens.'

'What do you want me to do?'

'Make a choice.'

Martin Dyce offered no indication he cared, or was remotely concerned by the information Max put to him, drawing lines on the desk jotter as the allegations stacked up. Max reached across and drew the jotter towards him. He counted the lines, 'You know what this represents?'

Dyce stared coldly. 'They're just lines.'

'Nothing's *just* anything, Martin. What this says to me is your indifference, as studied and controlled as you make it appear on the outside, is keeping the lid on something very tense. Or it could be you keeping track of how long you'll spend inside when we bring this to court and you're convicted.'

Tait leaned forward, checked the pad. 'I'd say both.'

Dyce sniffed, amused now. 'This is genuinely a first, the whole bullshit TV cop routine. Right in front of me. I've seen worse on Sunday nights at Up the Creek.'

'Can I borrow your pen?'

Dyce gave him the pen. Max crossed diagonally through the first four lines, then a second set of four, a third and a fourth. 'Fourteen for money laundering, ten for conspiracy to defraud, six for trafficking and exploitation. And that's before we get to murder.' He rolled the pen back across the table. Dyce snatched and missed.

'I don't think so.'

'You can't wish it away, Martin. I want whoever killed Fraser Neal. And if I can't get that, I'll get all of you for conspiracy to murder. That's still a life sentence. I know you were there. You were seen. I only have to prove you agreed with another person or persons to commit murder. And I can.' He reached down and retrieved the pen. 'It's a nice pen, got some weight to it. What was it, a gift?'

'They gave them to us when we came of age at St Mark's.'

'Of course, you're a local boy. Polished up your accent, though. Goes with the territory, especially if you're dealing with people like Gavin Slade. Stuart Slade, I'm guessing, not so much.'

A flicker of anger in his eyes. 'Don't try and play me.'

'But we never completely lose our roots, do we? I'm not fooled, Martin. Slade's furious about the headlines, pictures splashed over the news, hosing priests and kicking in church-goers with the company name on your backs. That's a very poor impression you created; you're deluded if you think otherwise.'

'We know who you are.' Dyce jabbed his finger to empha-sise the point. 'You're an agitator. You've built a career on manipulating people, lying to them, making them sell them-selves for your benefit. It won't work here.'

'Own this one, son. Deal with it before he leaves you in the shit.'

Dyce hardened, said nothing.

Max said, 'I can't convince you of any truth you don't already know, but I've got reliable intelligence Slade is moving on and moving up and you're not part of his plans. His ADC in the new world of gladhanding ministers, GLA politics and criminal capital has to be someone with a bit more gravitas. Like a former senior police officer, one who knows the patch. One who knows not to turn the hoses on a priest.'

Back on the street, Tait pulled Max aside. 'What are you saying?'

'You questioned Conway's approach to the Neal case, exces-sively hands-on, desperate to pin it on me and Special Operations, then equally keen to focus in the other direction. You asked me to go where you couldn't and this is where it leads. CCTV of Johnny Nunn was available from day one, but Conway didn't want you to find it until it worked for him. Those decisions might be justifiable in an operational context, but you have to admit, they are *helpful*.'

'To who?'

'Conway is planning a move to the commercial sector. It's a lucrative proposal. Slade takes his GLA seat with an eye to working his way upriver to Westminster in a term or two's time and keeps Conway alongside.'

'You can prove it?'

'Not with anything admissible in court. But if you don't believe me, ask him.'

58

Slade

SLADE LEANED BACK IN his chair, staring across the neighbours' gardens from the office he'd had installed in an upstairs room. Bare trees bowed and twisted in the wind. He owed Conway a call. It had better be in person. They'd spoken twice on the phone at length since the debacle at Pepys House and his mind was clearer as a result. Conway's strategy was to turn the protest to his advantage. He'd spoken to political contacts at City Hall. They reassured him, the closed-list candidacy was his come the spring. Nothing had changed. Assurances about the Deputy Mayoral post for Crime and Policing were more difficult to come by. Some people were harder to pin down.

With Conway's counsel, Slade recognised coming down hard on the protest at Pepys House could be sold as necessary enforcement, extreme but warranted under the circumstances. Still, there were investors to consider. Stuart had called to voice the concerns of their American friends. He said to assure them he wasn't in the business of disincentivising the community, rather moving them aside. As soon as the site was declared safe, they'd rip the guts out of Pepys House and start upgrading. The doorbell rang. Sophie answered, appearing at the door to the office a few seconds later. 'Martin Dyce is here. He says it's important.'

'Let him come up.' The time had come to stop dealing with these people.

Slade came out from behind the desk.

Dyce said, 'I called.'

'You did.'

'I left a message.'

'All good so far.'

'You need to get Lomax to back off. What in God's name is Conway doing if he's got evidence—'

Slade noticed a dullness behind Dyce's eyes. He'd grown threadbare, almost seedy over recent weeks. The suit, the shoes, the way he held himself. 'Sit down, Martin. It's not a problem. We'll deal with it. That's the benefit of having Conway onside, someone whose closest ally is set for the top job at Scotland Yard and is also Lomax's boss. It'll be dealt with.'

Dyce blinked. 'It makes me uneasy. Alison Barnes set that up on Monday. She must have known what would happen. I need to work out where the pictures were taken from. Nunn knows. That bothers me. How the hell did he come back and bite us on the arse?'

'According to you, none of your people had sufficient knowledge to cause concern.'

'Johnny Nunn's talking to Lomax. Downey jumps up with his righteous indignation. Why did the police drop the charges?'

'Because prosecuting a priest makes a bad situation worse. He was cautioned, that's enough.'

'It won't stop him.'

'Take a moment and think,' said Slade. 'You need to find out where Nunn is and deal with him. He won't be far. The rest will blow over, trust me. I'm lining up TV interviews for Sunday morning. It's an opportunity. Decry criminal behaviour, aggravated trespass, police infiltrator agitation. I'll tell them we've examined our processes and procedures internally. The actions of our people were to do with a lack of training and those responsible have been reprimanded. I'll outline our planned new training programme in partnership with law-enforcement advisors.'

'While he's advising,' said Dyce, 'why don't you ask Conway if his training programme covers Father Downey slagging us off by name from the pulpit at St Mark's? You've heard he's organising a day of action, gathering his flock from across London for an anti-Jamaica Dock protest march on City Hall?'

'You know the man, Martin. Speak to him. Say an act of contrition, whatever it is you do. Get him to forgive your sins. It'll make you feel better. *Deal with it.*'

59

Downey

THAT MORNING AT MASS a fox appeared at the rear of the church during communion. With the congregation gathered in the first half-dozen pews, the movement caught Downey's eye and he paused in reading the text. The creature – in good condition for a city fox – had appeared in the aisle and stole forward, but not too far, standing stock-still as if taking in the echo of his words. Instinctively he softened his tone: '...*in this sacrament Thou hast brought us near to an innumerable company of angels and to the spirits of the saints made perfect...*' As though it had heard enough, it turned and padded away. Downey completed the reading: '... *as in this food of our earthly pilgrimage we have shared their fellowship, so may we come to share their joy in heaven; through Jesus Christ, Thy Son, our Lord.*'

The 'Amen' sang thinly around the rafters. Downey meant to find and feed the animal after Mass, but he was tired. This last week he'd found himself sleeping between services, his pen falling from his fingers at his desk or, as on that morning, the book from his lap. They said it was the drink. They probably had a point. Though he hadn't felt right since the drenching on Monday, kept waiting in wet clothes in a police cell until they released him later in the day. The cold hadn't left his bones since.

His hour between morning Mass, breakfast and the mid-morning prayer service was precious. The fox reappeared in his dreams, but disappeared as mysteriously as before, turning its back at the company of angels.

He awoke abruptly, vaguely aware of having been prodded on the arm. A man came into focus. He wore a mask with slits for eyes.

Of course, the fox. Someone had left a door unlocked.

The man planted himself in front of Downey. 'Where's Johnny Nunn?'

Downey leaned over and retrieved his dropped book, a volume of T S Eliot's collected poetry. He'd managed the opening stanzas of 'Ash Wednesday', but no more. He replaced the postcard he used as a bookmark. 'It's a police matter. Nothing to do with me. Though I'm guessing you won't want to ask them.' He hoped Mrs Ajibade would bring his coffee. Usually she'd wake him around 10 o'clock. It must have been nearly that already, though perhaps it would be best if she stayed away.

'Bullshit.' The man came close. 'We warned you.'

Downey rose from his seat with the intention of returning the book to the shelf, get the man talking and, if not, he'd find another use for the bottle he kept there. The intruder shoved him, the heel of his hand hard dead centre of his chest, rocked him back in the chair. 'You know where Nunn is. You're supposed to be a good man. This way you save others from getting hurt.'

'If others are hurt, it's because you hurt them. This has nothing to do with whether I tell you what you're asking. *Nothing*. That's the trouble with you people, making bad choices, doing bad things and damn the rest of us. You have the gall to blame everyone else. You're the same as every abuser I've ever met, peddling your excuses. I'll tell you nothing.'

'But you know who I am.'

'No, and I don't care. Stop doing what you're doing in this community and leave and I'll pray for your soul.' He went to stand and his world was filled with pain, his nose cracked, instantly bleeding He kicked out with both feet and connected with the man's shins. He staggered to his feet and reached behind the curtain for his walking stick, swinging it around and lunging hard with the tip at the man's chest. The attacker was on him and wrenched the stick from his hand. He spun it around and brought the heavy handle hard across Downey's knees. Downey cried out and felt a fool for doing it. His guard dropped and he felt a second blow, hard across the side of his head. He threw up his arms in defence, but the blows kept coming down across his head and body. He was knocked to the floor, crawling under the chair, his face pressed against the rug, praying until the breath drained out of him.

The man dragged him out into the open. 'Where is Johnny Nunn?' The stick came down across his back, his arms, over and over, the blows punctuated with one question: 'Where? Where? Where?'

Downey pictured the fox, pictured the company of angels, until the pain was louder than his prayers and he couldn't bear it any longer. He held up a hand. 'Please stop.'

The stick came down. He didn't stop. Wouldn't stop until Downey was beaten into silence.

60

Max

THE PEPYS HOUSE SITE was silent, a raw December evening. An eerie absence of voices after weeks of catcalls and shouts carried across the estate. On the third-level scaffold, top poles creaked against the clamps. The wind had picked up the day after the site was cleared pending inspection. It had torn away at sheets of plastic covered in the Belmont Homes logo, a phone number, a website and now the Olympic rings. Slade didn't miss a trick. The night security supervisor had reported back to the office, the structure wasn't safe. Two scaffold planks had fallen through, missing him by a couple of feet, no more. *Replace the sheeting*, he was told. He complained. His team's job was to keep kids out, not fix what never ought to have been there in the first place.

Roofless and glassless under security spotlights, its unfinished state was worse for the neighbourhood than its being built. It took Max back to the urban streets he fought through on public disorder training. He'd left Gravesend bruised and disillusioned, but was back a year later, and every year since, for firearms training. A split second to distinguish the genuine threat from the innocent. That's what made him think he'd seen a figure at the window in Pepys House. Too many ghosts, he thought.

He made his way to the river. The waves sucked and slapped at the water's edge as the tide withdrew. Gulls stalked the mud. Time passed. The river rendered him speechless.

Ali found him there. She limped badly, fresh bruises marked her jaw, stitches holding her torn lip together. 'I'm sorry,' she said.

'I wanted you to know, we've been through Kerry Nunn's file. There's no fault attached to the police investigation at the time she disappeared. I can't see what more they could have done. Johnny's reputation had no bearing.'

'Thank you. I'll tell him.'

'When you do, you might want to pass on that she was seen working at a station hotel café in a town called Chaumont in north-eastern France the summer before last. Someone she knew at school saw her clearing tables. They spoke for a while. Said she seemed well, content.'

'That's good news.'

'The note on the file said they'd tried to find Johnny to let him know, but he was untraceable at the time. They found you, though. Let's call it an oversight.'

There was a silence. He'd said all he needed to say.

Ali came closer. 'Max, something I have to tell you, John's got a gun. It's my dad's. Dad says John thinks George Laska murdered Sam Downey.' She waited for a response. When none came, she went to walk away, but stopped. 'I think you and me weren't meant to know each other.'

'We didn't.'

The river separated Max from uncertainty. He called Tait.

Max made his way along Lower Road to the China Hall. This was the place Slade meant when he said he'd fancied a pub to add to his portfolio. Not this one, thought Max. Not the dockers' pub. Not the old man's pub. Gavin Slade's vision of Michelin-starred, gastropub dining, somewhere swish to swell off to his investors, would never work. The bastard would cut his losses and turn it into flats.

Fitzpatrick met Max at the door. There was intent in his

body search. Invasive, hands firmer than they needed to be, fingers probing his groin. A humiliation. The sensation stayed with him as he crossed the bar to where Slade and Dyce were sitting. 'I didn't think you two would still be talking.'

Fitz was behind him. Max stopped dead. Dyce gave the word and Fitz backed off, went to join Pallo at a corner table with Laska. Laska dabbed a gauze pad at a line of jagged stitches oozing across his cheek.

Max pulled out a chair. 'You wanted to see me.'

'I did,' said Slade. 'Against my better judgement, it must be said. You've been causing problems for my business, my professional life and my personal life. These allegations you've been punting around, you have to stop.'

'Nothing alleged about it. You're over.'

Dyce cut in. 'If you had a case and the witnesses to back it up, credible ones, we wouldn't be having this conversation. But you've got Johnny Nunn.'

Max said, 'The papers are formally with the CPS as of this afternoon. Copy to the Serious Fraud Office. I've had their initial charging advice and clearance to apply for a court order enabling Gilchrist Neal to release the names of investors in Jamaica Dock Development Corporation, Kingsdale Developments, Kingsdale Security, not that I need it, because I've got a good idea who your backers are, who they represent and their intentions. Commercial and political. I'm giving Mr Slade the same courtesy I gave you. Do the right thing.'

Slade bit hard. 'I want to know what will settle this.'

'There is no settling.'

Dyce was wide-eyed, spoiling for confrontation. 'Why don't you take us in now?'

'I know you love the sound of your own voice, Martin, but it fucking grates on me. You're out of your depth.' He turned to Slade. 'You know what the stakes are. Tell him. Tell him about your deals, the trade-off with Conway that makes him surplus to requirements. He thinks he knows. Same as them.' He raised a finger towards Fitz, Pallo and Laska. 'They think they've got your number. They haven't got the first fucking idea, have they?'

Dyce kicked his chair from under him. Max was already on his feet. 'All yours, Gavin. You know where to find me. And you can tell Stuart he's next for a visit.'

Half an hour later, he took a call. Dyce wanted to meet. He was waiting at the corner of Tooley Street and Tower Bridge Road when Max arrived.

Max was impatient. 'It's simple enough, Martin. There's enough filthy money sloshing round the system to buy half of London. With what I'll give them, we have people who'll go after accounts, contracts, investors, anyone or anything remotely connected with Slade and that includes you. But Fraser Neal, Sam Downey, Shelly Dowd, what happened to them happened because you or Slade gave the word. One or both of you are responsible.'

'Talk to Pallo Gashi.'

'We've got him for ABH minimum on Shelly Dowd. Any time we want.'

'That's never getting to court. You know Johnny Nunn worked for us, right?'

'I'm sick of people discounting that man's evidence, Martin. I'll decide what it's worth. What I want to know is which one of you animals beat an old man to death?'

The world had changed while Martin Dyce wasn't paying attention. The realisation dawned; he'd be the last man standing.

'There has to be some assurance. Whatever I tell you, it comes back on me. He'll know. I'll get a lawyer...'

'Enough.' Max walked away.

'He's got Conway.'

'I told you that, prick. And Conway's got him.' He came back and bunched his fist close to Dyce's face. 'By the bollocks.'

Max felt the drizzle carried in the wind off the river on his face. The station entrance had a too-bright welcome. He passed through the barrier. As he made his way down the steps, he put his hand in his coat pocket. The yawara slipped easily into his fist. He saw Laska first, which meant Fitz and Pallo were either behind him or waiting on the platform.

Ten steps to go, Max took the initiative. 'Tell Slade from me he's fucked up this time.'

Six steps. 'I don't think so.' Laska was a man in need of a scrap, sweating and snarling as he faced up and came forward. Max sensed Fitz behind him, Laska glanced over Max's shoulder and confirmed it. He turned and moved up two steps, took the yawara from his pocket and jabbed hard upwards, jarring his shoulder as the stick connected with Fitz's groin. He swept his free arm behind Fitz's knees and took his legs. Turning back, face to face with Laska, he moved inside the arc of Laska's punch and swung an uppercut, the stick connected under the chin, ripping the stitches. Max shoved past and headed for the platform. The train indicator read *2 MINUTES*. He met the gaze of a woman passenger, her partner drawing her away. Others followed, retreating. He gripped the yawara tight in his fist, waiting for them to come at him. He felt his palm sticking. There was blood on his wrist, running between his fingers, dripping along the yawara grain onto the platform. His coat sleeve was slashed across the forearm. Fitz limped towards him like a man who'd shit his pants. Max lost his grip. The yawara bounced off the concrete and spun over the platform edge, clattering onto the track. Laska closed in. Pallo from behind. The platform indicator showed *1 MINUTE*. He'd either be on the train or under it.

Max's head filled with noise.

'Wait.' The voice from the far end of the platform. Dyce running as they closed in. 'I said wait.'

Laska was no more than a metre away.

The train rumbled into the station and slowed to a stop. Dyce walked stiffly along the platform. 'I mean it. Leave him.'

Max boarded. As the doors closed, Tait and his team closed in from either entrance. Dyce, Gashi and Fitzpatrick were taken down fast. Before the train entered the tunnel, Laska had disappeared.

61

Max

SEDGEFIELD HOUSE WAS QUIET. Max waited in full view at the edge of the light spilling out from the hallway. It stood to reason that Johnny would be there. There were footsteps behind him in the dark.

'Laska went in about ten minutes ago. Are you on your own?'

'For now.' Johnny's hand in his coat pocket told Max all he needed to know. 'Probably a good idea if you give that to me.'

'In a minute.'

'Have you spoken to Alison tonight?'

'I'm guessing you have.'

'You should talk to her, John. She's got news. You'll want to hear it from her.'

'What I want is to come home, but he's made it so that can't happen, they all have.'

Max had half a mind to leave him to it. It was too cold to be standing out in the rain. The pain throbbing in his arm would need heftier painkillers soon. 'Laska didn't murder Sam Downey.'

'Who did?'

'I don't know, but it wasn't him. Tait's people have had him under surveillance all day. We'll have him, but not for that. We'll have them all.' Max reached out and gently put his hand on Johnny's arm, easing it from his pocket. He took the gun, flicked on the safety and slipped it inside his coat. Conscious of bodies moving in around them, he guided Johnny away.

Johnny looked at him, a question on his lips. 'You deal with these people all the time. When do they stop?'

'When the money's gone.'

Private section visible to Prosecution, Defence and 'Read Only' users.

CROWN V SLADE

ITEM 4. Exhibit 7 [Audio recording]

i. Transcript of phone message, FRASER GORDON NEAL, decd. To DETECTIVE SERGEANT MARK LOMAX. Sunday, 16 October 2011, 10.20 am

Max, it's Fraser. We're close, man, so close. But I need your help and I need that money. You've no idea what I'm dealing with. I swear they are watching everything I do... You need to get your man back down here. There's stuff getting talked about that's not come from me, stuff they shouldn't know. Only you and me know and if it's no' us, then who? I'm asking, last time. I need a grand by Thursday and I need to know I'm not getting a bullet in the back of my head. Call me back.

ii. Transcript of phone message, FRASER GORDON NEAL, decd. To DETECTIVE SERGEANT MARK LOMAX. Sunday, 16 October, 6.03 pm

Sorry to do this, man. I know what they're doing here. I need you to trust me. It's dark money. Bent money. I know I'm right, so do you [...] You want names, I'll give you names. ▓▓▓▓▓▓▓▓▓▓▓▓▓▓▓▓▓▓ ▓▓▓▓▓▓▓▓▓▓▓▓▓ *And I don't care who's listening. It's just the start, I'm telling you. I pulled you out from the rubble, Max. I pulled you out. I need your help, please.*

343

Part Four

4 August 2012 – *Super Saturday*

62

Max

MAX CARRIED HIS JACKET, covering the scar on his arm, as he walked home from an early screening at the Everyman. Forewarned by Kilby, he'd been expecting the call from Hannah Rees. He was pleased to hear her voice. She and her boss, David Bittman, were in London, renting a house in Hampstead for the Olympics. Bittman, it turned out, was a track-and-field aficionado. The games were a useful cover for meetings that would otherwise be logistically *problematic*.

'Sunday is social, Max. I promise,' said Rees. 'Come over for lunch. We're having something outdoorsy in the garden with wine.'

'Are you cooking?'

'Don't be ridiculous. David's hired a private cook for the entire visit. She's really good, I may take her back to the States. Anyhow, I'm counting on you. Do not leave me hanging.'

He'd be there.

If he hadn't been preoccupied trying to fathom Rees's actual agenda – there would inevitably be one – he might have been more guarded when a second call came in, this one from DS Tait. He'd certainly have read more into Tait's insistence it was time they settled their differences. Max agreed to meet later at his local.

The Black Lion was empty for a Saturday evening. As Max waited to be served, the TV showed highlights from the

Olympics opening ceremony. His thoughts turned to the magazine cover in Gavin Slade's office. *London Calling, The Olympic Dividend*. The cast of thousands filled the screen, the camera flashed up to the VIP section. Queens, kings, presidents, dignitaries and the mayor. There was some satisfaction in knowing Gavin Slade was not among them.

Slade's case hadn't made it to trial. A Senior Crown Prosecutor by the name of Clayton concluded the evidence was insufficient for a realistic prospect of conviction, a decision made late in the day. Someone had interfered. Kilby's reticence in probing further suggested he knew as much. Martin Dyce's case fell at the same time. It came too late to save Slade's political career. Forced to resign from the Jamaica Dock Development Consortium, investment in his business interests diverted elsewhere. The dark money backing another horse. Another name on Fraser Neal's list.

Max sipped his pint and found a quiet table away from the TV screen.

Tait walked in shortly afterwards, carrying the weight of his world.

'How's things?' said Max.

'Good. Kind of.'

'You want a drink?'

'Sure, whatever you're drinking.'

They ordered sandwiches. Tait ate quickly. He finished his beer and pushed the glass away. 'We didn't get a chance to talk after the case review. You were a bit bruised.'

'Wasn't much to say. You got what you got. You'd have had more if Conway hadn't prevented it.'

'It's not enough.'

'It never is. But Fitzpatrick and Gashi are down for drugs, trafficking and the assault on Shelly Dowd. And you put Laska away for his part.' Max rubbed his forearm.

'We got nothing on Fraser Neal.'

'Come on, Ben. Johnny Nunn swore blind Stuart Slade went into the alley before Neal arrived. Gavin Slade knew he'd seen their list of investors. It was a matter of time before it came to us. But you never rated Nunn as a witness. Didn't matter that he was willing to put himself at risk, or what I thought. You undermined him and Clayton knew it. You made his job easy.'

Tait wasn't convinced. 'Actually, that wasn't what I wanted to talk about. I've driven back from Bridlington. A woman who used to know Stan Moffatt got in touch last week. She seemed to think he was back up north.'

Stan had gone missing on release from hospital and Tait shared Max's concern he'd find himself back on the streets in the same trouble as before. A loose end for one of Laska's many cousins to clear up.

'She also recognised Martin Dyce. She'd seen him as recently as a month ago, staying at the hotel she works in on Kingsgate. She gave me a description of three men she witnessed shoving him in the back of a light blue Rover. The car was registered to Mr Alec Barnes. Only Mr Barnes passed away at the end of May. The car was found burned out in Epping Forest two days after she saw it in Bridlington.' He read from a notebook, *One was a big black feller, solid sort of a bloke, one in an army jacket, a bit handy and a bit banged up around the face. The one driving was in black jeans and boots, bit scruffy.'*

'What's your point?'

'She said Dyce was white as death, looked like he'd shat himself.'

Whatever it was Tait had missed until that moment became clear. 'You knew where Dyce was going, didn't you? You risked your career to find him and take them to him.'

'I don't see it that way,' said Max. 'Did you get a result?'

'If you mean, did Dyce turn up in Lewisham looking like

349

he'd been run over and confess to the murder of Father Sam Downey? Yes, he did. But Jesus, Max. Not like this. I've spoken to Payne, for what it's worth. And I can't find Nunn. No one knows anything. I wondered if you had an idea?'

'You won't find him.'

'You're very confident.'

'He's gone.'

Max finished his pint and stood up, jacket across his arm. 'Do yourself a favour, Ben. Move on.'

'Tell me why.'

'If you don't know, I can't explain.'

He left Tait at the table to think it through. He could have said it didn't matter, but he didn't believe it. In truth, he'd grown tired of Slade and Dyce and men like them. Dwight Payne wasn't letting what happened to his mother go unanswered and Johnny had waited for the chance to straighten things out. He could have gone at any time once Dominik Saski sorted his ID, but he'd waited until Alec didn't need him any more. Alison was staying for now. She had a decision to make. She'd most likely follow Johnny Nunn into history, or to France. What happened afterwards, Max didn't want to know.

A car drew up beside him as he turned at the top end of Broadhurst Gardens. Tait wound down his window.

'Where are you going?'

'Home. Turn the music up loud and get drunk.'

'I want something.'

Max kept walking.

'I want to come and work with you.'

Tait was away into traffic before Max could tell him to fuck off.

Max had a few days before Kilby returned from his attachment to the security services. Denny would return to Carteret Street officially from Tuesday. By the autumn, Commander Harding would be back behind her desk, gunning for control.

He owed Liz a drink at the very least for bringing Nathan Dowd home. Now he had tomorrow's lunch with Hannah Rees to navigate. He put Tait to the back of his mind.

It was a still, warm evening. A London summer people would remember. Darkness had fallen by the time Max made his way along Goldhurst Terrace. As he came close to 139, he was conscious of the rising pitch and volume of stadium noise spilling from open windows. He stopped to listen, taking in the rare sound of a nation feeling what it's like to win, and win, and win again. He climbed the steps and put his key in the lock.

Acknowledgements

The Last Days of Johnny Nunn is a work of fiction inspired by the reality of urban regeneration as experienced by many communities across the UK. Thanks to Roger Green and Malcolm Cadman at Voice4Deptford, campaigning to secure a better deal for local people on the Convoys Wharf development in south east London; and to Billy Dasein and Josie Moon at East Marsh United, together with their colleagues bringing hope to Grimsby's former fishing community. I'm ever grateful to Tina Jackson, friend, first-reader and truthteller-in-chief. Thanks to Philip Patterson at Marjacq and to Carolyn Mays, Polly Halsey, Laura Fletcher, Alice Grandison, Ion Mills, Steven Mair and all at Bedford Square Publishers / No Exit Press. Special Thanks to Sean O'Brien for permission to quote from 'Somebody Else'. Deepest thanks to Beverlea, as always.

A number of books and articles were extremely helpful in writing *The Last Days of Johnny Nunn*, notably: *Alpha City* by Rowland Atkinson; *City of Quartz* by Mike Davis; *Murder Investigation Team* by Steven Keogh. Steve Platt's *New Statesman* article 'Or was it a police riot?' helped sharpen detail and clarify memories of the anti-racist march in south London in October 1993.

About the Author

Photo Credit © Neil Holmes Photography

Nick Triplow is the writer of crime thriller *Never Walk Away* and south London noir, *Frank's Wild Years*. His acclaimed biography of crime fiction pioneer, Ted Lewis, *Getting Carter: Ted Lewis and the Birth of Brit Noir*, was longlisted for the CWA Gold Dagger for Non-Fiction and HRF Keating Award. Nick is also the author of the social history books, *Pattie Slappers*, *Distant Water* and *The Women They Left Behind*. Originally from London, he lives in Barton-upon-Humber and is co-founder of Hull Noir Crime Fiction Festival.

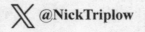 **@NickTriplow**